TIDAL RAGE

David Evans

LOUDHAILER BOOKS

preface

No day is a good day to die, especially when you are young, vibrant, and beautiful. The fact that it was not a single killer, but two independent killers unaware of each other made her chance of survival zero.

Elisa Cutler radiated the youthful self-confidence that comes with the knowledge that men and women admired her, both for her intelligence and her personality. Her flawless skin would flush bright red when admiring eyes cast over her face and body. Elisa was a virgin; she had just discovered boys, well one in particular.

Elisa stood at the stern of deck six of the cruise ship, to Skype her boyfriend. It was an area of relative privacy on a vessel with two thousand plus guests, and one where she could get a good internet connection for her iPad. She carried her tablet in a pink cover which matched the colour of her short dress

The day was on the verge of turning, the red tinge on the horizon announcing dusk. The day had unusually for the area been rainless and cool. The air was crisp as the sun dropped below the mountains that appeared as giant ice-cream cones. The cry from a bald eagle broke the steady hum of the wake of the propeller. The eddies had been the playground of a pod of orcas for the last hour.

Stretching from Puget Sound, Washington, through the British Columbia coast and into the Gulf of Alaska, the Inside Passage includes more than a thousand islands, seemingly endless shoreline, and a multitude of idyllic coves and bays. The ship had visited Icy Strait earlier that day, and was now just a little south of Juneau, Alaska.

2,043 guests, less 1, would depart the following morning on excursions. Many would go whale watching, others to view the magnificent Mendenhall Glacier, a sizeable minority no further than the well-stocked local bars. Juneau was the capital of Alaska and established before the big Klondike Gold Rush of 1898.

The scenery and the ambience meant little to the assassin. He hid in the shadows at the stern of deck six. He was a man, and like any other man, he admired the beauty of his victim, even feeling a little lustful. He was too much of a professional to let these thoughts get in the way; he had a job to do. She would have to die, and it was her brother's fault for meddling in his boss's affairs. 'A distraction' was how he described it; her brother and parents would call it devastation.

Elisa had spent the early evening dining in the stylish Swallow restaurant on deck three, followed by a drink in the music bar, as the excellent pianist plied his trade. Elisa was connecting the settings on her iPad to the ship's Wi-Fi system. Elisa had waited patiently to connect with her first and only boyfriend, whom she had met at college several weeks earlier.

The assassin began to move silently and stealthily, then rapidly moved back into the shadows, as his acute senses warned him someone else was approaching.

The captain was at the wheel, the chefs in the galley, and the ship's orchestra playing the theme to Phantom of the Opera to support the cast in the Seaward theatre. The pianist had finished his early stint in the music bar and was not due to play again for a further forty minutes.

Elisa turned, and ceased dabbing her fingers on the tablet, to see who was approaching her. It was a windless night, but the massive hulk of the ship displaced the air in front of it which created a gentle breeze. Elisa's hair wafted on the breeze, which only enhanced her youthfulness and beauty.

To the assassin in the shadows, it appeared that she knew the approaching man. He pondered whether he would have to kill them both. The man who was approaching was small in stature; the assassin considered killing them both quickly and silently.

For eleven years, the assassin had plied his trade. Not many things could shock him, but the events of the next thirty seconds did. Shock may be too strong a word, but he did feel admiration and surprise at the tradecraft of the individual with Elisa.

"Good evening, Maestro."

Elisa smiled as you would to an acquaintance, and died. The demure figure rabbit-punched her in the throat, and she let out one last gasp, before slumping dead on the deck. He rapidly pulled out a chunk of her scalp, carefully placing it into a plastic bag. He was much stronger than the assassin in the shadows had assumed. The executioner lifted her over the back of the boat in one fluid motion.

Job done, thought the redundant assassin; *money for nothing.* He rapidly moved back into the dark shadows of the stairwell.

Elisa's murderer walked past the assassin, and stopped for a second, as though he sensed another human being in the vicinity. He sniffed the air, but any trace was lost in the gentle breeze, and he walked off. It had taken less than forty seconds from arrival to disposal.

Elisa dropped like a stone, six decks into the wake. There were no windows, balconies, or open spaces on the five decks below, and no CCTV. The killer had picked his spot well. With only a single bald eagle as a spectator, the pod of orcas played with their new toy. They flipped Elisa's cadaver from one to another. Finally one submerged, with Elisa between its teeth. Elisa did not resurface, lost forever to the ice-cold depths of the Inside Passage.

Today was not a good day to die; it was destiny of a sort. Her life cut short; Max Cutler would never see his sister again.

chapter one

Sebastian was conceived in the sex pit of Patpong, a chaotic tangle of market stalls, shops, restaurants, and drinking dens in the heart of Bangkok. The mainstays of business were alcohol and sexual encounters. The demand for underage girls was constant, and many of them were either dead or diseased by the age of twenty-five.

Those that survived were much cheaper to purchase by the hour or for a night. In some cases, the boys had their Adam's apples shaved and their penises strapped tightly between their legs. Most times, you could not tell the boys from the girls. Some of the less discerning customers did not care, and some preferred their boys to look like boys.

The acrid aroma of sex was everywhere: the sickly stench of sour flesh and bodily fluids. The smell intermingled with the scents of dried shrimp and coconut milk emanating from the heady mix of food stalls that lined the streets.

A man (or indeed a woman) could have all their primal needs satisfied within this area: food, shelter, and sex. Not just any sex; there was a whole menu of the type, gender, transgender, size, and age, all of questionable quality, but copious quantity.

The sex workers of Patpong worked mainly from bars, controlled by a pimp who was primarily a bar owner. In some bars, they sat around the tables; in others, they were corralled together like cattle in pens, waiting to be picked by the multitude of lustful beings that passed them by.

Some men would choose the cheapest sex workers, who were generally unkempt, infested, walking skeletons, apparently afflicted by sexually transmitted diseases. These customers were playing Russian roulette with their lives; sometimes due to economics, other times by choice.

Somewhere beneath the neon lights in Silom Road, an overweight sex tourist, between visits to the Emerald Buddha Temple and the water market, heaved and sweated Sebastian into existence.

Sebastian's mother, Kim, was originally from a small village on the outskirts of Chang Mai, to the north of the country along the Burmese border. Kim was twelve when her father sold her to Luau Wan. He wanted her to work in his factory in Bangkok sewing teddy bears; that was the lie he had told her father. As soon as Kim's mother was diagnosed with breast cancer, he needed to decide. Kim's father needed money for an operation, and the 700 US dollars he received for Kim would pay for the initial treatment. He had no option but to sell his only daughter, who was not worth as much to him as her brothers; they could earn their keep in the fields, harvesting rice.

Kim never had a chance to work in a factory or a shop. Not yet a teenager, she lost her virginity to a US three-star general on leave from Vietnam. Luau Wan received 500 US dollars—the market rate for a confirmed virgin.

Unfortunately for Wan, he could only sell Kim as pure for the first year. Within twelve months, the heroin she was hooked on started to take its toll. To the discerning customer, it was noticeable that, although only thirteen, she was no longer fresh.

After two years, Kim had been moved by Luau Wan down to Pattaya, to his bar on Walking Street, preferring fresher meat for his establishment in Bangkok. Kim would sit on the wooden veranda one floor up, which jutted out over Walking Street. The street consisted of a multitude of two-floor wooden buildings facing each other, some five yards across over a dusty mix of tarmac and grit. The alley consisted of bars, money exchangers, Thai boxing venues, even more bars, and brothels.

From Kim's vantage point on the veranda, she could see the multitude of European sex tourists and American soldiers. The lustful intermingled with curious visitors. Kim was the near-nude centrepiece, and they would cheer as she was goaded into pole dancing to entice even more clients.

Kim had to make money to pay for her habit. She needed the heroin to survive and could no longer live without the white powder, even for a day.

Like most pimps, Luau Wan kept most of Kim's takings, leaving her with just enough for the drug and basic food. Kim would get laid or offer other services at least seven times a night. To fall short would mean a beating, but even worse was the withdrawal from the heroin she so craved.

Kim was sixteen years old when the scented condom burst, and she conceived Sebastian. The father was a twenty-stone German car worker from Hamburg called Fritz. Had the rupture happened twenty minutes earlier, the father would have been Joachim from Sweden. Had it been an hour earlier, it could have been Karl from London, or Gregg from Washington. These two had met in a bar and had agreed to share her and the price.

The magnetic appeal of child sex for some of the world's lowlifes was clearly apparent in this area of Bangkok.

Kim had been forced on the pill since she was twelve and had no idea how she became pregnant. After the first beating, Luau Wan had allowed her to have the child. Wan's parents had been religious, and although he had no qualms about dealing with child sex slavery, he could not cross the line into killing unborn children.

Sebastian was born on a hot and humid New Year's Day, the first day of 1972. Not the beautiful baby she had hoped for, but a heroin addict's child, with a defined harelip. Sebastian was an ugly child by any standard.

Kim rented an apartment situated above a Thai fighting arena, just off Walking Street and located next to Baby Doll night club. A neon Coke bottle flashed on and off continuously from the Spanky's bar opposite, filling the room with light and then plunging it into darkness just as quickly. Sebastian's crib was dark for two seconds, then illuminated for two seconds, and so it went on from 9 pm until 5 am.

The child suffered constant stress from interrupted sleep patterns, disturbed by the gasping, throaty noises of men in the throes of sex, men that Kim brought home each night.

Sebastian's existence was, from his earliest memory, all about survival. Other children suckled at their mother's breasts for milk. Sebastian was fed milk from an unsterilized bottle. The constant pulling, tugging, and bites from the men she entertained left her too sore.

Kim would feed him his eight ounces of formula with a tiny amount of heroin mixed in. It was the only way to quiet him down, or he would scream all night long.

Sebastian was the name his mother had called him. An English client insisted on bringing a video cassette along. He pressed play before heaving himself up and down on top of her. He watched episodes of the English drama *Upstairs Downstairs*. Kim heard the name several times over his grunting. She liked the name, so she called her half-Thai, half-European child Sebastian.

Events took a turn for the better in 1975. Sebastian was three years old, and his mother, Kim, was nineteen. Several sex workers moved away from the pimps and bars and bought in muscle to assist them. Needing to continue to work required developing a new marketing strategy; well, not new, but redefined. It was the time when the American GIs came to Bangkok; battle-weary and looking for beer, and lots of sex.

Sex workers waited outside the gates of the barracks that housed the American soldiers on respite from the terrors of the Vietnam war.

Kim found the GIs too rough; some liked to beat up their women, and they were often high on one drug or another. Kim used Don Mueang International Airport.Along with another dozen or so sex workers, she would wait for the flights from Europe, Australia, or America.

Kim's clients were usually overbearing Europeans, Australians, and a few Arabs who had a penchant for the likes of Kim. The rent boys at the airports would target lithe Nordic travellers, who preferred the ladyboys. Clients were predominantly men, some middle-aged, some positively ancient, some young, some married, some with wives in tow, and almost all wanting one kind of sexual encounter or another.

Kim, like many Thai women, appraised men differently than their Western counterparts. A paunchy belly in the US or UK is not the ideal shape for a man. Many women assume the man likes too many beers or does not work hard enough, whereas a Thai woman sees a paunch as a sign of wealth.

Hank McKenzie was such a man. He had been born in Portland, Oregon, in the United States, some forty years earlier. Hank was a victim of fast-food chains; it would kill him in the end, but not because of the food. He was a big man in every way, over six feet two inches tall, with a broad chest, and a more expansive waist and stomach. He was big, he was bald as a newborn, and fat. There was a reason he was in Thailand. Hank wanted to purchase a companion, and if it worked out, a wife. He had been here twice before and knew the lay of the land. He was determined this time was the right time.

On the day Kim and Hank crossed paths, she had her little Eurasian son in tow. Some men liked this; she knew. They thought that if a woman had a child, she would be drug- and disease-free, but this was not true in Kim's case.

"No waste time looking for other girls, they no good. I clean, no disease, we do fucky-fucky all night long. Then I clean and bathe you, I cook for you and then again, I love you long, long time."

Hank wanted a wife so badly. He was sick of going to work functions as one of an insignificant band of men who could not get a date, no matter how hard he tried. Hank had been to many social occasions where he stuck out as a lonely bachelor, the type the lonely ladies do not want. Unfortunately, his size and looks left him in the also-ran stakes of romance.

Hank was desperate and driven, and this may have clouded his vision as far as Kim was concerned. He could see she was young but had been at this game for a few years. He knew she would be drug-dependent and in need of more than a few doses of antibiotics, but as long as she was AIDS-free, he could get her assistance. The child was a bonus, a ready-made family.

Hank bought her for four weeks and told her she had to do anything he wanted in those four weeks. Hank showed Kim a $500 bill; she gasped. Kim had seen thousands of dollars cross the palms of the bar owner. The most Kim had ever held in her hands at the end of the month was $40. She had never seen so much money, nearly all of hers had gone to pimps. Hank ripped the bill and gave her one-half, he promised the other half in four weeks if she had pleased him.

Kim was no fool. These opportunities only came along once in a lifetime, if you were lucky, and she agreed to the contract. You can imagine her surprise when Hank had her and Sebastian go to Chiang Rai, 800 kilometres north of Bangkok. She asked no questions, as Hank had made it clear he was footing the bill, so it was his party. After landing, he drove in the hired car some twenty miles further into the interior to a large camp, which looked like a military base.

Hank, in the two days prior, had done his homework well. He had used his contacts from previous visits to arrange the treatment. Kim had no idea what she was going to be undertaking.

The camp was eighteen acres, surrounded by barbed wire and armed guards posted every forty yards. The recovery unit was an open secret. Colonel James Fallon had seen the drug abuse first-hand in Vietnam. Fallon knew wherever there was substance abuse, the military would need rehabilitation units. Men who had left home as fresh-faced GIs could not be sent back as gibbering drug addicts.

Colonel James Fallon took his retirement and set about creating a critical rehabilitation unit in the countryside outside Chiang Rai. He agreed to multi-million-dollar contracts with the US government to rehabilitate soldiers, and South Vietnamese persons of interest to the US government. The camp was also open to those who had problems and could afford the costs to undertake the treatment.

Kim had no idea what she had signed herself and Sebastian up for. At first, she was bewildered, but she wanted her other half of the $500 bill. Plus, she had promised she would do anything Hank wanted within that month.

Hank handed over the mother and child, explaining she was his wife, and that was all the attending physician required. Besides the thousand dollars for each of their treatments.

Hank flew to Bangkok, and enjoyed the services of several call girls over the next two weeks, as Kim begged and screamed to be released; screeching and begging for heroin. Sebastian cried and cried unmercifully. Although only three years of age, Sebastian would never forget the pain, or the experience, throughout his sordid life.

When Hank returned nearly four weeks later, he was more than pleased to pay a $1,500 bonus for successful completion. Kim was dressed in a blue and silver sarong and looked more like nineteen than thirty years of age, as she had when he had met her. She was clean, and she was calm.

Doctor Charlton was a young ear, nose, and throat consultant from Cambridge, had volunteered twelve months of free service through the World Health Organization to help the clinic. He undertook operations in the camp to rebuild septums in noses, or repair holes in windpipes from inhaled drugs. Doctor Charlton had screened Sebastian and felt sorry for the little Eurasian, drug-addicted boy with the harelip.

Hank was delighted to see Sebastian's harelip was now only a tight scar running from the repaired lip to the nose. While it was apparent Sebastian had undergone surgery—he looked different— he would not stand out so much in a crowd. Hank looked at the boy and saw cold, brown eyes staring back from the little boy's improved face.

Hank was a chemical engineer, a respectable and upright career with excellent remuneration and benefits. He was comfortable, with a healthy bank balance, all of which he explained to Kim. She heard the words 'marriage' and 'moving to England', where Hank worked.

Better to have one obese, sweaty man mounting her than the hundreds if not thousands she would have had to sleep with over the coming years. She would accept Hank's marriage proposal. She was clean, and she deserved to be looked after for once in her life.

Hank took a three-month sabbatical from work; his company were quite helpful over the matter. After all, Hank was an excellent engineer; so what if he needed to get some Thai call girl to marry him? The company thought Hank would be a complete salaryman when he was married. Hank had wanted to ensure that his new possessions, Kim and Sebastian, were clean and presentable before turning them into his new family, which he did in October of 1976.

<h1 style="text-align:center">chapter two</h1>

Kim was used to paddy fields from her hometown, and the stinking streets of Patpong. It was a significant shock to both her and Sebastian when, a few days after the marriage, they landed at Manchester Airport in the United Kingdom. The taxi sped eastwards along the M62 motorway towards their new home in Southport, on the outskirts of Liverpool. Once a bustling holiday destination, it had now grown quieter and more sedate, abandoned by the tourists who preferred the sun of Spain to the rain of northern England.

It was not the colour of Sebastian's skin that alienated him from his childhood peers and teachers at the infant school. It was his nature. Most children have their tantrums and take it out on other children. Teachers often turned a blind eye to such outbursts. But Sebastian had wild fits of temper which far exceeded the teachers' level of tolerance.

Sebastian's eruptions were met with a stern telling-off, and on occasion, a cane to the bottom. The teachers had no idea what Sebastian had gone through in his formative years. To them, Kim was a respectable mother. They didn't know he was the son of a reformed prostitute and reared on heroin.

While Sebastian's IQ was up and beyond that of his peers, his social skills were not. It was clear to him, even at that age, that the teachers did not seem to have the same affection for him as they did for the other children; not that he cared.

Another legacy of the prenatal addiction he had inherited from his mother was a compulsion to pull out and eat his hair. The doctors had put a name to this compulsive urge; they called it trichotillomania or trichotillosis.

Children of all types can be caustic and cruel to someone with an affliction, and Sebastian's peers were no different. It had started when he went to kindergarten, soon after he had come to the country, and the torment continued into junior school. They saw the remnants of his harelip, the tight scar running from nose to the top lip. More apparent were the tufts of black hair interspersed with bald patches where Sebastian had, over many months, tugged at his hair till it parted from his scalp, and then he ate the coarse threads. His compulsion had left him with a head full of scars and scabs. It got to the point where his hair would never grow back again in certain areas.

Sebastian was not one of those children who crumpled and ran to Mummy at the first sign of bullying. It was not in his nature to go to the school and seek help from people in authority, those who were supposed to stop this type of behaviour, but seldom did. Sebastian was a shadow child in the school, with neither friends nor confidants. He kept himself to himself. Sebastian was living in a dual world. There were the typical school relationships, and there were his, which were mainly fantasy. It was inevitable that the two worlds would collide someday.

One of the children who liked to belittle Sebastian was Geraldine Mills. She was a beautiful little girl with red hair, who also happened to be a bundle of trouble, a remnant of her Gaelic ancestry. Geraldine said what she thought, regardless of any fallout, be it a teacher or, more often, those classmates who were not in her little clique.

"Tufty, scabby, train-line lip," they would spit out at Sebastian, along with racial abuse.

Sebastian was not angered or perplexed by the taunts, which predominately emanated from Geraldine or one of her many friends. Sebastian was unemotional; he could detach himself and almost watch over the events as if he were an observer. The confused and angry boy did not blame the other children, as he disliked himself intensely, and often wished he had never been born. While immune to the insults, the bullies stuck out as people he notably did not like, and ones he wanted to hurt. Just the thought of it gave him pleasure.

A few short weeks after Sebastian began to give in to his fantasies, he wanted more realism. One day, he put a dead, dissected rat in the school satchel of Mike Mayer, a boy in one of Geraldine's cliques, and put it back in his locker. He waited excitedly to the side of the cabinets at the end of the school day and enjoyed the screams when the boy opened the bag and proceeded to wet himself.

It was time, Sebastian knew, to elevate the game to the next level. Mitzie was a black Labrador puppy that had been brought to school by Gwen Childs, a particular friend of Geraldine's, and one of Sebastian's chief tormentors. The puppy had extracted the oohs and ahs of the gathering schoolchildren. It brought out a universal outpouring of love that Sebastian found strange; in his country, it was a delicacy. He crept into Gwen's garden and had the puppy in his arms and away in a matter of seconds. He returned it that night and laid it out on their lawn. They never did find the puppy's head.

Hank had noticed that Sebastian had some strange oddities about him from an early age, but he also had talent. He could play Hank's small upright piano and pick up tunes just by listening. Hank insisted Sebastian go to music lessons every Saturday.

Hank enlisted Sebastian in a karate class held each Tuesday as well. He was wise enough to know a Eurasian boy with limited social skills may well need to defend himself as he progressed through the schools in the area.

Sebastian took to the piano and astonished his musical tutors with how quickly he could pick up tunes from listening, as well as his grasp of reading music. It was not long before he was singing in his local choir.

Sebastian's piano teacher, Miss Jenkins, would generally limit her lessons to the genre of Elton John or John Lennon, with *Imagine* being her favourite song. She made an exception for Sebastian. After hearing an advert on television, he gave a passable rendition of *Bagatelle in A Minor*, played at a moderate speed. The piece was not excessively challenging, but there are some slightly tricky runs in the last half. Sebastian played it note-perfect. From that day on, she introduced him to a variety of pieces from classical composers: Bach, Mozart, Schumann, Chopin and Beethoven.

Sebastian's all-time favourite was Wagner, who happened to have been Adolf Hitler's favourite composer as well. He could play the piano section of *Das Rheingold*, which is the first opera in the cycle of operas of *Der Ring des Nibelungen*. By the age of nine, he was starting on the second Siegfried.

Sebastian's talent enraptured Miss Jenkins, and very soon she was giving extra sessions, for which she did not charge her normal feet. She saw past his inept social skills and felt he expressed himself through his music.

Sebastian played in front of his school and won the school's talent show. Geraldine amended her taunts to, "Sissy, Chink, and scabby dog." She had no intention of relenting from her harassment.

Hank McKenzie decided to return to the United States. It was not an easy decision, but one he thought necessary, after a young girl from Sebastian's school went missing.

There was the intense activity of the police investigation; the questions and suspicion not only fell on the classmates of Geraldine Mills, but her parents, grandparents, and neighbours. This unfortunate episode changed the balance of the community, and trust between each other had turned toxic.

The year was 1981. The McKenzies had been in the country since 1976. Sebastian was ten years old, and by this time, completely bald.

Geraldine had failed to arrive home after school. Six hours later, the men of the area had been willingly pressed by the police to search streets, common land, and agricultural land; anywhere the child might be.

Several days later, and with Geraldine still missing, the interviews began. The first interviews were held in the school, with the children from Geraldine's class. Shortly afterwards, the known paedophiles, child killers, and drug dealers in the area were targeted. The police then interviewed parents of her classmates, followed by a further week of re-interviews with anyone who may have had a problem with her.

Following initial inquiries, it did not take long for the local constabulary to work out that Geraldine's peers had mixed feelings for her. She was popular amongst her small, close clique of friends. To others, she was an out-and-out bully. The list of interviews with children with possible grudges was a long one.

Sebastian was interviewed twice, along with his parents, as he fell within the group considered to have been bullied.

A month after Geraldine's disappearance, the police were no closer to solving the case or finding the body than they were on day one. She had just disappeared. One of the main problems for the police was the area. Surrounding Southport was arable farmland, so, in essence, there were thousands upon thousands of acres to search.

Hank had decided enough was enough. England was on the slide. He had thought this a safer haven than the USA, but where America went, Great Britain soon followed. Hank applied for the post of senior biochemist in the San Diego operation and was quickly accepted. It was not up for discussion. Kim and Sebastian would have to follow Hank's wishes. At first, Kim was frightened of the move. Sebastian was nonplussed, not at all interested in where he lived. He was pretty sure a different country, a different culture, would not make him any more responsive to people or their feelings.

They arrived at the southernmost city on the west coast of America, San Diego. Hank had taken out a three-year lease on a detached wooden house not far from the city's famous zoo, and the peripheral Balboa Park. The park was full of museums and natural gardens. In no time at all, Hank and Kim settled down very nicely into the area.

Hank had ensured that Sebastian enrolled with a new music teacher and signed up to one of the many self-defence classes springing up all over the city, thanks to the actor and martial artist Bruce Lee.

Sebastian joined a new school, but the same old problems trailed him. It did not matter that the school was full of Hispanics and Mexicans who had immigrated the few miles from the border to San Diego. He was some kid from Vietnam. He was the enemy, Viet Cong; it did not matter to the children that it was a different country, a different culture.

His trichotillomania had been a matter of concern to doctors and psychiatrists over two continents. None could modify the compulsive addiction that had control over Sebastian. As he was entering puberty, he found new tufts of hair to remove and devour. Sebastian would never have pubic or body hair in his life, for as it came through, he plucked it out, and after time, it never grew back.

Sebastian was twelve years old and was walking on the Cabrillo Bridge in Balboa Park near the San Diego Zoo when Hank decided to treat him to a McDonald's meal. This decision from Hank, apart from either a chicken or hamburger, would be his last on this earth.

Ed Huberty, from across the bridge, had decided that this day would change his life forever. He needed to express himself, and for that, he needed to ensure that there would be plenty of people there. Just before taking the bus to the zoo area with a haversack full of weapons, his wife asked him where he was going.

"Going hunting. Humans," was Huberty's chilly retort.

Sebastian had opted for the cheeseburger and French fries, and Hank went with the chicken burger. The first sign of trouble was when the door flung open, and the girl behind the counter seemed to explode in a mist of blood and guts. Huberty had begun his killing spree.

There was only one way out, and that was past Huberty.

"Slide along the floor and get to the toilets and stay there," Hank ordered Sebastian.

Sebastian crept into the bathroom and then locked himself inside the cubicle, sitting with his feet off the floor, hugging them to his chin as he sat on the toilet pan.

Sebastian stayed within the cubicle of the bathroom in McDonald's as the massacre continued. The semi-automatic weapon pumped out its deadly cargo. Once the ammunition was spent, the definite boom of a Winchester pump-action 12-gauge shotgun drowned out the screams.

Sebastian wondered with no fear or alarm if he would die that day. Would this be his last day on earth? If it were, it might well save lives in the future.

Sebastian had the Walkman portable cassette player that Hank had given him for his birthday. He loved the idea of listening to music on the move, in any situation, and as the shots rang out in the McDonald's, he put his headphones on and listened to *Gotterdammerung*, the fourth opera in the cycle.

The carnage on the other side of the toilet awakened something in him. Sebastian blocked out all the current, horrific events and placed the earphones of the Walkman on. He went back to that day six months prior in England; to that day that would shape the rest of his life, should he survive today.

He had listened to the same rendition of *Gotterdammerung* those six months prior. It was when his child-sized frame and limbs had strained to slide the heavy cover from the septic tank. And where he placed Geraldine Mills in her final resting place.

He remembered the same potent section of the tape, the smell of methane gas before finally easing the bag which contained Geraldine's body through the maintenance hole.

***

Sebastian had enticed Geraldine Mills to the woods behind the school by sending her a letter from Chris Coleman; everyone knew she had her eye on the school football captain. The note simply said: "Have been watching you for some time, would you like to be my girlfriend? If the answer is yes, meet me at Langton Woods near the pond at 4:30 pm after school. Come alone. Chris C."

So, it was her fault she was dead. She had not been dragged here screaming; she came of her own free will. Geraldine was like his mother, a little bitch. This was fate, thought Sebastian.

The lake was more of a pond than a lake. It was small, no more than fifty metres by twenty metres across. The lake was covered on three sides with thick foliage, and the western side had a clearing with a small bank to the water's edge, made up of mud and stone. It was a popular meeting place for children by day, and lovers at night.

Geraldine was dead three seconds after she got there. Sebastian had seen her arrive and waited in the foliage until she was no more than a body length from him. He sprang out of the foliage, and she began to turn instinctively to see what had caused the noise. It was already too late for her; she didn't see the hammer hurtling down towards her head.

Geraldine slumped to the ground; the claw of the hammer wedged between in the top of her skull. The blood loss was minimal, as he left the implement *in situ*.

As she lay there, Sebastian thought that it had been too quick, too easy. He would have enjoyed it more if she had suffered like the puppy he had beheaded. He had wanted to see her eyes as life departed.

Sebastian did not think insults had driven him to kill her; he was going to kill someone, somewhere, sometime anyhow. She was on his radar because she had a big mouth and was female.

He had not expected the release, the intense rush as the dopamine and adrenaline fuelled a high that swept over him from the moment he killed her. His hands shook as he felt her lifeless body, as the elation increased.

He would have liked to open her up, experiment on her, but time was a problem; he would have to account for his whereabouts, he was sure, when this all blew up. He also knew they would drag the pond in the woods for her body. He had seen enough murder movies to know waterways were always searched for bodies.

He had stolen a large canvas bag from the school the previous week. A group had come back after doing their Duke of Edinburgh

Bronze outdoor award, and it had been easy to lift one from the passageway as they had a debriefing in the hall.

Because his hands shook so much, it was not as easy to bundle the small body of a girl into the canvas coffin. But after a ten-minute struggle, he managed it. For several minutes, he enjoyed ripping out clumps of the shocking red hair and took another fifteen minutes to consume it.

Finally, he fought with the zip to close it. Geraldine's hair and part of her scalp and some fluids had become entangled in the zip. He yanked at it with all his strength, and a clump of hair fell out, attached to skin and roots.

He eventually got the bag onto his back. Although gaunt and slim, he was surprisingly strong. The hours at the piano had strengthened his fingers and forearms beyond his years. His leg strength was always there from a young age.

It was less than a quarter of a mile to his destination, although it felt more like five miles. The trail was sheltered, and not on the route for dog walkers, so it was quite remote. But still, he kept a careful ear out for others who might be on the trail. The air was crisp and cold, but thankfully it was not raining, as this would have added weight to the load Sebastian was carrying.

The trek took Sebastian through the woods. He stumbled along under the weight of the bundle for the final 100 yards on a track hidden from the public footpath. He finally entered the field, the lines of cabbages stretching as far as he could see.

Had someone approached Sebastian that day within a few yards, the game would have been up. Bloodstains from Geraldine's head wound had seeped through the canvas material, creating a dark, red stain on the outer membrane.

Finally, he reached his destination, tired and in need of hydration. He had been here the previous week. Sebastian had walked the route and stored a bottle of water under a bush by the cesspit, which he gulped down hurriedly.

On his previous visit, Sebastian had ensured the cover to the cesspit could be removed. It was 4:30 pm on a February afternoon, and at that time of the year, England is in darkness from around 4:00 pm. Sebastian had the cover of darkness to assist him with his deeds.

What Sebastian had not read up on and did not expect was the smell, the wretched smell that emanated from within the bag. The acrid smell of the detritus seemed to penetrate through the canvas bag and settle deep within his nostrils. Next time, he would be better prepared.

Sebastian had read up on fingerprinting and was confident that the slurry would destroy any prints that had been transferred to canvas.

But the best-laid plans do not always run smoothly, he found, after two attempts to open the zip. The zip was not going to ease, so he would have to leave Geraldine in the canvas bag. He had planned to place it with the contents in the cesspit, which served as a collection point for the farm's human sewage. In his haste, when putting Geraldine in her canvas coffin, Sebastian inadvertently dropped his closed, topped water bottle underneath the canvas bag in the pit.

After a few moments' thought, he wondered if the body would decompose as quickly in the canvas bag as it would if it were loose within the pit. From talking to local farmers, he knew cesspits in the area were emptied every three years or thereabout. This pit had been serviced the previous year; he had seen it while hunting for rabbits in a field nearby. It was one of the reasons he chose this particular cesspit rather than ones closer to the woods.

After two years in that environment, she would be soup at best, and the bag would have rotted down.

Sebastian pushed the canvas bag into the sewage and staggered a little as the fumes from the confined space made him dizzy, nearly sending him falling into the maintenance hole.

He retained sufficient oxygen and wits to replace and tighten the wing nuts on the cover before heading back to the woods.

In the dark, Sebastian stripped and washed in the pond in the woods. He took clean clothes from a bag he had left there previously and put the clothes he had worn into the bag. On his return home, Sebastian would burn all the contents, along with his parka coat and running shoes. With the flashlight retrieved from the pack, he scanned the area of the initial assault for signs of a disturbance. Once satisfied he scooped out water from the pond with his hands and washed away the small amount of blood on leaves, he had found under the glare of the flashlight.

****

He was shaken out of his trip down memory lane as the main entrance door to the toilets was kicked open. He heard muffled shouts, and then the deafening noise of several semi-automatics going off.

"He's down!" shouted a voice, followed by, "Is there anyone in here, shout if there is?"

Sebastian heard the commands over his Walkman and clicked open the cubicle door and emerged into a scene from a Hollywood movie. There was a man on the floor, obviously dead, going by the amount of blood surrounding him.

At first sight, Sebastian thought this was the killer, as the SWAT police officer still had his gun pointing at the dead man's head. Another officer put his arm around Sebastian and led him to the carnage while trying to shield his eyes from the death and destruction. Sebastian stopped by the corpse of his dead father, who had a gaping wound in his forehead and looked down without any feeling or emotion, as the policeman dragged him away.

That night, the news bulletin reported that five children and sixteen adults had been killed, with nineteen others injured before the SWAT team had dealt out instant justice to the killer.

Kim moaned and cried in the bedroom, not for the loss of Hank but the future, their future. The loss of Hank was initially a stunning blow for Kim. She had come to like Hank, could accept his love, and not grimace every time he made love to her.

The insurance pay-out Kim received from the company eased her fears about financial stability. There was enough in the fund to pay off the house and have a semi-comfortable living for the rest of her life. She still had her looks and her figure, although she knew these would not last forever. Maybe another three or four years, she guessed. The other silver lining was that there were still plenty of rich pickings in the area, either by the hour or long-term; she could always supplement the pot with regular top-ups.

Two years after the McDonald's massacre in 1986, Sebastian was fourteen years old, he and Kim still lived in the same house. Kim and Sebastian were watching television when a report related to the San Diego massacre was being discussed.

The widow of the killer James Huberty, Etna Huberty, tried to sue McDonald's and Babcock and Wilcox, James's former employer, in an Ohio state court for five million dollars. Etna Huberty claimed that the combined mixture of eating too many of their chicken nuggets and working around highly poisonous metals triggered the massacre. She alleged that monosodium glutamate in the food, combined with the high levels of lead and cadmium in his body, induced delusions, and uncontrollable rage. She lost the case.

chapter three

The millennium had come and gone, and the world and all its communication systems had survived.

Max Cutler radiated the youthful self-confidence that came with the knowledge that he was physically very capable of sports. His boyish smile and jovial personality meant he had many an admirer, both female and male.

Cutler was twenty-two years of age, six foot two inches tall, with the physique of a football player. He had short, blonde hair, which was the frame required to show off his piercing blue eyes. Cutler was blessed with a strong, square jaw, with a dimple placed amidships. He looked like an extraordinarily fit and better-looking young Robert Redford.

The looks came at a price: girls came and went for Cutler, and he left a trail of broken hearts, with the girls all too ready to fall in love, while Max was just after some fun. Long and meaningful relationships had no place in Cutler's world. Cutler had two women in his life: Mom, who made the best apple pie this side of the Rockies; and his little sister Elisa, who acted and talked more like a teenager than a ten-year-old.

At the age of eighteen, Cutler had entered the Case Western Reserve University School of Law in his hometown of Cleveland, Ohio. The school is among one of the oldest law schools in the USA, and Cutler had excelled in his admission exam to gain entrance to this prestigious school, much to his parents' delight.

The three years he spent at Case Western were the best three years of his life so far. The fraternity parties, girls, alcohol, lovemaking, torts, contract law, employment law, Latin, sex, criminal law, debates, and more sex, made it seem like the three quickest years of his life.

Every positive has a negative, and every high has a low. Cutler's was the guilt that his parents had worked for twenty years so they could lay out over $120,000 in tuition fees alone. Now that they had paid most of their dues for him, it had started again for Elisa's education, and never once did they complain.

The fourth year of law school had been on placement in Jeddah, Saudi Arabia, where he interned at Saudi International Solicitors, writing contracts and terms and conditions for several oil exploration companies. While the assignment lacked the after-hours activities of the first three years, Max did pick up Arabic as a consolation prize.

At the end of the fourth year, his parents' sacrifice paid off. Max came out top of his class and was awarded a Doctor of Juridical Science (JD), which in layman's terms is a law degree with an international bias. Even before the results were known, Max knew he had done well.

Throughout university, Cutler was on the watchlist of scouts from several of the leading football teams in the country, but today the scout who had turned up to see Max had nothing to do with sports.

Following the graduation, and before the festivities began in earnest, Max's professor invited him to his private quarters. Wasting no time, he introduced Max to the Secret Service headhunter. The professor, having done this several times in the past, left the bewildered Cutler in Wyatt Rockman's hands.

Wyatt Rockman was in his fifties, six foot five inches tall, with a typical Marine, close-cropped haircut. He stood upright, rigidly tall, with a military bearing. He wore a black Armani suit, a red silk tie, and sunglasses; a clear indication he was a man of standing, a man of precision.

Rockman had served time in the Navy Seals, qualifying out of the San Diego main base. He was placed in Berlin, Germany, for several years, carrying out missions in the Russian-controlled Eastern sector. Rockman had seen action—too much action—during the Vietnam War.

Rockman and his team had located and destroyed Cuban communication units which were assisting the Viet Cong to move their troops. Rockman undertook four separate deployments to this theatre of war, losing three men in the process.

Rockman rose quickly through the ranks and became one of the most highly decorated commissioned officers in the Vietnam War.

Following the end of the war, the Secret Service began a recruiting program. Rockman was a prime candidate, and so began a long career in the Service.

Rockman's face beneath the sunglasses had history etched into every line. Although middle-aged, he retained his handsome looks. He possessed a strong, square jawline, brown eyes, salt-and-pepper hair, and skin that had been continuously exposed to the sun, golden brown and thickly lined around the forehead and upper cheeks.

Rockman had developed his skills as an operative firstly in personal security detail, then progressing to recruitment. He had been in the Service for over twenty years.

"The Secret Service has a long and rewarding relationship with several of the leading law universities. The Service actively seeks out those students in law, as well as other disciplines. We look for students with a high IQ and a firm grasp of the subject. We only recruit alpha males," Rockman stated.

Rockman had been monitoring Max and two other students from year one. The other potential recruits, Lehman and Cooper, had failed to reach his exacting standards. Lehman had broken his leg falling from the window of his first-year tutor's bedroom and was not considered suitable material. Cooper was reported as using cannabis at a party by one of Rockman's spies, and he was no longer under consideration. Cutler had had many sexual liaisons at the university. Still, these were all within the parameters of what the Service deemed to be acceptable, and there had been no notices of drug use or deviant behaviour.

Max Cutler chose international law, although the options at Case Western had been vast and varied. He could have chosen a law doctorate pertaining to counterterrorism. The subject included war crimes, communication intercepts, etc.

Cutler was somewhat surprised at the initial approach by the Secret Service recruiter, as he had chosen international law, and pondered the connection between that and the Secret Service.

After the initial introduction, Rockman came straight to the point about wanting him to apply to enlist in the Secret Service.

"The widely held belief in America, and throughout the world, is that the Secret Service protects the president. In short, we are just bodyguards. That is not even scratching the surface of what we do," Rockman said.

"There was me thinking they just wore black suits and sunglasses," Cutler replied, humorously but respectfully.

"Yes, we do watch over the president, but we want you for the original reason the Secret Service was established. The Service is the oldest federal investigative law enforcement agency in the United States. The service was created in 1865 as an integral part of the Treasury Department."

Rockman paused to let this sink in, and then continued.

"The Secret Service was created the same year President Lincoln was assassinated at Ford's Theatre in Washington by John Wilkes Booth. The same year the Civil War, which had been going on since 1861, came to a bloody end.

"One of the primary reasons for creating the Secret Service was the severe problems the Civil War had created, not just national, but global problems, which could have had dire implications for the country.

"The problems were so severe that had the Service not been created, the number one superpower we now know may have been more like some of the poorer South American countries."

Cutler leaned against the windowsill of the quarters as he listened intently to the history lesson.

"To undermine the North and to be able to purchase weapons, the South produced counterfeit American notes. The South was not alone; some in the criminal fraternity employed those who had used their skills to help the South after the war.

"For the new United States emerging from the bloody Civil War, it was believed that up to half of all currency in circulation was counterfeit. It weakened the power of the dollar and the standing of the country itself."

Rockman poured himself and Max each a small brandy and took a sip before continuing.

"It was in 1901, following the assassination of another president, William McKinley, murdered in Buffalo, New York, that the Secret Service was tasked with its second line of operation. That duty was the protection of the president, for which it is now so well known.

"However, I am trying to recruit you into the counterfeiting unit, known as the CU. That is, if you agree to join us, and you pass an in-depth selection process."

Rockman stopped talking and quaffed the exquisite Napoleon brandy in his glass.

Rockman, the Secret Service recruiter, had certainly done his research. The criteria laid down by the powers above for selection were stringent and challenging, both physically and academically. No criminal record was permitted; even minor misdemeanours would mean failure, and the interview would not have gone ahead.

Cutler had been sent for a medical exam the month before. He thought it was to do with his football, as it was his coach who had sent him. He felt it had been unusually thorough, and now he knew why.

"You have been pre-assessed and have a clean bill of health, and as far as we can judge, you show no present physiological or psychological problems. You have excelled at athletics, have no eyesight or hearing difficulties, and are physically fit. You would be able to withstand the same physical rigours as a US Marine, which you will need to, to pass selection."

Rockman did not need to pick up the report on Cutler that was sitting on the desk. Rockman knew this background report verbatim; such was the time he had spent over the years managing others to groom into the Service.

Unbeknown to Cutler, John Redmond, his year third year mentor, was a psychiatrist, who had been evaluating the young Max Cutler at each session he had attended. Paul Edelman, his football coach, was not only part of Rockman's recruitment team, but monitored radicals that often walked the same career and educational paths of ordinary citizens. Karl Horst, Max's law mentor, had been a part-time code breaker for the Service for over forty years and was instrumental in Cutler getting the Saudi placement.

Both Rockman and Cutler now stood by the professor's open fireplace, the warmth filling the room. Rockman looked straight into Cutler's ice-blue eyes and said in a calm voice, "We have been keeping a close eye on you, Max. We think you have the skills required to pass selection and progress to becoming an agent."

Whatever Cutler had been expecting, it was not that.

"I don't know what to say, Mr Rockman. One minute I am enjoying a graduation drink with my professor, and the next I am being asked to enlist in the Secret Service. Why me?" Cutler asked.

Rockman bent down and placed a log on the fire before continuing.

"We only take on the smartest of the smart; men and women who are adaptable, brave beyond brave, so patriotic that they piss red, white, and blue, can adapt, change plans, and make decisions instantly. Are you made from that material?" Rockman asked. "Clever and patriotic, Cutler?"

"I'm as patriotic as the next man. I love my country, sir. As for being brave, I do not know. Brave is a word. Is it brave to run at the line-backers? This certainly isn't the bravery of a typical soldier in Iraq, so unless you can define brave, I don't know. I'm able to adapt quickly, but again, how long is a piece of string?" Max replied.

"Smart answer and you'll probably only find the answers through time, and your actions and reactions to circumstances. Cutler, we have an excellent profile on you, and we think you can cut the cloth, so to speak," Rockman retorted.

Cutler turned and went to the window overlooking the courtyard where graduates were enjoying themselves with families, friends, and lovers.

"I don't mean to be ignorant, but I have no idea what you expect from me. My life has been academia for the past few years."

Rockman sat down, filled his glass with more Napoleon brandy to just over the halfway point, sniffed the contents, and downed the contents in one gulp. He replied, "What would be required? Well, not wanting to keep you away too long from your family downstairs, let us see if I can give you a brief synopsis. New agent trainees are initially sent to the Federal Law Enforcement Training

Centre in Glynco, Georgia, where they enrol on the Criminal Investigator Training Program. This ten-week course is designed to train new federal investigators in such areas as criminal law and investigative techniques and provides a broad foundation for agency-specific training."

Rockman was now on a roll, with his back to Max, looking into the fire as he continued.

"Upon successful completion of the Criminal Investigator Training Program, new agent trainees attend a seventeen-week Special Agent Training Course at the Secret Service training academy, outside of Washington, DC. This course focuses on specific Secret Service policies and procedures.

"Trainees are provided with the necessary knowledge and advanced application training in combating counterfeiting, assessing device fraud, and other financial criminal activity, protective intelligence investigations, physical protection techniques, protective advances, and emergency medicine.

"Then you progress and undertake another part of the core curriculum run by ex-Navy Seals, sadists to the core. The training includes extensive training in marksmanship, self-control and crowd control tactics, water survival skills and physical fitness." Rockman took another full gulp of brandy and, after pausing to savour the contents, continued.

"After you complete the selection, which is only the very start of the process. Secret Service agents receive continuous advanced training throughout their careers. In part, this training consists of regular firearms requalification and emergency medicine refresher courses," he added.

Cutler turned back to the window once again to watch the antics of some of his classmates outside, with the knowledge that his time here at the university was at an end.

"Anything else I should know?" he asked Rockman.

"We would expect you to beat a lie detector while swearing white is black, be as fit as a Marine, and as skilled with a gun as a Navy Seal. You will need to learn new languages to add to your Arabic. Also, have the analytical skills of an accountant, the perseverance of a New York cop, the attention to detail of a top prosecutor, and the patience of a chess master. And finally, to put the country and lives of others ahead of yourself. In other words, be willing to die in the line of duty. I think that about sums it up, young Cutler."

Rockman topped up his brandy glass. He did not offer Cutler any; the young man had been so wrapped up in the interview, the original contents of his glass had not been touched, and it remained half full.

Before going to Saudi Arabia, Max had been clear about what his aims and objectives were. Three years as a junior in a Washington attorney's office specializing in contract law. Junior partner by year four, senior partner by year eight, and the $500,000 salary and benefits that went with it.

The dream began to wear thin during his twelve months spent in Saudi Arabia. At first, he thought it was the oppressive heat, then the constant air conditioning noise in the office. Maybe it was the view or the printer noise. No, it was the whole bundle, stuck in an office hour after hour.

Cutler had begun to fret that he would be unable to spend the next four years, never mind the next forty, chained to a desk doing law.

The offer intrigued and excited Max, who saw this as a way of putting his academic skills, matched with his physical abilities, to good use. Never one to jump in blindly or to decide, Max needed time to think about the offer. But then, after a short silence, he stopped the Secret Service recruiter in his tracks.

"I'll do it. Where do I sign?"

Rockman looked bemused. "Just like that, you'll do it. What about the recompense? What about the training?"

Max thought for a moment. "I can't influence either the money or the training; they'll be set in stone. And if you have come from Washington to see me, and believe that I am your man, well, that's good enough for me."

chapter four

Robert Stahmer was neither short nor tall. He was six feet in his stocking feet, yet the extra few pounds he was carrying around his midriff made him appear shorter. Stahmer had short, cropped, salt-and-pepper hair, more salt than pepper lately, making him look older than his thirty years of age, having been born in 1973.

Today was a day off, a rare day away from work, and that frequently meant putting away the suit, putting on his jeans, and working in his beloved garden. He was a tropical plantsman; his garden looked like it belonged in the tropics rather than in St. Neots on the outskirts of Cambridge, UK. Robert Stahmer loved his garden and knew his plants.

Stahmer was from Newcastle originally and still spoke in the North-Eastern twang. The years had not diluted his accent, and others from outside England thought the Geordie version of English was Australian or Scottish.

With more than ten years in military intelligence and investigations, Stahmer had had several offers of employment after leaving the army. Both intelligence agencies MI5 and MI6 had offered him the opportunity to work for them. To everyone's surprise, he opted for the Health and Safety Executive as an inspector and accident investigator. What most people did not know was that Stahmer's father had been killed in an explosion at the shipyard where he worked, and the investigation was lacking in fact and substance. Robert Stahmer wanted to make a difference.

Several years after joining the Health and Safety Executive, Stahmer had undertaken an accident investigation on a significant construction site in Newmarket. He had appreciated and admired the miles upon miles of rolling countryside interlaced with lazy waterways, and flora and fauna they supported. Stahmer's bubbly, lovely little five-feet-nothing wife, Louise, had fallen in love with the magnificent university buildings and majestic cathedral. Both decided to move lock, stock, and barrel down to the area.

Stahmer was thinking about his Gunnera, a sub-tropical plant which looks like a giant rhubarb, with huge, prickly leaves. The Gunnera plant likes boggy, wet conditions, and his local water authority had enforced a hosepipe ban, as it had not rained for two weeks. He pondered whether the Gunnera would survive. Robert Stahmer was honest and straight as a die, but he did consider sneaking out in the dead of night, hosepipe in hand, to illegally water the precious plant he had nurtured the past seven years.

His thoughts were interrupted.

"Her Majesty will see you now," said the suited employee of the General Department of the Royal Household.

Automatically Stahmer stood erect, today looking all of his six feet, and adjusted his tie. He suspected this suited man with a military bearing was not a footman or a butler, but he was not going to ask and look like a fool. Stahmer was a man of research; he should have researched palace protocol, such as who would greet him. Stahmer hated not knowing. He was angry with himself, as he should have looked it up.

"Your Majesty, Robert Stahmer, for your 3 pm meeting," the suit said.

"Ah, Mr Stahmer. I have been so looking forward to meeting you. Please, sit down and please be at ease. One has been briefed, but I want all the bits that I don't get told," the Queen opened.

"Ma'am, where should I start?" Stahmer asked, after a slight bow.

"First and foremost, with this pleasant Darjeeling tea," the Queen added, "and the Devon cream scones."

"Special Branch has warned me never to mention this, but I gather you are an exception to the rule," Stahmer said, knowing the answer.

"Well, I'm sure they have told you about the situation. No medals, I am afraid. Nobody wants this to come out; not now, not in a hundred years. We have had one Guy Fawkes, and we don't want another."

Robert Stahmer took several minutes and explained his background; that he had worked for the Health and Safety Executive as an accident investigator for the past eight years. The Queen, of course, had been briefed on his background, but she remained impassive and very professional as he described what she already knew.

She moved in her chair a little closer to Robert as he began to get to the exciting parts of his story.

"Ma'am, the member of parliament for Grantham requested that my department send down an investigator to the Houses of Parliament after the Deputy Speaker of the House had contracted Weil's disease and subsequently died."

"I know about this disease," the Queen interjected. "In 1978, the Health Minister at one of my garden parties told me a little tale. It appears that the masses at that time had begun to enjoy drinking Mexican beer out of bottles; not a pastime one would partake in," she said, amused. "Anyhow, as they began this, let's say, habit, Weil's disease began to raise its ugly head again. No longer the odd case of the sewer worker, but twenty or thirty cases a year. Evidently, the female rats in Mexico, on the ships, and in the British ports, had a penchant for relieving themselves against the bottles of beer in the cargo holds. Well, next stop would be the lips of the masses, and for those unfortunate enough to drink from the infected bottles, they got Leptospirosis, commonly known as Weil's disease." The Queen paused.

"Yes, Ma'am, but probably what you were not told was how the importers and producers got over the problem," Stahmer added, "without losing a penny."

"Pray, do tell," the Queen replied enthusiastically.

"They advertised the bottles of beer with a segment of lemon or lime, and the actors would rub the lime or lemon around the top of the bottle. Both citrus fruits are a disinfectant, and it killed off the disease. It caught on quickly, and the disease more or less disappeared overnight," Stahmer replied.

"Fascinating. So, all these up-and-coming city types with a slice of lemon in their bottle of beer think it is stylish when in truth they are masking rat urine. So, how did our illustrious Members of Parliament contract the disease? Most of them are more gin than beer; one would suspect," the Queen observed.

"On being appointed to undertake the investigation, my thoughts were that the Houses are on the River Thames. Where there is a river, rats will not be far away. However, when I met the pest control unit that is responsible for keeping the Houses pest free, they confirmed they had tests carried out on the rats they had caught over the last several weeks. The outcome of the tests: there were none with Leptospirosis or Weil's disease." Stahmer paused and took a sip of his tea before continuing.

"The first morning, I took the investigation to Parliament. I was escorted to the Lords' Chamber, the Clock Tower, Westminster Hall, the Central Lobby, the House of Commons, and the House of Lords."

"My, my… You may well have seen more than most of the Royal Household. Did you get to see the magnificent Lords Library?" the Queen inquired.

"No, Ma'am, the Lords Library and basement were out of bounds and roped off, as there was a program of asbestos removal underway. As you are probably aware, the Houses of Parliament had been stuffed to the gunnels with asbestos dating back before the Second World War, and further reinforced with asbestos during the war. Winston Churchill determined that he would not hand Hitler a propaganda coup by showing them on fire."

"Good old Winston. They filled the palace up with the heinous material as well," the Queen added, as Stahmer drained his cup.

"During the tour, I had become somewhat concerned about what I observed. I was escorted back to my car to get some bags and equipment. As per standing operating procedure, I put on a white coverall suit and took an FFP3 high-quality dust mask. The maintenance supervisor escorting me declined the use of the PPE; he probably thought I was typical Health and Safety and overreacting. I pulled rank and told him to put them on," Stahmer explained.

"What was concerning you to go all Health and Safety, Mr Stahmer?" the Queen inquired.

"Dust, Ma'am. On the benches of the House of Commons, I noticed fine fibres. Just a few, but they were there. On asking, I was informed the cleaners had cleaned that morning, so I assumed they had arrived there recently. In the Lords' there was evidence of wood dust. So, I went back and had the samples I took analysed.

"The analysis would take several days, so I started to do some desktop investigations. At first, I considered that it might have been poor craft and lack of professionalism by the asbestos removers. I got their details from the maintenance supervisor. From that point, I began to check the contractors out and look at their background." Robert paused to take a little bite of the delicious scone filled with the lightest cream he had ever tasted.

"The Office of Parliamentary Security was helpful and showed me all the criminal record checks on the principal contractor. There were eight of their men on the site, including the proprietor, Mitch Mills. All had sailed through the audit.

"When the sample results were returned and confirmed my initial concerns, I started to dig deeper. First, we stopped the contractor on-site and removed his and all his employees' passes. Whatever happened, they would never get back on site," Stahmer reported.

"Is that when you found it was the asbestos dust?" the Queen inquired.

"Yes, Ma'am," Stahmer replied.

"What made you think it was something other than an error or an accident?" the Queen asked.

"The dust I found in the House of Lords was MDF dust, Medium Density Fibreboard. This dust is banned in a whole host of countries and is widely known as a carcinogen: two separate materials, asbestos and MDF, both highly dangerous, and in both sets of Houses. Needless to say, Ma'am, my antennae were going haywire.

"After a day or so of hands-on research, I discovered that there had been a severe outbreak of salmonella in Bellamy's, the restaurant at the House. A week after this, one of the government whips received third-degree burns from an electrical shock from a kettle in his office; the grounding wire had come loose. All these random incidents in one place? Odds are stacked against it," Stahmer concluded.

"Is that when you had the Houses closed? The first time in an emergency for over a hundred years. Although I believe the excuse was it had been closed due to a gas leak," the Queen added.

"Yes, Ma'am. I could not be sure what was happening, just that something was amiss. Special Branch got involved and started to delve into Mr Mills. They discovered that his wife, Christine Mills, had been made bankrupt by HMRC over a £17,000 unpaid VAT bill. Evidently, she was a woman who was bipolar. Three weeks after the court bankrupted her, she went to her local tax office, poured petrol over her head, and lit the flammable liquid."

"How tragic! Did she die?" the Queen asked, somewhat saddened.

"Yes, Ma'am, she did. Mr Mills told anyone and everyone he would get some payback. The trouble is, this sort of thing doesn't come up in the criminal records check," he added.

"Once we had all the Houses cleared, I had specialist teams go in to check the whole complex over. We found crocidolite and amosite asbestos dust inside hundreds of books in the library. They are lethal, if not immediately, certainly at some time in the future. We found the same asbestos in the House records and papers. Further investigation found MDF dust and amosite asbestos in the House of Lords. If this was not bad enough, we discovered Legionella bacterium in the air conditioning units.

"We also found that Mr Mills was replacing the asbestos in the roof voids with fine acrylic powder, not one generally used in insulation. Dust and powder can explode if agitated enough, and we found fans up in the attic spaces. So although he is not admitting to it, we believe he was planning for an explosion at some time," Robert continued.

"Mills had easy access to MDF and asbestos. Several months ago, he did some work in a lab in Oxford where they were looking at diseases such as Weil's disease. They found vials of the stuff in his house." Stahmer paused for another bite of the scone.

"So, has everyone been exposed to these toxins?" the Queen interjected.

"Luckily, the weather has been unseasonably cold, so the air conditioning units had not been switched on. I think it is safe to say now, I believe that we dodged the bullet there. However, when they interviewed Mills, he admitted he had been placing the asbestos dust for weeks. The house has had many full debates, so we can assume an awful lot of people and Members of Parliament have been exposed," Robert explained.

"So, does that mean they will all die?" the Queen asked.

"Hard to say, Ma'am. Sure, some will die; not tomorrow, but in five, ten, fifteen years. The luck of the draw, actually; the older you are, and most MPs are, if you smoke, and many do, the bigger the chance of contracting it. They certainly have not dodged the bullet there.

"Of the previous incidents, an Under Secretary of State has had to have a kidney transplant after the salmonella outbreak, and then the whip has had some skin grafts after the electrocution," he said.

"We don't know how much of this you know, but we do know you have had to sign the Official Secret Act, so the least we can do is bring you up to date. Only a few in the House know what has happened, and that is the way it will stay; no use in worrying them.

"There will be no trial. Knowing my intelligence services, we think it is certain that Mr Mills will have an unfortunate accident sometime soon, and thus another secret that won't be available for scrutiny, ever."

"You have the thanks of a grateful nation, Mr Stahmer. No medals, alas, but the personal thanks of your Queen," she said.

"I appreciate that, Ma'am," Stahmer replied.

"So, is it back to the Health and Safety Executive? May seem a little boring after this," the Queen inquired.

"Not right away, Ma'am. It's my tenth wedding anniversary next week, and we are going on a cruise in the Caribbean."

Chapter Five

Sebastian had resorted to wearing wigs, expensive wigs, most people never gave it a second glance. The small fortune Sebastian invested made the wigs look like natural hair. To the more discerning and trained in the art of hairdressing, it was apparent they were artificial. He had no hair around his crotch, under his arms, or on any skin surface. Instead, he had blotches and scars where the hair had once sprouted. Once the compulsion could no longer be satisfied for the lack of body hair, he had moved on to stealing cats, removing their hair as they squirmed, screeched, and spat out in pain. Then once he had satisfied his lust and hunger, he would typically choke the life out of the poor animal, before removing the ligatures and disposing of the carcass in the nearest disposal unit.

In the spring of 1992, Sebastian had an interview and audition with Danish Cruise Liners. He played various tracks from Lennon and McCartney, and sang a ballad from the musical *Joseph*, and played an outstanding rendition of Ravel's *Bolero*. Even before he played *American Pie*, the panel had made their minds up. The panel consisted of two male entertainment managers and a female management representative. It was clear the interview panel thought the appearance of Sebastian strange. It was a warm, spring day, and nearly all the entertainers the panel had interviewed that day had come in T-shirts or summer dresses. Sebastian came wearing a long-sleeved shirt, and one interviewer remarked how his hair seemed strange. Another commented on the lack of eyebrows. What all the panel members did agree upon was that they thoroughly enjoyed the music and the singing.

The audition went well, as he expected, and within six weeks Sebastian had been offered the position of piano bar musician on the cruise ships the Danish Cruise Liners operated. Less than two weeks after the offer of employment, Sebastian boarded the daily Pan Am transatlantic flight to Heathrow terminal just outside London.

Sebastian had to attend a three-day induction course held at the Hyde Park Hotel. He did not mix with the other seven entertainers who participated at the same induction. One of the female performers was a dancer; an older male was a compere. Also present were five female musicians who had worked with orchestras around the world, and had now formed a group to play classical music in the dining rooms and atriums. Most tried to talk to Sebastian, but his replies were limited and unresponsive; they thought him extremely shy. Sebastian's demeanour was becoming a problem for the training manager. During the appraisal, she was dubious about Sebastian's people skills, thinking that she would probably not let Sebastian pass through the induction. Inevitably, this would lead to the offer to play with Danish Cruise Liners being retracted. Sebastian realized after his assessor's intervention that his interaction with the other entertainers might count against him, and he knew he had to do something to ensure he would be accepted.

On the final evening of the stay at the Hyde Park Hotel, and without notice or invitation, Sebastian sat down at the large, shining, white grand piano. He began playing a rendition of *Rocket Man,* the Elton John crowd-pleaser. At the end of the song, the genuine applause from the other entertainers and guests rang out loudly. Sebastian followed the rock classic by expertly delivering a rousing theme from Wagner's *Gotterdammerung*. Finally, in utter contrast, he finished with Billy Joel's *Uptown Girl,* before granting the audience an encore of music by John Mills. The reaction from the audience, and Sebastian's change from introvert to extrovert when he got behind the grand piano, convinced the training manager to rethink her decision, and grant Sebastian an initial contract.

Again, Sebastian had pulled it off. He put it down to his favourite quote by Leo Tolstoy, the Russian author, and philosopher: 'Music is the shorthand to the emotions.' In short, music could make a grown man cry, or in this case, change the mind of a doubting Thomas.

The following afternoon, the group of artists, having all been told they had reached an acceptable level to work for Danish Cruise Liners, collected their luggage. The musical group returned to the airport to board a flight to Barcelona to join the ship Aquatic Adventure. Sebastian and the remaining two sped southwards by coach down to the docks at Southampton to meet his new ship, the Majesty of the Waves.

Before applying for a position at sea, Sebastian had thought hard and long about working on a cruise liner. He had considered several different options, but every time, he came back to cruising. Cruise ships would be the perfect platform for his musical skills, as well as offering an opportunity for him to go about his business, with little chance of detection. Cats no longer fulfilled his desires;

he wanted more, much more. He wanted an adult experience like Geraldine, with the chance to satisfy his ever-present and demanding urges.

Sebastian knew that the perfect opportunity to indulge his idiosyncrasies and pleasures with minimum risk was across international borders, preferably in countries that lacked the facilities and expertise in the up-and-coming scientific breakthrough call DNA testing. Cruise ships passed through these areas every day.

The liner was undertaking a round-the-world trip from Southampton to Sydney. There would be short stops at Gibraltar, Cyprus, and the Red Sea port of Sharm El Sheikh, before moving on to Dubai. After an overnight stop in Dubai, the ship would be at sea for several days until it reached Phuket. The island was a holiday resort belonging to Thailand. Following an overnight stop, they would take the short hop down to Singapore and then to Sydney, Australia. On the return leg of the cruise, the ship would visit the South Pacific, visiting firstly New Zealand, later to Rarotonga, the most populous and beautiful island in the Cook Islands. The vessel would then travel onwards across the International Date Line and take in Cabo on the west coast of Mexico, before finally heading into the Port of Los Angeles. Sebastian was contracted to do the outward leg of the journey as far as Singapore. He would then have thirty-six hours of leisure in the area before flying home to San Diego for a short break before joining a ship in Miami.

The ship owners decided that entertainers would stay on board for a maximum of a month before being rotated to another liner, and rest periods every three months. This procedure ensured that the passengers received a variety of performers throughout the cruise. The most critical part for Sebastian was that he would then have thirty-six hours in Singapore before flying home.

During the cruise down to Singapore, Sebastian was playing seven nights a week, from 7:30-9:00 pm, and then 11:00 pm to 12:30 am. Occasionally, he would perform in the main lounge to back up the entertainers.

The ship had a gross tonnage of 101,500, and a length of 893 feet. It could cruise along at 21 knots, which equates to 24 miles per hour, and had accommodation for 2,750 passengers, with an average of two guests per room.

The ship had nine decks, with an atrium dissecting seven levels right through the centre. The second to top outer deck consisted of two bars, a bistro, a large swimming pool, three hot spas, and a multitude of deck chairs. Running through deck six was an avenue, an arcade of shops running aft from the atrium. Forward of the atrium on deck seven was the piano lounge, and this was to be Sebastian's working area, with the odd appearance on the main theatre or variety bar as planned by the entertainment manager, who was treated like minor royalty, while the captain of the ship was the king.

Sebastian was quite amused at how the entertainers were treated compared to the other staff. All ships have a hierarchy of respect and treatment from peers and others. The ship's officers, who dealt with sailing and engineering, came top of the tree. The crew captain came next, followed by the entertainers, then the chefs and waiting staff. The cabin boys and girls and laundry staff sat squarely at the bottom of the heap.

Sebastian received respect for his status as an artist, but behind the scenes some would sneer at his appearance and attitude. He was one of the few who had a single-person cabin, a real perk when you considered that the waiters shared four to a cabin. The single cabin status displayed the entertainers' standing in the pecking order.

The work was easy, and the temptations on offer were overwhelming. Sebastian could have had a multitude of older women guests; it was unbelievable how many middle-aged women would make it quite clear to Sebastian that they would appreciate a little more than *Atlantic Crossing* or *Rockin' Robin*. The lip scar and strange hairdo did not seem to put these women off. Music was the key to emotion.

His scarred lip mattered little. To sleep with the excellent pianist was a priority for some of the guests. However, Sebastian was not interested in sex; he was involved in another type of pleasure, the extreme joy which comes from being in control, to have the power to give and to take away life.

Sebastian used his spare time each day to research and look for an excellent opportunity to satisfy his ever-present needs. He studied the route and destinations of the cruise carefully, and maps of the ports. He researched towns near the cruise terminals, as well as some further afield. The place to launch his first attack had to be far enough away from the cruise port. The police force had to be limited in professionalism and lacking new technology.

Almost immediately, this ruled out Singapore, as the police force had been trained by the British and had the latest technology as befitted a first-world nation.

However, while the Malaysians had also had training from the British, their force, due to economics, was not as efficient, nor did it have the technological advances that Singapore enjoyed. The Malaysian police force was concentrated in the principal cities, such as Kuala Lumpur, and had far less coverage in the outlying areas and islands.

Sebastian had reconciled himself to Malaysia. The target area needed to have sufficient escape routes. It would be easy to get to and from Singapore by train and be within sixteen hours of travelling time. The area had to be somewhat remote, and far enough away from the main conurbations with increased police presence. Sebastian had worked out that he had thirty-six hours from beginning to end so he could be on the flight home on Monday that the cruise line company had booked him on.

Everything pointed to the kampongs on the islands of Penang or Langkawi. However, Penang was a much shorter ferry ride, and it also had a connecting bridge from the mainland, so Penang it was.

Sebastian had decided to carry out his attack in one of the kampongs. He knew these villages of bamboo and corrugated iron huts had little in the way of security. Sebastian needed a kampong that was on the tourist route. Even though he had similar colouring to the locals, he had Eurasian tones and looks, and with his scar on his lip, he would stand out in an area devoid of tourists. He needed the district to have public transport. There was no possibility of hiring a motorbike or car, as they would require a paper trail, and Sebastian's forgery skills were not up to that standard.

Although he was confident the police force had little training in the way of modern forensic science, he had decided not to leave any traces. He would have used a hair remover the day he left the ship, but none was required, as one had to have hair to remove it. Sebastian left the ship for his thirty-six-hour sabbatical before flying back to San Diego via Heathrow.

He had stood naked in his shower and spread soap and scrubbed vigorously with a scrubbing brush all over his body—under his arms, across his chest, around the pubic area, everywhere. After showering, he had inspected himself and was pleased with the outcome. He was sure the dead skin cells—which accumulate on all human beings and leave identifiable DNA traces when they fall invisibly—had been eradicated and had been washed away down the shower drain.

The day had come; the day he had waited for since Geraldine. Sebastian disembarked in Singapore. He had somehow managed to control his passions on the ship. Some of the men and women had beautiful locks of hair. What he wouldn't have given to have been able to tear out some of those strands and to gorge himself on it, the screams of the victim just an added pleasure he fantasised about constantly.

Sebastian had taken the train from Singapore, travelling the twelve hours north, until he arrived at the ferry terminal at Butterworth. The ferry would take him off the mainland of Malaysia to Penang, and on to Georgetown on the island. The ferry was the first of the day, and most people would be coming the other way to the mainland, rather than going to the island at this time, so it was relatively quiet.

On arriving at the island, Sebastian then took what passed for a bus to the Batu Ferringhi. It was 5:30 am when he arrived at the central town bus station, which consisted of a couple of sheds with corrugated roofing.

The bus station had a busy outside café that began to service several locals who were having breakfast before going to work. He smelt damp foliage and the unmistakable aroma of fish, along with the acrid stench of sewage, intermingled with the aroma of spices.

On the map, the kampong, Batu Ferringhi, was just off the main street, and offset a couple of hundred yards south of the market on the opposite side.

The market side was very civilized. There were seating areas where the locals drank tea, and local traders were readying their stalls with a variety of live, dead, and inanimate objects to sell.

While the bus station and local market were not precisely what Sebastian would consider American or British standard, they looked comparatively modern after he veered off the main road and onto the tracks into the kampongs. The concrete of the twentieth century ebbed away with every footstep.

The particular kampong Sebastian had chosen was ideal. There was a main road running from the bridge at Gelugor north, as you entered the sub-tropical island to the small town of Batu Ferringhi. The town was on the tourist trail, due to its proximity to one of the best butterfly farms in Asia. There was also the snake temple, and the area had excellent beaches. The road was sporadically littered with tired Seventies-built hotels, along with a few later models.

The light of the morning that welcomed him when he arrived at the bus station struggled to penetrate the canopy of trees on the narrow paths leading to the kampong. Sebastian began to sweat; the heat of the early morning began to intensify. It had reached 28 degrees Celsius before most people in the area had set off to work.

Sebastian had to traverse deep monsoon drains by a small metal ramp among the dead foliage that was on the dried, baked mud track. He heard the melody of monkeys that inhabited the canopies above. Sebastian was now in the jungle, passable jungle with defined trails, but jungle nonetheless.

There was dense foliage that consisted of banana trees, palm trees, and aloe vera and sisal plants, with their sharp, pointed, rigid, needle-type leaves overhanging and impinging on the path. On more than one occasion, Sebastian was stabbed by one tropical plant or another.

The environment did worry Sebastian somewhat. For all his careful planning, he had not been in this type of situation before. His childhood memories differed from the tropical forests he remembered in Thailand. Maybe it was the foliage that gave rise to the overwhelmingly humid conditions. The heat and lack of light in the jungle area were not something he had thought about when planning this. When he entered this jungle, he began to think about other hazards that had not crossed his mind in the planning stage.

Several rhesus monkeys swung overhead and squawked in a threatening manner; they appeared to resent the intruder's presence into their domain. Sebastian hoped the noise of the monkey's chattering covered all the sound he was trying not to make.

The route to the kampong, although semi-lit by the rays of the sun that penetrated the canopy in sporadic areas, was cluttered with dead foliage, and the multitude of micro wildlife including beetle and ant varieties. Sebastian followed the electric and telephone wires, which seemed out of place. They did not belong, any more than he did in the area. The lines led him to the main area for the huts. Telegraph poles sat in between the dense foliage on either side of the little square in the centre of the kampong. The early morning chorus from singing birds that jostled for space along the lines assisted in camouflaging the noise he made as he inched along the edges.

Sebastian began to sweat even more profusely, as the high temperature and humidity increased once he was off the main road and into the jungle. Due to the lack of hair on his body, the sweat ran in rivulets down his back, and cascaded in the crease of his buttocks and down his legs. Sebastian stopped when someone further down the track made a noise, and he sidestepped into the jungle a few steps, which was sufficient to hide. He stood behind a large, green banana tree, which had flowered with a deep, large red flower head and tiny bananas beside it. The brilliance of the colours was somewhat diminished by the smell of rotting foliage, and the sewage seeping through the green surroundings.

A young, athletic, and lithe-looking villager wearing a blue and red sarong passed along the track, unaware that only feet away hid the man who was planning his attack.

Sebastian emerged and closed in on the kampong. From observation on the perimeter of the kampong, and hidden in the dense green, he had sight of the only building not made of wood and corrugated metal sheets; it was the small, white Catholic church in the centre of the kampong. It was a remnant of another century, when missionaries had spread the wrath of God should the villagers not visit the church each Sunday, and each church occupied the primary position in the village.

As quietly as possible, Sebastian circumnavigated the kampong, looking for all possible escape routes and hidden snags such as drains or ruts in the mud. Monsoon season was still a month or so away, so the ground was hard and compacted away from the access routes, thus leaving access and egress routes that would leave no boot tracks, which was just how Sebastian had planned it.

Monkeys squawked, birds sang, dogs barked, and the noise of the multitude of crickets created a backdrop of routine, everyday sounds, that would not attract attention.

Sebastian settled down and hid under the leaf of a large, indigenous plant. Its foliage was as broad as Sebastian's ship cabin. He kept a careful lookout for snakes and the numerous large poisonous spiders that inhabited the island. He was angry with himself that he had not considered this when putting his plan together. The last thing he needed was a bite from one of these reptiles or arachnids to destroy his day and possibly expose him.

With the light increasing, Sebastian decided to make a move a few minutes past 6 am. He used his binoculars to watch the kampong stir into life. He was somewhat surprised as spotlessly clean children in neat and ironed school uniforms emerged from the ramshackle huts and went off through the tracks to catch their early morning school bus.

The men emerged from their shelters and went off to the fields and factories in nearby towns. By 7 am, the kampong appeared mostly deserted, apart from a young teenager who chatted quietly with an older-looking lady, possibly her mother. The older woman was slim, with her own teeth, and skin a little leathery from the effects of the sun. He surmised the woman was in her middle forties. They sat around a small, square wooden table that looked older than the woman, the varnish and wood stain a distant memory. It was not more than thirty minutes before the teenager left to go about her business.

He dismissed the idea of killing the mother when a younger girl, no more than twenty-two, emerged from the hut next to the one he had been observing. She was about five feet tall, with a beautiful, childlike, rounded face, and jet-black hair tied back with a rainbow-coloured ribbon. Sebastian knew it had to be her.

The old woman chatted with the young Malay woman for several minutes, while clearing the leftover rice and stinky fruit from that morning's breakfast.

After a further twenty minutes, the old lady emerged from her hut with reed shopping bags, and disappeared between the other shelters, obviously going out for the dinner she would serve up that evening.

Sebastian edged closer and closer, with only the movement of the leaves in his wake, and the noise drowned out by the chorus of the jungle. He stopped beside a bamboo wall that acted as a fence to one of the huts, out of sight and waited another ten minutes to ensure that no one else was around.

His condition was far from ideal, soaking wet with sweat from the high humidity, and sure he must be leaving DNA traces along the route.

Sebastian amended his plans to minimize any risk of being seen, or worse, caught in the act. There were several areas of chance and uncertainty. He could not be sure that there was no one else in any of the other huts so it would have to be silent, and death rendered almost immediately. While he would have preferred to have some foreplay, this was a risk too far today, so his torture fantasies were put away for another time—and they were many.

He had considered burning the hut on completion of his task but thought that would bring attention to bear too quickly. He was satisfied; his precautions were sufficient for the task at hand.

Today would have to be perfect. It was not some simple rite of passage. Not a quick, fumbled, devastating exchange like Geraldine. Here and now was the real deal; this was more like the fantasy he had had ever since he had killed for the first time as a child.

There was not, nor had there ever been, a message from God telling him to kill. There were no conflicting voices in his head. No purely sexual motive for what he was about to do. It was about who he was and what he wanted to do. The planning and the act were what made life bearable and exciting. It was simple: he needed hair, and he enjoyed the pain.

After stowing his rucksack under some bushes, he stealthily crept forward, until he reached the only entrance in and out of the hut. He gently knocked on the door, and the young, pregnant woman answered immediately. There were no eyeholes in the door to see who was there, no chain lock, for this was a simple hut in a Malaysian kampong, and what was the risk to her?

As she opened the door, she wondered who this stranger was, and looked astonished for a millisecond before she began to collapse. Sebastian had stunned her with a jab to the jaw; it had rocked the slightly built woman to the core. As she started to collapse, Sebastian pushed his way into the hut. He placed a hand over the woman's mouth, in case she gathered her senses and began to scream.

He noticed a wooden surround vanity mirror which could be altered to various angles, that the woman used to ready her appearance. With one hand, Sebastian placed this on the floor and redirected the perspective so he could see the face of the woman. She was on her knees with Sebastian behind her, also on his knees. He ripped off her sarong with one fluid movement, and the girl was naked underneath the garment. He would have to forgo the pleasure of seeing this beautiful girl in pain. He knew silence was the key, as there were possibly other villagers around. He would have to kill her quickly, which took the edge of excitement off a little.

The girl's naked body was perfect. He would start with the pubic hairs, which were few, and head upwards to the beautiful, long, shiny black hair. He would have her plucked like a chicken within the hour.

Sebastian transferred his left hand from her mouth to her throat and began to squeeze. This had a weakening effect on the woman. She struggled relentlessly, legs kicking at first, and then more of a convulsive shudder as she slowly choked to death.

Sebastian did not take his eyes off the mirror, watching her struggle to breathe, the eyes wide and terrified, and still he squeezed. She babbled on in her mother tongue, more a rasp, as the life was being choked out of her. Her hand was on his, trying to pry his fingers off her throat, the other was rubbing her stomach as if soothing the baby inside from the horror that had befallen her and it.

Just as life was leaving her, the door suddenly creaked and opened slightly. Sebastian jumped up and let the choking girl fall. In a fluid movement, he stamped down on her throat, extinguishing her spark of life. Sebastian was furious that his experience had been interrupted. He was fast and no sooner had the visitor creaked open the door then he pulled her in.

It was evident now that the older woman he had seen earlier had forgotten something, and on her return had heard the commotion in the hut.

The elderly lady's eyes opened in terror at the sight of her naked neighbour spread-eagled on the floor. Her eyes were wide open; it was clear she was dead. The woman went to scream, but the scream would not come out. What she had not realized was that her brain had not accepted the death delivered to her a second earlier. Sebastian struck her with the clenched heel of his palm.

He hit her directly under the nose, and the force knocked the cartilage upwards until the nasal bone was pushed backwards into the brain.

Sebastian was enraged. He had not had time to think; the kill was a reflex action to a situation he had not expected. He had killed two women but had not had the explosion of pleasure he so wanted and needed because he was disturbed by this woman.

Sebastian lost several minutes of memory while he delivered his fury through his feet to the lifeless body beneath him. Gone was the pleasure. Gone was his meticulous and flawless planning. His lack of control startled him back to reality. He had blood spattered up his legs, and his white training shoes dyed into a bloody, slick red. Quickly he checked the slat which passed for a window; there was no other movement, and for that he was thankful. He turned his attention back to his victim, and with a firm grip, he tore away at the young girl's hair, pulling out clumps of the scalp along with the strands of dark hair. Each tuft took Sebastian several minutes to gulp down.

Bloodied from the splatters from the women, and the constant leaking of sweat from his brow, Sebastian's face and clothes were streaked. He took a bottle of water that was placed on a rickety table and began to wash away the evidence from his legs. His training shoes proved more resilient to the water. Once most of the blood was removed from his legs, he began to reformulate his plan. There was a pool of water mixed with blood on the floor; there were streaks of blood over the wooden slats of the door and on some of the furniture.

Sebastian took a deep breath. His original plan was always open for adaptation, but this was going to be one hell of an adjustment. He would have to burn the hut and destroy what evidence was there; if he could make it look accidental, all the better.

The hut had what passed for two rooms; a bedroom with several beds in it where all the family slept, regardless of age, and the main room, which was both a living and cooking area.

As in most hot countries, the occupants would cook on open fires outside the huts. But in times of monsoon there needed to be a backup. In the corner was a 13.5 kg butane gas bottle attached to a basic camp stove, which consisted of two rings. On the table were a packet of cigarettes and a box of matches. His plan was formulating and taking shape.

Bordered by a pair of bodies and blood evidence, it was time to take his predetermined route back to the main road before the village folk heard the explosion.

As Sebastian boarded the bus to Georgetown, he heard a dull thud in the distance and could see wisps of smoke from over the tree line from the direction of the kampong. The cigarette Sebastian had lit as the ignition source married with the gas from the ruptured rubber line leading from the gas bottle to the two-ring stove. The explosion blew the hut apart and pieces of the dead women lay scattered over a two hundred metre circumference amongst the burning trees and foliage.

No DNA, Sebastian thought. He doubted the police would search for it, as this was a simple, tragic accident. The bodies incinerated beyond recognition he hoped, their injuries obliterated.

From Georgetown, it took fourteen hours to Singapore Central Station. From the train station, Sebastian took a taxi to Orchid Road, had some Singapore dim sum with noodles, mixed with a couple of strands of his victim's hair, and ate the strange concoction hungrily. Following the meal, Sebastian hailed a taxi to Changi Airport. By this time, the fire that had engulfed the kampong and obliterated seventeen other huts close to the murder scene, and the lives and possessions of those two family members, mothers both, were finally extinguished. The final death toll had been four: the old woman, the young, intended victim, a child who had missed school through chickenpox, and her grandma who had been looking after her.

Three hours and two airport showers later, Sebastian boarded a Boeing 747 on the way back to San Diego, via London.

chapter six

ax Cutler was twenty-four years of age in 2005. During the previous five years, he had been through all the recruitment training, and then some, at the Secret Service training academy outside of Washington, DC. Graduating from the course in the top two percentile, he was marked down for the fast track for exceptional officers. He had quickly learned the advanced application training in combatting counterfeiting and could identify a forged dollar bill within seconds. His marksmanship was assessed as sniper level, and he relished and excelled at water survival skills and physical fitness. The slight blemish on his record from the course was the inability to keep his manhood in his pants when a beautiful lady, in this case a female instructor, came a-calling.

Within a year, Max had had several excursions into the field, as part of a covert team investigating counterfeiting and the organizations that undertake such activities. He had had cause to draw his weapon twice in the intervening years and had shot in retaliation once. The Romanian he had cornered with $25,000 in counterfeit bills was not going to come easy and had shot at Cutler and his colleagues three times before Cutler put a 9mm projectile between the Romanian's eyes.

The Secret Service offered mandatory counselling, as they did for all agents who had participated in a shooting that had led to a fatality. His debrief was short, and the kill was good. Cutler felt no remorse; the guy was trying to kill him. After the shooting, he was no longer treated as the new kid on the block. Cutler had earned respect for his aptitude and attitude from day one from his peers and superiors, but the way he handled himself had built up new levels of respect and admiration from others in the Service.

He had been leading an investigation unit comprised of three agents and himself for the past year. At twenty-four years of age, he was amongst the youngest team leaders the Service had had since the Second World War.

Cutler and his team had been investigating a German gang of counterfeiters for much of 2005 and into 2006.

The Berlin Wall had been dismantled in 1989, which led to the demise of the East German Ministry of State Security, commonly known as the Stasi. Trained by the KGB, the Stasi had a reputation for being one of the most ruthless of any government department, even outstripping the KGB in some ways.

Reforming and restructuring the Soviet Union, known as Perestroika, had been Gorbachev's legacy, and one of the turning points in the twentieth century. On the downside, hundreds of highly trained East German intelligence operatives had been put out of work overnight. Some of them would be tracked down and prosecuted over atrocities they had committed in the name of the East German government. Some had been taken on by their West German counterparts; most had set up criminal operations and utilized other ex-members or trained up new ones.

Cutler had begun to investigate such a gang, which originated in Dresden, in the old Eastern section. When the police started to close in on them, they moved base, setting up operations in a beautiful small town in Bavaria, Bad Reichenhall, right in the foothills of the Bavarian Alps. The area was as stunning as it was quiet, just fifteen minutes from the Austrian border and Salzburg, the same distance up the steep, winding road to Berchtesgaden.

Cutler was on their trail and set up his base in Berchtesgaden. Following the second world war, the USA created a significant military presence in the area and built a large army camp, on the foot of an alpine peak. This town and camp were situated below the lodge known as the Eagle's Nest, a birthday present for Adolf Hitler in 1939. The American military and CIA had several safe houses near the base. Cutler chose a pleasant Bavarian chalet between the river and salt mine, which was once an SS brothel in the Second World War.

The third day of June 2006, Cutler had travelled some eight miles along the alpine road to Konigsee. The scenery was outstanding: tree-lined, with Bavarian chalets interspersed with woods and fast-flowing rivers of ice melt from the looming alps, which served as a picture-postcard backdrop.

Their destination was an alpine lake with green slopes and wildflowers surrounding the bright expanse of water. Apart from the top of the Alps, the snow had receded two months earlier. Where there had been crisp, white, virgin snow in March, the hillsides had transformed and were alive with the vibrant colour and fresh smell of resplendent alpine flowers. The flora was glorious and all-encompassing. The impact on the view was stunning, with several shades of green interspersed with the blues and whites of the alpine flowers. Cutler had excellent hearing, and the chorus of birds and insects drowned out the radio, which was on low. The most evocative of his senses were sight and smell. The aroma took him back to his childhood, days of skiing in Lake Louise, Canada. The crisp, white snowmelt raced past in the river that ran beside his car. Sweet, aromatic flowers, combined with fresh bread from a bakery some several hundred yards down the road, overwhelmed his senses. His sense of wellbeing was in sharp contrast to what he and his team were about to do.

On the same day, several hours earlier, Sebastian, under the cloak of darkness, dropped Cutler's sister Elisa still-warm body over the stern of the cruise ship. He had finally succumbed to his passion and killed a guest, a very special person to the Cutler family and her friends.

Cutler and his team were close to closing this ex-Stasi gang down once and for all. He had his team plant microphones where he assumed, they would meet in the parking lot leading to the lake. He placed one of his team behind the ticket office for the parking lot, and another elevated on a slight rise in the Alps, hidden by several pine trees. The third was in the café opposite the lake, and Cutler headed to the alpine ski area with its magnificent bobsled run.

Seppi Werner was the ex-Stasi agent in charge of the operation. He was a typical Aryan, with short, blond, cropped hair and blue eyes. At six foot one, Werner looked squat due to muscle, which appeared to weigh him down, lowering his centre of gravity. His operation was simple; he had acquired, through fair means and foul, as many one-dollar bills as possible. Werner used an American airline stewardess to import a thousand one-dollar bills from the States each month. He had an American US Air Force mechanic who could bring in another eight hundred through his contacts, an East End London car broker could ensure seven hundred and fifty per month, and others besides.

On average, the gang was collecting over four thousand one dollar bills each month. With their technique, equipment, and knowledge, they could convert the one-dollar bills into hundred-dollar bills.

This operation in Bad Reichenhall was generating them $480,000 per year. They received fifty cents on the dollar from other couriers, who would use and spread the hundred-dollar bills as genuine. The gang was clearing $240,000 per month from the counterfeit operation.

The bills were of excellent quality, as the main ingredient was the unique paper, of which they had a steady supply. Neither Cutler nor his superiors had ever seen such high-quality bills, and they were concerned, as it would be easy to integrate the bills into the economy of the USA.

The technique for bleaching and over-printing of the bills was perfected in a building in the Tierpark in Berlin, which was Stasi-controlled, and was now the German-Russian Museum Berlin-Karlshorst.

Along with its Russian counterpart, the KBG, the Stasi planned to flood Europe with hundred-dollar bills. Ironically, the United States had given the Russians the idea of flooding other countries with its currency to destabilize the country.

The Americans had told the English in the 1950s that if they did not leave Egypt and give up their stranglehold on the Suez Canal, this is what they would do to them. Their only problem was, the Americans controlled their output of money carefully, and to flood Europe with sufficient dollars to cause the Americans serious problems would prove impracticable. That is when the Stasi came up with forging the money.

Once the plan was evaluated, the Russians put it on the back shelf; it was assessed that the amount of counterfeit money generated would not impact the American economy sufficiently to destablise it.

However, the Stasi, with Werner leading the counterintelligence, was not willing to put it away so quickly, and had been working on the plan and converting dollars for five years before the Berlin Wall came down. If not for the communist cause, Werner was happy to proceed for his own greed.

Cutler stood in the warm sunshine at the bottom of the concrete bobsled run. He was just another tourist visiting this place of past sporting triumphs and beauty. The difference was he was looking through his 10x50 WB Swarovski binoculars at the parking lot instead of looking at the lake. The binoculars were amongst the best in the world. They gave Max a clear view of the Mercedes van as it drew up alongside the white Ford transit van with the oval Austrian vehicle registration sticker, designated by the black letter 'A' on the white oval background.

Cutler knew from previous observations that the counterfeit money would be moved from Konigsee, a few miles to Obersalzberg, down the steep, cobbled Alpen Strasse until it flattened out on the outskirts of Salzburg. Then it would be on the autobahn down to Vienna and then moved on again in several directions to their distributors in Hungary, Slovakia, Italy, and Switzerland.

The counterfeit dollar bills in ten large brown packets were being transferred from the Mercedes to the Ford, which took several minutes. It took far less time for the five suitcases filled with $100,000 in genuine bills to be handed over from the two men from the Ford. Werner went inside the Mercedes van, to check the suitcases. Five minutes later, Werner emerged and nodded to the drivers of the Ford, who already had the engine running and ready to go. Cutler observed the transactions.

Cutler, in liaison with the local police, had three police vans waiting on the Alpen Strasse to set up a roadblock immediately after Cutler gave the go-ahead.

Cutler's third team member was in a blue Nissan Micra, a nondescript car which would not draw attention. He would follow the Ford van, and radio Cutler when they were approaching the section where the police vans had parked. Cutler would then inform the commander in charge, and the van would be hemmed in on both sides, with nowhere to go. Where the roadblock had been situated was not Cutler's choice or first option, but in line with working in partnership with the German police, he had reluctantly agreed to the commander's choice of location.

The route was steep and cobblestoned, with minimal turning opportunities. There were sheer rock walls on the driver's side and deep gorges on the passenger side.

Werner and his two henchmen would be going in the opposite direction. They would retrace the road Cutler had taken from Berchtesgaden. Cutler fell in love with the area with its small, picturesque villages with chalets adorned with paintings on the side of a man baking bread, or working the field, primarily depicting what the trade of the family that lived there.

As the road started to descend outside Berchtesgaden, you could either continue the high route towards the Austrian ski resorts, or take the road leading down to Bad Reichenhall. As the gang's headquarters was in Bad Reichenhall, Cutler had set up a similar trap on this road just north of a small town called Bischofsweisen.

Again, the German commander had chosen the area to block, which was the village's alpine railway crossing, a natural place for a roadblock, the leader had told Cutler. Again, it would not have been Cutler's first choice.

Radio masts were few and far between, and not allowed in the alpine area. As a result, the reception was abysmal. Still as a precaution, Cutler had agreed with the police to ensure the masts were offline while the operation was underway. He knew Werner never used mobile phones as he did not trust them, but his men may have them as backup.

Because of the separate vans going in opposite directions, the last thing Cutler needed was one van to inform the other they had fallen into a trap.

Cutler, from earlier stakeouts of the gang, had already identified that they used shortwave radios with encrypted transmissions. Werner had taken technical equipment and weapons from the Stasi armoury on its demise. The problem was the technology was outdated and Cutler could listen in unhindered to their transmissions. The lack of new technology was a flaw in the gang's communication capability—a significant weakness, as far as Cutler was concerned.

The Ford van navigated the cobblestoned hairpin bends slowly, as the road almost came parallel with the road back, which was now several metres higher. As soon as they had cleared the bend, they could see the police cars some hundred metres ahead.

Maybe it was the ten years they were almost certainly going to face in prison that made them make the foolish decision to try to navigate the roadblock. On the other hand, maybe as they came round the corner, the roadblock was on them too quickly, and they could not reverse, nor did they have any other escape routes.

In the blink of an eye, they skirted the roadblock, the left front and back wheels teetering on the edge of the cobbled road, the left-hand tyres spinning in open space above the 200-metre drop.

The centre of gravity is a moveable, invisible force, and gravity is forever the winner in battles of height and open spaces. The weight of the van and lack of support on the left-hand side began, slowly at first, to incline the van downwards over the open space. The right-hand tyres' grip on the road began to slip, and the force trying to keep it on the road was not sustainable.

The two occupants, the driver and his accomplice, were both hard men. When not plying their illegal trade, they visited the gym and worked out for most days of their adult lives. They were large men, with T-shirts that were stretched taut against their bulging muscles. They were men who had known violence, had seen grown men pleading with them as they had beaten them close to death. Today it was they who screamed like frightened little boys, tossing around as if they were in a tumble dryer as the van spun slowly and hastened its descent onto the boulders below.

Immediately upon impact, the two men were no longer screaming. Both men had died immediately on impact, their heads no more than a wet stain inside the demolished vehicle.

Fire needs three things to ensure that ignition can start and maintain the inferno. First, it needs oxygen; the clean mountain alpine air, sweet to taste, if a little sparser than at sea level, would do. Fire also requires an ignition source, and there were certainly enough sparks as the van hit the stony bottom of the gorge. Finally, fire needs fuel, and the petrol tank ruptured giving way to a deafening explosion, milliseconds after the engine was forced through the car, exiting the car's rear. Once the petrol had been spent, the fire sought out other sources of fuel to maintain the fire, and it found some. The cartons of money that were in the van seconds before the explosion now rained down to earth on fire. The vehicle's plastic components plus the fat and muscle of the two occupants, all added fuel to maintain the fire.

While the fire consumed the Ford van, Agent Johnson had come down from his observation point behind the trees on the hill. Johnson had joined Cutler in an unassuming Opel. They drove out behind the Mercedes van in which Werner and his bodyguard were exiting the parking lot.

Cutler was not worried that Werner or his crony would see the Opel. Such was the width of the road. The van would have been closely followed by several vehicles under any circumstances on any day.

At this stage, Werner sped down Berchtesgadener Strasse approaching thew town of Bayerisch Gmain, Cutler still tailing several cars back. The dull thud of the Ford van explosion was barely audible as it travelled through the alpine passes from four miles away. Cutler was unaware that the counterfeit dollars had gone up in smoke.

Werner was an astute operative. Unlike his dead Austrian counterparts, he would always put his faith in the justice system rather than risk his life by running or trying to skirt a roadblock. After all, Werner could always buy someone, either with money, or information he held on them from his days in the Stasi, and thus minimize any charges, or make them go away entirely.

Cutler had discussed the details with the German police commander on the ideal place to set up the roadblock. Both had finally agreed to locate the barrier half way around the steep hairpin on Haniel Strasse. The road narrowed and turned back on itself down a steep incline. The road had been blocked by police cars at both ends after Werner left to ensure no other traffic was coming from either direction.

Cutler, using the shortwave radio, gave the order to close the trap, as the Mercedes van approached the roadblock.

Werner was more surprised than alarmed when he saw the roadblock taking shape with only one car between him and the blockade. Werner was driving and reactively slammed on his breaks and skidded sidewards on the steep incline. Vlad, named after Vlad the Impaler, a name he revelled in, had an outstanding warrant against him for kicking to death a Turkish immigrant in

Berlin. He was not so ready to comply with the commands to exit the vehicle.

Werner was as surprised as anyone to see the Benelli M4 Super 90 12-gauge semi-automatic shotgun. Vlad had adored the Benelli at first sight. The gun lacked the traditional solid fixed stock and had a collapsible buttstock and was widely used in the US Marine Corps, favourite with the Navy Seals. The gun was robust, and the action was reliable and quick, and Vlad was just about to test it again.

"Dummkopf!" Werner shouted and attempted to grab the gun, as Vlad began to exit the passenger door, with the weapon rising to its firing position.

Too late. The snipers perched on the rocks above the roadblock and those hidden amongst the tree had unobstructed views through their telescopic sights. The leader gave one click on the microphone, which was heard in every sniper's headset, it was the order to open fire. It was seconds before the policemen at the roadblock could react.

A hail of bullets cut Vlad almost in half. He thought himself immortal and had survived several battles against other gangs, and once before with the police. But unfortunately for Vlad, this specialized squad had trained with the GSG9 German special forces, and the training had been comprehensive and drilled time and time again into the members of the unit.

Cutler got to the vehicle after the commander had issued the order to stop firing. He opened the door, and Werner fell out of the driver's seat into Cutler's arms. Cutler lowered him to the ground. Werner was struggling to breathe as air and blood escaped through the gaping hole in his throat. He had been hit by a single bullet that had entered the driver's side window, passed through the side of his neck, through his windpipe, and out the other side of his neck before exiting the rear side panel of the Mercedes van.

Cutler considered and assessed the scene before him and could immediately see that if he did not act quickly, Werner would not be around for the trial. Cutler moved over to Vlad laying in the middle of the road and proceeded to rip the shirt from the half-severed torso. Although the shirt was blood-soaked, Cutler's last thought was cross-contaminating Werner with Vlad's blood. Cutler was willing to help him, but there were limits to that help and he was not about to use his own shirt. He wrapped the blood-infused rag around Werner's throat, trying to stem the blood. The German snipers looked on impassively, wondering why the American was trying to save this scumbag's life.

Gasping and gurgling Werner could not get the words out. He knew off Cutler's interest in his operation. He had set in motion events which would no doubt see Cutler return home. He had not expected Cutler to act so quickly. Werner last thought before he lost conscious had been was his misjudgement on how far the investigation had advanced.

Within minutes, the air filled with the noise of sirens. Police cars and ambulances arrived from the temporary police base at Berchtesgaden.

The first helicopter to move off was the air ambulance. Werner had been transferred on a stretcher into the interior, and as it took off, he had several paramedics working on him, trying to save his life.

After the initial onslaught of police cars, officers, and paramedics, the commandant identified where Cutler was and approached him.

"Herr Cutler, thank you for your assistance with this successful operation. Both our governments will be pleased with the outcome."

The commandant continued, "I have received instructions that you are to go in the helicopter immediately to Munich. It will land near the American consulate; you have been summoned." Cutler looked a little bemused as the commandant steered him towards the Puma helicopter.

After a twenty-five minute flight through the alpine foothills and skirting Chiemsee, a large lake on the main route to Munich, the helicopter landed in the nearest green space, which happened to be Hofgarten. The local police had secured the landing area and removed the children that minutes before had been playing there. The vast green flat area was accessible to the Puma helicopter. The children laughed and swayed exaggeratedly as the downdraft from the rotors washed over them.

Hofgarten was a mere few hundred metres from the consulate.

On exiting the Puma, Max stooped down automatically to shield his face from the downward turbulence of the spinning rotors. Cutler walked to the waiting Land Rover, which had a small United States flag sitting proudly on the hood. He was met by a huge, black-uniformed military policeman. "Sir, you need to come with me immediately."

Cutler was a professional; he knew that whatever was coming up was not good. In his time with the Service, this was the first time he had been summoned to a consulate or embassy.

The military policeman had hands as large as the steering wheel he manipulated on the short journey to the corner of Schönfeldstrasse and Königstrasse, where the consulate was situated.

The military policeman guided Cutler through the lightly guarded consulate reception area to the police changing rooms, where he gave Cutler a new shirt.

"Consul is a graduate of Kogod School of Business, not seen much blood I'm afraid, sir," the military policeman said, as Cutler changed into the slightly large starched, crisp white shirt.

Cutler was directed through the marble corridor and up the stairway to the floor housing the consul's office.

Kalvin Ryan was a small, bespectacled man with hair receding from his forehead and wispy, straggly hair at the sides. Cutler thought he must have family connections or an extraordinary brain, as he was not the typical suited and booted official representative of the American government.

Ryan rose and introduced himself as the American consul from Munich.

"Max—you don't mind if I call you Max, do you?" the consul asked.

"People usually call me Cutler; it's been a long time since anyone has used my Christian name, Mr Ryan."

"Very well, Cutler it is," the consul responded, as he cleared his throat.

"First and foremost, I've been brought up to speed with the operation to stop the ever-resourceful Werner, and I believe congratulations are in order."

"Thank you, but I'm pretty positive you haven't brought me here to massage my ego," Cutler replied.

"No, it's not the main reason, I'm sorry to say. I'm afraid I have some disheartening news, Cutler; news from back home."

"Is it one of my parents?" Cutler asked, controlling the rising fear emanating from within his chest.

"No, it's not about your parents, although it does concern them. You see, they were on holiday, more specifically a cruise out of Seattle. From the little information I know, they were cruising the Inside Passage in Alaska with your sister, Elisa."

Considering what Cutler had gone through that day, his heart rate had remained a steady sixty-five beats per minute; now his heart raced and was beating at ninety-two beats per minute. He knew bad news was on the way.

"I believe she's eighteen years old," the consul said. "It seems your sister has gone missing, Cutler. Off the coast of Juneau. Very little information at this time, I am afraid," he said, far more quietly.

Cutler looked confused and asked, "You're telling me my sister is missing in Juneau, Alaska?"

"Not in Juneau. The ship had not docked at the time she went missing. It appears she disappeared from the vessel while at sea. She is not on board. It seems she may have gone overboard, the captain thinks," the Consul explained, with all the sympathy he could muster.

"Overboard?" Cutler repeated, incredulously. "You realize what you're telling me, Mr Ryan? It's June, and the water around there will still be freezing. She would not last five minutes. You're telling me she's dead."

"You need to go home, Cutler. You need to be with your family. There is a flight out tonight from Munich; one stop in Gander, Newfoundland, arriving at La Guardia at 7 am, then a connection on from there. You should be home in twenty-four hours."

"I'm not going home; I'm going to Alaska to find my sister," Cutler whispered.

chapter seven

Cruising was becoming much more popular and accessible to the working and middle classes due to supply and demand forcing the prices downward. As the ships got larger, with increasing numbers of cabins, prices for cruises fell. Presently, a full-board cruise with flights would cost anywhere between eighty and a hundred dollars a day for the holiday makers. For those wishing outside cabins with balconies, the price rose to several hundred dollars a day, and up to tens of thousands a day for those who could afford the extra luxuries such as suites and butlers.

The affordability and multitude of cruises and geographical locations had pushed America into prime position for cruises. Old and new cruise ships headed north out of New York to Canada and south to Florida. On a weekly basis, ships left the East Coast and Florida to ports to the Caribbean and South America. On the western coast of the United States, they sailed from San Diego to Hawaii and Mexico and beyond; from Seattle to Alaska and Japan. America had grown into the hub of the cruise line industry.

It was inevitable at some stage that Sebastian would either land at one of these ports by ship or fly into one to board a ship for local destinations.

His acclaim as a cruise pianist was extremely high, and he was in constant demand. Sebastian was ahead of the pack. He was much sought after, because he could double up, perform classics with the onboard orchestras on the large ships as well as undertaking his piano bar sessions each night.

Sebastian was in demand and could choose to work for any of the cruise lines. To date, he had worked on three different cruise lines out of America over the past five years, and it would soon be time to find new pastures.

Sebastian had berated himself after the fiasco in Malaysia. That had been seven years ago, and it still angered him to think of the stupidity of it all. Although nothing was ever traced back to him, it had been messy, and not fulfilling in any satisfactory way. It was an act which was flawed. Sebastian recognized that he had been detailed enough in his research, but subsequently had not reconnoitred the area accurately and thoroughly. He also concluded that to go so far from the ship was not the intelligent option he first thought; it gave numerous people the opportunity to see him along the way.

Although the harelip had been operated on, Sebastian could not hide the distinctive tram-line scar over his lip, which he knew was a definite identification marker. Someone might also notice his wig. Both facts set him aside from most other people. Sebastian could hear the conversation in his head.

"Yeah, I saw a guy, white, no, maybe Asian. Cannot remember the colour of his hair or eyes. Could have been anywhere between five foot five, to six feet tall. Oh, yeah, had a scar above his lip, like he had surgery on a harelip or something, and he had weird hair."

So, an excursion out and about to fulfil his desires was not the way to go. In fact, if he wanted to get caught, this would be a sure way of ensuring that happened. Sebastian did not want to get caught.

His eureka moment came on his second cruise on the *Duchess of Shetland* cruise ship, those seven long years ago. During the first two weeks of the journey, a passenger had gone missing in the water surrounding the French Reunion Island. The island is located in the Indian Ocean, to the east of the African coast.

Jill Cooper was in her fifties and had simply gone missing. She was observed entering her cabin on the first Saturday night of the cruise, and then she was gone, declared missing by Sunday morning. Following a full search of the ship, no trace or evidence of her or what had happened to her was discovered.

Jock Walker was an old sea dog who hailed from Glasgow. Jock was still, at forty-two years of age, a cabin boy; he was Sebastian's boy. He was a five-foot-two Glaswegian with shocking red hair and a pockmarked face, with an old knife scar running to the side of his right eye; a legacy from a drunken advance toward Moira of Paisley. Unfortunately, Moira's husband did not see the funny side of this drunken encounter. Jock should have been in a more senior position after his twenty-three years at sea, but the drink and his antics had ruined that, as well as the few brain cells he had started life off with.

Jock had been raised up in the urban sprawl of Glasgow. In his youth, he frequented the streets and alleys of Hill Street and Renfrew Street in the dilapidated city centre. The large three-floor sandstone houses were in much need of tender loving care. When Jock was thirteen, his school organized a day's outing to the beautiful Trossachs National Park, about an hour away by coach, but a million miles away by contrast.

The stunning area was spotted with a multitude of breweries interspersed with Dickensian villages that still discharged large plumes of smoke out of chimney stacks. The scenic locations, nestled in along the banks of Loch Lomond and between the Munros, as the Scots called their mountains, were a magnet to tourists. The master brewers utilized hundreds of years of inherited knowledge and skills to convert the icy-cold, crystal snow-clear water, and brewed the magical whiskies by the vatful. Jock had been introduced to the lovely malts of the beautiful national park by one of the older schoolchildren on that trip. Jock had been given a lifelong legacy on that day trip all those years ago, as he became hooked on the firewater. While it was well-known in the ships Jock had served on that he had a drinking problem; hangover or not, he always got up to do his duties. But he was a crew assistant and kept away from the passengers and on a tight leash.

The first cruise lines were British, and being British, they automatically included a class structure. Not just between passengers, such as first and second class, but also between the crew. It was always officers first and everyone else after. But the entertainers on board were treated as if they were royalty. Sebastian, as a headliner, was considered amongst the elite contingent of the crew, which entitled him to the same standard of service as the passengers.

Jock was cleaner, carrier, general dogsbody, and scandal sheet to several of the entertainers, including Sebastian.

Within twenty minutes of the first news that Jill Cooper had gone missing, Jock had relayed the news to several of his wards.

He knocked on Sebastian's door before entering to find Sebastian sitting at the small desk, reading some music scores.

"Aye, staff captain told the chief steward who told Roily the senior steward that she was a single woman in her fifties. She was supposed to be here celebrating her divorce," Jock said, giving a knowing wink.

"Obviously looking for a little action. They become invisible at that age, so probably ended up with a gin and tonic rather than a roll in the hay. Probably drank a little more; gin is a well-known depressant. Finally the sixty-foot drop into the dark ocean below. Probably seemed like an excellent idea at the time." Jock added, "Silly bitch," as an afterthought.

"Captain sent out three lifeboats to search for her this morning, but she could have jumped twelve hours ago. Anyway, with the number of sharks around here she's dead meat, and her next appearance will be out of the rear end of a tiger shark sometime soon," Jock said, as a matter of fact.

Sebastian was fascinated by the unsubstantiated jumps to conclusions, and lack of facts that Jock had just presented to him.

"Not wanting facts to get in the way of a good story, Jock, this woman spends $2,000 to come to the other side of the world to jump into a sea to be eaten by sharks? Why not just take a swig of methanol or a couple of packets of sedatives? Is the captain sure she wasn't murdered and dumped or something?" Sebastian inquired.

He addressed Sebastian by his surname, as was his custom, "Mr McKenzie, we never have a murder on a ship, you should know that. We have *incidents*, we have *accidents*; we never have killings. It's a bit like an actor saying 'Macbeth'; we don't even think it."

"What about a police investigation?" Sebastian asked.

"No police out here, sir; only police in five hundred miles are the ones in the Reunion Islands. On the high seas, the captain is the police. He says it is suicide, then suicide it surely is. He reports it to the police and to the company, and that's the end of that. On to the next cruise."

"Does this befall people often, Jock?"

"Aye, I have been on cruise ships some twenty-odd years now, transferred from an old cargo ship company. The first I ever witnessed was an eighteen-year-old, straight out of college he was. Whenever someone crosses the equator for the first time, we call it crossing the line; well, we threaten them with stuff, and mostly carry out the threats. Martha, the third engineer, whose real name was Marty, had scared him shitless. He had told the lad he was going to gang-fuck him with a couple of mates. The boy, believing this, hid in the freezer down at the rear of the galley; idiot didn't know you couldn't open it from the inside. Found him next day as solid as a leg of New Zealand lamb. Missing his mom, committed suicide, the captain said. Dropped him off at the nearest port, which was Aden, to be shipped home; never seen again. Lads reckon the locals turned him into dog food. Since then I have seen too many suicides and accidents to remember, but not one murder." Jock took a breath.

"Not one murder, not one domestic squabble that leads to a fight and death?" Sebastian replied incredulously.

"You have to remember we have a fair amount of the walking dead that come on cruises. Generally old people, those who want the journey of a lifetime before the cancer, cirrhosis, or whatever ailment they suffer from gets them. We get the depressives, we get the drunks, we get the idiots; there're a thousand ways to die on the sea, and I've seen most of them," Jock replied.

"Do you mean like once or twice a year?" Sebastian probed.

"No, I mean like once or twice a *cruise*. It's just kept quiet so as not to disturb the guests. Disturb the guests and they don't spend money, my old captain used to say."

Sebastian's modus operandi altered; the discussion had assisted in Sebastian's evolution. In future, there was no need to go off the ship, no need to take risks and chances. The sea was a massive dumping ground, with little hope of the body's discovery, and the captains and cruise line companies had a blind spot for murder.

Several years later, Jock was diagnosed with pancreatic cancer, caused by his drinking. He took the coach to Callander in the Trossachs. On the outskirts of the town sat a medium-sized brewery. The brewery was fed water by the local stream, which cascaded down a small waterfall into the catchment area. The smell of hops was overwhelming from the large brass vessels. Jock had broken into the brewing area and the brewery manager, on investigating a blockage in the fermenter the following morning, found Jock dead, evidently drowned in the vat. The manager related to anyone who would listen that Jock had a smile on his face. Jock became immortal as the ghost of Callander Brewery, and the children of the area shivered when his name was mentioned.

The body of Jill Cooper was never found. She had thrown herself overboard in despair, mid-air she knew it was a mistake. The fall killed her instantly, like hitting a block of concrete. It had taken all of the thirty minutes before the sharks had ripped her limb from limb. The small remnants of body tissue after the shark fest fed the smaller fish and eels.

chapter eight

Cutler had one stop on the way into Tacoma International Airport in Seattle. The plane had a soft landing in Gander, Newfoundland, and would be on the ground for two hours. Gander airport had been a Canadian Air Force base that had many years previously allowed civilian aircraft to land to refuel. The highlight for most passengers was Gander's famous ice cream. During short stopovers most passengers headed towards the small store within the steel-framed building that sold the treat.

Cutler did not register the frigid Newfoundland wind chill as he walked down the aircraft steps onto the aircraft staging area. Most of the long flight had been a blur since he had heard the news of his sister's disappearance. Once inside the sparse building that passed for a terminal, he headed for a seat as far away from the humanity around him as possible.

A little girl approached him. She had blonde hair tied into two small ponytails sprouting from above each ear, her tiny frame in a floral printed dress displayed like a vase of summer flowers against the cold, hard interior.

"You look sad, mister," she said innocently, in a tone that was sympathetic beyond her years.

"Macy, Macy, come away and leave that man alone!" boomed the voice of what Cutler assumed was the girl's mother. He gave a little smile as the girl ran towards her mother with a quick backward glance.

Cutler could remember his sister in ponytails, wearing floral dresses that his mother would make on her little sewing machine on the porch of their house. His mind wandered back to Elisa when she was a kid, wanting to hold his hand wherever they went. Sometimes it had been restrictive; he was five years older than she was, and having a young girl hanging onto your arm was a topic for his friends to prod him with jibes.

He remembered the first time he had pitched a tent in the garden at their house in Cleveland. It had been an old silk parachute that his father had got hold of. Cutler did not know it was purchased so his mom could make a First Communion dress for Elisa; she must have been six years old. Boy, the telling-off was worth it to see the joy on his little sister's face when she had charge of her first playhouse. She was playacting the mom, ordering Cutler about. "Clean the dishes! Mop the floor!" He had to endure the warm water flowing from a plastic teapot into a plastic cup and was made to drink every last drop of Elisa's unique tea.

Elisa was every inch as clever as Cutler and had become an honour student at Cleveland High. Cutler's mother did not leave a single item out of what she had done, how she had grown, who was making eyes at her, in the long letters she wrote to Cutler during his absences. On his return, Cutler would spoil her, spending a significant amount of his salary on her in Abercrombie and Fitch and other high-end clothes shops.

As he sat there in the minimalist terminal building, he was in no doubt his little sister was either in severe peril or dead. From his experience, he knew the crew would have searched the ship thoroughly.

Cutler had been involved in searches on ships looking for counterfeit dollars off the coast of Tampa, and he knew the crew would have a thorough understanding of all the places she could be on the ship. If she had injured herself, or knocked herself unconscious, they would have discovered her by now. He was certain she was no longer on the vessel.

"Boarding will commence on the British Airways flight to Seattle in twenty-five minutes," the loudspeaker announced.

His mind had settled on the fact; she was definitely not still on the ship. That meant there could only be two possibilities. One: she was abducted onto another boat from the vessel, and that was highly unlikely with the watch-outs and the size of the vessel. Plus, the assailants would have to traverse the side of the hull and bypass the sophisticated radar. In essence, he calculated, one of the two possibilities was highly unlikely. Not impossible, but highly improbable.

All that remained was that Elisa had, by one means or another, fallen overboard. Certainly not by her own hand; suicide was not an option. She was a happy girl. He had seen her only four months earlier, and she was looking forward to the gymnastic competitions that she was entered in that summer.

Cutler's parents were sure Elisa would make the national team for the vault, such was her skill at the sport. Cutler was almost sure; she was too well-adjusted to ever consider suicide. Even in the unlikely event his eighteen-year-old sister had a major problem in her life, she would not consider suicide.

Cutler took out his pen and notebook and scribbled down a reminder for himself to investigate the events involving Elisa's life leading up to the cruise.

"Sir, you have to board; we're waiting for you," said the flight attendant he barely recognized from his aircraft.

Cutler looked up and was surprised to see that the terminal building was almost empty.

"Sir, you're the last person; we have to board," she emphasized.

"Sorry, I was deep in thought. I didn't hear the boarding announcement," Cutler apologized, as he stood up and began walking toward the terminal door with the flight attendant.

Under normal circumstances, he would have noticed the utter beauty of the stewardess—black hair, perfect almond skin, large brown eyes—but today this was lost on him.

They boarded the aircraft, to the background muttering from a young, suited banker type in the second row of business class.

"Always one person to keep you waiting," he said, looking around at the same time to see if he had any back slaps or support for commenting.

Cutler was certainly not in the mood, and the business type visibly shrank in his seat when Cutler gave him a look that said, 'Don't mess with me today, you may regret it.'

Cutler did not feel the upward motion as the wheels lifted off the ground, for he had returned to his thoughts. So, not suicide; one hundred percent rule that out. That means she had gone overboard by what means? Could she have fallen over by accident?

Cutler had a fair understanding of the requirements under federal law for health and safety of maritime vessels. This was one of those series of lectures he had had to undertake along with other, what he considered at the time, lame subjects, but he now appreciated the background.

As far as he could recall, guardrails around outer decks on the lower levels with decks above would normally be 950mm to 1150mm, above waist height. On the upper, open decks above the ship would be enclosed in glass panels, where the wind strength was the strongest. Guardrails again a minimum 950mm at the stern. What this meant was that it would take a physical action on Elisa's behalf—or someone else's—for her to go over the barriers. It would not be an accident. The deck with the lifeboats would have removable guardrails for loading in the event of an emergency, but these are locked into position.

Again, Cutler took out his notebook and wrote, 'Check logs for the lifeboat drill that day,' just in case someone had not locked the guardrail in position.

Cutler had spoken to his father courtesy of the consulate satellite phone before leaving the building in Munich. Stephen, his father, had stated that the last time anyone saw Elisa was 11:30 pm on her way to her cabin, which was next door to theirs. Cutler concluded that any lifeboat drill would have been completed in daylight hours. To him, it was kind of inconceivable, but again not impossible, that the guardrails could have remained unlocked for such a period, considering the inspection systems on-board. He took out his pen and wrote, 'Check inspection log aboard vessel.'

"Sir, can I offer you a drink?" asked the stewardess who had escorted him onto the airplane.

"Erm, sorry, yes, can I have a malt whisky. Glenfiddich if possible, no ice, make it a double, please," Cutler replied, as he finally made eye contact with her.

"Sir seems very preoccupied; is everything all right? If you are afraid of flying maybe I can get you something," she offered.

For the first time in many hours, a shadow of a smile crossed Cutler's face.

"Thank you. I am not afraid of flying. In fact, I have over eighty parachute jumps to my name. I'm going home to a family crisis; my sister is missing," Cutler said, not really knowing why he was opening himself up to this stewardess.

"Oh, I'm sorry. I did not mean to pry. I don't know what to say, apart from forgive me for interfering," she said, embarrassed.

"No, it's okay. In fact, thank you. I needed to tell someone before I burst. I don't mean to come over as someone in need of your pity, or vulnerable at the moment. I've had a long trip back with this on my mind," Cutler said.

"She may well have turned up by the time you get off this plane," the stewardess added hopefully.

"Somehow, I do not think so; she has gone missing off a ship, just off the coast of Alaska. I think in all probability she is dead. There are two possibilities: she has gone overboard, either alive or dead. If she went into the water, she's dead. If she was kidnapped, there is a possibility she is still alive," Cutler said, finalizing the logic and fear that he had been dwelling on.

The stewardess sat down in the empty business class seat alongside Cutler and put her slim, light hands over his large, left masculine hand, ever so lightly. It was like his hand had a feather resting on it.

"Oh, I'm so sorry. This may not be the time to say this. When you've been flying for as long as I have you hear all sorts of things, and sometimes missing people turn up in places you would not have dreamt possible."

Cutler half-turned towards her and looked deeply into those beautiful, dark eyes. He could tell she had honest eyes, beautiful and soulful.

"Have you come across people going missing on ships?" Cutler asked, without any hint of sarcasm.

"Actually, I have a couple of times. It's more common than you would think," she replied.

"And did they find any of them alive?" he inquired.

"Once, a lady in the Bahamas with dementia wandered onto a supply boat. She had wandered off and gotten into a restricted area. Once in the area she had access to and got on the boat unseen, only to turn up in Nassau three days later, not knowing who she was and what country she lived in," the stewardess explained.

"My sister is eighteen years old and in control of all her faculties. The others you mentioned; what happened to them?" he pressed.

"Oh, I don't really know about all of them, just a few," she said, somewhat flustered.

"All of them; how many is all of them?" he asked, with a growing sense of bewilderment.

"Well, you understand it's not all me, it's other flight attendants as well. When something like this crops up on a flight, you typically find out because the relatives are upset and often talk to a cabin member when asked if they are okay. Well, they tell one person, who tells another, and before you know it, we are all aware. Sometimes people add a little in to spice it up, most times not. It is a closed environment in the airline industry, and we do get to know an awful lot of what goes on. All in all, I've heard of about ten or eleven different cases."

Cutler sat upright at the mention of the number of instances. "And of these, how many outcomes do you know?"

"Most..." she replied hesitantly.

"And how many turned up alive?" Cutler took hold of her hand. "Please be honest with me," he continued.

"Just that one I told you about, the lady with dementia," she said quietly as she squeezed his hand.

"Thank you for being honest with me," Cutler said, as he reluctantly let go of her hand. The warmth and silkiness of her skin had soothed him for a millisecond until the nightmarish thoughts returned to haunt him.

Cutler sat quietly for the rest of the flight back to Seattle, his training helping him to control his emotions, mostly. The fear in his gut, the tightness of his chest and the lump in his throat gave way to an eruption. A sob cascaded up like a flow of lava. He fought to quell the volcano of emotions until he knew he was at his limit.

Cutler took himself to the on-board toilet and sobbed for the first time since he was a child, and for the last time in his life. He washed his face and returned, in control of his emotions, to his seat.

It was not long before the flight attendant came over with another double Glenfiddich.

"Thought you might need this," she said tenderly, looking at his red swollen eyes, guessing why he had spent so long in the lavatory. "On the drink napkin is my phone number. I am not that crass to be trying to pick you up when you are obviously in a deeply worried state, but if you ever want to talk, my name is Cathy Lavine. I live in Seattle when I am not flying. No strings; phone me, use me as a sounding board, any time, night or day."

"You're a very special lady, Cathy. Thank you for your kindness. You might be sorry you gave me the number, as I might be phoning you sooner than you think," Cutler replied, already thinking she may be a good contact for information should he need it. Somewhere deep down within him it registered that she was beautiful, and it would be nice to spend time with her, but his brain would not allow him to process the thought amidst his trauma.

chapter nine

Sebastian had been away from the American hub for several years, and lately had spent two years in the Antipodes circumnavigating Australia and New Zealand several times. His tally of murders was now at twenty-five; twenty-three since he had first signed on the cruise ships all those fourteen years ago. This equated to one killing every eight months. Sebastian knew he had hit on a vein of gold when he had cemented the idea and plan of his killing spree.

Sebastian was not stupid; he knew if there were too many deaths, sooner or later someone would work it out, and his way of life would have to change. Eight months was about the maximum length of time he could go without killing. He had once got to nine months, but, on the other hand, had also killed three women in a one-year period in 2004, two years previous.

The ship was called the *Oyster*, a nine-decked, three-year-old cruise liner owned and run by the Wave Runner Cruise Company, and they were undertaking the Caribbean circular route.

Guests that night sitting around his piano had been a mix of Canadians and Americans, with a single middle-aged Japanese woman. The tip jar was full, as was the request docket sitting atop the white mini grand piano. The requests varied from country and western to *Phantom of the Opera*, *Lucy in the Sky with Diamonds*, and *Piano Man*. He would certainly do the music, but he would not be singing the lyrics to *Stand by your Man*, as the Japanese guest had requested.

It had been a laborious night, made worse because everyone spoke English, and this meant he had to converse with them at a level, something he profoundly did not want to do. He had enjoyed cruising out of Hong Kong several years earlier on the Red Star Cruise Line, as most of the guests did not speak English, so there was no need for any chit-chat.

Sebastian had perfected his killing, but although quick, he had never quite reached the peak of enjoyment, he knew there was more to come.

He had noticed a young couple sitting at the back of the bar the previous two nights. She was petite, with a slim figure and very light hair; maybe dyed, but Sebastian thought it looked too perfect to have come out of a bottle. Her companion was of medium height, medium build, cropped hair, liked his beer, nothing special. He did have a tattoo on his forearm, which had an eagle on a crest, so Sebastian hazarded a guess that he was either English or German; he later confirmed German. What was apparent was that the couple argued most of the time.

Having open access to the ship and its records meant Sebastian could quite easily discover who was staying in what cabin; all he needed was a name. Sebastian had access to the ship's computer and had previously heard a bartender call the man Herr Shultz. From there on in, it was just a matter of time for both Herr and Frau Shultz.

Over the next week of the cruise he kept a close eye on the couple from a distance and waited patiently for his opportunity.

On the Tuesday—Sebastian knew it was Tuesday as the cleaners changed the carpets in the glass elevators that had the day of the week on them—the *Oyster* anchored off the port of Samana in the Dominican Republic. The port did not have sufficient depth for the *Oyster* to berth in the port so she anchored off in deep water, a half-mile from the harbor.

The tenders were small boats from the island, which came across on the starboard side, and there they picked up all the guests going on shore.

Sebastian noticed that the young German man was without his young, fair, beautiful Germanic frau as he boarded a tender in an ungainly fashion, due to the swells beneath the small boat. He noticed because he had duties on many occasions to wave off the guests on their various excursions, as did a lot of the entertainers. It was excellent customer service, as far as the cruise captain was concerned.

As soon as his duties had been discharged and all the excursions had departed, Sebastian headed for the Pearl Deck, which was the name given to deck four. This deck was an accommodation deck only. The deck had long corridors running down the port and starboard sides of the ship, with breaks every forty-five yards or so to enter the open area where the stairs and elevators were sited. On the outer side of the corridor the cabins had ocean-view windows; opposite them were the interior cabins, with pictures instead of windows or portholes. The cabins had a bathroom immediately as you walked to the left or right, depending on what side of the corridor the cabin was situated on. A small desk and chair under a television hung on the wall. Opposite this were two single beds with a little night table in between. Under the window of the porthole or picture was a day couch, which could convert into a single bed if required.

Frau Shultz had cabin 4092, which was an ocean-view cabin, but this was irrelevant to Sebastian's plans, as ocean-view cabins had a view through a window, but the portholes or picture windows were locked down with bolts. There was no CCTV in the accommodation deck corridors or in the stairwells.

Sebastian checked on the location of the cabin stewards; in a corridor this size there would almost certainly be three cabin stewards. He knew he didn't have to worry too much about guests, as nearly all the ship had gone ashore, with only a few staying on-board, enjoying the sun by the swimming pool on the Lido Deck. As luck would have it, he saw a sign on the canteen noticeboard on the lower decks that the stewards were on lifeboat drills and would be late starting their cleaning schedules this morning.

The door of 4092 had a 'Do Not Disturb' sign on it, but this did not deter Sebastian from knocking. He knocked several times before a dishevelled and obviously weepy Frau Shultz opened the cabin door.

"Good morning, Frau Shultz. I'm one of the entertainers, and as a lot of the crew have shore duties today, I have been allocated communication duties on-board," he lied.

"Ja, I know you from the piano bar. What is it you want?" she asked sleepily.

"Can you accompany me to sick bay? Your husband has had a fall. He is okay, but he has broken his ankle. We need you to come down to the sick bay and fill out some forms and details, plus see your husband," Sebastian continued.

"Broke his ankle? I wish he had broken his neck. Only six weeks married, I wanted a ship day. He leaves me here on-board while he goes off to the island, not to see lovely sights, but to drink beer." she said, more upset than angry.

After some more exchanges, she excused herself, retreated into her cabin and tidied herself up. She exited the cabin a few minutes later and followed Sebastian a few yards down the corridor to a service door which had a 'No Entrance' sign. Explaining this was the quickest way, he led her through the doors and down the levels to deck one, which at this time of the day he was sure would have no members of staff around. Deck one was where the refuse holds were, and he knew the trash collectors worked around here at night only.

The light was dim and there was a large door in front of them. Frau Shultz started to turn to ask him what a first aid station was doing in this dimly lit place. The stench hit her as soon as he opened the door. Sebastian had directed her to the garbage room. Each evening, the elevators would be filled with bags of garbage generated from the multiple bars and restaurants, and throughout the hours of darkness the bags were thrown into the room.

The garbage room was a large metal hold that looked like the inside of a massive container, but with one side bent in the shape of the hull. It ran the length of thirty-four cabins and was two decks lower than the guest cabins. There were metal grids on the ground to allow some of the sickly-sweet ooze that spilled from the garbage bags to drain. The grids had drains that directed the stinking fluid into receptor tanks, which were cleaned and emptied into the sea most nights.

The lighting was subdued and background only, with orange lights in steel enclosures and glass on the side of the hull.

Inside of the giant disposal receptor, the garbage bags were piled up unevenly, some ten high on the starboard side. On the port side was a six-foot hull door that was opened and used to remove the bags to waiting garbage wagons when they arrived and berthed in ports.

Frau Shultz knew immediately something was amiss. She turned sharply on her heels to retrace her steps at a pace. Sebastian placed his middle and forefinger of his right hand swiftly on the pressure point in front of her left shoulder by her neck. This pressure point is an acupunctural pressure point that Sebastian had learned by studying and practicing the Chinese martial art of dim mak. The pain was intense and agonizing for a millisecond; Frau Shultz was unconscious before the scream could escape her mouth.

Sebastian dragged her deeper into the garbage room and closed the heavy hatch door. It was pitch-black once the doors were shut. Sebastian retrieved a pencil flashlight from his pocket and clicked it on to light the way ahead down the narrow aisle through the bags of garbage. He dragged the limp body over the metal steel decking and through the slime of the ooze that had leaked from the bags.

He was in no rush; he knew no one would come down here until night. He put on his disc player with earphones to listen to Wagner; this way he would not have to listen to the sounds of death. While the act of murder was euphoric, the sounds of the human body dying disgusted him a little. He really did not enjoy the groans, the moans, or the gurgling and bubbling as the fluids escaped the body. Wagner was much more appropriate to support what was to follow.

Slowly she regained consciousness and tried to scream, but no cry came out, only gurgled nonsense. She realized quickly that her arms had been tied behind her back with her own dress, and a piece torn off and strapped around her mouth. She was naked and dripping in the fetid garbage ooze. Frau Shultz urinated involuntarily with fright; she now feared the worst, except what she feared was not the worst.

As Frau Shultz regained some of her senses, she realized she was naked, and that her private area and under her arms stung intensely. She could not move her arms as they were tethered. At first, she could not work out why her lower regions were covered in blood, as she had only days ago finished her cycle. Clarity only came as her eyes adjusted to the dark room and she saw the shape of a man; he was eating. Several seconds later her terrified eyes achieved full night vision and she realized *what* the man was eating. No, not eating but eating and balking at the same time. His meal of the day was hair, her pubic offerings.

Not content with his meal, Sebastian moved over to her wriggling, constricted body. With all his strength, he grabbed a handful of hair and yanked it so hard a large piece of scalp came away with the entrée.

Frau Shultz was in agony and endured this torture for a further hour. When Sebastian could eat no more, he continued with the hair extraction, taking pleasure in the tears and terror reflected in her eyes.

Finally, Sebastian made her watch him as he placed his hands around her throat. He strangled her to the point of unconsciousness, and then relaxed his grip. This went on for a further thirty minutes until Frau Shultz's brain could take no more and shut down again for several minutes.

Sebastian had been getting more and more exhilarated as she became more petrified and fought for her breath. He removed his headphones that were attached to his portable music player. Wagner blared out through the earphones. Sebastian placed the headphones several yards away from Frau Shultz, worrying that what he had planned may ruin the player.

Sebastian walked over to the bulkhead, where a fire hose was bolted to the hull. He pulled the hose and tugged it the two yards to where the naked, bloodied, spoilt body of Frau Shultz lay.

Sebastian ripped the gag from her mouth and slapped her several times to bring her around. As soon as she started to regain consciousness, he forcefully shoved the one-inch diameter hose deeply down her throat, while her teeth that had been knocked out by the force filled her cheeks like a gorging hamster. Her once immaculate, straight, white teeth were now dead bone. He turned the valve on, and high-pressure seawater began to flow, flooding both the lungs and the stomach as he destroyed the individual tubes within her throat.

Her eyes opened wide in absolute horror as she was jolted back into consciousness. The water being forced into her lungs and stomach was a terror too far. Mercifully, her heart gave way and her eyes rolled towards the top of the sockets as she died a most horrendous death, a death fit for no man, woman or animal.

Sebastian removed the hose just before it burst her lungs and pinched her nose with his fingers while covering her mouth. Her lungs were full of seawater; it looked like she had drowned. If her heart had not given out, it would be put down to drowning.

Sebastian's emotions were running riot. He had such an intense high; Geraldine, the skier, the other twenty-odd bodies were nothing compared to this. He had found his path, his way. He had enjoyed her death. He was elated.

An hour, it may have been more, Sebastian was not sure, and the elation subsided. The burning heat inside his head began to cool down, and he returned to some semblance of sanity. As his logic returned, his first thought was about the clean-up. He redressed the body.

During the killing, the blood had pumped out of her when she was alive. It leaked out of her when she had stopped breathing. Sebastian was not worried about detritus—blood and faecal matter—on the metal deck, as this intermingled with the natural waste fluids from the waste bags. Sebastian knew you could, if you looked carefully, see human matter, but this would be diminished and cleaned before anyone would notice.

He slowly opened the small hull door, so it was open enough for him to see out, but not open enough to draw the attention of any tender boats in the area. The waterline was not more than ten feet below his position. On looking around, he could see there were no tenders bringing back early visitors. Although the tenders would draw up to gantries on the other side of the vessel to offload their human cargo. It was always a possibility when there were too many tenders for the available gantries that they would lay off on the other side of the hull until some of the tenders had departed from their positions.

On peering down into the crystal-clear water, Sebastian could see that the water extended well below the hull. However, even if he weighed Frau Shultz down, the water was so clear her body may be sighted or discovered if she floated out. The water was too clear.

He decided then that he would hide the body under the bags of rubbish and come back later when it was getting dark, but before the garbage porters started their nightly duties. By the time he had achieved this task he was matted in grime, blood, and a mixture of human and food waste. He washed himself down with the hose in the warm seawater and stood there with just his swimming shorts on. As he had done with his body, he rinsed his clothes in the seawater to remove the blood. He placed the clothes into a waste bag he opened and pushed it down amongst the pile of over a hundred refuse bags. Sebastian had retrieved Frau Shultz's cabin key and washed off the blood.

After the exertions of hiding the dead weight and the warm flow of seawater over his body, he took a few minutes to settle his pulse down. Sebastian did not want to look flushed or overexerted on his way back to his cabin.

Quietly he closed the waste hold door and walked up the two flights of internal stairs before emerging from the door with the 'No Entrance' sign on the front. He walked from the restricted area, and it was only seconds until he was seen by staff and by a cruise guest. A man walking through the corridor in his swimming costume does not raise suspicion or alarm on a cruise ship, Sebastian knew; it was an everyday occurrence. Sebastian walked back to his cabin; no problem, just another guy who had been for a swim on the Promenade Deck.

After a quick shower to remove the salt from the seawater that he had rinsed himself down with. Once dry he put on fresh shorts and a Bermuda shirt and went back to the tender area in readiness for the tenders returning.

It had been three hours since he had left the tender station; it had felt a lot quicker to Sebastian. He was due back at the arrival deck in one hour, as the half-day excursions would be returning within the next hour. And he would be there to greet them. Sebastian went back early to the unmanned station.

Before Frau Shultz was allowed on the ship on embarkation, there had been several formalities she would have had to complete to ensure the company's procedures had been followed.

In the embarkation hall, she would have an imprint of her credit card taken, and a check to see that she had sufficient balance on it would be made. Then she would have her photograph taken, and the image transferred to a database on-board the ship. She would then be issued a cabin key; the key would also act as her on-board embarkation and disembarkation pass. Every time she got on or off the ship, she would be identified by inserting the pass into a computer terminal.

Each time she bought a drink at the bar the key would be swiped, and her photograph would appear on the screen in the bar till; it was an on-board credit card.

Sebastian knew there was one flaw in the system; the embarkation and disembarkation system for excursions merely recorded access and egress from the ship; it did not record the time the individual left or came back on-board.

Sebastian retrieved Frau Shultz's pass and inserted it into the terminal. For all intents and purposes, Frau Shultz had exited the ship and disembarked. Minutes later, the key was cut into ribbons and deposited on the tide of the Caribbean Sea.

That evening at 6 pm he heard the announcement over the on-board speakers.

"Mrs Shultz, report to the Purser's Office, immediately."

Sebastian knew this was standard procedure if someone was back late or had not returned past the last boarding time. He knew that soon they would be telling her husband she had not returned from shore and, as per company policy, they would not wait and put themselves behind schedule. Anyone late back would have to make their way to the next port of call and rejoin the ship there, obviously on their own dollar.

Sebastian was almost sure that no matter what the argument was that had caused Herr Shultz to go ashore alone, he would not stay on the ship while his wife was not on-board. He would think her late back and would want to be there for her. Once it was clear she was not on-board, Herr Shultz did decide to go ashore to look for her. He was put on the pilot boat and taken ashore.

Once the ship was on its way and the light began to fade, Sebastian went out again in his swimming shorts, with a towel draped over his shoulders. Once inside the garbage room, he opened the hull door and observed the waves swelling up to about two yards below the hull door.

Sebastian retrieved the large refuse bag containing the remains of Frau Shultz. He dragged her lifeless form out of the bag and to the door and waited. The ship rose and fell on the swell, and the water line changed with each cycle. Sebastian waited until the ship fell and quickly slipped the body out of the bag and through the door.

The draw of water from two massive bronze propellers is enormous, and no sooner had she entered the water than she was drawn to the water flow towards the propellers like a magnet. There was a slight shudder and a little kick, and Sebastian knew she had met this kiss of the giant bronze propellers. The body would now be in edible chunks for the reef sharks.

"Job done," he whispered to himself.

If anyone had night vision glasses, and a bird's eye, sea-level view, which was not possible in the light conditions, they may have spotted the flush of red water, the dismembered arm, part of a foot with two toes and half a heel, for that was about all that was left of Frau Shultz.

While Herr Shultz was pleading with the police to find his wife in the Dominican Republic, Sebastian was playing with vigour in the piano bar. He seemed to really enjoy himself. He was on top of the world.

Several weeks later, and three nights spent in a mosquito-infested hotel, Manfred Shultz returned home with the finger of suspicion hanging over him, as Frau Shultz's body had never been found. Certainly the Dominican police thought he was the prime suspect, but they had no evidence to detain him.

His team leader back in Munich thought it highly unlikely Manfred had anything to do with his wife going missing. They had sent a detective from their team over to assist, and he could not find one sighting of them together on the island. The detective found it strange that no one at the port or on the island had seen or could remember Frau Shultz.

Manfred Shultz had been drinking far too much beer for the past three months. He had been part of a mission hunting armed thieves who had held up a jeweller. They had cornered the remnants of the gang at the central train station in Munich. They had their sights trained on them. One of the gangs, smaller and lighter than the others, and still wearing a black ski mask, turned towards Manfred and his team, the gun glistening and visible.

Manfred Shultz had not thought twice before shooting two bullets into the chest area of the criminal. Once they had detained the rest of the gang, who gave up readily after the shooting, he moved over to the body, which was outstretched at the top of the entrance to the subway lines. Travellers in the area had screamed and backed away from the entrance to one of the many food outlets in the station.

Shultz removed the mask; it was a young girl of Albanian descent, no more than thirteen years old. He just stood there, motionless, staring as the blood seeped around his boots.

German beer is good; too good. But it could not take away the pain Shultz felt. The guilt over the child, along with the guilt over arguing with his wife before she went missing, consumed him. He knew three things; he did not kill her, and she would have never killed herself and murdered their unborn child, and thirdly, the beer was not helping, so he had stopped his drinking.

Manfred Shultz was six feet of muscle, with an athletic build, fair hair, blue eyes, and Germanic features. Post 9/11 he had run away at sixteen and joined the Foreign Legion. He was annoyed that the German Army could not participate in any retaliation, and he wanted revenge. His older brother had been in the South Tower when it collapsed. Manfred had trained and fought with the Legion over Algeria and other countries they were not supposed to be in. He returned in 2005 and joined the elite squad of police.

Time was cruel; a lot had happened in a year. He had passed the police entrance and subsequent German Special Forces training. He had gunned down a child, married his childhood sweetheart, and lost his wife and unborn baby. Now the first week back on duty here he was, in the same train station he had shot the young girl. Had the shooting given him post-traumatic stress syndrome, or had it been the loss of his wife? Manfred knew he had reached the bottom of the barrel and did not have the energy for the fight back up. Manfred stepped off the platform as the 8:28 am to Nuremberg was leaving the station, wanting the pain to stop. Large hands grappled at his shoulders and dragged him back from the rail lines. Manfred turned to see the sympathetic look from the station master; Sebastian had not claimed another victim.

chapter ten

utler landed at Seattle Airport tired and irritable. He was met at immigration control by Conan Dreyfuss, a Secret Service agent based in the city of Seattle. Brad Hemmingway, Cutler's head of department, had arranged the assistance for Cutler, knowing his prodigy would need as much help as possible when he arrived.

Dreifuss brought Cutler up to date on the location of the *Oceanic Discoverer*, the ship Elisa had disappeared from. The ship was due in Vancouver within the next four hours. Dreyfuss relayed to Cutler that his parents had insisted on staying in Juneau while the sea search continued.

He did not have to tell Cutler that thirty minutes after entering the water she would have been dead from the intense cold of the water. Instead, he just raised his palms upwards in a gesture of futility.

Dreyfuss stayed with him until Cutler boarded the 11:30 am flight to Vancouver, a flight of less than one hour in duration.

He had organized a Canadian police officer to pick Cutler up from Vancouver International Airport and drive him to the seaport where the ship would be docking in the next hour. The officer tried to engage Cutler in banal conversation; he gave up trying when it became apparent that his charge was not in the best of moods for trivia.

Cutler watched the ship dock from beneath the overhang of the roof of the embarkation hall. The Victoria rain put a watery curtain on the scene, with high visibility coats hanging onto ropes and securing the boat the quay.

Accompanied by the Canadian police officer, Cutler was able to bypass the security checks and they walked through the baggage reclaim area, which was a big, empty space with a roof and gray aluminum panels for walls. There was a hive of activity as dockside porters offloaded the never-ending stream of small, medium, large, extra-large, massive, blue, brown, and polka-dotted bags. The bags had been placed in lanes in readiness for the guests to depart.

Immediately Cutler's spirits dropped, as he had not realized this was the disembarkation port, the final destination where everyone left the ship. He thought the last port would be Seattle, the port from where all the guests had embarked.

Cutler bypassed the long, high escalator and took the stairs up to the main terminus. He needed security passes to gain permission to enter the vessel from the immigration officers on duty. The police officer remained in the terminus, relieved that he was able to get a hot cup of tea.

Cutler was escorted the short distance across the enclosed gantry, which rose at a slight angle to emerge on the ship's fourth deck. He was escorted to the captain's quarters. Cutler had to wait for half an hour before the captain came down and invited him into his office adjoining his quarters.

The captain was a stocky man, his perfectly crisp white shirt straining at the seams. Captain Jjordsen was of Viking descent and followed a long tradition of Nordic captains. He sported a silver beard and moustache, which was also the colour of his dense, cropped hair.

Captain Jjordsen confirmed everything Cutler had been told previously: Elisa had been on the ship, and then she was gone the following morning. The ship had been searched thoroughly, and the captain assured Cutler she was not anywhere on the vessel. There was no evidence of any foul play. And he had an open mind as to the cause of her disappearance.

Cutler probed Captain Jjordsen on the siting of any CCTV cameras. To Cutler, it appeared that there were cameras which pointed down the port and starboard side of the hulls in case of illegal boardings and yes, because of the odd suicide attempt. However, on further questioning, it was apparent that there were blind spots, so the captain admitted. The CCTV had been reviewed, and although there were sightings of Elisa in the common areas, there was certainly none of her jumping off the ship.

Captain Jjordsen angered Cutler immensely by acknowledging that the only people who had been questioned over Elisa's disappearance were her cabin steward and Cutler's parents. However, Jjordsen did stress that most of the crew had been involved in the search for Elisa.

"Captain Jjordsen, I know my sister would not commit suicide, so that leaves an accident or murder. If she was killed, it is highly likely that the murderer may have been a guest or an employee, most of whom can disembark this vessel today without being investigated!" Cutler seethed.

"Mr Cutler, I'm very sorry for your loss, if indeed she is dead. We have two thousand guests leaving today, eight hundred members of staff, and you want them interviewed? You do the math. You would need two hundred officers all day, every day, for the next week, and that's just for interviews!"

Cutler knew he was hitting a barrier, a barrier he could neither influence nor order around. He could argue till he was red in the face; the captain was not about to launch a major investigation which would cost his company millions of dollars, and anger a couple of thousand guests, for what they probably thought was probably a suicide.

Max thanked Captain Jjordsen for his time, knowing he might need more information from him in the future. He did not want to leave him with bad blood between them.

No sooner had Cutler disembarked the ship than the police officer sped him back to the airport with his blues and twos flashing.

To get to where he wanted to go, Cutler had to hire a seaplane from an Alaskan charter based at Vancouver International Airport. The operations manager of Orca Airlines warned him to delay the flight for a couple of hours due to bad weather, but Cutler could not wait. Luckily for Cutler, Captain Mantis had been flying seaplanes in this part of the world for twenty-five years, and a little storm would not stop him from flying.

Cutler's cup was refilled by the co-pilot from the thermos he had wedged down the side of his seat. The plane see-sawed over the large glacier below, then back out above the open sea of the Gulf of Alaska.

Cutler sat in silence, weighing up what he knew already, which was not a great deal. If someone goes missing on a cruise ship, the local authorities investigate. By the time they investigate their possible crime scene, it has moved to another location, along with any suspects, of which there is a poll of thousands. Any one of the guests could be a killer, and they will have dispersed to the four corners of the world. The easiest solution all round is a proclamation of a suicide or accident.

Rolls of black, angry clouds rose thousands of feet above the red 1983 Cessna 4 Turbo U206 Amphibian seaplane. Suddenly the plane dropped as the currents that lifted the plane ceased to exist, and then rose several hundred feet as the plane bounced off the rising bubble of air. Then it was gone, and the plane plummeted. It felt like the biggest rollercoaster Cutler had ever been on.

Cutler balanced his coffee in his hand as best he could, as the plane tried to maintain ten thousand feet across the Gulf of Alaska. Cutler needed the coffee, he had not slept in the two days since he had left Munich after learning the devastating news. He hardly registered the burning sensation in his hand as the seaplane lost another five hundred feet in height in a split-second.

The plane fought against the winds, and it seemed impossible for the pilot to land it in any chosen spot, but land it he did, right alongside the quay in Juneau in the sea harbour port. Abundant numbers of seals swam around when the propellers of the plane ceased to rotate.

"Welcome to Juneau, Mr Cutler. You may want to button up your coat. The temperature is around fifty-one degrees," the pilot announced.

This was Cutler's first visit to the Alaskan city, and Juneau was not what Cutler had expected. *National Geographic* was Cutler's only previous exposure to the state, fragmented from its homeland by the country of Canada.

Cutler thought of glaciers and whales, and he was not disappointed, as they were certainly in abundance. The pilot had pointed out a pod of humpback whales blowing water from their blowholes as the plane had come in low over Stephens Passage on the way to Juneau. As for glaciers and mountains, the beautiful Mount Juneau perched over the city, with remnants of snow from the harsh winter still in evidence.

What Cutler did not expect was the homeless shelter and Alcoholics Anonymous centre next to the largest pub in town. *It may be a pristine environment, but it is contaminated with human beings,* Cutler thought.

Stephen Cutler was a tall, erect man, with large shoulders and cropped black hair. He did not look tall today when Max met his father in the reception area of the Bears Paw Hotel. Stephen Cutler was stooped; it had only been a few months since Max had seen him, and he was shocked by what he saw—his black hair had turned white.

Cutler's father put his arms around him and tried to speak, but only croaks and sobs came out. Max never had in all his years witnessed his father like this. It was clear to him his dad was broken-hearted; he was spent. He loved his father and always thought him a strong, safe pair of hands in any situation. He had never factored in the situation where this proud man would lose his little girl.

Cutler was hurting like he never had before; his father was being eaten alive.

"Where's Mom, Dad?" Cutler asked quietly with resignation.

"Erm," he cleared his throat with a cough, "Bartlett Regional Hospital, ten minutes away." He slumped down into a chair and put his face into his hands. "She's sedated. She was distraught. I thought it better we stay here to wait, but it hasn't helped; if anything, I think it has made it worse," Stephen said, as he raised his head slightly.

"Now that you are here, I can take her home. I have used the insurance and have a private ambulance plane coming in tonight. I've got to get her home, away from this place," Stephen said through his pain.

"Probably best," Max replied.

Cutler senior took a deep breath and in a shaky voice continued, "We both know there's no hope, Max, waiting to drag a body up from out there." Stephen pointed towards the direction of the sea. "It's thousands of feet deep. Could be some time, could be never," he spluttered, with the tears dropping in large globules from his eyes.

"Dad, we both know she's gone, but you have to be strong for Mom, although I know it's killing you," Max said, as he embraced his father.

"I don't care what they say, she never committed suicide. She was happy right up to the time she went to her cabin. She never committed suicide," Stephen said, with more steel in his voice.

"Dad, I know. I do not want to upset you any more than you already are, but it must be an accident or more likely murder. After walking through and around the ship today, I think it would be hard to fall overboard by accident. The captain assured me the lifeboat gates had been locked, so to fall over the barriers is nearly impossible. Did Elisa have a drink that night?" Max inquired.

"She had cola all night, that's all she drank," Stephen replied.

"So that leaves out accident by shenanigans under the influence. The captain said you would be amazed how many people kill or put themselves at risk under the influence at sea," Max said.

"He's blowing smoke up your arse, Max. We told him she had not touched a drop of alcohol. You could tell he did not believe us or did not want to believe us. Convenient excuse if you ask me," Stephen said, with an equal amount of anger and tears.

"Well, that just leaves murder. You understand that don't you, Dad?" Max said plainly.

"I do, and so does your mom. We knew the moment the captain said they could not find her anywhere on the ship. She'll never get over this, son, you know." Stephen continued, "We're proud of you, Max. We know how much you enjoy your job, and what skills you have. Give your mom and me some hope. Use your skills to catch the bastard who did this; make him suffer, whether it's death row or from your own hands, you make him suffer," Stephen said, his fists clenched.

"Dad, I promise if it's murder, I won't rest. It is not going to be easy. It may be the hardest thing I have ever done. But I promise you I will try. I'll do my utmost to get him," Max promised.

"You've never broken a promise or failed in anything substantial, so that will do for me," Stephen said, as he tugged Max's head toward him and kissed him on his forehead. To Cutler, it felt as if his father was saying goodbye.

Stephen sat next to his wife in the ambulance as it went the very short distance to the seaplane, which had been equipped as an air ambulance. The seaplane bobbed up and down on its mooring as the rough sea beneath it swelled and sank. With some difficulty the paramedic, pilot, and co-pilot transferred the stretcher to the dedicated flat area at the back of the plane.

Max had been walking the streets, talking to anyone he could. He showed anyone who would look a picture of Elisa. "Have you seen this girl?" he had asked a hundred people.

He arrived a few minutes before take-off to see his parents off. "I have a meeting with the police chief in fifteen minutes, and over the next few days I'll go out to the area where Elisa disappeared, so I need to arrange for a boat," Cutler told his father. "I'll come home in a day or two to update you and see Mom," he said, as he stroked her forehead. She had been under constant sedation and had not woken all that day.

The noise increased dramatically, and the propellers sprang to life. The little seaplane started off slowly and fought the swells of water. Eventually, the plane gathered sufficient speed against the drag of the water and wind and staggered into the air.

Cutler could see the aircraft's wings swaying as it fought to gain height. The clouds reflected Cutler's mood, dark and angry, with an undertone of violence. Cutler knew he had to control his emotions if he was to keep a clear head and fulfil his promise to his father.

Two hours later, Cutler had showered and changed and was in with Gregg Wayne. The police commissioner, while not a tall man, certainly looked like he had seen his fair share of action;

Cutler guessed ex-military. A scar ran from his left ear to the corner of his lip, the result of close-quarter combat with a grizzly the previous winter.

Cutler thought it was like being back on the ship with the captain. Although eager to help, the story was more or less the same, possible suicide or accident, no plausible evidence for any other conclusion.

The phone rang and Wayne's eyebrows had lifted before he replaced the receiver. Before he could say anything, the phone rang again, and this time his face did show some concern.

"I have some bad news, Agent Cutler," the police commissioner said.

"Have they found Elisa's body?" Cutler interjected quickly.

"No. Sometimes when shit happens, well, it has a way of luring you into a sense that nothing else can go wrong. Well, bad news is not like that; it keeps on a coming. Sorry, Cutler; the air ambulance carrying your parents has gone down in rough seas, just off the coastline of Seattle. It disintegrated, and I'm afraid no one got out alive."

Cutler looked dumbfounded.

chapter eleven

Werner survived. It was touch and go for a while whether he would succumb to his injuries. He had been as strong as a bull, but now was as weak as a kitten after several operations to repair the bullet wound to his throat. He knew he would almost certainly have died had not the tall American agent tied a shirt around his neck to stem the flow of life-giving fluid that had oozed from his wound.

Werner was not grateful to Cutler, for that was an emotion that he had long since lost the ability to feel. He was not angry with Cutler, either; he had been doing his job, just as Werner was doing his. He was, however, enraged by the bloody fool of a bodyguard, Vlad. Trying to shoot his way out of the trap was stupid. It had led to Werner's woes. It was a good thing Vlad was no longer in the land of the living, as he would have been exposed to pain as he had never suffered before.

Werner knew the name of the American agent, Max Cutler. Werner had been warned that he was under investigation, but he thought he had it under control. After all, information was power, and he had many sources of data. The problem was, Cutler knew who was on the payroll and who was not, and he had controlled who knew what and when. It was and had been on a need-to-know and just-in-time basis. It had been a success, as Werner had been completely surprised that he had been targeted by the German and American authorities without him knowing.

After Werner had been shot and struggled for life, the German commander had the stricken counterfeiter transferred to the hospital. The ambulance and armed police cars took him to the beautiful spa town of Bad Reichenhall, some five miles away. The town was in the foothills of the Bavarian Alps and had the primness of a German town, with the stunning backdrop of the hills of green and explosion of spring flowers.

The German commander had posted two heavily armed guards outside the hospital theater; two in the reception area of the hospital, and a further two were posted in the Bad Reichenhall train station situated some three hundred yards along the road.

Following the assessment of risk by the German commander, he set up a perimeter around the town. Within the vicinity, there were three white and green BMW patrol cars. One monitored the access and egress to the town from the autobahn. The second was situated in the parking lot of the last Gasthaus on Thumsee Strasse in Karlstein, noted for the mural on its side of a twenty-metre-high bakery scene.

Karlstein was a micro-town, which mainly consisted of houses, a bakery and the odd guesthouse, a town you would normally see through the car window. The fact that all traffic going up to Schneizlreuth or returning had to pass through this small town made it a choke point for anything coming down from or arriving in through the alpine passes from Austria. Thus, they had all the main routes covered, such was the concern arising from housing a notorious ex-Stasi gangster in their midst.

The medical procedure went as well as could be hoped. It was damage limitation rather than renewal. After several days, the morphine that had kept the pain at bay was reduced to a level which brought the reality of the situation clearer to Werner.

Werner thought he knew pain; thought he had conquered the fear of pain. He had tortured numerous prisoners as part of his Stasi job description, watching them scream in terror and in agony, for that was his duty, and often, his pleasure.

He had been injured once before; he had dislocated his shoulder while beating up on a prisoner whose crime was using graffiti as a tool against the puppet East German government. Werner was enraged; he could accept the pain. What he could not accept and what angered him immensely was that this prisoner had seen him wince and had grinned at Werner's discomfort.

It was fortuitous that evolution had given the human form two sides of the body, as Werner used the working right shoulder to raise his arm that held the stool that was placed nearby. He deliberately smashed the stool against the wall.

"You think this is funny? You think my arm hanging down from its socket is hilarious?" Werner had inquired sinisterly.

The activist watched through bloodied eyes as the stool broke into several pieces, and then as Werner kicked one of the larger remnants around the room in pure rage. Werner slowly knelt, and with his good arm, retrieved what was once the leg of the stool. Through a mist of pain, Werner could see the prisoner smirk at him. Werner looked intently at the splintered end, which had a point like a dagger. He turned it around in his fingers, studying it and formatting the next stage of his plan.

With the quickness which belied his injury, he had reached his prey in a millisecond, crossing the space between them with the prowess of a lion. He was on him and used his weight to pin down the man's shoulders and arms. The victim tried to kick his leg and dismount Werner from his upper torso, but the guard had been well trained, and brought his truncheon down on his right knee. The unmistakable sound of hardwood cracking bone lasted only a second before the man screamed in agony.

Werner took a breath, enjoying the pain, his pain and the prisoner's pain. The detainee was stubborn and brave; he fought to gain control of the pain and after a minute, grunted and grimaced rather than screamed. It was Werner's turn to smirk.

Werner waited a few more seconds, relishing the look of agony and arrogance in the man's eyes before violently and efficiently forcing the splintered, sharp end of the stool leg down the activist's mouth. The force of the blow , breaking his teeth and ripping through his voice box before emerging from the back of the neck close to the spine.

***

But, back to reality, back to today. This pain was something else. It was like nothing he had ever experienced before. Maybe it was this kind of pain the prisoner had felt, he thought, but then his pain lasted minutes rather than the constant pain Werner had endured since the morphine had worn off.

Herr Braun, an eminent ear, nose and throat specialist, explained that the bullet had destroyed Werner's voice box and he would have to perform a laryngectomy. Herr Braun continued in a soft, professional tone in which he detailed that the operation removed his voice box and had permanently left a breathing hole in his neck.

Werner tried to interject, but only frothy, blood-infused spittle gargled out of the breathing hole.

Herr Braun further explained that the only hope of communicating verbally would be through an artificial mechanical larynx.

Werner shook his head; Herr Braun took this as meaning he did not understand, when Werner was thinking, *you better sort this or I will kill you.*

"Basically, after a week or so, when your throat recovers some more, we insert a small vibration plate and give you a handheld microphone which will pick up vibrations. And after several months of practice and rehabilitation, this will let you communicate," Herr Braun continued.

Werner was shaking his head violently from side to side. The nurse handed him a pen and paper.

"Unfortunately, your oesophagus was severely affected and presently, and for the foreseeable future, this will be the only means of communication. Technological advances are happening all the time; we never say anything is forever," Herr Braun said optimistically, as Werner scribbled on the notepad.

Werner showed him the paper. "Sort this out and get me off fucking baby food."

"Solid food is not viable as a food source; not now, and probably not in the future," Herr Braun replied, as again Werner scribbled away frantically.

"You want me to eat fucking baby food?" he wrote down and thrust the paper up under the consultant's face and struggled to get up closer to him.

The consultant remained calm as one of the police officers forced him back onto the bed.

The consultant was not used to such venom, such anger; after all, he was trying to help this patient. He turned on his heels, followed by the nurse and policeman, and left the windowless room.

Werner waited several minutes before pulling the assistance cord for the nurse. The nurse was male; this was by design rather than chance, due to the fact that no females were allowed to be alone with Werner at any time, such was his perceived risk to members of staff.

Werner wrote a phone number on his paper and below the number was another, but this had a monetary value.

"Ten thousand euros for you to call this number and just let the person on the end of the phone know my whereabouts."

The nurse shook his head from side to side vigorously, declining the offer. Werner pointed at the name badge, ripped up the previous page and on the virgin-white paper wrote, "I know your name, Nurse Hessler. You must know who I am and my reputation? How long will it take for my friends to find you outside this hospital? The police will not guard you; they can't guard you forever."

Nurse Seppi Hessler spun around, scared, and walked out. Hessler had thought maybe thirty minutes, but the nurse had fought his predicament for over an hour before he returned. The nurse wanted to know how and when he would be paid and got Werner to rewrite the telephone number.

After the nurse had scurried out, Werner turned his thoughts to the other two outstanding issues that needed immediate attention. He had over twenty-four million dollars in cash hanging around, genuine dollars he had been paid for the counterfeit notes. The money was stashed in a safe in a townhouse in Bad Tölz.

The spa town based in Tölzer land was a favourite of Werner's. The resort spa hamlet sat in the alpine foothills, nestled between the alpine lakes of Bad Weissee and Lake Starnberg. Werner would visit the town when he could no longer stand the pain and irritation his gout brought on. Werner swore by the healing capabilities of the mud baths and visited at least four times a year. The resort was within easy driving distance of Munich, but far enough away from the metropolis to not fall under the watchful eyes of the Munich Police Department, an easy selection for a safe house.

The house and the six-foot-high wall safe was a concern; it was only known to him and two other people. *They* were his two issues, his concern. Once they knew of his position, his vulnerability, who was to say they would not take the money and disappear? For now, they would be too frightened to move against him, but it would not take long before news got out about his predicament.

It was as clear as the Aegean Sea to Werner he would be serving some time in police and prison custody. Eventually, he knew he could ride the surf; his contacts would put pressure on those in power, or one of his henchmen would get to a juror. But for now, he was still some time away from freedom, perhaps years.

Werner was all consumed by the thoughts that while on the outside, no one dared to undermine him. But when Werner's cronies heard of his injuries and incarceration, well, they may think he was no longer a credible force. He needed to address this situation, and he needed to sort it out now. He needed to secure the money, for money could buy power, and he was going to need that when he got out, broken man or not.

His first port of call would be his political contact; she was more a hidden partner, as she had profited by more than ten million dollars from their partnership. It was now time she started to earn her keep, no matter how high her status.

Nurse Hessler walked two hundred metres past the tall stone buildings with black-topped Germanic roofs to the phone booth. It was just outside the large, glassed swimming hall complex. He called the number Werner had written down.

"I'm in the hospital in Bad Reichenhall, Herr Werner is injured but not terminal. Get Attorney Von-Baer to visit me and see what you can do to alleviate this situation," Hessler repeated the message as instructed.

"Do you know who I am?" the strong female Germanic voice inquired of Nurse Hessler.

"Nein," he responded.

"Destroy the number you have, immediately. Never repeat the number or this conversation if you would like to keep breathing the wonderful fresh air down there," she demanded.

Nurse Hessler continued, "Yah, I will destroy the number, but Herr Werner said I would be paid ten thousand euros for my trouble."

"And so you shall. In two days, travel to Munich and go to the English Garden. You will be met there at 6 pm. We don't need your name, for your security of course, but we do need to know what you look like so we can pay you," the female said.

Evidently Hessler thought if he went in his nurse uniform, he would stand out sufficiently to be noticed, and that is exactly what he told her he would do.

Delegate Frau Uebering replaced the phone.

"Damn Werner, giving out my number! He knows better than that," she muttered to herself.

Frau Uebering had also been brought up in the old East Germany and had been recruited as an informant by Werner. She was a full member of the Communist party and a junior member of the East German Government.

She would get and relay information to Werner. The information varied from petty to serious, any information; who was screwing whom, was anyone spending more than they could afford, any homosexuals, lesbians, whoremongers or pedophiles; any information, obviously for a price. Sometimes money, sometimes power.

Had the East German government survived another year, Frau Uebering may have become too powerful and in an elevated position for her to ever be considered for a post in the Bundestag, the unified government following the fall of the Berlin Wall.

It was not that Werner had a stranglehold over Delegate Frau Uebering, which he had; it was her need for a constant flow of money that kept her on the darker side of politics. Elections do not come cheap, and mediocre politicians never reached the top of their profession. Frau Uebering was determined to get to the top of hers.

Communism was a means to an end for her. She was and always had been a socialist; that of the Nazi kind. When she one day became chancellor, she would use the European Union as a means of controlling immigration and the dilution of the Aryan gene pool. For now, she was a delegate, a woman of power, a woman who would be listened to. She reckoned she was ten years away from the top job.

Frau Uebering took out a prepaid, throw-away mobile phone and rang Kurt Bauer, who was another ex-Stasi agent and now freelanced as a killer for hire. Both she and Bauer were based in Berlin. Frau Uebering lived on Unter den Linden, while Bauer lived a short distance away near the historic Alexander Platz.

"We have a rat, meet me in two hours at the Zoological Gardens, outside the reptile house," Frau Uebering ordered Kurt Bauer.

She was comfortable there at the Gardens, as there were areas in the zoo where they could have complete privacy, out of sight and earshot of any member of the public or security services.

The phone call from the nurse did not take her by surprise. Through the Berlin grapevine, she quickly learned that Werner had been involved in a shoot-out and had been taken to the hospital. For her to have pressed the matter further could have raised questions as to her interest. She now knew his location and understood what was required.

In the Zoological Gardens, Kurt Bauer had listened intently and taken the orders from the delegate. Both Werner and the delegate knew that they had a rat in their house, someone who had intimate knowledge of the transference of the counterfeit and actual dollars. Only two other persons outside of Werner and the delegate had sufficient information that would have led to the compromising of their operation. This had resulted in the shoot-out that had destroyed Werner's voice box. Schweinsteiger, and Dietmar Richter. It had to be one of those two.

It mattered little to Bauer that he knew both his targets and had worked with them in the past.

Schweinsteiger was based in Cologne; he occupied an apartment just behind the magnificent Gothic twin-spired cathedral. Originally built in 1248; the towers were added in 1880. It was a huge cathedral that barely survived the Second World War. Cologne's tallest building had been lovingly rebuilt to dominate the skyline, hovering magnificently above the roofs and chimneys of the city.

Bauer crossed over the Severinsbrücke Bridge, which ran parallel to the Rhine river. A hundred metres further on he turned right and found a parking spot near the Church of St George. Bauer put the coins into the parking meter, as the last thing he needed was a parking ticket to identify he had been there at all.

Bauer walked the short distance to Severin Strasse and found the large brick house. Ensuring no one saw him, he entered the main door and walked up the three flights of marble-capped steps to Schweinsteiger's apartment. Bauer knocked heavily on the solid wooden door of the apartment. Schweinsteiger opened the door after a slight pause after he had looked through the peephole in the door. Schweinsteiger was happy to let Bauer in; after all, they had worked together many times, and he assumed that this would be for a new job.

Schweinsteiger was the bag man; he was the man the cash came to. He would be the delivery man to take it from several cities to Bad Tölz, where he would hand the money over to Richter.

Bauer explained quickly to Schweinsteiger that he had been sent by Werner with orders for him and the accountant.

Schweinsteiger had been like a rudderless ship since Werner had gone off the radar several days before. He had collated the information, counted the money, ensured that every cent was accounted for, and he had completed three deliveries to Richter in Bad Tölz.

Bauer accepted the offer of a Jägermeister, and Schweinsteiger turned his back on him to prepare the drink.

"How is the boss? I heard—" Schweinsteiger was cut off mid-sentence.

Bauer had put on thin rubber gloves, and in a fluid, motion removed a clear plastic bag from his pocket. Before Schweinsteiger finished his sentence, he had a bag put over his head and was kicked in the back of his left knee. Bauer pushed him down into a kneeling position, facing away from him. Schweinsteiger knew his time was up and who had ordered him dead. Schweinsteiger struggled for the best part of a minute, his strength depleting every second. Schweinsteiger's last thoughts were of his father, who had been executed many years before as a war criminal.

I'll be seeing you soon, he thought, and then he expired.

Bauer had previously wiped the interior of the bag with an amphetamine so Schweinsteiger would inhale and ingest the drug in his dying breaths. The bag puffed out weaker and weaker as Schweinsteiger fought for the oxygen that was no longer available.

Once Bauer was satisfied Schweinsteiger was dead, he placed the body on its back. Bauer looked intently at the vacant, dead of eyes of Schweinsteiger, now a cadaver, a piece of meat, not human anymore, just a problem.

Bauer removed the contaminated plastic bag from the head. He retrieved a piece of amphetamine-contaminated orange from a small plastic container in his left pocket and placed it between the dead man's lips. Bauer then put the original plastic bag back over the cadaver's head and pulled the drawstring tight.

It would be several hours before Schweinsteiger's hands would go stiff with rigor mortis; Bauer manipulated his fingers on his left hand onto the drawstring. He then undid Schweinsteiger's trousers and pulled them down to below his knees. He manipulated the right hand of the dead man around his penis. He took a final look around the apartment for any incriminating evidence. Finding none, he left.

Bauer had used this method several times, and the result was the same every time. The family wanted it all hushed up with minimum investigation; bad press on a loved one with the morbid hobby of masturbation and strangulation is not one many would want as an epitaph.

Bauer drove out of the city of Cologne, joining the E43 Autobahn, passing Frankfurt and Nuremberg down to Munich. He had rented the Mercedes under a false name using false identification documents, provided by the same expert who produced the counterfeit notes.

Shortly before 6 pm, he entered the English Garden, and immediately noticed the man in the garb of a nurse on the far side of the park, sitting on a wooden bench. Bauer manoeuvred his way around the park out of Nurse Hessler's vision until he stood no more than a few yards behind him.

Bauer scanned the area three hundred and sixty degrees to ensure he was not being watched. He quickly covered the two yards to the back of the bench while removing the weapon of choice from the inside pocket of his black leather jacket. Bauer expertly thrust the ice pick into the nape, killing Hessler instantly. The pick had been out of his pocket less than a second before it was replaced, and Bauer was already ten yards away from Nurse Hessler, who remained sitting upright.

Bauer returned to his car, not wanting to stay in the city longer than he had to. He had to get to Bad Tölz, to kill Richter. It was just another hit for Bauer, but the instruction to kill him immediately after Schweinsteiger and Nurse Hessler was intriguing. Never before had he been contracted for three separate hits to be carried out in three different places in one day. But that is what he would do; it was suicide to double-cross Werner or the delegate.

Dietmar Richter was the gatekeeper, the money genius, the holder of the keys to the million-dollar fortune. The only thing he feared more than Werner was the thought of being tortured or locked up for years on end. He was only five foot two; a small, rotund man with a face that resembled a million other businessmen that had gained too many pounds after becoming overly enthusiastic for German food and beer.

The large mobile phone with extended antenna had been muffled. Richter removed it from the small drawer on the end table which sat beside the stressed brown leather loveseat he used as an armchair. He was nervous as he touched the phone, as this was the first time it had ever rung.

"They have killed Schweinsteiger. My guess is they are on their way to kill you, Richter. Get the money and get to the safe house in Bern. Leave now," the voice said.

"How, who?" Richter begged.

"I don't think they know you're working with us," the voice said.

"Working with you? I am not working with you; you threatened me with a life term in Stadelheim prison, leaving me a bitch for some psycho! I'm not working with you; I have been pressed into service!" Richter blurted out.

"I don't have time for this. I have pressing matters of my own. Get the merchandise now and leave, or by the end of the night you'll be maggot food," the voice commanded.

"This is my life; how do you expect me to just up and leave with all the money? I will be hunted down and killed within the week!" Richter pleaded.

"Look, you idiot. You will be dead by tonight. If it had not been for my colleague watching Schweinsteiger's apartment we would not have known, but right now Bauer is on his way to gut you," came the stern reply.

"Can you come or send someone to help me?" Richter's voice was two octaves higher.

"I am a continent away and you will be dead before one of my men get to you. Do what you're told," Cutler said, as he handed the phone back to Captain Wayne. Cutler, stunned, left the small Juneau police station.

<h1 style="text-align:center">chapter twelve</h1>

The last three years had been good for Sebastian. His reputation as an outstanding performer whom the cruise crowd liked was at a high, and he was in demand. When demand outstrips supply, the cost of the service increases, and Sebastian found himself in the top tier of paid performers on the ocean waves.

He sometimes played in the piano bars, but due to his popularity, he was in the main theatres on the ship doing one-night performances more and more. His specialty was that the audience would shout out a tune or a song, and he would then play it. He played the Beatles, the Beach Boys, and George Michael. Other times he would be on stage backing up the in-house team of entertainers who would put on short musical snippets from the West End or Broadway. He would play *Phantom*, *Miss Saigon*, and *Les Misérables*; there was no classic he could not do. It was much to his disappointment that this never included Wagner, who was deemed a little too Germanic for most mixed audiences.

The upside to his newfound popularity was that on some occasions, he might only be on-board for a week or two. He would then be flown to another port to board another vessel to ply his trade.

This made the killings much more random, and they increased in number, to feed his appetite. In the last three years he had killed thirteen times. Always someone who had long hair—dark, blonde, auburn—it did not really matter to Sebastian. He found difficulty in identifying which type of women he enjoyed killing more, so variety was the spice of life, as long as they had clean and ample hair.

Of the thirteen kills, only six had been conscious when he had deflowered their hair. It was only with these six that Sebastian had reached the euphoria he so desired and needed.

Disposal was an art form, and one that varied ever so slightly, depending upon the cruise line and vessel. The introduction and expansion of CCTV had been a thorn in Sebastian's side, and he had to find innovative ways to circumnavigate the visual recorders.

There were also some close shaves. Vivien Trench, a blonde he had met and killed on the cruise ship *Heart of the Orient* was one. He had weighed her down and dropped her over into the South China Sea, at the mouth of the Pearl River Delta prior to docking in Hong Kong Harbour. Unfortunately, she had surfaced before the ship left port two days later. Surfaced several times in different locations, in fact. Her body had encountered a Star ferry crossing from the harbour on the short trip to Kowloon. Part of her was wedged between the hull and propeller, while several other parts bobbed up around the ferry, to the horror of its passengers.

It was clear she was off the ship, and the police delayed the departure for a full day while they investigated. The outcome was that it was deemed an accident, as the seas had been heavy on entrance, and it was possible she was leaning over and fell. Her skull had been cracked open like an egg by a propeller, and the wounds and lack of hair had been blamed on the sharks.

He often fantasized about Rachel Jones, who had mousy hair, feline looks, and beautiful, dark, almost-black eyes. They had met on the *Dream Catcher*; Sebastian thought they should rename the ship *Nightmare of the Seas* in honour of Rachel. He had dragged her into a lifeboat on deck six in the middle of a storm as she was seasick. The noise she made was drowned out by the tempest in the Great Australian Bight.

Rachel's mistake was to wander out on the deck during a storm when no one else would, apart from Sebastian. She went over the side some two hours later, lacking most of her hair and part of her scalp, just seven miles off the coast of Fremantle in Australia. Sebastian was pretty sure, storm or no storm, the sharks and other predators of the sea would devour her before the week was out.

Miss Daphne—this was how she insisted on being addressed—was a young woman of breeding and standing. Born in the Channel Island of Guernsey, her father was a banker who plied his trade in London and came home on weekends. As it happens in so many cases, he met and fell in love with someone other than his wife, and young enough to be his daughter. When the banker's wife found out, she shipped daughter Daphne on a Balkan cruise with her close friend Gemina Montgomery while she tried to calm the waters back home.

Daphne was eighteen and had vivid red hair with rosy good looks; she looked like a flower ready to pluck, to Sebastian. Gemina was handsome rather than pretty. She was lean bordering on malnourished and had closely cropped black hair. She was of no interest.

Gemina was getting ready for the return to England, so it was not much of a problem to find Miss Daphne alone. She had a habit of walking around the pool deck at night-time, enjoying a glass of Chablis, when most people were watching the shows.

Sebastian reconnoitred the area. In the last year, closed-circuit cameras had been introduced into some cruise ships. These were in communal areas, and predominantly based around the casinos. There was one or two around the decks, but none covering this area. At the stern of the ship on this deck was a Crazy Golf course within some netting, with a storage cupboard built into the bulkhead the ninth hole nestled up to.

Sebastian knew from previous nights she would show up around 9 pm—only problem was, she did not. He had to wait a further twenty-four frustrating hours to take his pleasure, and he made her suffer for making him wait. He was furious when he finally got her; for she was a fake. He killed her quickly in disgust, as there was no hair to remove. Daphne was nearly bald from alopecia and wore expensive wigs.

"False little bitch," he said, as he threw her from the top deck on the starboard side. He could not throw her over the stern, as there was an open-air restaurant on deck five, and there was the possibility of someone seeing her body fly by. The best option was starboard, as there were no balcony cabins this far back, and the chances of someone spotting her falling were slim. Even if they did, it would be assumed she had jumped.

Her torso ended up on a remote beach several miles up from Golden Sands on the Black Sea coast of Bulgaria. The Bulgarians flew investigators out to the ship. The investigation lasted twelve hours, six of which the investigators spent enjoying the cuisine in the breakfast hall, at lunchtime, and again in the early evening. After a cursory Bulgarian investigation, it was closed with the outcome she had probably committed suicide. They reached their conclusion based on Gemina telling the investigating officers about Daphne's parents' problems.

Melissa Rodrigues had lush, jet-black hair that flowed freely down her back and sat in a straight line, converging into a sleek, smooth wave nestled on the rise of her pert buttocks. She needed some Vitamin D in the form of sunshine to help her hair and skin bloom. She got her vitamin D aboard the cruise ship *Bonny Prince Charlie*.

This was an old Cunard ship that had been too old for service in the Cunard fleet for the past ten years. *Bonny Prince Charlie* had been purchased by the Belgium Cruise Co. and transported her guests around the Red Sea.

Bonny Prince Charlie would start her journey from Sharm El Sheikh in Egypt and cruise along to the ports in Jordan, so the travellers could pay exorbitant prices to walk in the footsteps of Lawrence of Arabia, or visit the beautiful but fly-ridden shores of the Dead Sea. Or for the more adventurous, taking the trip down the narrow gorges to Petra, the ancient trading city built into the hills in the desert.

Sebastian had taken the soft option and joined the multitude of visitors to the Dead Sea, where he first observed Melissa.

What attracted Sebastian was her demeanor. While not that tall and with a lithe, slim body, she seemed to take up all the space around her as the long mane of black hair swirled from side to side as she alerted everyone in line of sight to her presence. She showered beside the walkway down to the Dead Sea, swatting away the numerous flies from her skimpily covered body, which had the eyes of every heterosexual male between the ages of ten and ninety fixated.

When Melissa immersed herself in the Dead Sea, she jumped up and yelped a little as the salt initially stung her openings. The second wave of pain was caused by the areas she had shaved prior to departing the ship that morning. She settled down and soon followed the others in the dense salty water, trying to float. They were not floating *in* the Dead Sea, but on top of the sea, as it is virtually impossible to submerge oneself in the saltiest sea in the world. Her hair turned white, as did her slim body as it was covered and baked in the salt.

Looking down at her from the hill overlooking the spot was a stone structure, supposedly the remains of Lot's wife, as this was the setting of Sodom and Gomorrah. Lot's wife died because she looked back to the forsaken city. Melissa would be killed for just being there, and not by God, but by ice-cold Sebastian.

Sebastian was not one to strip off and get in the water. He did not want everyone to know his hair-pulling habit, and had he stripped, the scarring over his body would have been a clear indicator that something was not right with the pianist. The scar tissue was still there after many years of abuse, tender to the touch, and Sebastian would be in agony in the water.

Sebastian watched Melissa from the comfort of the air-conditioned balcony of a bistro while sipping on a lime and soda and chewing on the cashews the hotel provided for free.

He shielded his eyes from the intense glare of the sun behind his mirrored Ray-Ban sunglasses, watching Melissa intently as his excitement began to grow.

Melissa would be an important kill, Sebastian realized as he sat on the balcony. It was the stalking of his prey; the hunting and planning were becoming an important and exciting part of the experience. Plus, her hair spread over her body from her head to her waist in the saline sea, the strands magnificent even coated in the salt.

Sebastian was patient; he followed Melissa and her husband back on to the *Bonny Prince Charlie*. He saw the security officer insert her cabin card key into the computer, to check her identity and allow her back on-board the ship. The database was updated as soon as a card was swiped, and this would show who was on board, who had returned, and who had not.

"Welcome back, Mrs Rodrigues," Sebastian heard the security guard say. He now had a name, and thanks to his access to all areas on the ship, in an hour he had the cabin number.

Sebastian waited five more days before he attacked her in her cabin. Mr Rodrigues was a man of habit; each morning after breakfast, at 8 am, he would swim ten lengths of the short pool, and then sit in the warmth of the Jacuzzi. He was several decks above her when she died.

As with all his kills, Sebastian had planned it down to the last detail. First, he gained entry purporting to be room service; borrowing the black pants and white top room service wore.

Melissa did wonder why room service would bring a laundry trolley into her cabin. Before she could raise the question, he immobilized her by forcing the heel of his hand quickly and violently to her forehead. Melissa dropped like a rock He pulled her to the shower and within fifteen minutes she was plucked clean. The pain had awoken her from the concussion only for Sebastian to kill her with a fist to the throat. It was quick; too fast for him to reach the elated state he yearned for, but he could not afford to take longer.

The inside cabin was on a lower deck and to the rear of the passageway. He placed her inside the laundry trolley, placing the sheet from their bed on top of her. Sebastian exited the cabin with the trolley across the passageway and into the service area. This area was restricted to staff. Sebastian knew at this time of the morning they would all be in the lower deck canteen, enjoying breakfast before the start of another long day.

Once inside the restricted area, he placed the trolley into the service elevator. Sebastian was on his way to the waste disposal area on the bottom deck of the ship. He had discovered that all ships have garbage dumping zones, and they were nearly always in the lowermost deck of the vessel. This was his favourite, and well-used means of disposal for cadavers.

Problems began to emerge for Sebastian as the elevator slammed to a halt between decks. Sebastian was aware of the dangers this created and wondered at the lack of fear he felt.

Did this mean he wanted to be caught? Or was he just fearless? He thought he would soon find out. It was a half-hour before the elevator began to move to the lower deck. When the door opened, Sebastian was met by a young Romanian engineer, Alexandros Blaga.

"Fuse had blown; hope you weren't too worried in there," the engineer said.

Sebastian moved away with the trolley, shaking his head no.

"Hang on, you're the pianist! I watched you play last night. They let us grease monkeys up there now and again. Are you doubling up as a cabin boy now, or have you got a little smuggling project on the go?" the engineer said as he walked toward Sebastian.

"You got me," Sebastian replied.

"Well, let's see what you have in the laundry trolley; that will decide the levy," said the now eager engineer.

The engineer was of medium height but was solid, obviously through either training or steroid abuse. He would be capable of putting up a good fight if required. But slogging it out fist to fist, body to body, was not Sebastian's way. As the engineer's eyes opened in shock when Sebastian pulled back the covering, he turned automatically towards Sebastian. That was the final act of his life; not that he died there immediately. It took time for his brain to bleed out.

Sebastian used a 'phoenix eye punch', or feng an choi, as it is known in its country of origin. Sebastian had instantly and sequentially closed his fingers into a fist, with the little finger on up to the middle finger, and then folding his forefinger back upon the support of the thumb. This pushed the knuckle of the forefinger outwards, and Sebastian thrust this not once but twice in a rapid movement into the left temple of the engineer. The engineer's eyes widened in shock and pain; he felt his vision going and began to fade away into unconsciousness. Just before his legs gave way, Sebastian steered his body into the laundry basket atop the dead girl's body.

The trip to the waste room was uneventful after that, and Sebastian set about disposing of the bodies.

His original plan was he would have returned sometime later for the disposal, but he could not wait, as the engineer would be missed, and his last whereabouts were on this deck. He opened the access hatch on the port side of the hull slightly and looked out. He could see they were navigating the Suez Canal. He knew it was the canal, as the banks of the canal side were only some six metres away from the hull hatch. The bank was two metres above him, but he could see there was no one in the vicinity looking down on him.

Sebastian slid her body out first, and then after a little struggle, he dropped the engineer into the water. As with Melissa, the engineer was immediately sucked down beneath the massive hull and into the spinning bronze blades of the propeller.

The other vital lesson Sebastian learned on that trip was that the cruise company investigates the loss of an employee far more thoroughly than that of a guest. It may have something to do with death pay-outs, but the cruise liner sent company representatives to the Port of Suez to investigate.

Due to the depth of the Suez Canal and its position, it was not long before both bodies had been recovered. The bodies were surprisingly intact due to the nature of the canal structure. There had obviously been a propeller strike on the female body, as her left arm and head were missing, stated the post-mortem carried out by a local Egyptian pathologist.

The local police took several weeks to conclude their report. They said it was a clear case of murder. It could not be an accident, as post-mortem showed that Melissa had been killed before she hit the water as there was no water in her lungs.

The engineer had a previous conviction back in Romania for putting his hand up a waitress's skirt on a drunken night out. His conviction had been noted down as a sexual assault, and this had emerged during the investigation. He had lured and attacked Melissa down there in the depths of the ship; she had died during the attack. When the engineer tried to get rid of her body, he had slipped in and been dragged under the steel hull.

The owners of *Bonny Prince Charlie* paid out a sizeable sum to Melissa's husband. The story got six lines on page nine in the pages of a tabloid in England, and page two in the main broadsheet in Romania, which had a readership of less than five thousand.

Sebastian realized that it was not that he was fearless, it was just a matter of expediency. He would kill anyone who got in his way; woman, man, boy or girl.

He carried on his killing spree. Jane was dumped into the Pacific off the coast of Hawaii. Helga in the deep Atlantic Ocean west of Madeira; Serena in the waters of the Persian Gulf; Deborah in the English Channel; Corby in the Aegean Sea; Crystal in the Bay of Biscay; Ulrika in the Bay of Islands in New Zealand; and on and on.

Sebastian was a most proficient serial killer, probably one of the leading serial killers at large in the twenty-first century, he thought.

chapter thirteen

The months that followed seemed to pass by in a haze for Cutler. In some respects, he felt guilty because he was happy that his parents had died together, and he had what was left of his parents' bodies there to bury. The same could not be said for Elisa. After months had gone by there was still no evidence of her body. Still nothing had washed up on shore, and the longer it went on, the less likely it was that he would ever have some part of her to bury.

Cutler's parents' funeral went as well as a funeral can, but what should have been an occasion to celebrate their lives turned into a barrage of non-stop questions from family and friends concerning Elisa.

A few days later, he attended the funerals of the pilot in Vancouver and the paramedics in Frazer Island, as a mark of respect.

Cutler had thought long and hard about a memorial service for Elisa but could not quite get around to organizing one. This was due to the finality of the process; Cutler still hoped as each new day dawned that news would come about Elisa. He was not naïve and knew she was not coming home alive, but to have a body to bury would help him come to terms with his loss.

As would be expected in any walk of life, the escalating bad news and tragedy had affected Cutler's work. He had done what needed to be done to keep the loose ends of his inquiries to a minimum.

A week after the funeral, Cutler took the US flight from Seattle to Chicago, where he had boarded a United Airlines flight to Geneva to visit Richter. The plan was to use the money Richter had fled with to force Werner's partner's hand. Cutler's goal was to bring down the silent partner who hid behind the scenes. Cutler knew it was a delegate in the government, but it could have been any one of three, and Cutler needed to know who.

Richter had been panicking; he had no idea what was going on in Cutler's life, nor did he care. The money was placed in a Swiss bank with Cutler as the signatory, less one hundred thousand euros, which would keep Richter in house and home for the next few years.

Cutler had brought a whole new identity along with him for Richter. He had a bona fide English passport and driving license for him, courtesy of his English counterparts. They flew into Glasgow Airport from Geneva, and as Cutler expected, had no problems with the border officers.

Cutler had used his contacts in the American embassy to find him secluded cottages in the rural area not too far from Glasgow. He had picked the area as an unusual place to put an informant. They had found a cottage on the outskirts of a small Scottish town in the highlands, called Newtonmore. The town was busy enough to have a good transport network. The population was small in the winter but increased through tourism in the summer. The cottage lay on the road leading to Aviemore, and his nearest neighbours were a mile away.

It was a week Cutler could have done without, but he had to stay with Richter to mentor him in his new identity. He accompanied Richter to the local pub, and generally ensured that he was accepted. For all intents and purposes, Richter was Karl Smitt, an immigrant from Dresden, who moved there after the fall of Communism. He was a technical author, someone who drew up plans for buildings, and thus could work from his home.

Richter was uneasy when Cutler finally left, but with the rent paid for three years and enough funds to keep him in sufficient comfort for several years, he was not that unhappy. Cutler had promised more funds later if he kept his nose clean and his head down. For now, any thoughts or plans involving Werner and his delegate partner would have to be put on hold.

Cutler had been given permission to use any surplus funds from the Werner operation as needed, to bring the gang down; pay informants, hire in specialists as required, etc. Nobody asked how much that was, as they wanted the deniability on the operation should it turn sour. Cutler never offered the information that he had put twenty-four million dollars in the bank. The money he had paid Richter had more than been made up by interest payments.

Four months after Elisa had gone missing, four months since that horrendous flight back from Germany, he arrived back in Seattle. With Richter settled in Scotland, he had to move forward. Cutler felt like he was walking through wet mud, and he needed to feel lighter if he were to get on with finding his sister's killer.

In all that time, his only comfort had come from Cathy, the stewardess on the awful flight back from Germany, hours after he had heard of Elisa's disappearance. Cathy had been pleasantly surprised by the phone call from Cutler, and even more so when a couple of days later he was true to his promise and visited her in her apartment in Seattle.

Cathy lived in a spacious, second-floor apartment on Westlake, near the Space Needle. Due to its location near the landmark tower, Cutler had found it quite quickly, and was able to park his rented sedan quite near to the building.

Cathy had just completed a flight back from Moscow and, although tired, outwardly she looked stunning when Cutler arrived. She wore a starched, crisp white blouse and a short, navy blue skirt and she looked every inch the glamorous flight attendant. Cutler felt guilty as, for the first time in months, he had looked at a woman and had immediately had the subconscious conversation with himself; the answer was yes, he definitely would like to get closer to her.

He initially had set about visiting her for some additional information. The conversation Cathy and he had on-board the flight back from Gander had played on his mind ever since. She had been a revelation, although he did not know it at the time. The comments about the number of missing persons from cruise ships had become more profound as time passed; maybe she would be able to tell him more.

Ever the gentleman, Cutler took Cathy to the local bistro, where they ate and exchanged small talk. Cathy flirted with Cutler; she was attracted by his strong outer shell, and she had seen the soft centre on that flight several months previous. She looked at him in a new light. Although apparently coping with grief, he still radiated energy and made her feel safe. He was good-looking, tall, and boyish; he would turn heads wherever he went.

Cathy had changed from her work outfit to go out. She had dressed to attract; a short, snow-white dress, which accentuated her long, black hair as it cascaded down onto her shoulders. Her almond skin was faultless, and there was not a freckle or spot that Cutler could see on her exposed skin. She was twenty-eight years old but had the skin of a sixteen-year-old; he could see her cheeks redden when he complimented her on her beauty. While he drank his Jack Daniels, he could not break contact with those enormous, oval brown eyes.

It was inevitable. For the first time since he had heard Elisa had gone missing, Cutler felt something like his old self. Her skin was magnetizing for him; he wanted to touch her, touch her anywhere, as long as he could feel that silky skin beneath his hands. She wanted to press her lips tightly around his, to connect with him, to feel more excited than she already was.

They had half-undressed each other by the time they had got through her apartment door. The lamp on the table just inside the door fell to the floor and broke into several pieces as they meandered blindly backward towards the bedroom. Cutler had pulled the straps of the white dress over her shoulders, and this now lay on the floor beside the shards of glass from the lamp. Inexpertly for a woman of her age, she struggled with the belt on his Chinos. Her bedroom was on the same level, and she steered Cutler blindly toward the door while still locked in a passionate embrace. By the time, they fell on the oversized bed he was left in his stretched Pierre Cardin white boxer shorts, and she had a flimsy pair of white satin panties being gently pulled down over her thighs.

Cutler was a generous lover. Repressing the massive urge to make love to her, he waited; he kissed her, he touched her. Taking his time he caressed and fondled her gently until her back was arching as she climaxed. Eager to please, he brought her to another, more intense orgasm. It was Cathy who could not wait any longer, and she flipped him on his back and mounted him. She sat astride him; she had control of the pace of their lovemaking. She was in awe; she had felt Cutler reach his peak, but he just kept on going, and going.

All the men she had slept with previously—and there had been eight of them—had either turned over and gone to sleep or needed a good hour to recover. Cutler just carried on for the next forty-five incredible minutes.

Finally, they slept. For Cutler, it was the first solid six hours of sleep he had had in months. Cathy was on her left side, with Cutler sculpted into her curves, and both slept in a semi-foetal position.

It was a repeat experience the following morning; the difference was they ate a hearty breakfast Cathy prepared instead of sleeping after they had made love.

Finally, Cutler got around to the main reason he had come to see Cathy. Cutler wanted to know if she had heard of anyone who had got through the red tape and ignorance surrounding those who had disappeared at sea, and could she give him any pointers or assistance.

Cutler was an experienced investigator. He knew that if he were to find out what had happened to Elisa, he would need help;

he would need someone who could navigate the problems and get him to see the right people—someone in the know.

Cathy had heard of an organization; in fact, she had had a full discussion with the founder last year on a flight back from Egypt. Cathy retrieved the black, leather-bound diary from under the cushion of her white cloth sofa and began to scan through it.

"Cheryl Ross lives in Everglade City down in Florida. Her husband went missing several years ago while leading a school trip on the *Large Pink Boat*," Cathy explained.

"*Large Pink Boat?*" Cutler asked, confused.

"Out of Fort Lauderdale, Nassau registered. They gave it the name thinking it would attract the youngsters, and it does. Drinking age is twenty-one on land. Go five miles offshore heading to the Bahamas and it comes under the law of the registered authority, and that happens to allow drinking at eighteen years old. Parents organize trips for the kids when they pass major exams, pass their driving test, you name it. They have to be sixteen to travel without a parent and believe me, it is full of them," Cathy continued.

"Cheryl's husband, Don, went missing during a cruise on the ship, and no one could throw a light on his disappearance. To cut a long story short, Cheryl launched an investigation when no one would help her."

"You mean no one investigated this, either from here or in the Bahamas?" Cutler asked incredulously.

"No, no one was willing to investigate it. She hired private detectives from New York. I met her on a trip back from Egypt. She had gone there to talk to a family who had been on the ship at the same time and had witnessed an altercation. She was convinced her husband had been murdered. Last I heard she had taken a file to the police in Fort Lauderdale on the case, but as it was in Bahamian waters, they said it was out of their jurisdiction. I think she's still trying to get the Nassau police to investigate," Cathy explained.

Cutler wrote down the name and address and jotted down notes; this was routine. It was not that his memory was poor, it was his training that had been instilled in him.

They were not Cutler's strong points: commitment, and goodbyes. He assumed Cathy would take it as fact that he would come back and see her soon. Cathy fretted she may have slept with him too quickly. Maybe he had tasted the forbidden fruit and now would move on to the next orchid.

Cutler realized he could not settle down until he had kept his last promise to his father, to find out what had happened to Elisa. The night of love and passion had brought Cutler some semblance of clarity, for the first time in months.

***

Werner was locked up and not going anywhere for months. Richter was safely resettled in Scotland, and the money was safe in a Swiss bank in Geneva. Cutler could afford to let the Werner investigation simmer on the back burner for several months. Cutler wrote out his request for a six-month sabbatical to his senior in the agency. He was sure there would not be a problem; after all, his boss knew he was not 100 percent committed in his present state of mind.

chapter fourteen

Cheryl Ross was in her early thirties. She had outgrown the youthful lustre of life, and the loss of her husband had etched some sorrow lines around her eyes. She could be described as growing older gracefully, certainly in her appearance and dress code. She was petite, at five foot two, but looked taller in the high heels she wore at any time of the day. She wore Burberry with long, silk scarves and matching accessories.

Elisa had been missing five months by the time Cutler met with Cheryl. He had taken a flight down to Miami. After a quick transfer from the airport, he settled down for the night in the Thunderbird Hotel on South Beach.

Following an early morning swim, he picked up the Hertz rental car, a Chevrolet. The two-hour drive across Alligator Alley, until he reached the turning for Everglade City, was stunning but uneventful. The lush green foliage on either side of the road contained perched eagles scanning the ground for snakes and rodents.

Everglade City was not what Cutler expected; it was a small town on the edge of the Barron River on one side and Lake Placid on the opposite side. He drove down Copeland Avenue, which had stilted houses interspersed with some local businesses; he passed the white wooden buildings with small green lawns surrounded by picket fences. Cutler turned left on West Broadway until he went as far as he could, then he came to Riverside Drive.

The intense humidity, as compared to Miami, hit Cutler straight away as he exited his air-conditioned rental. Cutler had found the address quite easily in what was a small town; the name Everglade City was an exaggeration off the scale.

Cheryl lived in a timber-built house that rested on stilts. Her Range Rover, parked under the stilts, rested alongside a small airboat. He climbed up the fourteen white wooden steps till he emerged on a good-sized, square balcony, equipped with a refrigerator for beers and a swinging hammock. Cutler could see there was netting that could be rolled down on all three open sides to keep the hordes of mosquitoes and other flying parasites out after dark.

Cutler did not need to tap on the external netted door, as the dog barking from within had announced his arrival. After the initial introductions, which included a brief introduction to Spike, a black Shar-Pei with enough wrinkles to keep a plastic surgeon busy for life, Cheryl escorted Cutler out onto the rear balcony which overlooked the Everglades.

Cutler accepted a Coke from the outside fridge while admiring the two enormous pelicans perched on the balcony surround, eagerly staring into the mass of water, waiting for their next feed to swim on by.

Cheryl explained that she had been a financial auditor for a large multinational firm prior to her husband Don's death. Several months after he went missing, and because of her constant searching for the truth, she had suffered what has been described as a nervous breakdown. She lost the high-paying job and saw her five-year-old daughter, Esme, removed and placed in foster care. To this day, two years on, she had been unable to get her daughter back, as the authorities still felt she had mental health issues. Cutler discovered these supposed mental health problems had more to do with her drive to find the truth about her husband than the perceived paranoia the mental health representatives had labelled her with. Cutler knew exactly how she felt, as he had been going through the same emotions and feelings over the past several months.

Within a couple of hours, both Cheryl and Cutler had settled into conversation. The talked about their losses, and family, things they had not discussed with any other living soul. The clarity created an honest and open discussion that would normally be restricted to the closest of friends and confidants, rather than two people who were virtual strangers.

Cheryl explained to Cutler in no uncertain terms that the lost ones and dead at sea had virtually no rights. They crossed national and international borders, and this caused responsibility issues. There were problems with who investigates and where to investigate, as the missing person could have disappeared miles away from where it was reported. She also discovered that police forces are not set up to investigate such disappearances.

Many disappearances are put down to misadventure or suicide, with the odd exception where someone had seen an altercation and witnesses came forward.

After Cheryl's husband had gone missing, she had approached her local police, the Bahamian police, the FBI, even Interpol, all to no avail. She pestered them, harassed them, and this was one of the reasons she was not allowed her child back. When she mentioned Esme, a sadness fell over her.

Cutler explained that he had been hitting brick walls since Elisa had gone missing as well. Furthermore, with his background and contacts, if there were anything to know, he would have got the data, but the information was just not there. Yes, there were missing person's reports, but not a whole lot more. All the checks and counterchecks generally undertaken for a missing person or murder on the mainland were simply missing for Elisa, and it seemed for most individuals who went missing at sea.

Cheryl told Cutler that she had travelled to Egypt before her nervous breakdown. One member of the ship's crew had anonymously sent her a letter saying that an Egyptian couple had mentioned that they had seen a fracas on deck, and it might have involved her husband; they gave the forwarding address of the family.

Cheryl had travelled to Cairo to meet the Yacoub family. They met her in a café overlooking the plains of Giza. Any time before her husband's disappearance she would have been amazed at the sight of the three pyramids, with the Sphinx placed forward of them and lit up by the setting sun, but not now.

Mr and Mrs Yacoub met her in the café at the appointed time. Over Egyptian, apple-infused tea, they explained they had seen two young men beating up an older man. The Yacoubs confirmed it was Cheryl's husband from a photograph she showed them. Mr Yacoub expressed his regret and shame; he said he had been worried about his wife, and ushered her away. He had been cowardly, he said. The next morning, Mr Yacoub reported the incident to a steward. They had not known the elder man on the floor receiving the beating was missing until they received the phone call from Cheryl.

Cheryl had at first been bemused, as the ship owners denied having received any reports of any incidents on that cruise, apart from the report that her husband was missing. Cheryl thought that a crew member had not bothered to log it, or it had been glossed over by the company. In the end she believed it was her husband's cabin steward, Emilio, who sent her the letter but try as she might, he would not agree to see her.

Cheryl and Cutler were so deep in discussion they had not noticed that the sun had gone down over the Everglades. The light came on automatically and illuminated the immediate area. Outside the balcony, the darkness was intense due to the overwhelming over-illumination you are exposed to in any other city. The oppressive heat of the day was replaced by the humid atmosphere which envelops the Everglades at night.

After several bites, Cheryl pulled down the fine netting to keep the mosquitoes and other night-time parasites away from them. She took a short break, leaving Cutler with a Budweiser, and returned with sirloin steaks and a bowl of salad. Cheryl turned on the gas grill, and after coating the thick steaks in olive oil, she threw them both on the grill.

"Medium rare," Cutler asked politely, as his nostrils flared to take in the aroma of the cooking steaks.

They both ate in comparative silence, enjoying the food and the noises of the night kept at bay by the net.

Over the next few hours, they discussed their options in detail. They brought up both sensible and outlandish ideas; the problem was, it always came back to money. Neither the governments nor the ship owners were willing to finance investigations nor were they prepared to have the publicity that went with it. This was definitely not the case of any publicity is good publicity.

Cutler had known within two weeks of Elisa going missing that there was no set organization to investigate people lost at sea. It was a Bermuda Triangle; facts went into one police force or another, and nothing ever came out. He also knew that if he was going to keep his promise to his father, he was going to have to take some considerable time away from the Secret Service. In fact, what he had planned may mean a permanent break.

Cheryl was smart, driven, and sane, as far as Cutler could make out. All too often people in authority make the mistake of underestimating or categorizing driven people as mentally unstable. Cheryl had suffered a nervous breakdown due to the stress and loss of her husband, and subsequent revelations concerning his death.

She explained to Cutler that she had, with some difficulty, purchased a photograph of everyone under the age of twenty who had been on the cruise. It had not been easy; she had single-handedly tracked down the photographer from the cruise her husband had undertaken. Matt Rice, known to all his friends as Basmati, no longer worked for the cruise line industry. He now worked as a crime scene photographer for the crime scene unit working out of Tampa.

Once Cheryl had tracked Basmati down, he was a mine of information. The digital age had revolutionized his trade, and he kept a digital record of every cruise and of every photograph he had taken.

The reference he filed it under was 12987, and this was the disc with everyone's first photograph aboard the ship. The cruise lines ensure that about fifteen photographs and more are taken of every guest on-board, but it can be a bit hit-and-miss. What is not hit-and-miss is the picture captured by the digital camera for their ship's pass, and Basmati downloaded these images, as well as keeping his own. He loaded them onto his computer and entered a filter. Within the hour, he had a download of every picture of males under the age of twenty-one on the ship that week; one hundred and twenty-nine young men in all.

"I had shown all hundred and twenty-nine photographs to Mr and Mrs Yacoub, when sitting in the moonlight a hundred yards away from the Sphinx. The Egyptian couple meticulously studied the photos and identified the two boys. Two days and several hundred dollars later, I had a notary sign the Yacoubs' statements in front of them all to say they were true accounts," Cheryl recounted.

"You had good, solid leads," Cutler replied.

"On my return to the States a few days later, I gave the statements to the police in Fort Lauderdale. They basically said it was up to the Bahamian police force, as it had happened in their waters. The Bahamian police refused point blank to investigate anymore. They also claimed the investigation had been closed and recorded as a suicide, and, therefore, no crime. I tried every law enforcement agency I knew, but no one wanted to know."

"The evidence was circumstantial, but strong evidence. You have sworn statements and two names to go with, and no one wanted to know," Cutler said, somewhat perturbed.

"After that I tracked down one of the lads. His name is Bernard Rothhelm, and he lives in Palm Beach. I went there but could not get past the security at the gate. The place just oozed money. I wrote to his parents and explained the circumstances, and within two weeks, I had been institutionalized, and had Esme removed. It took nearly a year to get out of the institution, and I still cannot get Esme back. I'm ashamed to say I have been fighting that for the past two years, not concentrating on my husband's death."

"Sounds like exactly what I would want you to do, if I were the boy's parents," Cutler said.

Cheryl offered him a room for the night, as it was clear to them both they still had more talking to do in the morning, and Cutler had drunk several Budweisers. She retired to her room, leaving Cutler on the veranda drinking a final beer, and with an awful lot of thinking to do.

When Cheryl arose early the next morning, she cooked a Canadian breakfast of thick bacon, eggs, hash browns, and pancakes with maple syrup. She was surprised to find him still on the veranda, with a stockpile of empty Budweiser bottles.

As they sat down to breakfast, Cutler had the look of a man who had seen the light. He waded through the meal with gusto.

"Cheryl, it's obvious no one cares. Even in my position, where I have access to different investigative authorities, I am clueless on where to go and who to see within the present system," Cutler said with resignation.

"That's exactly what I've been saying!" interjected Cheryl.

"Well, when one meets a wall, one must find a way to get around that wall, even if that means building a new bypass," Cutler said.

"In English please, Max," Cheryl said.

"Everyone calls me Cutler, Cheryl. I'm kind of used to it now," Cutler said gently. "In plain language, we need to set up our own investigation team, set up a company that investigates across borders and across police forces. If the police don't investigate, we will do the investigations. If they don't act on our findings, we will take out advertisements; go to the local television stations, etc." Cutler went on.

"That is all well and good, but that takes money. I'm barely hanging onto my house after paying for my own trip to Egypt after the loss of my job," Cheryl said dejectedly.

"I have money, easily enough money to set this up, and to bankroll investigations for several years to come. Plus, we could take donations," Cutler said.

"You have money? You never said," Cheryl inquired more excitedly.

"Well, let's say I have *access* to a fund. The less you know about it, the better. But it is nothing illegal," Cutler explained, half-heartedly believing it.

Cutler had fought his conscience. He felt he was betraying everything he stood for by using the money. He listed down on one side of a piece of paper all the reasons not to do this; on the other hand he wrote down all the reasons he should follow this course of action. He had four reasons not to move forward, and twenty-five reasons why he should. His mind was settled; he knew he had no option.

chapter fifteen

Attorney Seppi Von-Baer was the legal brains of the outfit; Delegate Frau Uebering had corrupted him when he was still at school in Dresden. Von-Baer was their one and only attorney. Von-Baer knew the set-up; he knew their secrets. And, above all, they owned him, lock, stock, and barrel.

He was the delegate's lover. Before that he was her son's friend, and then foster son. He had been besotted with her, even as a young boy of twelve. Delegate Frau Uebering had ushered him to her bed a year later, and he had become her constant plaything, her boy toy, their relationship a carefully guarded secret.

Delegate Frau Uebering had need of sexual release. It was not the normal man-woman relationship, as she dominated every man she had ever met. But he satisfied her in a way she had not experienced before. She would show him how she wanted pleasuring, and he would obey. She knew the Kama Sutra inside out.

Von-Baer's mother had grown up with Delegate Frau Uebering, and they had been at school together. It was not long before she had pieced together the change in her son's attitude and the way he talked and looked at the delegate. Out of friendship, she approached the delegate and told her to stop enchanting her son, or she would destroy her career by exposing her underage sex to the media.

Two days later, and without her adolescent lover's knowledge, Frau Uebering had her friend killed. The task was easy enough for Werner; a phone call and order to a minion, and then the next day a minibus hit her side-on outside the school as she waited for Von-Baer. He saw the aftermath; his mother's body contorted and bloodied, her brain oozing out of the crushed forehead.

Von-Baer became an orphan at fourteen. It was not difficult, nor did it raise any eyebrows when Frau Uebering fostered her son's friend. In fact, it was reported in the *Bild* newspaper how magnanimous she had been to accept this responsibility. Three weeks after he moved in, she moved Raphe, her son from a previous marriage, to a boarding school outside of Frankfurt; her husband had been discarded years before. She now had a foster child and a lover, all to herself, and she did not want Raphe getting in the way.

When Von-Baer graduated from school, she put him in the best law school that money could buy, in Berlin, and close to her. He went to university on the condition he came home each evening.

University was a lonely place for him. Forbidden to mix with other students by the delegate, he cut an isolated figure. The other students would harass and mock him at first. Once he had broken down and wept in front of the delegate, and admitted he was being bullied because of her insistence on isolation. This behaviour stopped immediately when the delegate sent a couple of Werner's men around to pick him up outside the university. One of the minders walked up to Jon, the main antagonist, and a punch later Jon was sprawled out on the ground and his nose would never go back to its original shape.

Power was everything to Von-Baer and he had none of it. He adored the thought of a powerful woman dominating, both in and out of bed, and the delegate certainly did this with aplomb.

To the outside world, the delegate was a doting, caring, and loving mother and stepmother. No one apart from Werner knew the depths of their relationship. He was not blind and had a fair idea of her need for unconventional sex. This knowledge was acquired through first-hand experience. Indeed he had once shared her bed—only once, as Werner was a missionary sort of person, and this did not raise the delegate's pulse rate one bit.

Never once had anyone ever thought of them as anything other than mother and stepson. Her biological son had, after completing school in Dresden, been ushered to England, to Oxford to study medicine, and he decided to stay in Cambridge, visiting his mother less and less over the years.

Von-Baer knew the damaging impact of the loss of the counterfeit operation after the arrest of Werner, not just this part of the business, but to the organization overall. The immediate impact was the capture and confinement of Jan Eichmann, the gang's master forger. It would take a considerable amount of time and effort, not to mention the financial costs, to get another master forger. Von-Baer and the delegate also lamented the loss and subsequent seizure and destruction of their operational equipment, the best that money could buy.

Jan was known as The Professor, although he did not have one solitary qualification. He would spend the next decade in prison. The thought that Jan would turn state's evidence against them was unviable, as the only high-level contact he knew was Werner.

He had never heard or seen either the delegate or Von-Baer. His wife would wait for him, and his children would be teenagers by the time he came out. Jan was as sure of this as he was that they would all be killed if he ever said a word in or out of court against Werner.

All the power and all the connections would not help Werner. Von-Baer had explained in detail to the delegate as he raised his head from under the white cotton covers once he had satisfied the delegate's daily requirement of cunnilingus. Werner had been caught in the act; by this fact alone he was implicated. Somehow, Von-Baer had to ensure that Werner had the shortest time in prison. He was good, but even he could not get him out of prison on bail. His best chance was to have the proceedings dismissed, and he doubted he could achieve this with the publicity surrounding the case. If Von-Baer could not get a dismissal, then a not guilty verdict would suffice, but he doubted he could achieve this, even with the delegate's assistance.

Probing the delegate carefully, Von-Baer raised the possibility with her of having Werner killed in the prison hospital; basically, solving a major problem, and the only link back to them both. The delegate had dismissed the idea immediately. Werner was the only connection other than Von-Baer. He made the money on the ground, and he was her general. To attempt to elevate one of his lieutenants into a more senior position as a replacement for Werner was to put the delegate at risk.

She was powerful because only a handful of confidants knew of her past, and even less about the present. And the overriding factor for not having Werner killed was that he had many contacts.

He would be sure to find out if there were a contract out on him, and he would surely turn this around so it would be them that would most likely be terminated.

Von-Baer visited the prison and was used to the searches and security measures that were in place. He was escorted to the hospital wing, which was decorated in sparkling white and green tiles from floor to ceiling. Werner should have been on a ward with other prisoners, but such was his reputation that he was housed in a separate room, a private room normally reserved for terminally ill prisoners.

Von-Baer was visibly shocked at seeing the once strong, enigmatic, and overbearing presence of Werner now diminished. Werner had shed a significant amount of weight; it had wasted away from his enormous chest and shoulders. Werner was aware that his size intimidated people, and he had worked on it every day in the gym with weights, reps, bench presses, etc. All this was a thing of the past these few months, as he had to regulate his breathing through his damaged airways. Werner's skin was pallid and wet with sweat as he fought off the never-ending small infections that blighted his recovery. He had a white lint elastic bandage around his neck with what looked like a white plastic valve where the voice box should have been. Von-Baer stood there, shocked, for several moments.

Werner was determined not to talk in his metallic voice with Von-Baer. Werner would only speak through the ghastly, machine-generated voice when he had mastered it, or technology had caught up with his requirements; a real voice.

Werner insisted on having paper, a pen, and a shredding machine in his room. The shredder had cost him several thousand Euros to the prison guards' so-called benevolent fund.

"She wants to know where the twenty-four million is, Werner," Von-Baer began.

Werner wrote rapidly and once finished, he pushed it under Von-Baer's nose.

"Where do you think it is, you little pip-squeak? Fucking Richter has disappeared with it." Von-Baer put the note into the shredder, and the machine chewed it up.

Von-Baer ignored the insult and continued. "What have you done to retrieve the money?"

Werner wrote the next message down angrily. "Forget the money for now. What are you doing to get me out?"

"For now, nothing. You were caught red-handed. We have the German government watching the outcome of this prosecution, we also have the American government. The best we can hope for is to get to a juror, and then again if we do, I think the government will want an inquiry. In short, you may have to stay in prison, as even our friends may find it impossible to help you. Naturally, the twenty-four million would help," Von-Baer said, in a calm, quiet voice.

Werner began to scribble hurriedly. "You organize to get me out of here one way or another, and quickly. As soon as you do, I will start the task of finding Richter and the money. No freedom, no money." Again, Von-Baer shredded the message while he digested the contents.

"Obviously, I'm not in the position to say what will happen next. I will discuss it with, well, you know who. She will make the decision about how we go forward," Von-Baer replied.

"Tell her Operation Muscat. Tell her I want the same; she will know what I mean. And tell her we stand together, or we drown together," Werner had written.

"I have no idea what Muscat is, and it is not a good idea to be using threats, Herr Werner, not a good idea at all, given your present predicament," Von-Baer said more sternly.

Twenty seconds later, Werner was ready with his message. It covered quite a section of the page. "Listen to me, rent boy. Do you think I do not know about you and the delegate fucking yourselves to death every night? I have contacts you have no idea about. If I don't get Muscat, then you will learn about it the hard way. I will have someone tattoo the meaning on your cock, except it won't be attached to your body any longer. And I'll send it to the delegate so she can get it mounted as a memento of what you both had. Do I make myself clear, rent boy?"

"Crystal, Herr Werner. I will return within the week with her answer," Von-Baer said as he stood and immediately walked towards the cell door, which was opened by a nurse guard on the opposite side.

chapter sixteen

Over the weeks since Cutler first had the meeting with Cheryl, he had laid out his plans in more detail, culminating in a full business plan. One of the main aspects was discussing Cheryl's level of involvement. After several meetings, Cutler offered her a paid position as a researcher and director of the company. He had been impressed with her determination, and he had a genuine need for her research and audit skills.

Together they advanced the business plan to include human resource requirements; how many people they would need, what expertise and specialties would be required. The only thing that was not discussed was finance. Cutler had sorted it, and that was good enough for Cheryl.

Several days before incorporating the company, Cutler put in his formal resignation to the Secret Service. He travelled to Washington to meet Wyatt Rockman, his recruiter into the Secret Service. He discussed in detail what he was planning, leaving out the financial aspects. Rockman listened and gave advice but was not wholly convinced it was the major problem that Cutler thought it was. Rockman put this eagerness down to the loss of his sister. He assured Cutler that, should he ever want to return to the Service, he would assist him to get back in.

On his return to Florida, he discussed the need for investigators. Cutler told Cheryl he had put out some feelers and had several recommendations. Cheryl recommended Matt

Rice, the photographer who had helped her. He was well known in the cruise line circles and could assist them with getting some inside information, and they could use him for his forensic and photography skills.

A photographer would not have been the first recruit in Cutler's mind, but the more he thought about it, the more it made sense. Cutler was impressed when Cheryl got him Matt Rice's curriculum vitae. Matt had learned his photography skills as a coroner's assistant in Tampa; with luck, he would have picked up some forensic skills as well.

Over the next few weeks, Cutler spent a lot of time with Cheryl. He had her join him on trips to Geneva, where they set up a new office for the company, which they had decided to call Marine Investigations Deaths at Sea, or MIDAS for short.

He was not overly worried about the Secret Service or the American government, as they had no idea about the $24 million lodged with a Swiss bank. The only person who knew was Richter, and he would not be popping up anywhere soon, as Werner would surely have a contract out on him.

Cutler was going to leave the main deposit to use to flush out the German politician who had run Werner. He was going to use the interest to run MIDAS, to recruit the personnel he needed and pay the expenses required. He had set aside $5 million in shares and amounts of $250,000 in small banks throughout the world as working capital for MIDAS. The remainder was to be placed in Switzerland. It would generate $1.7 million dollars per year in interest at current interest rates, plus whatever dividends the shares would bring. On the advice of a close friend on Wall

Street, Cutler had purchased three thousand shares in a web-based search engine company called Google. This was the first release of shares by Google, and Cutler received the whole allotment of ten thousand Class A common stock shares at $85 dollars a share. Little did Cutler know that within twelve years they would be valued at $577.27. The original outlay of $855,000 would generate $5,770,000; he just had to stay alive for twelve years to enjoy it.

Over the next month, Cutler used all his resources to identify potential new agents for MIDAS. Cutler used his network of contacts in the security services, Special Forces, and specialists in the United States and abroad to identify potential new MIDAS recruits. The process took months of sifting through their backgrounds and interviewing the shortlisted candidates.

With Cheryl's help, he set up an office in Everglade City. This was an odd place for an office, out of the way, and some two hours from the nearest big city of Miami, but in Cutler's mind, it was the perfect place. Yes, it was hot, humid, and sticky for most of the year, but it was a one-road town with everyone knowing each other, and tourists and unwanted visitors could easily be identified. Secondly, he did not want Chery relocated away from her home, not while she was trying to win back her daughter.

For his European office, both he and Cheryl opted for Geneva. The options were limited; they needed somewhere with a lack of regulations and prying into large amounts deposited in their banks' vaults, and Geneva was the natural choice. After several weeks, Cheryl, who was accompanied by their first recruit Matt Rice, decided on a location in a small suite of offices on the

Rue des Pâquis. She had decided on the area, as it was the most reasonable for leasing costs, its location was central, and what were once farm fields were now an exotic mixture of shops, restaurants, and nightclubs. Matt Rice readily agreed when he discovered a small but exquisite sushi bar just around the corner.

Naturally, all the money and accounts would be run from the Geneva office. Cutler wanted many of his intelligence operations based there, away from American jurisdiction, as he knew what he had planned was not entirely legal and would be frowned upon even more in the United States. He had indeed crossed the threshold and wanted freedom to undertake some activities away from the highly organized and intrusive security services in the Unites States.

Cutler had used his Italian and Swiss contacts to recruit a technical specialist. Ideally, he wanted someone with high levels of IT skills, with a detailed research background. Fabienne Asper, a large, butch Swiss brunette with shoulders wider than Cutler's, and a plain face bordering on masculine, had all the skills necessary, and a whole lot more.

What Fabienne lacked in feminism, she more than made up for with brains. She was a technical wizard, whether handling databases, setting up a website, or finding something or someone through search engines. She had a PhD in computer security and had gained this through hacking numerous sites, whether private, commercial or government, as part of her research into site security. She had seen nations' secrets, and not once had she tried to gain through her knowledge. Fabienne's mother was English and Fabienne had been recruited and worked for the British intelligence services, specifically for GCHQ, their information and intelligence gathering agency. She had seen information that could bring down governments and individuals. Fabienne had been instrumental in identifying suspected Al Qaeda terrorists based in Italy and Germany by breaking into a coded website and deciphering their discussions and plans. As this was the year after the 9/11 atrocity, she gladly shared the information with the United Kingdom's MI5 to bring them to justice. At that time, she had no idea that justice was a cell in Guantanamo Bay.

Cutler had his business partner Cheryl on board; an excellent administrator, and although a novice, she had proven quite adept at investigation by tracking down her husband's alleged killers. Together they had recruited a forensic photographer in Matt Rice, and now they had a first-class researcher in Fabienne. Now Cutler turned his attention to investigators of the highest quality, as for what they were about to undertake, only the best of the best would do.

Cutler had heard through a friend and CIA contact, Kale Fray, about the English Health and Safety investigator, Robert Stahmer. Kale had explained to Cutler that Robert was the investigator who had averted an attack on the Houses of Parliament. It had all been very hush-hush, but there was nothing that happened in London that the CIA did not find out about.

Kale had explained that the safety inspector was not only a first-class investigator with a dogged and determined attitude; Stahmer also had a vested interest in Cutler's project.

While Cutler and Kale enjoyed a pint of Guinness in the Elephant and Castle in London, Kale, with intelligible clarity, revealed the misfortune that had been inflicted upon Robert Stahmer after the Parliament incident.

Stahmer had been given several months' paid leave after the Parliament incident as a little but well-received gesture of thanks. For years, he had promised his wife a Caribbean holiday. The brochures he chose from the local travel agent made Dominica looks like a tropical paradise. Stahmer wanted to surprise his wife, with little hesitation and unbeknown to his wife, he booked them on a two-week, all-inclusive holiday, their first in ten years.

The hotel was everything he had expected; safe and secure, with three pools, the largest an infinity pool which appeared to merge with the clear blue crystal waters of the Caribbean Sea. Stahmer would never forgive himself for not doing what he did every day, and thoroughly investigate what and where he was going. Two days into the vacation, his beloved wife was taken from him in a most horrendous way.

Cutler approached Robert Stahmer. He described to Stahmer the outline over his own loss, and the problems he had encountered in trying to investigate his loss. Cutler omitted telling Stahmer where the funds to finance MIDAS had originated, and Stahmer did not ask.

Throughout the interviews, Robert Stahmer never discussed any detail about the Houses of Parliament attack, which reinforced Cutler's initial belief that this man could be trusted with a secret. Robert Stahmer was, however, more forthcoming on how he had tracked down the drug-infused local who had followed his wife into the restroom at the back of a jewellery shop they had been visiting.

The drug addict had attacked Stahmer's wife with a machete, dismembering the arm so he could retrieve the bracelet her loving husband had just purchased for her. The piece of jewellery would pay for his next few fixes. Mrs Stahmer just plain bled out, blood pumping profusely from the open arteries that seconds before had been connected to the amputated limb. She died on the bathroom floor. Her severed arm, stripped of the bracelet, was discarded a hundred yards away where the killer had dropped it.

Stahmer was angry; mad at himself for not having the foresight; angry he was not there in the bathroom to help her; and even angrier that he didn't know who did it, as he wanted to rip him limb from limb. Stahmer had lost both his parents the previous decade and thought he knew about grief; he did not. The pain and constant ache, and the emotional rollercoaster he suffered; he had never known before. The nightmare kept him awake, until sleep overtook him. When he awoke, he thought it was indeed a nightmare, and his beloved wife would come striding through with his morning coffee in hand, just like she had done for all their years of marriage.

Stahmer returned home to bury his wife. The funeral was not an end to his ordeal; it gave him no finality, only despair. A few days after the funeral, Stahmer returned to Dominica, determined to get the person who had cruelly taken his wife away. He was not sure what he was going to do; only that he would not and could not rest until he had him.

On his return, Stahmer ensured he was on one television or radio news station or another for several weeks, complaining about the lack of information from the public, and how this could affect tourism. In the end, it was money, bribery, and persistence that finally unearthed the information. It had taken seven weeks of stubborn adherence to the gruesome task.

Stahmer was not oblivious to the danger he was in. The island's publicity and façade are one of Caribbean beauty, white sandy beaches, and rum-infused nights. Go several hundred yards away from the tourist routes and you were in a third-world, poverty-stricken, violent country. Stahmer had hired a local who was an enormous mountain of a man, all muscle, but one Stahmer was assured he could trust. Joe Frazier had been named after the world boxing champion and probably, Stahmer thought, would have given a good account of himself with his namesake in the ring, even in his heyday. Stahmer began calling him The Champ after he knocked two drug dealers out cold who took offense to the questions Stahmer kept on asking their clients.

Finally, after a month, it was the shop owner who came forward with a name. He feigned terror of reprisal if he came forward but had now suddenly found his backbone. Stahmer disbelieved him. After physical intervention from Joe Frazier, and the threat of much worse to come, the jeweller admitted he had been approached by the killer with a false name of a rival, and they were going to split the reward. It did not take Joe very long to get the correct name from the jeweller. Stahmer would honour the reward to the jeweller, as he would need it to reconstruct his jaw and replace the teeth he had lost, not at the hands of Joe, but Stahmer.

More money passed hands, and Stahmer was permitted to go with the six police officers to observe the arrest. They broke down the door of the wooden hut and pulled out Nero, as he was nicknamed. Stahmer recognized him, not from the jeweller's, but as someone who had been paying them attention several hours before his wife's attack.

"You want him dead, boss? Five thousand US dollars," the senior officer inquired.

"No, I don't want him dead; that's too easy. After seeing the state of your police station, I gather your prisons are inhumane. I am going to pay you a thousand dollars a year for as long as it takes to keep him locked up. I want guarantees that no one will pay to get him out, or I will pay the same amount to someone else to settle the breach of contract with you. Do you understand what I'm saying?"

"Yes, boss, I send you proof every year. We keep him alive barely."

"Good, I want a copy of his fingerprints and his footprints, and each year for the next decade on the anniversary of my wife's killings you will cut off one of his digits, so I may verify them when I come back. I also want access to him in the prison to see him," Stahmer said coldly.

Nero began to beg, and the officer slammed his gun into his gut, knocking all the wind out of him.

"We don't feed them in prison. They rely on relatives. This guy will have no one once word gets around, he is not getting out ever. I'm afraid that will cost you another five hundred dollars a year to make sure we can sustain him and pay for some antibiotics, as his stumps will get infected," the officer pressed.

Stahmer handed over the fifteen hundred dollars to the officer as the first installment and kicked the recovering Nero as hard as he could between the legs.

Cutler had asked Kale Fray how he had come across this information, as he had found Stahmer quiet, proficient, and professional, and not someone that would give up private information easily.

"That's simple; Joe Frazier is ours. He's been our informant for many years. We owed Stahmer after the Parliament affair. He would have hit a brick wall in Dominica without Joe. We ensured, without Stahmer's knowledge, that Joe had his back," Fray replied.

"Nice to see chivalry is not dead," Cutler concluded.

Cutler knew that as well as brains and investigators, he would need muscle. The investigators would need someone to accompany them; muscle, and brains, to have their backs; specialists willing to go the extra mile.

Stahmer requested Joe Frazier as his minder. Cutler at first, was reticent. After getting the clearance from Fray, Cutler interviewed Joe and made it quite clear that if he worked for him, his days of reporting back to MI5 were over. He also asked him if he were up to the odd task that walked the line of legality.

"That's my specialty. One other thing; if I'm to give up my security with the British, I want US citizenship," Joe said. Cutler realized that the Jamaican jive Joe talked was a put-on, and he spoke with a very passable English accent.

What Cutler would learn over time was that Joe was as loyal a person as you could get. He also had a marvellous ability to speak in most accents and could mimic individuals. Sometimes Cutler wondered if he was talking to a colleague on the phone, or if it was Joe up to his tricks again.

Following the acquisition of Stahmer's and Joe's services, Cutler turned his attention to a security company in Atlanta. Custodela Incorporated was set up by John and Nick Commons. John was ex-Seal, and Nick was ex-Secret Service. This was the pond they fished in for their operatives. Custodela, as a name, was picked as it translated from Latin to 'guard', and this is what they did; they guarded the world's VIPs in areas of trouble. The company was initially set up to send out bodyguards to protect the green zone occupants in Baghdad; it had now widened its scope to other theatres of war.

It took a $50,000 introduction fee to Custodela to get Tuck Walters and a further $50,000 to release him from his contract. Walters was known just as Tuck. He was ex-SAS trained Special Forces. Tuck had worked with John Commons in a joint operation in Afghanistan to locate and call in drones to dispose of two leading members of the Taliban.

Cutler had thought the ex-SAS man short for Special Forces, at five feet eight, when he had appraised his file. However, on meeting Tuck, it became apparent that size did not matter. The man looked tough; he oozed power and presence. Tuck was of Maori descent, olive-skinned, square-jawed, and black hair. He was all muscle and was shaped like a V from the waist up. Originally from Rarotonga in the Cook Isles, he had found the life too peaceful and sedentary; others call that paradise. Tuck had emigrated and signed up for the New Zealand Armed Forces until finally being shipped off to the SAS training grounds of Hereford in the United Kingdom.

Tuck had seen action when stationed with the British in Kuwait, Iraq, and undercover in Iran and Sudan. He had gained a reputation as a dependable member of the team; fearless, fierce, and uncompromising. Lately he had been providing personal protection for oil executives from the UK and the States in Iraq, and had saved several from assassination attempts, leaving a dozen or so activists bereft of breath.

Tuck was to oversee the security team, and as such, wanted to recruit his own men. He wanted a wing man, and immediately put forward and hired Hoagie Finberg, who towered over Tuck at six foot five inches. The pair had worked together on several sorties, each had saved the other's life on at least one occasion. They had a bond; where Tuck went, Hoagie followed. This cost MIDAS another $50,000 introduction fee to Custodela. The company was quite willing to let their operatives leave for finder fees. As it stood, they now had an abundance of veterans from the Seals and SAS on their books, looking for high wages, and the need to get away from the boredom of civilian life.

Hoagie was as good-looking as Tuck was tough-looking. Short, blonde, salt-and-pepper speckled hair, and a striking facial resemblance to George Clooney. Due to this doppelganger legacy, he seldom left a pub or nightclub alone. The problem for the army of women admirers was, he always left with men, as Hoagie was gay. This perceived and outdated blemish on Hoagie's curriculum vitae led to his dismissal from the United States Navy Seals, and his subsequent twelve months in prison for striking the officer who blew the whistle on his sexual preferences.

Another recruit was a twenty-two-year-old graduate from Harvard: Ghislaine Lyman nee Farouk. She was of Palestinian extract, born in the Gaza Strip. Her parents had been killed when a retaliation raid for an earlier bomb attack on a bus station in Haifa. The result of the bombing had prompted the Israelis to send over ten times more explosive power in the form of rockets into the Gaza Strip. Unfortunately, one such missile blew up the family home. Ghislaine had been dragged from the wreckage of what was left of the house by an American volunteer for the World Health Organization. By hook and by crook, the American volunteer had gotten Ghislaine back to the States, where he and his wife had adopted Ghislaine Farouk, who several years later took on the Lyman name.

What Cutler had been looking for was a linguist; someone who could speak several languages. Cutler had a good grasp on German and Arabic, but that was all. Tuck could speak Maori and Aborigine; how useful that would be, they did not know. Fabienne could speak her native Swiss, plus English, French, and German.

What Cutler had not expected was Ghislaine's sheer presence; she was as striking as she was gifted. She had jet-black hair that flowed like layers of silk in the wind. Her olive skin had the red blush of youth and was faultless. She was five feet nine inches tall, and the heels she wore made her look more like six feet. When Cutler met her for the first time, she wore a two-piece white trouser suit which defined her slim, hourglass figure. The suit also accentuated the lustre of her hair against the whiteness of the suit. Ghislaine wore round Gucci sunglasses, her bright green eyes shining through the polarized layers of glass.

Cutler and Cheryl now had their initial team for MIDAS. Cheryl would be the researcher based in Florida who would be responsible for initial research. Matt Rice was their photographic expert. Fabienne in Geneva was responsible for building secure IT systems, research, and building search engines to assist Cheryl. Tuck and Hoagie were security, surveillance, and counter-surveillance. Robert Stahmer was his deputy lead investigator. Ghislaine was their translator.

Finally, Cutler transferred the first $1.4 million across to the MIDAS bank account. This was the interest earned on the initial deposit and would be the running fee for the pristine organization. This was the same day Fabienne completed the new MIDAS website, with the first appeal to anyone with information on Cheryl's husband's death and subsequent disappearance from the *Large Pink Boat*.

Cutler would wait a month or so before putting up a page for his missing sister Elisa. He thought he owed it to Cheryl to try and solve that case first and put the whole of his team on it.

He had worked for several weeks trying to identify and locate other potential investigators. One person he had not considered was Detective Manfred Shultz from Munich. He had collaborated with him in the Werner case and had almost forgotten about him. The news about his sister Elisa had overpowered him to such an extent that he had overlooked an obvious and capable investigator.

Cutler had known Shultz for eighteen months while working on the Werner case. Shultz had been responsible for identifying the master forger and the first tenuous link with an unknown government official. It was unfortunate that six months before they arrested Werner, Shultz had gone off on holiday and then disappeared off the radar. The German police did not offer an explanation to Cutler at the time, and appeared to be hiding something from him.

Cutler was enjoying a Wiener schnitzel and Weiss beer with Enrich, the German police commander Cutler had worked so closely with on the Werner case. The meeting in Munich had originally been set up as an update on the counterfeit gang. The commander was aware that Cutler had left the Secret Service and set up MIDAS. They had become good friends during the lengthy investigation.

Having enjoyed the main course, they moved on to the apple strudel, washed down with a double helping of Jägermeister. In the pauses, when they were neither eating nor drinking, Enrich briefed Cutler on the progress of the investigation. In return, Cutler explained how he had now left the Secret Service and had set up MIDAS, and on the revelations, or lack of them, surrounding his sister's disappearance. As an addendum and a throwaway remark, he asked Enrich if he knew of any first-class investigators looking for a well-paid and varied career.

Not really expecting any quick reply, Cutler was caught a little off guard when Enrich directed him towards Shultz.

"We kept this from you and within the department for his sake, and for the benefit of the department. Shultz's wife went missing on holiday, and he spent some time under investigation as a prime suspect before being repatriated to Munich for lack of evidence."

"My Lord, I didn't know!" Cutler replied.

"It was several months before your terrible news concerning your sister. You had enough grief to deal with without giving you more bad news, as I know you both got on well," Enrich said, between sips of his Jägermeister.

"Is he still with the department?"

"No, I'm ashamed to say. The bad publicity… he was released for lack of evidence, not cleared. My overlords deemed this sufficient to terminate his employment."

Cutler thought for a moment before replying.

"He was a damned good investigator. What is he up to now?"

"He undertakes private investigations, affairs and divorces, mostly. But he is not happy in his work. I think he would be exactly what you are looking for, considering the remit of MIDAS."

Cutler ensured that Enrich had the details of his new office in the Everglades, and in return he received the napkin with Shultz's address and telephone number.

Cutler took a day to consider and assess the data Fabienne had accessed on Shultz. Knowing the man, and with Enrich's advocacy, he gave careful thought and felt that the evidence before him was full of holes. He was willing to do what the Munich authorities had not done—give Shultz the benefit of the doubt, and the opportunity to come on-board with MIDAS.

They met at the Olympic Stadium. Cutler guided him past the lake and up the knoll while exchanging pleasantries. Cutler did not think it appropriate to ask him the questions he needed to be answered, nor did he want to be overheard while explaining the position available.

Atop the hill, with the BMW factory with the four buildings shaped like car pistons in the background, Cutler asked him about the circumstances of his wife's disappearance. Cutler was stunned by the closeness of the situation surrounding Shultz's wife's disappearance and Elisa's. Once satisfied he was telling him the truth, he outlined the vision of MIDAS and the offer on the table.

Shultz needed no more than a minute to absorb the implications and changes the offer would make to his life and accepted immediately. He had one proviso, however; that at some stage, MIDAS would investigate his wife's disappearance.

Cutler accepted the proviso but thought they had three open cases now: Elisa, Cheryl's husband Don, and now Frau Shultz.

"One more thing; the job may not always be safe. We are looking for killers. You need to make a will; we have insured each operative for one million dollars. In your contract, there is a 'volenti non fit injuria' clause. In simple terms, you accept the risk willingly."

Shultz agreed to fly to the Everglades the following week for induction, technique training, and to meet the team. From there he would travel to Geneva to see the set-up there, and then he would be allocated his first case.

Cutler drove from Munich for several hours in his hired C-class Mercedes and met his next appointment at the service station of the A12 Autobahn. Unbeknown to Cheryl, Cutler had recruited one more investigator. The position was not for MIDAS, it was for his conscience. While his primary concern was MIDAS, and finding out what had happened to his sister, he could not forget that there was a senior politician in Germany authorizing the manufacture of counterfeit American dollars along with her gangster counterpart, Werner. Cutler felt he had a duty to continue the investigation; maybe it was the money he had taken, but he did not think it was guilt. He felt it was the right thing to do.

Cutler had come across Philip Cortez on an investigation into American forged bonds three years earlier. He had first met Cortez in Alicante, on the Costa Brava on Spain's Mediterranean east side. Cortez was an undercover intelligence officer who had penetrated the Basque separatist group who had brought terror to Spain for decades.

The cell had been working seventy miles to the south of Alicante, in the town of Guardamar. As well as forging American bonds, the cell leader, Alonso, wanted to make a statement. Not a written statement, but one that used Semtex as its ink, and ball bearings as its paper. The explosion some ten miles further down the coast in Torrevieja was a dud.

Alonso had panicked on seeing a police car patrolling the area. He had left the device on the beach, which was busy with both Spanish and other European tourists. The conditions on the beach were blustery, and the sand had been whipped up to a mini sandstorm. This affected the timing mechanism. The explosion happened on a near-deserted beach some six hours later. The single casualty was a black and white mongrel searching for leftover scraps.

Cortez had been an undercover agent in the cell but was kept in the dark over the bombing. When he heard it had been a trial run and they were going to use a much bigger device on the bustling beaches of Benidorm, he took immediate action. He placed the timer in the remaining Semtex and put the explosive back in the backpack under the table. He told Alonso and his sidekick that he was going into the town to get a packet of Marlboro cigarettes. Two minutes after leaving the remote property, it disappeared in a cloud of dust and black smoke as the noise of the explosion echoed off the hills surrounding the compound.

Cortez knew that would kill off the investigation into the bonds, both his and Cutler's work was for nothing. But he had to do something, and quickly. Cortez was an embarrassment to the Service, while Cutler and his operatives had seen Cortez as a good operator who did what he had to do.

Cutler engaged the ostracized Cortez and offered him the chance to make some money and do some good. The six-foot-one, dark Spaniard—an Antonio Banderas lookalike—jumped at the opportunity.

chapter seventeen

lassical Canta Libra was the latest addition to the fleet of the Jules Verne Cruise Line Company. It was at the forefront of technology and innovation. The ship cost $900 million, and within its structure had twenty-eight conventional elevators and six glass elevators, which rose up through the centre of the vessel from the concourse on deck four to the outer leisure area on deck fifteen.

All internal and ocean-view cabins were several square metres larger than its competitors. Balcony cabins had an eight-foot-square patio, and the mini suites and suites had separate office areas with a desk.

The fourteen separate bars and music lounges were spread around the ship's plentiful and lush surroundings, seating, and decor.

The outdoor swimming pool on deck twelve was half the size of an Olympic swimming pool, and the bright-blue tiles shimmered through the crystal water in the brilliant sunshine. The pool had been fitted with a series of computer-controlled paddles to create a wave pool on the hour, every hour, between 8 am and 7 pm.

The *Classical Canta Libra* was hailed as the greatest ship ever launched, and during the ship's inaugural year, 2009, Sebastian had been invited on its maiden trip to ply his talents.

The maiden voyage would take it and its passengers from its homeport of Genoa, on the west coast of Italy, and sail south the short distance through the Liguria Sea, into the Tyrrhenian Sea, to its first stop in Cagliari, on the island of Sardinia. After a twelve-hour stopover, the ship would feel the first laps of the waves of the Mediterranean before sailing northeast into the Sea of Marmara to berth at Istanbul. Anchoring in the Aegean for twenty-four hours so the masses of guests could visit the beautiful attractions of the Blue Mosque and Grand Bazaar, among others.

The following day, the *Classical Canta Libra* entered the Bosphorus Strait, the Strait that divides the continents of Europe and Asia. The ship sailed under the two bridges spanning the channel. The Faith Sultan Mehmed, at 3,576 feet, was some 50 feet longer than Bogazici Bridge, which was completed in 1973. The captain steered the massive vessel with the help of the Turkish pilot through the strait, bypassing boats, and fishing trawlers the *Classical Canta Libra* dwarfed, and into the Black Sea.

The route would take them to Nessebar in Bulgaria, to Odessa and then Yalta, both in the Ukraine, before its final Black Sea stop of Sochi in Russia, then returning back to Genoa with a stop at Kusadasi in Turkey and the Isle of Capri, close to its home and final port of Genoa.

Sebastian had been allocated the Ice Bar to perform in. The bar was luxurious and sited on the fifth deck aft, a short walk from the theatre with its fifth-floor entrance. The theatre also had entrances directly below on deck four, and above on deck six, as it straddled the three decks.

The Ice Bar was known as the Martini-Pimm's bar by the guests, and it served over fifty cocktails. The other additives of the cocktails depended upon how blitzed the guest wanted to get, or how much money they had to waste. The most expensive martini included ten-year-old Morpheus XO Cognac, which retailed onboard for $120 and made the hardiest connoisseurs weep at the cross-contamination of the nectar.

The stunning, white baby grand piano was situated in the central part of the bar, and slightly elevated by the round marble stage, which was just large enough to sit the grand and a stool for the pianist. Semi-circular leather couches embellished with the Jules Verne Cruise Line logo spread out on all four sides of the stage to form a circle. There were gaps in between the couches for people to circulate. They went back seven rows, and there was a standing area at the bar.

The bar counter was magnificent; it looked like it had been plucked off a mountain in Alaska. To the naked eye, it was completely made of ice; in reality, only twenty percent was made of ice, but you would never know it. The mirror that adorned the area behind the bar was highly polished ice. The bar staff wore white shorts and jackets with fur collars to complete the style. Sebastian had been told previously to purchase and wear white suits only when playing in the Ice Bar.

While the guests marvelled at the gildings all around, Sebastian was more interested in other features. Sebastian noticed that there was a new design element to this ship, which far exceeded security arrangements he had seen before on any of the other ships.

The cause of Sebastian's concern was the use of internal and external closed-circuit television cameras, or CCTV. The tell-tale signs were the black, bulbous glass protrusions on the ceilings. This type of camera gave 360-degree coverage in all communal areas; in lounges, bars, swimming areas, and in each of the many long passageways to the ship's cabins. There were cameras placed on the starboard and port sides at intervals to cover the whole sides, as well as to the aft and stern of the ship.

If Sebastian were to continue in the same vein as previous cruises, he would have to discover the weak spots of the ship. He needed to see what the cameras covered.

During a meal on the second night on-board, Sebastian positioned himself alongside the third engineer and within the conversation, which brought up the coverage of the cameras. He was somewhat relieved to find out that the only active monitoring was in the casino and other areas such as the main lounges.

There were just too many cameras for active surveillance; the ship would need an army of CCTV operators to cover them all. Sebastian discovered that half the cameras were carcass cameras only; they were false cameras. This reduced some eighty-four cameras down to forty, of which ten were based in the casino alone. The port and starboard sides of the ship were covered with active cameras, as were the stern and aft.

The third engineer explained in a hushed manner to Sebastian that, apart from the casino and main reception, the other cameras were for recording purposes only, for evidential use only. The cameras could store recordings for twenty-four hours before being erased or transferred to the central computer in the case of an incident. If there was an altercation or someone jumped from a balcony into the sea, the camera being unmonitored would not assist but would be used to help the following inquiry and would form part of the investigation.

The trip out to Nessebar in Bulgaria was smooth; more than slight movement on the hull would be counterbalanced by the sea stabilizers. The waves of nearly three feet high would rock any other ship of this size, but not the *Classical Canta Libra*. You could put a tennis ball on the topmost deck, and it would not roll one inch, such was the computer-controlled environment. Even the sea could be calmed on this Leviathan of a ship.

Sebastian was joined by two of the female singers from the ship's on-board entertainment team, Christie, and Pam, both English. Sebastian had met Christie on previous cruise liners, and he nodded to her as the pair sat on the stage perimeter in the Ice Bar.

"*I Believe*, please maestro," Christie said to Sebastian.

Sebastian began to play the haunting melody *I Believe* from the musical *Miss Saigon*, a duet between Molly the American wife and Mella the Vietnamese girlfriend. Christie and Pam sang the parts perfectly.

"Yes still, I still believe, I know as long as I keep believing, I'll live, love, and die," they sang in unison.

Sebastian thought he liked the idea of them dying better, as he had no concept of what love should feel like; he did not believe.

The two performers received a standing ovation from the large crowd in the Ice Bar. They, in turn, raised their arms in Sebastian's direction as he remained sitting at the piano, in recognition of the expertise with which he had played the song. The crowd cheered, and Sebastian rose and gave a slight bow to the audience.

Christie and Pam went to the bar and waited while Sebastian finished the evening session with a rendition of *Sweet Caroline*, which allowed the guests to approach the piano and put their dollar bills into the tip glass that sat atop the baby grand.

After collecting the tips, Sebastian walked across to the two female performers at the bar. They walked over to the Vineyard Café, one deck up from the Ice Bar. The three sat down in a cubicle that was reserved for officers and entertainers for a little privacy. Two lattes and one espresso coffee immediately appeared from the waiter; it was his duty to know what each of the officers' and entertainers' favourite drinks was.

All the male eyes between the ages of four and a hundred and four turned to the two beautiful entertainers. The two gay men admired the dresses and makeup, and the heterosexuals admired the low-cut sequined dresses which displayed smooth, fulsome busts, and the high hems that were scant and gave little coverage of the long, bare, tanned legs that seemed to go on forever.

Christie turned to Pam. "Can I introduce you to Sebastian, the Grim Reaper?" she said. Both Pam and Sebastian looked bemused.

"Sorry, are you referring to me?" Sebastian said, somewhat in shock.

"Don't take it personally, Piano Man. I have been on three ships you've played on, and on each ship, we've had passengers die or go missing. You're jinxed!" Christie explained.

"Conversely, you have been on three that I have been on, and I have just found out that on those cruises, passengers have died or gone missing," Sebastian lied. "I think maybe you're the jinx," he said.

Pam giggled at the quick retort.

"Yes, I suppose what's good for the goose is good for the gander. I hadn't thought about it like that," Christie said.

Soon after they had finished their coffees and split the gratuities, sixty percent for Sebastian and forty percent between the two singers, Sebastian retreated to his large but single cabin on deck three. He sat down on the daybed to collate his thoughts. While not having the capacity to worry, he did not like loose ends, and Christie had become a loose end. Pam had been there as well, and while it may have seemed to be banter, she had heard them, and could relay the conversation to anyone at a later date.

Sebastian knew he had been on a killing spree in the last fifteen years and if anything, he was surprised he had not been the butt of speculation before. His mistake was to stay with the cruise company Christie had worked for and to remain for two years. The contract was the longest he had stayed with any one cruise company. Jon Deloitte, the chief executive of the Jules Verne Cruise Line, had signed him to an exclusive contract, with no freelancing for any other company for the two-year period.

This was a wake-up call, a revelation to Sebastian how sloppy he had become. He thought himself extremely intelligent and forensically aware. He had taken some chances, but, overall, he thought he had covered his tracks as well as anyone could. Staying two years with the one company had put his careful planning at risk, and he had not considered this in his risk analysis.

Sebastian kicked the chair in front of him and launched into a tirade of self-recrimination and abuse. Once he calmed down and collected his thoughts, he knew some things would have to change; he would not make this mistake again. He liked this ship, but what he was planning meant that he would have to move on after the three-month tour was up. But before handing in his resignation letter, he had loose ends to clear up.

Several days later, the *Classical Canta Libra* left Odessa, the principal port in Ukraine, and would soon be anchoring a short tender trip away from Yalta on the Crimean Peninsula.

Some guests, no matter where they were in the world, would not stray too far from the restaurants and bars on the ship. Many of the guests had taken full advantage of the historic stop in Yalta.

The tender boats from the port had been transporting the tourists all morning, from the ship to shore, over two thousand souls. Some would go off to 4x4s, discovering the mountainous routes in the area. A significant number of the older guests would visit the Livadia Palace, the venue for the historic Yalta Conference between Russia, America, and Great Britain, the aim to have their photos taken in front of the palace between the white marble lions, not far from the famous picture of Roosevelt, Churchill, and Stalin.

Those with no interest in history would board the coaches transporting them to the Swallow's Nest. The fairy-tale castle perched perilously 130 feet above the Black Sea on a mountain which had cracked during an earthquake and closed the Nest for 40 years. An entrepreneur had poured his roubles into stabilizing the crack and refurbished the Nest into a restaurant. The balcony on three sides of the Nest overhung the sea and gave the impression of being on a cliff edge looking far below into the sea. From the balcony, some mile out to sea, the *Classical Canta Libra* stood proudly on the still surface of the water.

All crew members, including the entertainers and officers, would have to attend compulsory evacuation and lifeboat drills. The exercise would include boat practice, taking the boats a thousand feet offshore and circling, with members of the crew acting as guests.

Sebastian knew that the entertainers that were part of groups or teams would be placed together for the drills. It had been quite simple to get the drill emergency plan and staff allocation list, as it had been published on the sophisticated Intranet the ship used as one of the tools to communicate with staff employees and entertainers.

Lifeboat four was located with other even-numbered lifeboats on deck six, starboard side. The groups quickly gathered at their allocated lifeboat stations and stood in orderly lines on hearing the alarm sound seconds before.

The captain had decided to continue with the exercise, even though most of the CCTV for the external areas had stopped working several hours before. The control box with the main fuses for the system had suffered a minor fire, cause unknown, and this would put the system out for repairs for the next sixteen hours.

Six persons were allocated to each lifeboat, plus the pilot. The lifeboats swung down on their hoists, known as gravity davits, level to the deck. Crew members removed the guardrails, and the allocated participants started to embark onto the lifeboats. Odd-numbered lifeboats on the port side were lowered down first, with even numbers on the starboard side following shortly after.

The first boats lowered had detached the harnesses that attached them to the gravity davits and were pulling away from the ship as the even-numbered boats hit the water on the other side of the ship.

Lifeboat four, with Christie, Pam, and four other singers and dancers, pulled away swiftly after hitting the water. The smell of the diesel became apparent less than a hundred feet away from the ship. In fact, as soon as the engine had started, the smell became apparent. The pilot was not too worried, as they may have a leak, but diesel was hard to ignite and it would need more than a little spark to ignite the fuel. Murat, the Turkish seaman who was piloting lifeboat four, turned off the engine, following his training to the letter.

"Diesel leak on number four," Murat said in English over the radio to the first mate on the bridge of the *Classical Canta Libra*.

"Don't worry, people. We have a slight problem with a fuel leak. Crack open the exit to get rid of the fumes while I investigate the leak," Murat relayed to the six entertainers.

Sebastian was on lifeboat one. Typically you could not see that much out of the small portholes, as the Perspex would be scratched by the salt water and become opaque with time. These were brand-new, so he had clear sight of the other lifeboats to the starboard. He could see one had stopped dead in the water and craned his neck to keep sight of the boat as his steered to the port.

Murat approached the hatch to the engine, which was located on the floor between the seats in the fourth row. The boat rocked in the slight swell without its power. Murat looked confused, and then alarmed. As he pulled up the hatch in the deck, he saw the end of a flare that had been attached to the catch. The active part of the flare dropped into the dark, dank liquid below. The flare at first struggled to ignite, but then the bright green and yellow of the intense heat source ignited.

"Abandon—" Murat's screamed order was cut off in mid-sentence.

The flare acted as the ignition source, the diesel fuel and the oxygen from the boat and the flow from the open door combined to give the three necessary elements for a fire.

The large *whoosh* and explosion and violent swell that followed told Sebastian his plan had worked. He took no satisfaction in this, his most major kill to date. The slaying was a necessity and gave him none of the pleasure he got from a close-up kill.

Murat and the six entertainers died within five seconds of the fireball. The beauty of Christie and Pam that had been so admired the night before was now turned to blackened, charred, ghastly leather in a millisecond; they were dead, the screams frozen in their throats.

The inevitable inquiry that followed the explosion and sinking of lifeboat four was as flawed as it was useless. The Russians retrieved the lifeboat and the charred remains of the six cadavers. Most of the interior was burnt out; the heat had set off all the remaining flares, so the ignition source was not apparent.

It was several weeks before the inquiry findings were made public. The Russian marine investigators put it down to a leaking diesel pipe, probably a fault at the manufacturing stage due to the newness of the boat. The ignition source was probably the pilot or one of the entertainers having a cigarette, which was against all standing orders.

Sebastian attended the on-board wake, and played *I Believe.*

chapter eighteen

Fabienne Asper, the MIDAS technical expert, based in Geneva, had been an excellent addition to the company, Cutler congratulated himself. He was, however, bewildered at how Fabienne parked her large frame in the computer chair, ripples of muscle and fat spilling over through the apertures and gaps of the swivel chair.

"The database is now complete, Herr Cutler," she said in excellent English, with just a slight Swiss twang.

"Fabienne, you are a genius," Max replied honestly.

"Over the last six months I have input all the data from the past ten years; every cruise that has been undertaken has been recorded. I must admit, I have used several students from the local technology college to assist in inputting the necessary information while I have put in the more delicate details. You also know I had Ghislaine with me for several months, and she helped with the differing languages and interpretation," Fabienne explained.

"How on earth did you get the missing persons and death at sea information? I can't believe the cruise line operators offered these up to you freely," Cutler said.

"They are not NASA or the FBI, and their firewalls and security systems for electronic information are no match for my talents. These companies record the ship's logs, crew names, guests' names and addresses, and abnormal events such as deaths, illness, and missing persons, all of which I have accessed," Fabienne replied.

"That's great work, Fabienne. When will you start adding the filters to start looking for trends of persons going missing or having died at sea?" Cutler asked impatiently.

"We have started already with the easiest filter; those who have died naturally. And let me clarify this; those who had heart attacks and the like, where post-mortems have been carried out independently and verified as natural causes. To explain what I mean, if there has been no post-mortem, or if the causes of death have been undetermined, they have been excluded from the filter," Fabienne explained.

"That is very impressive, Fabienne. I'm a little concerned we're only going back ten years, as we may miss some trends that go further back," Cutler commented.

"Without a doubt, that will be true; however, your initial briefing stated that you wanted a working system up in six months, which I have delivered. We could go back another ten years if you give me another two quarters. Give me a couple of years and I will include all those who died on the *Titanic*," Fabienne said, with a trace of sarcasm.

"Sorry if I have offended you. The work you have done is amazing in the time given. However, if you could keep those students of yours on, we will fund this, so if possible, let's start putting the information in from the previous decade," Cutler requested.

"My little darlings don't need paying; to learn from me is payment enough. I will do as you wish, Herr Cutler, but I assume you want me to start analysing the data we have stored already?" she continued.

"Yes, that would be my wish," Cutler responded.

"Good, and what a job we have to do. In the past ten years there have been over 707 deaths and missing persons at sea," Fabienne divulged to a stunned Cutler.

"Seven hundred and seven?" Cutler asked tentatively.

"What you must remember is that many guests on these ships are elderly; indeed, some are dying of cancers, heart disease, syphilis, boredom. What I'm trying to say is the numbers are bound to be high because a percentage of the passengers are the walking dead and would die anyway, whether at home or sipping a gin and tonic on a boat in the Pacific," she lectured Cutler.

"Okay, I understand this, Fabienne; tell me how many of these deaths you can rule out as natural," Cutler replied, a little irked at Fabienne's cold analysis.

"Logically we will keep in all those lost at sea or missing, including your sister. Those number 72 souls, which leaves us with 635 souls. Then we take away all those who have died and had post-mortems, and we can deduct another 510. Thus, that leaves us with 125 deaths that may be suspicious. They may have died of natural causes but at this time, it is hard to say. But we say 72 missing persons is obviously suspicious," Fabienne articulated.

"Where to next, Fabienne?"

"Over the next few weeks, I will add the filter for causes of death for the 125 and categorize them and look for any suspicious trends. The missing person filter will take longer, as there are so many fields, variables I have to take account of in the database; age, sex, cruise liner, age, personal history, medical records, plus a whole heap more."

"Very well, Fabienne. I'm not trying to repeat myself, but this is excellent work," Cutler emphasized.

"That's not everything. I have some news about Cheryl's husband's case," Fabienne surprised Cutler.

"News? What news?" he asked eagerly.

"I have extracted a statement given by an Emilio Antonelli, given to the captain the morning after Don, her husband, went missing. I have another from the captain's log which identifies both boys who had been involved. After accessing the Bahamian police records, they said they knew nothing of the alleged attack. And I have a memo from the first mate to the police saying there were no suspicious circumstances concerning his disappearance."

"This gives us the name of the second boy," Cutler stated.

"And some more vital information. Six weeks after Don Ross vanished off the *Large Pink Boat*; it went into dry dock for a refurbishment. The work was subcontracted to a small shipyard in Portland. I have a memo from them that was stored on the cruise line files which states they found several teeth and a ring in a small drain, a drain which is precisely where the alleged assault on Don took place," Fabienne qualified.

Cutler took several seconds to think before turning back towards Fabienne.

"Teeth and a ring; without the physical evidence, it doesn't have any real significance," Cutler specified.

"Normally I would agree with you, but Northwest Marine Services, this shipyard in Portland, Oregon, has an ISO quality accreditation. In short, they have procedures which are audited by an international body," she said.

"Where is this going, Fabienne? Procedures, ISO... I don't get it," Cutler replied, a little bemused.

"Quite naturally, I looked up their online procedures and found retention of property process. They keep any items found in the vessels, such as jewellery, for five years. When did Don Ross go missing?" she asked Cutler.

"Four years ago, I think; no, four and a half years," Cutler confirmed.

"That's what I figured. I accessed their database of retained property. It goes without saying that the teeth are long gone, but the ring is still in their lost property section, and there is a description on the report. The ring is a school ring, one with a unique motif of the school. The school is Palm Springs, the same school a certain Mick Hilton and Bernard Rothhelm go to. That's the same two boys identified in the first mate's report as those most likely to have been involved in a fracas on deck," Fabienne said with a hint of smugness.

"Wow!" exclaimed Cutler.

"Indeed," affirmed Fabienne.

"We need that ring. It may still have DNA on it, and if we can get the ring as proof, I have friends in the FBI in Palm Springs," he said, more to himself than to Fabienne.

Cutler moved from the hub, as Fabienne called the office that was packed from floor to ceiling with electronic equipment, to the office next door. In stark comparison, this room had just a desk, a telephone, and views of Geneva Lake, with the world-renowned fountain in full view.

Several minutes later, Cutler connected with Robert Stahmer.

"Afternoon, Robert, it's Max Cutler. And to cut to the chase, I need you to get on a plane from the UK and head over to Portland."

A short while after that, Cutler explained to the ex-Health and Safety Inspector that they had come across evidence of immense importance, but which had not been accessed in a legal manner. Cutler explained that although the initial computer search would not stand up in a court of law, Northwest Marine Services had a lost and found section on their website, and the ring would be listed. It was obvious to them both that the teeth would be disposed of by now, but the ring had not been claimed. There may be blood evidence on the ring.

"Once you download a picture of the ring, go to Judge Norman Freeman in Oregon. Tell him you work for me, and that we have evidence of a fatal assault; the ring could be evidence. Use the statements from the Yacoubs, who witnessed the attack. We've had Basmati working under the tuition of an independent crime laboratory in Miami for the last six months. He should be up to speed now, so I'll send him with you to secure the ring and ensure that the chain of evidence will stand up in a court of law," Cutler declared.

Immediately after the call to the MIDAS investigator he called Matt Rice, aka Basmati, and gave him his instructions. The next call was to his other investigator, Tucker Walters, the stocky ex-SAS New Zealander.

"Tuck, its Cutler."

Several moments later, after pleasantries had been passed, Cutler continued.

"Be careful what you say, as I know Cheryl is likely to be in the office with you. It concerns the disappearance of her husband.

Note down these names: Mick Hilton and Bernard Rothhelm. We know about Rothhelm already, but Hilton is new to us. Dig up what you can and try to get in their faces a little. No rough stuff but let them know they are in our sights. You know the drill."

Tuck looked at Cheryl's face as she sat opposite him. The large window in their office in Everglade City was sited along the banks of the Barron River, and Tuck could see a large pelican with a fish in its bill. The bird was sitting proudly on the wooden veranda.

"On it, boss," was all Tuck replied.

Cutler returned to the hub, where Fabienne delicately removed a slice of Aargau carrot cake and quaffed it down in one movement, followed by another.

"On the private matter, Fabienne, have you managed to look at Von-Baer and Werner's history, to identify who his political partner is?" Cutler inquired

"As you know, Herr Cutler, my German is good, but this guy has contacts all over Europe, and the translation takes time. If you let me have Ghislaine back I can get you an answer quicker," Fabienne responded.

"No, as much as possible I want MIDAS operatives kept out of this. I only asked you because you could save me hours of research," Cutler stated honestly.

"Well, I have several names, all delegates in the Bundestag: Guttmann, Heimlich, and Uebering. All seem to have had extensive business links with Werner," Fabienne reported.

"Thanks, Fabienne, keep digging if you would, please. Use a freelance interpreter if required; I'll fund this. Make sure the person is not from mainland Europe. Werner's tentacles stretch far and wide."

Cutler exited the hub once again to return to the desk to the phone. It took nearly twenty minutes to track down the handsome Spanish investigator, Philip Cortez, who was looking into the German connection.

"Hola, Philip, como estas?" Cutler used his more than adequate Spanish.

"Muy bien, gracias, my American friend. If you are phoning me, you must have something for me. It has been a while," Philip Cortez stated.

"Busy setting up MIDAS, Philip. You know how in-depth any new operation can be. However, you are always in my thoughts. I know you are self-reliant and wouldn't want me phoning you every week to catch up with you. The e-mails you send over are descriptive and informative. You're making real progress, the news about the link with the solicitor and political ally was excellent." Cutler continued.

"I think it may be fortuitous that you have phoned, as some information has come forward this morning which is disturbing," Cortez said.

"What information?" Cutler asked intuitively.

"There has been a contract out for Dietmar Richter, as you well know, for the past year, posted by Werner. This morning, one of my little spies tells me the word on the street is that Richter is in the UK. By tonight, half a dozen hitmen who want to earn a small fortune will be on their way, hoping for a lucrative payday."

Cutler was startled at the information. "Thank you for the information. I'll look into this."

"And what do you have for me?" Cortez asked.

"Guttmann, Heimlich, and Uebering, all delegates in the Bundestag. Mean anything to you?" Cutler probed.

"Yes, I know all three, all corrupt in their own way. But Uebering stands out. Her name has come up several times in my investigation and cross-referenced to Werner. She is certainly a person of interest and will move to the top of my list now that you have asked about her by name," Cortez indicated.

"Look into her first, and if you don't get anywhere, investigate the other two. Thank you for the information, Philip, and I will speak to you soon. Ciao," Cutler signed off.

Cutler redialled.

"Twice in one day, boss; what gives?" Tuck asked.

"Is Hoagie there with you?" Cutler inquired.

"No, he met a gay hairdresser in Hooters, of all places; they've gone for a love-in for the weekend to Saratoga Beach. I can use the emergency phone we've been issued."

"Use it, please, Tuck. Tell Hoagie to get his ass on a plane to Glasgow. Tell him I will be there in the Thistle Hotel in Sauchiehall Street. One more thing; text me his ETA," Cutler ordered.

"On it, boss," Tuck said, knowing the rage that would consume Hoagie, as this had been his first lover in six weeks; such was the workload Tuck had set him.

Cutler pressed 'end' and redialled.

"I don't know what the fuck you've been up to, but you've been made!" Cutler spat out.

On the other end of the phone, the ex-German gang accountant Dietmar Richter began to shake.

"They know where I am," Richter said tellingly.

"They know you're in the UK, and as we speak, half a dozen sociopaths are on the way there to dismember your useless body!" Cutler was getting angrier by the moment.

"I have to go out, shopping, a quiet drink. How could they know I'm here?" Dietmar said quietly.

"Don't you lie to me, you piece of shit! I need to know where you've been, so I don't send you somewhere you've been spotted. Now tell me the truth, or I'm cutting you loose."

"Last… last month I went to Edinburgh and visited a pub called the Three Headed Man. I met a girl… I didn't know she was a call girl," Dietmar stuttered.

"You thought she was after your body; you deluded idiot? What did you tell her?" Cutler demanded.

"In the passion, I may have told her I was a German gangster in hiding."

"Couldn't impress her with your tiny cock, so you played it big. You are a moron, and I should leave you to the consequences!" Cutler stormed.

"Please, Herr Cutler, I'm sorry. A man has needs. Please, Herr Cutler, you must come and get me. Werner's men will tear me apart, and under pressure, I may have to tell them what we did with the money," Dietmar declared, gaining a little of his composure back.

"You can't blackmail me, Dietmar. There is no trace of the money, and they will think you are lying to save your skin. The next time you try that ploy with me it will be me you are running from. Now I want you to go to the Thistle Hotel in Glasgow, between Hill Street and Sauchiehall. Register under the name Smith and order room service. Make sure you do not leave your room until I get there; do you understand?"

"I understand, Herr Cutler. Thistle Hotel in Glasgow, between Hill Street and Sauchiehall. Mr Smith, and stay in my room," Dietmar repeated.

"Go, now!" Cutler said as he slammed the receiver down.

Cutler walked the short distance to the hub and calmed himself down. On entering the hub, he saw Fabienne looking lovingly at a slice of tarte tatin, the slice bulging with apples entombed in caramel, and then it was gone.

"Fabienne, concentrate on Uebering. Look at bank accounts and assets and see what you can come up with."

Fabienne just nodded, as she was still masticating the tarte tatin.

horny. You have been reticent, my sexy lover. Your mouth has been at rest. On your knees and finish me off," she said, as she lifted the hem of her houndstooth dress.

***

Kurt Bauer, ex-Stasi agent and now freelance killer, had spent three years as a sniper for the Stasi. Many times, he crossed over to West Germany, where he would stalk dissidents and kill them, sometimes from as far as a thousand metres, such was his expertise. He had a variety of weapons but preferred the US ArmaLite 50 circa 1997. His second weapon of choice was not a sniper's rifle but a get-out-of-shit weapon, the Barrett XM109 semi-automatic 25mm grenade launcher.

He had trained up several snipers over the years, both before and after the Berlin Wall came tumbling down. His longest-serving compatriot was Roderick Friedman, whom he had met and trained during his Stasi days. Friedman was tall and gangly, with sparse tufts of hair. But the most distinguishing feature was the glass eye in the left socket, with a thick, rugged scar running down the length of his face. The loss of the eye and acquisition of the scar came after a run-in with an African American Marine, who did not take it lightly when Friedman had spat the N-word at him. Friedman was a bigot and a racist and took extra pleasure when his victim was non-white. Friedman's choice of weapon had changed in 2005 from the German DSR-1 to the Canadian C14 Timberwolf rifle from the Prairie Gun Works.

Lothar Gottschalk was another oddity in appearance. He had been born with the hereditary disease albinism. The traits of the condition were the lack of pigment that normally gives colour to the skin, eyes, and hair. He had ultra-white skin and white hair, and his eyes were white. Normally an albino has eye problems, and Gottschalk was no different, which made him an unlikely sniper. He had 20/20 vision, which was rare in albinos, but suffered from photophobia: light sensitivity. In normal day conditions, he could not hit a bus with a shotgun. This meant you never saw Gottschalk without his dark Ray-Ban sunglasses. With the glasses, he could take out a mouse at five hundred yards. Gottschalk's weapon of choice was the German Blaser R93 tactical straight pull bolt-action rifle.

The latest and youngest recruit was Falco Jager. The ex-gang enforcer and nightclub bouncer was twenty-six years old. He was also the silver medal winner of the World Rifle Championship of 2008. Kurt Bauer always attended the championships looking for potential recruits. Jager was a solid hulk of muscle, which again was unusual for a sniper. He had short-cropped brown hair speckled with blonde patches. The pupils of his eyes were enormous; he had deep, black eyes that gave little room for the off-white irises. He had a hooked nose which gave him the nickname 'ule', or in English, Owl. Jager was even a better shot than Kurt Bauer, which was some achievement. His choice of weapon was more modern, and he preferred the Swiss bolt-action SSG 2000.

Kurt Bauer had initially laughed at both Roderick Friedman and Lothar Gottschalk as snipers; their names were antonyms. Friedman's name translated means 'peacemaker', and he certainly was not. Gottschalk means 'God's servant', and he was anything but. The only name which reflected their personality was Jager, meaning 'hunter'. Bauer's own name reflected his heritage: 'peasant'.

Werner had been moved from the hospital in Bad Reichenhall to Landsberg Prison. The medical facilities of the prison had been identified as ones that could support Werner to adjust from the horrific injuries he had suffered. The prison was in the handsome little town of Landsberg am Lech and had previously been designated Prison Number One to hold convicted Nazi war criminals by the United States. It was located sixty-five kilometres west of Munich.

Delegate Frau Uebering had taken a particular interest in Werner's case. She had used influence and money to ensure he had the best of medical help and facilities. She could not help with the food, as everything he ate was blended, and as he said in his robotic voice through his electric larynx, "Tasted of shit." Werner had the small electric shaver-like device, which assisted him to talk by placing it on his neck, with him always.

Delegate Frau Uebering knew Werner was being moved to the courts in Munich for the first day of his trial, as she had paid for access to the records. She also knew the prison wagon would be accompanied by two police cars.

Kurt Bauer had been informed by the delegate that the convoy would travel east along the Romantic Road until it connected with the E54 and would skirt past Lake Ammersee and the town of Inning on Ammersee. A few kilometres further on, the main road cut through a tunnel under the fields and the two-lane motorway. The convoy entered back into daylight as it exited the tunnel, and they emerged with grass banks on either side, a concrete barrier a few metres high down the centre median.

They had stolen a motorway traffic truck with illuminated signs on the back. Bauer had enlisted Klaus, an old hand, and Heidi, his wife. The husband-and-wife team had done dirty and wet work for Bauer in the past.

Klaus turned up twenty minutes early, and waited on the roadway about a hundred metres before the prison convoy was due.

Bauer, Gottschalk, and Jager had arrived the previous night. They wore full camouflage gear, and it was an overcast evening, with no moon or stars for illumination. Using their infrared night goggles, they created their hides in less than two hours. Any sweep of the road prior to the prison convoys would have driven straight past them; they had simply blended into the flora and fauna.

Friedman, the fourth sniper, arrived at the same time as Klaus. After stashing the C-class Mercedes Benz he had travelled down in from Berlin, he took the C4 explosive from his black knapsack and crossed the carriageway to the opposite side when no cars were visible.

Friedman positioned the explosive on the base of a large coniferous tree and held it in place with tape. Once he had activated the remote-controlled censor, he returned across the dual carriage motorway, again unseen. He went on digging his hide some 300 metres away from the other snipers and opposite the tree.

Friedman, Bauer, Jager, and Gottschalk, the four-man hit team, had undertaken previous operations together in the past. They had left sufficient space, although very limited, so they could move to their side very slightly should they need to urinate. They had clingfilm with them to catch any number twos. They would leave no evidence of their DNA, and the filled cling sewage packs would be taken far away from the scene before being disposed of.

In the earphones, Klaus and the four snipers heard the one click. This was the premeditated sign from Heidi that the convoy had been spotted and was less than five kilometres away.

Klaus placed no entry signs in the lanes and the innermost lane had a sign slanting down to the left to display that only one lane was in use. A flashing 30-kilometre sign flashed, and five cars that passed the sign slowed down immediately. Klaus then took out his Zeus binoculars and had clear sight of the three-vehicle convoy that had no other traffic before them.

Several minutes later, the convoy slowed down on seeing the sign. They moved to the outside lane and decreased their speed in tandem. Klaus clicked his transmitter twice to forewarn the team that the convoy had entered the tunnel. Klaus then changed the sign to 'No Entry Due to Roadworks' and manoeuvred the vehicle between both lanes. After a few minutes, Heidi joined him, and they started to make their way on foot through the tunnel, as had been the agreement.

Two clicks in the earpiece were also the instruction to blow the tree, and Friedman clicked his remote. The noise was lost on those in the tunnel, but the initial explosion and cracking of the tree was audible for a couple of kilometres. The tree crashed onto the two lanes on the offside traffic. It landed on a Volkswagen Passat, with immediate fatal injuries delivered to the driver and passenger.

Three other cars screamed to a halt behind the Volkswagen, each with their fenders bumped or split by the slight collisions.

The first phase of the plan had been completed; the outside traffic had been stopped, and their view of the other carriageway was blocked. They were also too busy trying to exit their vehicles. Friedman saw a young woman of no more than twenty-two putting her mobile phone to her ear, apparently to call emergency services. The C14 Timberwolf rifle spat the bullet out silently that a millisecond later exited the back of the young woman's head. She was dead before she hit the ground. The drivers and passengers who witnessed this dove for cover, and as far as Friedman could tell, no one else had a mobile phone or dared to put one to their ear.

The first police car exited the tunnel, followed closely by the prison transport van, and thirty metres away the second police vehicle.

Bauer targeted the lead vehicle. He raised the Barrett XM109 semi-automatic 25mm grenade launcher. The grenade hit the side of the first police car, blowing it sideways across both lanes of the carriageway. One of the policemen was dead on impact; the other had lost both his lower limbs and did not pose a threat.

The prison transport van screeched to a halt and simultaneously Jager and Gottschalk fired. The firing sequence was the tried and tested double tap; two rapid presses on the trigger and their victim received one kill shot and one for insurance.

Jager took out the driver of the prison transport van, and just as the thought process of the second guard sprang to life, his brain became scrambled egg as the double tap hit him between the eyes.

Gottschalk went through the same process with the police driver. But when he attempted to double tap his colleague, the German Blaser R93 tactical sniper rifle had a blockage; the ammunition was faulty. The second officer reached for the fixed car radio, and just as he was about to report the incident, the back windscreen was splattered with blood and brain tissue. Friedman had been covering 300 metres further down the road and realized the second officer was still alive and his training took over. Two shots in succession and the second policeman was no more. That quick.

The whole operation, from the first patrol car exiting to Werner being removed from the prison transport van, had lasted less than twenty seconds. All three snipers were known to Werner, and had run to release Werner, while Friedman covered their operation from his hide.

Heidi and Klaus emerged from the tunnel and ran towards the group excitedly. Just as planned, Friedman dropped both as they reached Bauer. Jager and Bauer lifted them unceremoniously into the back of the prison van as they headed off toward the car. Just before they went over a small knoll to their vehicle and joined Friedman, Bauer turned and fired a grenade into the van. The explosion was loud, and the inferno intense.

"Shame; I liked them," Bauer said.

Werner placed the small shaver-like voice resonator to his throat and spoke in his robotic voice.

"Bauer drop off these three at the nearest station. They should have their passports with them as I ordered."

"Yes, Herr Werner, they have come prepared."

"I want you three to take the next flight to London; you will find the address in London where I have arranged for you to pick up some weapons. Leave your guns in the car, and Bauer and I will ensure safe storage," Werner strained to say in his metallic voice.

Werner then led Bauer to one side. "You are to drive with me down to Turkey. For this, you will need to purchase a campervan. Once there, I have arranged for a close security team to take over my protection, as I have other things for you to do, Bauer."

chapter twenty

Judge Norman Freeman had known Cutler for seven years; the judge was a prosecutor for one of the counterfeit cases Cutler had previously worked on. The counterfeit gang from Portland had abducted the prosecutor's niece as leverage. Cutler had mapped out all the group members and their hideouts. He had assisted the police in identifying who would be responsible, and where they may well be. The remnants of the band, those that had not been prosecuted, were the lower tier gang members. Their brightest and best were on trial.

Two days later they had identified the property, and Cutler had gone with the local police to rescue the girl. When they had forced entrance there were two gang members there; one was watching baseball on television, and the other was trying to assault the courageous young girl. The couch potato was arrested with no injuries and gave up readily, surrounded by the armed police officers. The second assailant, of Hispanic descent, kept the girl as a human shield over an hour. She was battered and bruised, but had barely, just barely, avoided being raped. He did not get off so lightly after he gave up, the police officers left Cutler with him in the room for five minutes. Cutler broke his jaw and his arm and stamped so hard on his testicles that his sperm count was dramatically reduced for life.

A year later, prosecutor Norman Freeman was invited to be a judge. He never forgot Cutler's help, and for a man with few friends, classed Cutler up there with the best.

Robert Stahmer had employed a local attorney to draw up the subpoena warrant for the ring based on the open evidence on the shipyard's database and backed up with the Yacoubs' statements. The attorney was amazed when the warrant was granted by Judge Norman Freeman, as the evidence was tenuous at best.

Stahmer had gone with Basmati to the shipyard owners and had the ring in their possession within two hours. Basmati videotaped himself placing the ring in a clear plastic bag. He then sealed the bag with white tape and asked the receptionist from the shipyard to sign the tape. He had now secured the chain of evidence, and his job was to get it back to Miami and to the laboratory for analysis.

Stahmer decided to stay around a little while longer to meet some of the workers in the local bars. He hoped he could glean a little more information.

Tuck Walters had taken up a small hotel suite in the Embassy Suites in Palm Springs. He had years of living out of a sleeping bag in jungles, drains, and any other sewer you could imagine. Those days in the SAS were over, and he decided if he were away anywhere, he would be sleeping in a nice room with clean sheets and a coffee maker.

Bernard Rothhelm was a known quantity; he was seventeen and a bully. Cheryl had traced Rothhelm down after viewing the photographs Basmati had taken. She had hit a brick wall. The US authorities did not want to know, and the Bahamian police had no cause to investigate.

Cheryl's own private investigator had been threatened when he started to examine young Rothhelm. The investigator had first been threatened legally for prying into the adolescent Rothhelm. In time, he had a visit from a couple of heavyweights who left the private detective in no doubt what would happen to him if he did not back off. He did, and Cheryl was left only with the reports and the bill from the investigator.

The elder Rothhelm was rich; he had built a fortune in selling unwanted asbestos to third world countries. As soon as it was banned in 1985, he knew he could buy it for pennies on the dollar and sell it on for an enormous profit. He had also collaborated with a French company that reformulated the asbestos and sold it back to Europe, mainly the United Kingdom, as Artex or decorative coating. He had no conscience about the death he was selling; there was a profit to be made.

Mick Hilton was seventeen and was an altogether different animal, Tuck had discovered. Hilton came from moderate means; his father worked six weeks on and six weeks off on an oil rig in the Gulf of Mexico. The mother worked two jobs; secretary in the daytime, and small business bookkeeper at night, so they could give Mick the education and chances they never had.

Bernard Rothhelm came from a wealthy family, but there was a stench of the new money and where his father had got the money from. He was not welcomed into the clique of the cool kids in his school, all with super-rich parents. He had created his own group, mostly those who were on the edges of the clique but just could not break through. Mick Hilton would never get in, as they classified him as a working-class kid. To Bernard, he was someone he could push around and use. Both were disenfranchised and had underlying personality problems; Rothhelm was the leader, and Hilton was the disciple.

Tuck Walters undertook all the background investigation. He knew more about these two kids within a week than their own parents knew.

Once Robert Stahmer and Basmati had the ring, Tuck knew he had to get DNA samples from the two boys. From his initial investigation it was apparent that they had insufficient evidence to go the legal route; he needed to get samples any way he could.

Tuck spent several days following the boys around. It was obvious to him there had been schism between the two. When they left their school, it was never together. When they went out it was with different friends. In fact, over the following weeks, the two lads totally ignored each other, even when they left school at the same time.

There was another problem, and Tuck spotted it almost immediately. The Rothhelm boy was being tracked by a pair of minders; he was sure the boy did not know. The minders were professionals, but not in Tuck's class, as they did not make him. When Bernard Rothhelm visited the local McDonald's, the pair would be in straight after he left and would remove his spent cup. The only reason they would be removing this would be because of a DNA trace.

Back in the Embassy Suites, Tuck had set up the whiteboard he carried around in his car; it was his brainstorming tool. He listed all he had learned in the week. Flowcharting the information he rearranged some of the data.

Several espressos later, he was satisfied with his conclusions. He checked his watch, calculated the time difference in the UK— five hours later—and worked out that it was 10 pm in the UK. He picked up the landline and dialed. After a wait of several seconds, he connected with the hotel receptionist, who then diverted his call to Cutler's room.

"Hi, Cutler, how goes it with you?" Tuck inquired.

"As you know, we got Richter out of Scotland and have moved to Newcastle, where I have a contact to get him an American passport. Will be another few days before that's ready," Cutler replied.

"Is Hoagie still with you?" Tuck asked.

"Yes, he's downstairs in the bar keeping a lookout. We only just got out of Scotland before Richter's old place was torn apart. Both Hoagie and I think there may be up to four contractors on our tails. We also believe that with Werner's extensive network, most of the airports will be watched, but we can cross that bridge when we come to it. Anyway, how is your investigation going?" Cutler questioned.

"I think Mr Rothhelm has been flustered by the initial investigation a couple of years ago by Cheryl's investigator. It's also possible he knows what his boy has done. He has two minders clearing up any DNA evidence after him, and you don't do that if you have nothing to hide," Tuck reported.

"Yes, I would concur with that, Tuck. What about the other kid, Hilton?" Cutler probed.

"That is a whole different situation. No minders, and unaware he's under any sort of investigation. He and his mother ate at

Wendy's in the city last night; I was in the next booth and retrieved a cup he had been drinking Coke from. Have sent it down to Basmati's lab by courier," Tuck announced.

"Good work, Tuck. You know, we'll have to get a sample by hook or by crook from the Rothhelm kid," Cutler retorted.

"Working on it, boss," Tuck said, as he disconnected the call.

The following afternoon, Bernard Rothhelm exited the school with two other young men. Tuck followed them from a distance and watched them enter Costa Coffee. The two minders waited across the street, with a clear view.

Tuck entered Costa Coffee and pushed in front of the three guys in line, receiving a torrent of abuse from all three. In an instant, he slapped Rothhelm lightly, ensuring he pulled out several of his hair strands as he withdrew his hand. Then he quietly walked out as the three astonished boys looked on in shock.

From across the street, the two minders had seen the altercation. Tuck knew that they would not both leave the Rothhelm boy to follow him, but he anticipated one of them would.

To the right there was an underpass, and Tuck turned and entered it.

"Hey, you! Stop there or I'll break your fucking neck!" shouted the minder.

The minder towered over the five-foot-eight Tuck by nearly a foot. He also had a good four inches more around his chest than Tuck. Slowly and deliberately, Tuck turned towards the advancing minder, who had murder in his eyes.

"What do you think you're playing at, Geronimo?" the minder spat out.

"If you weren't so stupid, you'd know the difference between a Maori and an Indian," Tuck said as a matter of fact, as the minder closed to within reach.

With all the subtlety of an elephant, the minder charged at Tuck. He recognized the mode of attack; the guy was an ex-football player without any military training, pure brawn, and no brains.

Tuck sidestepped the charging bull and flicked his right leg out straight, connecting with the minder's right knee. The pop was audible as the knee dislocated from the socket and the minder went down screaming. The minder scrabbled in his pocket for what Tuck thought was a weapon. Tuck circled the injured minder and warned him in no uncertain terms of the consequences if he tried to continue the attack. He bent down to the wounded man and caught the hand as he extracted a pistol; with his right hand he punched his flat hand into the outstretching arm, snapping it immediately. The pistol fell from the man's grip and Tuck kicked it over to the other side of the underpass.

"Now, no more problems, I think. You tell old man Rothhelm his son killed one of our friends, and we're going to get him, no matter what. Tell him we also know about the other kid, Hilton. Things are not going to go well for either of them," he said, before turning on his heels and heading back out of the underpass.

Going on what Tuck knew from his research, Rothhelm Senior would not let anyone get in his way. He would not tolerate a slur on his name, and he would not accept the thought of his son going to prison. Tuck had just hung a big come and get me sign around Hilton's head, and he was certain Rothhelm Senior was not above killing the kid.

chapter nineteen

Operation Muscat was to be accomplished with some slight changes. Delegate Frau Uebering was sitting on top of the naked Von-Baer. She was still dressed in her houndstooth dress and leather boots; the only item missing was her cotton underwear that Von-Baer thought, but dared never to say, looked like granny knickers.

She gripped the top of the red velvet headboard and rode him slowly and deliberately. Apart from the intermittent shudder of her body, she articulated the plan to her young lover. She ignored the limpness she felt inside her and forced herself down harder, grinding on Von-Baer's manhood. He knew he could not pull out or he would face the ire of the delegate. Von-Baer heard only intermittent parts of her plan as he concentrated on fantasizing that it was Ursula, the blonde, slim, and beautiful Polish teller from his local bank that was swelling his aching and friction-burnt member back to life.

When she had finally sated her lust, the delegate stood up and removed a wet wipe and cleaned her private area. She threw the used wipe at Von-Baer and told him to clean himself and meet her in the kitchen.

She ignored the pain-grimaced face and hobbled walk that Von-Baer had to undertake.

"Operation Muscat will take place this afternoon. The team is in place, and Werner will be moved from the hospital wing. This is the best part of being who I am. It is exciting, and it makes me

He would get what he needed by whatever means possible, and he would go back to Cheryl with information. They had been working closely together for the last four months, and Tuck was not sure when he had fallen for her, only that he had. He would have done his job regardless, but this may just help him with his plan for Cheryl.

Tuck had shaken the tree, he'd set the Hilton kid up, *Now let's see what falls from the branches,* he thought.

chapter twenty-one

Sebastian was oscillating on the tightrope of sanity. The overwhelming desire to fulfil his needs, and the pressing need to ensure he was not linked with any of the murders, was all-consuming. With hindsight, he realized that sabotaging lifeboat four and the subsequent killing of the seven people on board was a mistake. He had reacted to the Grim Reaper tag without foresight and control.

The seven killings had given him as much pleasure as eating a hot dog, food he never consumed. Sebastian needed another victim and he needed one fast, just to maintain his fragile sanity. He was still on the *Classical Canta Libra* and had another month of the tour to do; to take a victim from this ship would be foolish, as it had only been three weeks since the lifeboat disaster.

Jules Verne Cruise Line, the owners of the *Classical Canta Libra*, had launched its own investigation into the tragedy on the ship's return to its home port of Genoa. The accident investigator was used to dealing with outbreaks of norovirus or food poisoning, or the odd physical fracas between staff. But he had no previous experience of anything of this scale.

On board the ship, the atmosphere was tense; everybody from the staff and crew knew someone on lifeboat four. Gossip as to why the lifeboat caught fire abounded. The pilot of the lifeboat smoked, so the staff surmised the cause through accusation, while the crew would defend the pilot as being a professional who would not dream of lighting up while on duty.

Only Sebastian knew the whole truth: that he had killed seven people because of a tenuous link, a throwaway comment from a fellow artist. Calling him the Grim Reaper had sealed their fates. There were seven people dead, and not one ounce of pleasure to be absorbed by Sebastian. He had an itch that he could not scratch, the irritation burning away at him day in and day out.

Providence took a hand; Sebastian was called up to the captain's cabin. The cabin was not akin to the other crew cabins on the ship. It was more a suite enjoyed by the richest of guests.

"Sit please, Sebastian," the captain said, while pointing out the leather chair which was somewhat lower and less luxurious than the one the captain sat upon, opposite him across the large mahogany desk.

"The past few weeks have not been easy for any of us. We have all suffered the loss of our shipmates. Unfortunately, Sebastian, I must compound the sense of loss with worse news. I am afraid I have had a word from our agents, they were notified of your mother's passing yesterday. I believe she was only fifty-three so it will be a shock for you," the solemn captain said.

Sebastian just sat there, not feeling any loss or sorrow, but aware that he should be doing something, showing some emotion in front of the captain. The problem was, Sebastian had never encountered these feeling in his life; he had no history of emotion to call on, and he continued to sit there.

"Shock. This must be quite a shock for you. You have my condolences. We have arranged a flight back to Seattle today for you. A tender will pull alongside the ship within the hour to take you to shore," the captain informed Sebastian, as he stood and led him to the door of his cabin.

"Not a lot of time, you need to pack your gear," directed the captain.

The flight from Genoa to Seattle was via Heathrow. In total, the trip had taken him twenty-seven hours, and Sebastian had slept for eight continuous hours on the cross-Atlantic stretch.

After visiting the family home in midtown and depositing his luggage, he took the keys to his mother's small Toyota and headed for Scripps Mercy Hospital, where his mother had died.

Doctor Nicholas Remy, a large, robust character, confirmed Kim had died of cirrhosis of the liver, brought on by an infection of hepatitis B many years before when she was a child prostitute. Sebastian declined to see Kim's cadaver; however, he identified her from a video feed from the mortuary displaying only the cold, hard face of death.

Once the formalities were out of the way, Sebastian steered the Toyota down Cabrillo Freeway and cut through onto University Avenue until he reached Morley Field dog park, which was slightly down from Balboa Parkand opposite the San Diego Zoo. He parked up on the lane behind the Balboa Tennis Club.

Sebastian walked the lane between the wooded areas that skirted the San Diego Velodrome, shielded by the incline of the ridge of a hill.

Considering the thousands of people visiting Balboa Park less than 500 yards away, and the zoo a little further across the street, the area was quiet and isolated. The day was clear, with blue skies overhead and a warm wind blowing off the Pacific.

Sebastian wore short-sleeved white shirt and lightweight, taupe-coloured trousers. Putting his hand into his pocket, he felt the switchblade. A little further ahead was an older woman walking a greyhound; she was not Sebastian's type, he moved into the bushes to avoid face to face contact. A little further on, the only other dog walker in sight was a girl of no more than thirteen years of age.

Gwen had tightly curled, mouse-colored hair, which looked natural. She walked the dog each day as part of her routine to reduce her weight. Over the past year, she had lost over thirty pounds, and she was determined to lose even more. Gwen was not the ideal candidate for Sebastian, but she would suffice. The designer French bulldog was of no concern; at best it could take a nip out of his ankles.

Sebastian followed her for a short while and saw a deserted copse which would suffice. He quickened his step until he was a few yards behind the unsuspecting girl. It was the dog that noticed Sebastian first, and the dog could sense the danger in the man.

Gwen turned to Sebastian, startled, and the French Bulldog growled and barked.

"I'm sorry, mister. Mitsui isn't normally like this," Gwen said, as she bent down to stroke the forehead of the agitated dog.

Sebastian felt the knife and took a quick look around to see if he was clear.

"She's protecting you, little girl," Sebastian said, as he removed the knife, hidden in the palm of his left hand.

Sebastian turned on his heels and walked back towards his car. "Mission accomplished," he thought.

Sebastian was satisfied. He had set up for the kill and he had been able to walk away; he had left her alive. He needed to gain control before the monster managed him. He would kill on his terms, in his time and for pleasure, not malice.

The killing of the seven crew members on the *Classical Canta Libra* had left him feeling uncontrolled, taking unnecessary risks, risks which would get him caught if he continued.

Sebastian visited the McDonald's where his father had been killed, his mind wandered back two decades to his first kill, Geraldine Mills. He still got a buzz, as his mind dissected the deaths.

Once he had played through his fantasy and his coffee and fries had been consumed, he again reinforced himself about not taking risks, and how he had been uncontrolled and hot-headed.

Sebastian had no idea how insightful he had been as he disposed of the coffee cup. An ocean and continent away the captain of the *Classical Canta Libra* sat in the company's headquarters in Genoa with several board members.

Following a month of leave, Sebastian was flown to Santiago, Chile. He had no sooner landed in the bustling city than he was whisked away from the airport to Valparaiso Harbour to board the *Classical Expedition.*

This leviathan of a cruise ship had seventeen decks. Decks fourteen and fifteen were comprised of indoor pools and hot tubs mirrored on the outside decks. A huge screen towered over the blue mosaic-tiled swimming pool, showing concerts and movies under the night sky.

Once the moor lines had been cleared, the ship headed south to its first port of call, Puerto Montt, Chile, which was reached through the Canal de Chacao. Then the ship navigated the Chilean fjords.

Following the spectacular views of the fjords, the ship entered the Canal Trinidad to see the Amalia Glacier, originating in the southern Patagonian ice fields and reaching into the sea; aqua-blue ice shimmering in the summer sunshine. Following a further day at sea, the ship moored out in the bay, and the guests tendered in small craft to Punta Arenas in Chile. Most guests went off to see the Magellanic penguins particular to this area.

Next stop was through the historic Beagle Channel, named after the ship, that carried Charles Darwin on his voyage of discovery in 1831–1836. Once in the channel, the *Classical Expedition* steered towards Ushuaia in Argentina, an ex-convict settlement with around eighty thousand inhabitants. The bustling city is set against a backdrop of snow-capped, densely forested peaks that looked out onto glacier-clad mountains on islands that were the last in the South American continent.

Sebastian had some time off and joined the cruise tour to Tierra del Fuego National Park. During the trek across the peat-sodden landscape interspersed with large beaver dams blocking the rivers and acidifying the surrounding area, he first met Mona Cross. Ascending a slippery incline up the mountain trek she had slipped, losing her footing, landing heavily on the soggy earth.

Mona was caked from ankle to knee in the sodden remnants of a million-year-old peat bog. As with all groups, some found the sight amusing, others had empathy, and some offered wipes to clean herself. The Argentinian guides had seen it all before.

Sebastian told the guides to carry on up the path and pick him up an hour later their return, and he would see that Mona was okay. Being more than happy to oblige, the guides and group took off again up the mountain.

It was clear that Sebastian needed no introduction, as he had seen the plump, plain girl of no more the five feet and aged around twenty-five at his nightly performances in the Piazza piano bar amidships on deck five. She blushed and was apparently pleased to have Sebastian assisting in cleaning her up.

Mona was not used to the attention of men, especially those with the talent that Sebastian had. She would watch him entertain every single night of the cruise; she would sit alone at the back of the bar. She had come on the cruise alone; everyday girls did not attract girlfriends, neither male suitors. While she lacked good looks and height, she had a sweet, innocent personality, and in starkness to her experiences, she was a trusting person.

Mona from Calgary, was a computer games writer for Eldridge Software Company. She had just completed a new game called Attack of the Android, which was massively successful. Her boss, Norah James, was a robust and reliable businessperson, and while not overly generous, she knew she needed Mona more than Mona needed Eldridge.

After the initial launch of the game and the first profit and loss projections had been evaluated, Norah had given Mona a 100,000 US dollar bonus, and had bought her this South American cruise. Mona would come to work in sweaters with penguins on them;

she had a fluffy penguin hanging from the mirror of her old Mini Cooper car. It was not hard to figure, nor did it take any particular research to know that Mona would love to see the penguins in their own environment. Following Mona signing a new, extended contract of work, Norah had delighted her with the cruise tickets.

Sebastian was strangely aroused, an experience he had seldom felt unless killing someone. Washing the mud off her right shoulder, his hand had inadvertently brushed her breast. Mona did not flinch; she quite enjoyed it. He had not thought of killing this girl. It never came to mind. He was talking to someone properly. This had not happened since his childhood, as far as he could remember.

After he had helped clean her up, she cupped her hand around his chin and gave him slightly more than a peck on the lips, certainly not a full-blown tongue-down-the-throat kiss, and thanked him for his help.

As the guides and group of walkers came into view, she asked him if they could meet up again sometime. Sebastian explained he would try; he was not allowed to date guests of the cruise ship, but he would try.

Mona attended the piano recitals in the afternoon in the Fellowes Lounge and Sebastian's musical performances in the Piazza piano bar at night; Mona often putting requests on napkins with her favourite songs to play, which Sebastian did almost every time.

As the ship rounded Cape Horn, the most southerly tip of South America, and the nearest landmass to the Antarctic, Sebastian received a request for him to join the on-board band to do a Beatles tribute. This was to be held that night in the nightclub on the seventeenth deck.

The club was named Stars, and was a circular dome that sat uppermost on the ship at the rear. The nightclub was isolated from the other decks by a starlight spangled tunnel with a moving escalator to take the guests to the club.

The band had requested Sebastian, as he could mimic John Lennon nearly perfectly, and did a fantastic rendition of *Imagine*. He followed this with *Penny Lane* in the unusual voice of Paul McCartney in his camouflaged northern England accent. What the band had also requested was that Sebastian sit at the rear of the group, as they did not want to turn it into the Sebastian show, which was always a possibility.

Simmie Lan was a South Korean businessman who drank too much and thought his money could buy him anything. He was the cruise pest, waving his money around and pestering female guests. He wore dark, round glasses on his lean, bony nose and puckered-in face.

All Sebastian saw was Mona in the nightclub and Wan gripping her bottom and kissing her, and then they were gone. He thought they had left to complete what they had started. At that time, her fate was sealed. What Sebastian did not know was that Wan just jumped in and went for it, hands on bum, tongue in the mouth. After a moment, a stunned Mona had pushed Wan off and fled the club with the lusting Wan after her. She turned on the escalator as Wan hurled himself at her drunkenly and she brought her right knee up to his thin, wasted groin. Wan collapsed instantly in agony, groaning, his hands clutching his precious testicles.

Later during the evening performance, Sebastian played Elton John's *Circle of Life* from *The Lion King*, a favorite of Mona's. Sebastian cast a glancing smile at her at the back of the crowded bar. She had no idea that Sebastian had witnessed what appeared to be a groping in the club. As per usual, she walked meekly to the piano to hand in her requests on a paper napkin. Sebastian deftly handed her one back. It read, 'Don't tell anyone, and hand this back to me later. Will meet you at Brandon Road, Stanley, at 10 am tomorrow. Bring walking gear.'

Half-hour later she returned the napkin with, 'Can't wait.' Sebastian then played another Elton John song, *Norma Jean*, the relevance of the song lost on her.

Mona hardly slept all night with the excitement; she believed this could be the start of something wonderful. This, she thought, could be a new beginning in her life. She fantasized that she could just as easily create computer games from her powerful laptop on any ship she would follow Sebastian around on. Surely these entertainers could bring spouses on board.

The fantasies expanded, and before long she was pleasuring herself, which made the fantasies appear realer. When eventually morning came, she studied the port of Stanley on the Falkland Islands guide and found Brandon Road. It was several streets back from the 1982 war memorial, an easy twenty-minute walk, and off the beaten track.

The Falkland Islands, as the residents and its British protector call it, or Las Malvinas, as the Argentines proclaim it as their own, had seen a short but brutal war fought in the spring of 1982. It had been a British Protectorate since Britain had exerted the right in 1833. Stanley, named in 1845 after Lord Stanley, Secretary of State for the Colonies, was the only town on the island, with a population south of three thousand inhabitants. Stanley was the next port of call.

Sebastian hired a moped from the local hire shop just opposite the East Jetty Pier where the tender had brought him from the anchored ship some mile out in the harbour. He had ensured he had also taken two helmets. A driving license was not required, just cash and a credit card imprint in case of damage.

The majority of the cruise passengers queued at the tour buses to take them to see the gentoo penguins that frolic off the shore, or the smallest species type in the world, the rare rockhopper penguins, in a colony along the Berkeley Sound. Sebastian navigated through the throng and saw several of the guests walking along Ross Road to the memorial, those that were too set in their ways to pay the inflated tour prices. There was no one around when Sebastian picked up Mona, and insisted she wore the helmet.

***

It rains or snows in the Falklands for 250 days a year, and the wind chill from the wind and gales swept up from the Antarctic make the island inhospitable if you are not equipped with the right, heavy-duty outdoor clothing. Ned Jones knew this, as he had been here in 1982 fighting; at first against the poorly equipped conscripts, and later the better equipped and trained regular Argentine soldiers.

It was after the bloody fight at Mount Longdon. They were facing a heavily fortified Mount Tumbledown, the last hill stopping them from recapturing Stanley from the Argentine invasion force. The advance area had been mined heavily, as had a large part of the surrounding area.

Battalion headquarters knew Tumbledown was held by regular Argentine troops, and they had gun placements all trained on the advancing British troops. The Argentines expected that out of the attacking force of four hundred British troops, half would be dead or dying after the attack. The one advantage was the Argentines never put their ranking officers in the field or line of fire; they were all back in Stanley enjoying beer in one of the town's three well-equipped pubs.

The British commanding officer had other ideas. The projected death count was too much to pay, and the political ramifications back home would have been severe. Between his forces and Tumbledown, where the Argentines had occupied, the Argentine junior officers had deemed a little hill called Sapper Hill, as a non-strategic point, and not worthy of troops.

The commander had the seventy Royal Marines who had initially fought off the Argentine invasion in Government House. He had been captured by the overwhelming Argentine forces, returned to the UK, and who on landing insisted on coming back on the troop ships. They crept over to Sapper Hill under the cover of darkness with as much ammunition as they could carry. They placed mortars at the bottom of the hill with several squaddies, with the orders to make as much noise as possible and create the illusion the main attack was coming from their position.

When the Royal Marines obeyed and kicked up a rumpus that made them sound like seven hundred and not seventy, they complied with the orders.

The 2nd Scots Guards, 4 troop Blues and Royals and Ned's own 42 Commando Royal Marines then marched westward to the sea. They bypassed the minefields and tabbed seven miles.

At one stage, they had been pinned down by machine gun fire for several hours, and thankfully the peat surroundings absorbed most of the energy from the mortars being rained down on the troops.

A brave corporal attacked the gun position and killed the troops; at the same time, he had been shot several times in both legs. In a strange reversal, the corporal had been carried down off the mountain and, full of morphine, had been laid up against a rock. Four deserting Argentines had given themselves up to him and they now were kneeling with their hands on their heads. He maintained his gun on them for several hours through the pain and morphine, and for his bravery that day received the military medal awarded in the British army. Had he been an officer, he would have received the higher award of Medal of Honor. This ignoble practice was only outlawed after this conflict so soldier and officer would attain the same award regardless of rank.

Ned had been nineteen years old when fighting in this conflict. The last charge was one that would change his life forever. The orders were given by Major Kiszeley, "Fix bayonets and charge!" the officer in charge assessing that he would lose fewer men in a charge than being picked off by mercenary snipers and regular troops.

Killing a man from an airplane or mortar or even a rifle is one thing: it is sterile. You do not see the man's eyes close or the agony that the round or shrapnel has caused him. You miss the visual effects of the blood, the shards of bone and torn flesh.

Using a bayonet is an entirely different matter. Ned was as professional as the others and charged. He plunged the bayonet into so many bodies, saw the horrors of war close up, and like so many that day, it never left him.

Ned was nineteen at that battle and had since suffered from post-traumatic stress disorder. With horror, he had re-lived that battle most nights for the last thirty years. Neither the pills nor the countless visits to the psychiatrists had helped. This was a last-ditch attempt to cure him. It had helped other sufferers from this battle in the past. He had received funding for the trip to Stanley from the fund set up to help ex-soldiers.

***

Two days prior to the *Classical Expedition* weighing anchor in Stanley Harbour, Ned had flown into the airfield at Stanley. The first thing he noticed was that the vast crater from the historic Vulcan bombing of the landing strip was no more. Ned met a local guide. Geoff, who had been a civilian in Stanley at the time of the conflict, now worked as a battlefield tour guide and volunteered in the museum. He also helped veterans from both sides of the conflict.

Ned met him at the Globe Pub and found the surroundings strange. Machine guns mounted on the wall, Union Jack and St. George flags adorned the ceiling, with autographs of members of battalions who had served at the time of the conflict. Geoff gave Ned two options; a short visit to Tumbledown, or he could camp over for a night or two. Geoff assured him that seeing the mountain when it is at peace and the area tranquil would help him deal with the nightmares. Ned opted for the camping.

Geoff gave Ned a black Nissan SUV and directions to get to Tumbledown. In the back of the SUV were lightweight camping equipment and a stove, plus enough food and water in a backpack to last the short trip.

Ned parked up where Geoff had told him to and quickly saw the stone which had a Union Jack painted on the face. This was the stone the severely injured corporal had lain against with his gun pointed at the four prisoners some thirty years ago, now enshrined in history by the local islanders.

Geoff had been right; the serenity of the mountain had been an enormous help. Instead of setting up the tent Geoff had supplied, Ned took out the shovel and did a scrape as he had done every time, so he could get some sleep during the conflict. A scrape is where the soldier scrapes out enough earth for him to lie down in and cover it with his Bergen. Ned slept that night under the stars without the nightmares. The following day he trekked across to Mount Longdon, ensuring he kept clear of the minefields, which thirty years on were still all around the island. He thought he would stay one more night.

It was a little after 11 am, and Ned was just packing up his gear, when he heard the muffled cry. It was not a loud cry, more a muffled sob; just the one, and then it was no more. Ned could not be sure that he had heard it, or if it was in his head. Sound carries across these mountains, and if indeed it was a cry, it could have been around the corner or half a mile away. He could not be sure, so that is why he went to investigate.

Ned could not believe what he saw as he appeared over the ridge. There was a man overlooking what looked like a dead, bloodied hairless woman. Sebastian had scalped her to enjoy his present at length. Ned shook his head. Was his mind playing tricks, or was this for real? Nevertheless, he ran towards the man.

Ned was now forty-nine years old. He had been ultra-fit in his day and close combat trained, but that had been thirty years ago. He had kept some semblance of fitness, and the fighting skills never really go away, but the reactions and strength diminish with time.

Sebastian heard Ned running at the last moment, as the peat dulled the sound of the pounding boots. Sebastian swung his knife arm around towards the noise and was completely surprised that the thrust was blocked, and the blade knocked out of his hand.

There was a thirty-pound weight difference between Ned and Sebastian, and that extra ballast assisted Ned as he landed on top of Sebastian and started to pound each fist into both sides of Sebastian's skull.

Stunned and bloodied, Sebastian dug out the long-ago learned martial arts skills. He managed to get his hand out from under the hulk above him and pinch down on a nerve at the side of the neck, enough to make Ned yelp and lose the dominant position on top of the assailant.

Sebastian stood erect for a moment to gather his wits and strength. Almost immediately, Ned sprang back up and attempted to grab Sebastian by the arm to pull him in closer. Ned was going to try a bear hug to suck the strength from the lighter man. Sebastian was too fast, and he swerved one hundred eighty degrees on his right foot, thus making Ned lean forward, slightly unbalanced. Sebastian had his left fist up by his shoulder. He grabbed Ned's arm with his right hand and brought down the left elbow straight on Ned's forearm, snapping it immediately. Ned registered the pain, but adrenaline assisted him in carrying on with what started as an attack and was now a matter of defence.

Sebastian threw out his left hand in a classic karate chop; it was aimed at the bridge of Ned's nose. Ned managed to block the attack with his good left arm and immediately tried to pull up his right to guard his throat and right side of his face, but the right arm would not work. Instantaneously he felt the searing jab to his Adam's apple, and his knees crumpled under him.

Ned gasped for air, but none came. Sebastian knew it would take several minutes for the man to die. Never once did he consider putting Ned out of his misery; he just watched the man expire, slowly.

Finally, Mount Tumbledown had claimed back what it thought was hers thirty years prior.

A quick search of the body revealed car keys and Ned's wallet and passport. Sebastian moved both bodies under a rocky outcrop, leaving them hidden from view. He retraced Ned's steps, which were not easy to follow in the peat, and after thirty minutes he found Ned's gear. A further ten-minute trek found the black SUV.

The sight of the four-by-four was the first thing to go right all day. There was no one to be seen for miles as Sebastian eased the vehicle up over the hill towards the bodies. He stopped at Ned's camp and stowed all the gear into the rear compartment, and then completed the drive to the corpses. He placed Mona in the rear section and the man's heavier body across the back seat. Sebastian was pleased to see that the tracks of the vehicle had almost disappeared as the peat sprang back, helped by the massive amounts of water encased below. He backtracked to where he had left the moped and, after checking the road, which he could see in both directions, lifted the moped-on top of the camping gear with some considerable effort.

Sebastian had travelled less than two miles before he came across the area he wanted. To the right, between the road and the sea was a minefield, depicted in pictures and words on signs and two small road barriers on either side.

Again, checking the road for several miles in each direction, he stopped a little short of the minefield. Quickly he removed the moped and two helmets from the back. It took several minutes to move Ned's corpse into the front driver seat and place the foot on the gas.

Sebastian leaned through the open passenger's door. The car was an automatic, and after setting the steering wheel in the right direction, he checked that the car was in the park. He leaned across and started the engine. Half-hanging out of the car, he placed the gear lever in drive and released the handbrake.

The car went at speed as Sebastian exited and had sufficient force and power to break through the flimsy fence surrounding the minefield. The car had travelled less than fifty yards into the field before small anti-personnel mine exploded, which destroyed the door of the car but did not stop the car's forward movement. Then it hit the real thing, not anti-personnel that would blow a soldier's foot right off, but the dug-in mines that would stop a tank.

The explosion was heard back in Stanley, and then the second after the car was flipped over and did a full three-hundred-sixty-degree turn in the air, it landed on another tank buster. Diesel takes a lot to ignite, but what was left of the car and surrounding peat were blazing away in the middle of the field.

Sebastian had not accounted for the noise of the detonation being so loud, never mind a second one. He looked in the mirror of the moped. His face was a mess from the pounding under Ned's fists, and his clothes were a mess from the fight and exiting the moving car. There were sure to be police and fire engines on their way from Stanley coming to the sound of the explosions, and there was only one way in and one way out.

He had seen a farm on the map down the other way towards Two Sisters Mountain, and some help could be coming from there, too. There was no way the moped could make it over the peat bog the way the SUV had, and he was running out of time.

Mounting the moped, Sebastian kicked the engine into action. In the distance, he could hear the sirens screaming towards him. He drove a hundred yards down the road towards Stanley and turned around towards the burning field. He drove the moped at ten miles per hour and aimed for the untouched fixed guardrails that notify you that there is a minefield adjacent. The moped hit the barrier, and the helmetless Sebastian flew over the moped and over the barrier, landing in the mesh of the minefield fence.

Sebastian moved his hands to ensure he had not damaged the means to his living, and to his murderous hobby. New blood oozed from a deep cut over his eye and his left ankle was broken, then he passed out.

Sebastian awoke in the hospital several hours later with his ankle in plaster and several stitches to the gash above his eye; he also awoke to the tall, gangly policeman, Inspector Green.

The inspector had been employed by the Falkland Government and had previously been a detective in the London Metropolitan Police. He had been encouraged to accept the post, and there had been hints from his chief constable of fast-track rise through the ranks after his two-year stint, of which he had only served one month.

Several days and three interviews later, the inspector was still not satisfied. The *Classical Expedition*, like all cruise liners, waited for neither man nor mouse. If you were not back on-board on time, staff or not, it sailed. The company's agent, on hearing Sebastian's plight, had passed the information to the company headquarters, and they authorized payment of the hospital bill. They also gave him the services of a local attorney when it became apparent the inspector believed that Sebastian had something to do with the deaths of Ned and Mona in the minefield.

"It doesn't make sense; you hire a bike with two helmets, yet you say you were out there alone. The young lady was off your ship, and we know she liked to watch your performances. Ned had been on the mountain for two days, and we checked the mileage on the SUV. There was no way the distance indicated that he had been back to Stanley to pick up Mona, and no connection between them," the inspector said accusingly.

"It's all ifs, buts, and maybes. And wasn't the soldier guy suffering from some mental defect? You have nothing to connect my client with the accidents apart from the fact that he witnessed the car go through the fence and lost control of the moped," said James White, the rotund attorney the company's agent had hired.

"That may be at present, but I want your client's fingerprints, DNA, and passport. We're sending the remains back to a crime lab in the UK to see what they come up with."

"But that could take months! Are you going to keep my client here, in a jail cell, for several months?"

"No, there are enough hotels and bed and breakfasts on the island, and your company is more than capable of funding that. But till I get the DNA tests back, he is not going anywhere, and certainly not out of Stanley. I want him tagged as well, as a condition of his release."

"It's an outrage!" the sweating attorney said.

Police Inspector Green said he especially liked that comment, as he sat down in the Globe Pub with the attorney and the island's only two magistrates later that night to enjoy a very special Johnnie Walker whisky the management had flown in. The bill was on James White, as the retainer the agent had put him on would pay off very handsomely if this case lasted a few months.

chapter twenty-two

Cutler, Hoagie, and the German accountant Richter took the train across from Glasgow's Central Station. Two and a half hours later, the trio emerged from Newcastle's Central Station into the cold breezy northern air.

Richter bemoaned the walk down from the station towards the quayside and across the Millennium Bridge towards Gateshead.

"The bridge looks like a giant bear trap without the teeth," Richter spluttered out, with puffs of vapour.

"Shut up and concentrate on walking, Richter. The last thing we need is for you to collide with one of these cyclists and cause an incident," Hoagie said.

Cutler walked behind the pair, scanning the area, making sure they were not being followed. Newcastle, although a busy city, consists of a small and compact town centre. They would need a couple of days here for the passports, and Cutler didn't want to be so centrally based. Better to keep a low profile and stay off the radar.

Appearing in such a public place was an open invitation for Werner's henchmen. Cutler was under no illusion that Werner would have put the word on the street, a description of Richter, and a hefty bonus to anyone who gave him up. Werner's contract on Richter would have circulated in the underworld from Scotland down to Lands' End and across the Irish Sea.

Obscurity was the number one priority. Cutler had decided to walk the short distance to the Millennium Bridge from Newcastle to the Quays at Gateshead. The distance from the station at Newcastle to the Quays took less than fifteen minutes to walk.

Gateshead Quays were in a transitional stage; old warehouse buildings, once housing the fruits of the empire brought from the entire world to the Tyne, now museums and art centres. The trio passed the 1930s' Baltic flour mill, now converted and called the Baltic Centre for Contemporary Arts.

Richter struggled up the south bank steps and complained under the strain of the gradient. Several minutes later they walked past a deserted warehouse opposite the Gateshead College. They entered the Ramda hotel, Richter bent down, trying to draw in a breath.

Cutler had pre-booked two twin rooms using an alias. He had booked two twin rooms so Hoagie or himself could always keep an eye on Richter. The girls in Newcastle are known for their beauty; Cutler did not want Richter going off on a frolic with one of them.

Hoagie and Richter stayed in the shadows while Cutler registered at reception. Cutler got the room keys; he took the first room. Hoagie had the double bed, Richter the single, in the shared accommodation. Cutler went to the computer area of the hotel located on the ground floor, the only place he could get a Wi-Fi connection for his laptop.

Ghislaine's face filled the screen as Cutler connected with her via Skype. He had small headphones on so the other two Wi-Fi users in the area could not overhear them.

After several minutes of video conferencing with Ghislaine, Cutler knew they were being tracked within the UK. Ghislaine had reported several of Werner's operatives had entered the country; the last report was that two of them had flown to Glasgow. Cutler knew it was a matter of time before they tracked them to Newcastle, but he was in a catch-22 position; Richter's passport would not be ready for several more hours.

Finally, as night drew in, Cutler left the hotel and walked down to the Quays. He crossed the Gateshead Millennium Bridge, across the River Tyne. He walked southwards down the quay on the Newcastle side and under the Tyne Bridge. It swallowed up three-storey buildings under its main brick supports on the quayside. Walking up a steep cobbled street called The Side, he went towards the historic Castle Keep Black Gate and Moot Hall, which was undergoing restorative works. The area was dimly lit and isolated.

Cutler approached the archways of a railway embankment. He passed a Chinese restaurant; the aroma of duck and ginger tingled his senses. Cutler glanced into the restaurant and observed the staff setting up the tables for the evening; they were the first people he had seen since entering the cobbled street.

Two archways down, he entered through the door of a small outlet, which stated office supplies. Cutler spoke to a young man called Imran; he was of Indian extraction. Cutler requested to see Bruno, the shop owner. The young man eyed him suspiciously, and Cutler instantly thought he did not trust him.

Imran did not speak a word to Cutler but ushered him through to the back office to where Bruno, a thin, small man who looked ashen, sat. Imran retreated out of the door.

"Who's the young man, Bruno? Haven't seen him before," Cutler inquired.

"Not one for small talk, as usual, I see. Imran's an apprentice recommended by some friend from Goa. He did good work there, forging UK passports for illegal immigrants, good enough to get past border force. If he can forge UK passports, he can forge anything," he replied in a raspy voice.

"You should give up the cigarettes, Bruno; you don't sound too good," Cutler remarked honestly.

"That's why I need an apprentice, had half my lung removed earlier this year," Bruno wheezed.

"Do you trust him?" Cutler inquired.

"In this game, you don't trust anyone."

"Did he know I was coming?" Cutler continued.

"Yes, he did the work on the passport for your friend," Bruno replied.

"Does he know who I am?" Cutler pressed.

"He doesn't know your name or what you do, just that you need a passport. As I said: I trust no one," Bruno retorted.

"Is the passport ready?" Cutler replied, as his level of alarm increased.

"The picture you sent digitally was of good enough quality for me to download and put into the correct format. Imran has done a perfect job. We used the name of a Polish immigrant who has a green card for the USA. Unfortunately, the Pole died in a car crash on the first day he revisited his home in Warsaw via New York," Bruno said without emotion.

"What about his fingerprints? They would have taken them at JFK," Cutler said.

"We have a copy on file. The Agent we use knew his identity is worth more if we have his prints, very efficient in that part of the world. For an extra two thousand dollars, you can have the latex overlays, which are undetectable when applied to the fingers correctly. But you know that already, Cutler, as this is not the first time we have done business. But it has been a while," Bruno responded.

Cutler did not like doing business with the likes of Bruno, but he was a CIA and Secret Service asset that they had worked with in the past, and would no doubt use again in the future. Cutler understood that to catch major counterfeiters; you had to work with the likes of Bruno.

Cutler handed over the $10,000 in total for the passport and the latex fingerprints, after carefully checking the authenticity of the document. He had to agree; Imran had done a first-class job. Even Cutler would struggle, and would need high-tech equipment, to confirm it was counterfeit.

Cutler decided to take a circuitous route back to the hotel instead of retracing his steps. He exited onto a minor road at the top of The Side and passed the ancient black gates of the Castle Keep. There was temporary construction fencing surrounding the entrance to the gate, and Cutler noticed somebody had breached one of the fence panels. Had Cutler needed to spy on someone in the area, he would have placed one of his men up high within the construction site, but he would not have left the panel ajar.

The site elevated towers would have been a perfect location on high to watch the entrance into the archways.

Cutler could not take a chance he was being observed. Nowadays, with mobile phones, his picture could already be with Werner, if someone were indeed watching him. He cursed himself; he should have sent Hoagie, who would be unknown to Werner. Cutler's hackles were up; he could not tell why, and it was always hard to explain these often correct but tenuous feelings of danger, but he knew he had to check it out.

He side-stepped between the construction barriers and veered to the left into the darkness of what once was the moat. He knelt there for several seconds and listened intently. The sound of footsteps crossing the small drawbridge confirmed his fears; he had been observed. The stalker had seen him exit the archway and was now making his way onto the street to follow him.

Just before the observer exited through the gap in the panels onto the street, Cutler pounced out of the darkness of the moat. He hit the man immediately with a rabbit punch to his jaw, dragging the big muscle-bound man down into the grassy moat. *A street fighter rather than a professional,* Cutler thought. Cutler assumed he was local hired help rather than one of Werner's assassins due the ease with which Cutler had been able to sucker punch him.

The bloodied man tried to headbutt Cutler with the back of his head, but Cutler dropped his head down so the bottom of the observer's cranium encountered the top of Cutler's forehead. While the blow made Cutler stumble, it laid the man out flat. He would not gain consciousness for several more hours.

Cutler went through the unconscious man's pockets where he discovered binoculars, a mobile phone, and a flick knife with a seven-inch blade. He found the man's wallet, which contained his driving license and security pass with the man's photograph on it and the words 'Door Security', which confirmed to Cutler the man was locally hired.

Cutler read through the latest phone messages. It was clear that he had been followed, as the observer had relayed a message to a second assailant. The message said, 'Go to high ground on the Gateshead side of the bridge to track him on the way back.' There was a picture of Cutler on the smartphone, but it was too dark and pixelated to make out his face.

Cutler took out his phone and texted a message to Hoagie to bring him up to speed.

Hoagie, on receiving the text, immediately went to a local map of the area he had retrieved earlier from reception. He scanned the map and highlighted two areas on the map which he would choose if he had been on a reconnoitring mission. The first had been on top of the Baltic Mill overlooking the bridge and the other, the Sage. This modernistic building is a large, cultural centre holding concerts, displays, and galleries. The building has three pyramids in clear glass which are cocooned atop by reflective rounded panels. From a distance, they looked like clouds. The Sage sits atop a small plateau some 150 yards away from the Baltic centre and Tyne, and with a good view down to both the Millennium and Tyne bridges.

Hoagie ignored the constant requests from Richter for information about what was happening while Hoagie changed into a black tracksuit and handmade, black, lightweight army boots.

Richter began to complain again to Hoagie, who in the meantime retrieved two plastic restraints from his rucksack. Richter looked confused as Hoagie neared him.

"Yes, you deserve to know, but I need to whisper it to you, Richter. You know the saying, loose lips sink ships," Hoagie said quietly.

He put his lips to Richter's ear and in a swift movement had pressed his finger into a pressure point on the side of Richter's temple. Richter collapsed unconscious onto the bed. Hoagie secured his wrists and ankles with the plastic strips and placed a gag around his mouth.

Hoagie left the hotel and walked through the darkness of the parking lot. There was a small wall he hurdled, which took him down Mills Road. He hugged the wall on the far side in darkness until he crossed the road to the Baltic building. He circumnavigated the building, and it became apparent that this building was closed for business that evening. Hoagie noticed the whole building perimeter was covered with closed-circuit television cameras and excluded this observation post as too dangerous for any type of operation.

He retraced his steps towards the hotel until he entered the parking lot to the Sage. To anyone watching he was just one of the many people either entering or exiting the parking lot, and Hoagie was pretty sure the other observer would be watching the bridge for Cutler's return, and not the parking lot.

Cutler retraced his steps and re-entered the forger's premises under the archway. The look of shock on Imran's face told him everything he needed to know. Cutler swept the side of his right hand into Imran's throat and as he gasped for breath, Cutler pushed him through into Bruno's office, where he collapsed.

"We've been doing business a long time, Bruno. You know who I work for and know not to cross them, so I gather it's this little shit who gave me up," Cutler said, maintaining the pretense he still worked for the United States government.

Bruno stood up with the aid of a walking stick and looked at the forlorn figure on the floor. "You would guess right. I do over half my business with your government, and you don't bite the hand that feeds you," Bruno replied honestly.

"So that leaves you," he said to Imran, pushing him with the toe of his shoe.

"What pictures do you have of me, and have you sent them to anyone?" Cutler growled.

"I do not know what you're talking about, mister. Please do not hurt me!" a very scared Imran replied.

Cutler did not need to react, as Bruno crashed the walking stick down onto Imran's hand, breaking several fingers.

"This customer represents the American government, my clients, Imran. This is a customer you don't piss off; it only ends one way. If my friend here says you set him up, then you did. If you want to walk away from this, I will advise you to stop the lies and tell him the truth. If your fingers hurt, wait to feel the pain from your new arsehole when I relocate it," Bruno wheezed and growled; forcing the walking stick down onto Imran's broken fingers, as he screamed in agony.

"The gang that brought me to the UK placed me here with you, Bruno. They give me orders sometimes!" Imran cried out in pain.

"A picture was circulated yesterday, and I was told to contact them if he turned up. It was the picture this man sent through. I had to tell them, or they would kill me!"

"Clean your mess up, Bruno. I want any closed-circuit television or still pictures destroyed. If any of them get out, you will be getting a visit from one of the CIA clean-up squads. Do I make myself clear?" Cutler lied.

"Don't you worry, sir, no pictures will be getting out. And this mess will be cleared by tonight. I am very sorry; this is the first time I have had a client compromised this way," Bruno swore.

***

Hoagie had circumnavigated the Sage. It was clear the observer would not be inside, as there was a Schubert rendition underway in the centre and it thronged with business.

At the far side of the building, there was a grassy knoll that was hidden from view, and it was where Hoagie would have set up an observation post. He crept silently behind the mound, keeping close to the ground. He scanned the area with his infrared binoculars. He picked up a heat signal some fifty yards down and twenty yards to the left. Hoagie studied the area carefully, although he could not see anyone, he could see the end of a rifle and scope jutting out what seemed from the hill itself.

It was obvious to Hoagie that the object of his attention was much more than an observer; he was an assassin. The sniper had gouged out a hide and was wearing camouflage; it was only the slight heat trace that had given him away.

Hoagie had only the flick knife as a weapon. Cutler had insisted that they should not have any arms, as it was a mandatory five-year sentence in the UK for carrying weapons without a license. And since Cutler had left the Secret Service, he would have no one to turn to should they be stopped by the local police.

The rifle made the sniper's intention clear. While the picture the first assailant had taken of Cutler did not display his face in sufficient clarity, it did display his approximate height and clothing. It also had their original location as Gateshead. Hoagie was not willing to take a chance that even if Cutler changed his clothes he would not be picked out as he tried to cross either the Millennium or swing bridge by foot.

Two yards away from the sniper's hide, Hoagie was startled. This sniper was experienced. He was astute, and he had laid a trap in a hundred-eighty-degree semi-circle around his lair. Falco Jager, aka the Owl, had taken Heineken beer bottles and broken them into small pieces. The green colours of the bottles matched into the surrounding grass and were almost indiscernible in the night. Even Hoagie's night vision glasses could not pick out the shards. The crunch of the glass under Hoagie's foot was lost in the sound of the wind that always blew around the Tyne, but loud enough to alert the sniper.

Hoagie had used this basic type of motion sensor himself, and he scolded himself for not being more cautious. Cutler had mentioned an observer, not a sniper. If he had known what he was dealing with, he would have taken extra precautions.

The Owl swung around deftly and fired a single shot from the ArmaLite he had bought from one of Werner's English contacts in London. His beloved Swiss bolt-action SSG 2000 was in his gun safe back in Germany as Werner had ordered. It was much safer to buy weapons in a country than to transport them across the borders of Europe, especially into the UK.

Hoagie owed his life to his swiftness of feet and to the fact that the Owl had not had the time to find an isolated area where he could have tested and honed the rifle to his requirements.

Hoagie twisted to his left as the rifle targeted him. The bullet passed the fleshy part of his right forearm, missing the vital brachial artery, but tearing away the flesh in larger amounts from the exit wound. Hoagie landed heavily on the glass-strewn area and was glad the injury was to his right arm, as his left gripped the flick knife he had been holding onto since the observer morphed into a sniper.

Glass shards embedded themselves into Hoagie's left side; large enough to cut, small enough to not cause any serious injuries. In a fluid motion, he used the strength in his back and legs to jump from a prone position to an upright stance. His timing was perfect, as a second bullet from the ArmaLite passed between his legs where his head had been a millisecond before.

Adrenalin surged through Hoagie's veins. Gone was the pain in his arm; gone were the nuisance cuts from the glass. It was fight or flight time, and Hoagie had never fled in his life.

Falco Jager, aka 'the Owl', was a world-class rifleman. The medals he had won were a testament to his skills. He was also an excellent street fighter; he had honed his skills providing security outside dubious establishments in Hamburg, and at twenty-six years old was in peak physical condition.

Hoagie had two inches in height over the Owl. This was important, as it was two inches less to cover the ground to get to him. More importantly, Hoagie was an ex-Navy Seal, who had trained for six years with the elite unit until his sexual orientation forced him out of the job he loved. He was six years older than the Owl but maintained a fitness level of a pre-thirty-year-old. The drawback was, he was injured. Although the pain was masked by adrenaline, the mobility of his right arm was down to approximately sixty percent of normal use.

The Owl spun onto his back, the camouflage sheet now beneath him. Hoagie did not hear the second shot as the silencer had done its work, but the spit of fire was evident.

Pouncing, Hoagie landed on top of the Owl, trapping the rifle between their bodies, ensuring the Owl could not aim and put pressure on the trigger. It would be a lottery as to which one of them would be hit, had the gun fired. The Owl tried to use brawn rather than brain by an attempt to headbutt Hoagie. Hoagie rode with the force of the headbutt, dropping his brow down slightly to take blunt the energy and protect the bridge of his nose.

Stunned, Hoagie grabbed the gun from Owl and threw it sidewards away from the Owl. A mighty hand grasped around Hoagie's throat and twisted him, so Hoagie was now under his assailant. The grip was firm, and the Owl was trying to pull

Hoagie's windpipe out. It was a grip Hoagie was sure he could not break clear from. *Time to end this,* Hoagie thought. Rapidly he swung his knife hand around the Owl's back. With a quick incision and scrabbling round of the flick knife into the base of the Owl's skull at the top of his spine, Hoagie disabled his assailant, and this quickly led to the Owl's death, as the base of his brain was little more than shredded offal.

With a little effort, Hoagie rolled off the corpse and observed his handiwork. He pulled the camouflage sheeting from under the Owl and covered the body. He crawled underneath the ample camouflage and took out his phone. The light of the screen shielded by the camouflage; he began to text Cutler.

Fifteen minutes later, Cutler turned up at the Sage parking lot amidst the throng of guests leaving the concert. He knew from the text that Hoagie was to the far side of the building and out of sight. Once the main crowd departed, he made his way to Hoagie's position unobserved.

Cutler took in and evaluated the situation without either of them saying a word. He quickly removed the dead sniper's leather jacket, wiped it down, and gave it to Hoagie to put on to cover his wounds. While it was ample in width, it was a little short in the arms but far less prominent than a man with blood-stained clothes entering the hotel.

In silence, Cutler strapped the rifle to the corpse with the dead man's belt. He signalled to Hoagie that he was going to scout the area to find a means of disposing of the body.

Cutler carefully made his way down in the darkness to the edge of the Quay. There was a single-storey building that looked official, as it had a security fence around it, it seemed deserted. Cutler veered off to the left and circumnavigated the building's perimeter.

The building was HMS Calliope, a naval reserve centre. The British treated such premises as an extension of their Navy, hence the Her Majesty's Ship Calliope name.

The security fence gave Cutler the cover from the isolated late-night revellers who crossed the Millennium Bridge in small numbers. He retraced his steps back up to Hoagie.

Silently they sat there for an additional hour until they were sure the last remnants of guests and entertainers had left the Sage building. Cutler did not want the casual observer seeing them carrying a body-sized object down the hill down to the side of Her Majesty's Ship Calliope.

The Tyne was at high tide and flowing fast. It took both Hoagie and Cutler to lift the body over the quay wall and drop it into the rapid flow of ice-cold water. The Owl was not the only body to enter the Tyne that night; several hours later, an unconscious Imran followed him in with the aid of three of Bruno's accomplices. Not entirely what Cutler had meant by 'Clear up your mess.'

chapter twenty-three

Tuck received the call at 11 pm local time. He grabbed the phone from the bedside table and listened to Cutler explain some of what had occurred that evening.

"Sounds like you're having fun, is this a job I don't know about?" Tuck inquired.

"It's a clean-up job from my days in the secret service, Tuck," Cutler said.

"What's your next move?"

"We're flying from Liverpool to Shannon Airport in Ireland and are catching a flight to Miami via Chicago within the next hour. We had to avoid the major airports in case of another incident. I need to update you on some other stuff that's cropped up. How's the stakeout going? Cutler replied.

"I've got Stahmer sitting on Mick Hilton; we're taking twelve-hour shifts. It's been two days, and if I read this right, Hilton will be getting a visit soon from Rothhelm's people," Tuck reported.

"I need Stahmer for another job I'm afraid, Tuck. We've had a cruise line owner on the phone. They spoke to Fabienne. It seems they had a mysterious fire on a lifeboat last month, which killed quite a few employees.

"The families of the dead are not satisfied with the initial investigation and have been reaching out to several news stations in several countries. In turn, the bad publicity is hitting the cruise line hard, so they want us to investigate," Cutler explained.

"Christ, a cruise line asking us for help. Never thought I'd see the day," Tuck replied.

"Put Basmati on your case, but get him some backup, as he's not a muscle man," Cutler ordered.

"I know a guy in Nassau, used to work for the local drug enforcement. Trained by us and now freelance. His name is Nathan Colton, an African American. He's a big black guy, and he's good in a situation," Tuck announced.

"If you are recommending him, that's good enough for me. Get him on a flight as soon as possible. Pay him his standard contract rate, and we'll evaluate later whether he would be an additional asset to the team if he wants a full-term contract." Cutler hung up, and called Cheryl.

"Hi, Max, what do you need?"

"Fabienne has been on the line; evidently, there was an incident last month. A lifeboat exploded, seven dead crew. Jon Deloitte, the chief executive of Jules Verne Cruise Line, has asked us to investigate the incident. Fabienne says she believes the company's insurers are baulking at a multimillion-dollar payout to the families of the deceased, and pressure from bereaved families." Cutler relayed.

"Yes, I heard about that on CNN news report," Cheryl replied.

"The internal investigation was flawed, and no conclusions were drawn, although the report stated 'accident'. Appears my old recruiter, Wyatt Rockman, is an advisor to the insurance company and passed our names over as 'a company they could deal with'," Cutler quoted Fabienne.

"Not what we precisely set up to do, Max. We wanted to investigate the failings in these companies, not work for them," Cheryl said, a little irritated.

"Doesn't matter how we get to the outcome; the end goal remains the same. Same horse, different jockey," Cutler replied.

"What do you need me to do?" Cheryl asked.

"Send Stahmer over to Genoa where the ship is berthed for the next few days. Also, send Ghislaine, as some of the crew don't speak English, and he'll need a translator."

"What about Tuck?" she inquired, knowing she was being kept out of whatever he was doing at the moment. Even though they were lovers, she would never compromise him by asking him directly.

"Tuck is on other duties at the moment," Cutler replied.

"I know that Max; we're partners, and we're supposed to know what operations are going on. Keeping me in the dark is unlike you, so I can only assume the job has something to do with my husband's case," she continued, as Cutler grimaced at the words. *My husband.*

"Cheryl, I'll let you know when we know something. Let Tuck get on with his job, and as soon as I have something to tell you, I will, but not before. See you when I get back, our plane from Liverpool goes in an hour," Cutler stressed, before switching the phone to flight mode.

Tuck showered. Before he had time to dry off, his phone rang again.

"Hi, Tuck. Stahmer here."

"I know who it is. I don't know anyone else in the world with an accent like that."

"Ah, very droll, Tuck. Anyway, I think you need to get your butt out here, a car has pulled up outside the Hilton residence, the men don't look friendly."

"On my way in five minutes," Tuck replied and pressed 'end'.

Tuck contacted Nathan Colton, who had just finished two slugs of local rum; what he called lunch. Colton was happy to get the contract and said he would be on the next plane bound for Miami, and should be with him before morning.

No more than half an hour had passed when Cheryl was ready to leave. She quickly tidied the crumpled sheets and bedspread, and went to turn off the television, when a breaking news headline caught her eye.

"Terrorist attack at Liverpool John Lennon airport. Twelve persons confirmed dead at the scene. Local police and army are at the airport," the scrolling news bar at the bottom of the screen displayed.

Cheryl desperately tried to phone Cutler back, but received only the automated answer message.

chapter twenty-four

erner sat in his palatial villa; it was one of a pair of grand buildings sited next to each other at the highest point accessible by road on a hill overlooking the semi-circular bay of Akbuk, Turkey. The slope was like most hills around the area, strewn with olive groves and stone-domed, covered water wells. If you removed the sporadic villas, it would have looked the same as it had a thousand years ago. The general area was known as Didim, and was situated between Bodrum and Altinkum.

The area had been chosen with care, both for its beautiful panoramic view and the isolation from the major resorts: Kusadasi to the north, and Bodrum and Marmaris to the south. The resorts were densely populated, and there was the possibility of Werner being recognized.

The journey to Akbuk had not been comfortable. Bauer had purchased an American Winnebago for the trip. At some eight yards long and three yards high, it encompassed a large double bed so Werner could rest on the trip. There was an equipped kitchen with a new blender purchased to turn Werner's food from solid to a more liquid state. There was also a fully stocked first aid cupboard jam-packed with antibiotics and sterilizing equipment to neutralize the infections.

Bauer had driven the Winnebago across the German border into France near Strasbourg, as there was less of a police presence in this area. They were expecting him to try to cross into Austria or

Switzerland, according to information supplied by Delegate Frau Uebering.

Bauer had needed a rest break when they arrived at Chamonix, the French ski town nestled below the looming Mont Blanc. The game was nearly up before it started as an astute French cop wanted to know why Bauer had parked the van in the parking lot beneath the cable car. The sign clearly stated in several languages 'No Campervans Allowed'.

The cop wanted to see Bauer's driver's license, and then checked over his radio that it was not stolen, and Bauer's credentials were real. Had the cop looked inside the Winnebago he would have seen a familiar face staring at him from a sitting position on the van's large bed, for he would have seen the face in the picture that had been circulated that very morning from Interpol. Luckily for Werner, the cop was sloppy.

From Chamonix, and with his ears still ringing from the metallic lambasting from Werner for his stupidity, Bauer drove through the Mont Blanc tunnel, paying the fifty-euro toll fee at the entrance. Crossing over to the Italian side of three mountains, the vehicle emerged high up, driving on the valley floors of the large, peaked mountains on either side. Stopping only for fuel, Bauer carried on driving past Lake Como before he was forced to stop at Lake Garda for a few hours of sleep. This time he found a campervan park on the lake shore and just signed in as himself, showing his passport.

The next day he took the motorway down to Venice and bought an Anex ferry ticket for the two-day sailing to the port of

Patras in Greece. The port authorities did not check the interior of the vehicle, so Werner remained hidden inside as they boarded.

The Winnebago was directed into the bowels of the large ferry and parked inches away from the next campervan. What they had not expected was that Bauer was ordered out of the vehicle, under protest, as they did not allow drivers to stay with their vehicles. Once Bauer exited, another campervan was directed to park inches away from the driver's door he had just exited, thus trapping Werner in the vehicle for the two-day crossing. Bauer tried to get down to the deck later that day but found all access routes locked. He fretted away the two days in the bar, purchased a cabin to get some fitful sleep, and ate and drank some more.

They docked early in the morning, and it was thirty minutes before he was allowed on the vehicle deck. Bauer was unable to get into the vehicle, as he had to wait for the campervan parked alongside to disembark. Eventually he climbed in through the driver's door, and the stench of urine and detritus hit him.

"Dummkopf!" was his metallic greeting from Werner.

Bauer could see that the campervan was in a total mess, and the carpet outside the toilet was stained with urine.

"Nothing in the fucking van works without a hook up to electrics or off the leisure battery, which is immobilized when you lock the goddamn door!" Werner fumed.

"They got me out so quick; I didn't have a chance to do anything!" Bauer pleaded.

"You locked the door, asshole, no lights, no water, and no toilet flush. I have had to live off the bottle of water by the bed because I couldn't see what food was in the cupboards. Do you know how dark it is down here when they close the doors and turn off the lights?"

Ten minutes later they had disembarked the ship with no immigration to go through due to the open borders of the European Union. Bauer parked a mile along the beach road and began the clean-up of the van on Werner's orders.

They crawled the hundred and eighty kilometres to the port of Piraeus, due to the Greek government running out of funding for a new toll road, and which was now renamed the 'road of death'.

On arriving in the port that serves Athens a short distance away, Bauer bought a ticket for the Winnebago and himself. This time, the Blue Star Ferry that would take him overnight to the Greek island of Kos had a motorhome deck, where the owners could stay with the van, as it was open on one side and well ventilated. Only the use of liquid petroleum gas for cooking was banned, so the trip was far more pleasant than the initial crossing.

The shock came when they purchased a ticket for the Turkish Sea Line ferry from Kos to Bodrum. The ship was not a ship, but a converted wooden gulet, which had enough room on the back for two vehicles or one motorhome. The access ramp was moving, and would rise up three feet or so on the dockside with the swell of the Aegean, almost causing the Winnebago to topple off as it hung on with two wheels on and two wheels off the gulet, in a precarious position.

Werner sat in the toilet as Bauer took an hour to complete the document control and purchase motor insurance to cover Turkey.

They had been warned beforehand that customs would pop their heads into all incoming vehicles for a brief look, which they did, but it took all of three seconds.

Akbuk was mainly a Turkish resort with a minority of Brits and French expatriates. For ten months of the year, the crystal-clear turquoise Aegean Sea shimmered in the sunshine. The traditional Turkish restaurants would deliver their splendid cuisine daily; unfortunately for Werner, this had to be blended so he could consume it.

Kurt Bauer stayed with Werner for three months while he set up a network of Kurdish minders, men with whom he had a long-standing relationship with. With the help of the Kurds, he also set up links with corrupt local police officers, who would relay any information that may affect Werner's stay in the area.

The team of six Kurdish minders was split into three shifts to ensure that there were always two of them with him, for twenty-four hours per day, three hundred and sixty-five days per year.

Werner had grown stronger under the healing rays of the sun. He had gained back his ruddy complexion, and regained a little of the weight he had dramatically shed. The only major frustration for Werner was the intolerable voice box he had to hold to his throat to speak. It somehow decreased his power and the respect he was held in, or so he thought, as paranoia was another legacy of that awful day in the Bavarian Alps.

Delegate Frau Uebering was a regular visitor; taking time out from her duties in the Bundestag to ensure her other main business was maintained. Whenever she visited, she would bring along her lover and attorney, Von-Baer. It would annoy Werner that quite often they would contaminate his pristine swimming pool with their bodily fluids as they cavorted unashamedly.

Jan Eichmann, the gang's master forger, who had been arrested at the same time as Werner, had served only two years of his ten-year sentence, thanks to the intervention of Delegate Frau Uebering, using her contacts in the judicial system. Eichmann had, under the delegate's and Werner's instructions, begun the reproduction of hundred-dollar bills. They had set up a workshop on a farm just inside the Hungarian border with Austria, with easy access to Vienna and the autobahns back into Germany.

Werner, Delegate Frau Uebering, and Von-Baer sat around a white cast-iron table on lavishly cushioned chairs beside the dazzling blue, thirty-metre swimming pool. The Kurdish minders maintained a respectable distance from the table at the entrance to the property, out of earshot.

Von-Baer gave a short report on the business and growth. He discussed all three areas of the enterprise; counterfeiting, prostitution, and what he called security, but which might more accurately have been described as extortion. The business had been run without going anywhere near drugs, as they believed drugs led to turf wars, and attracted the most attention from the law enforcement agencies.

"Well, it appears we are back on track, Werner. We can put all that nasty business behind us now and look to the future," Delegate Frau Uebering said optimistically.

"Not before I get that little shit, Richter; no one steals from me," Werner replied, in the droning, tinny voice.

"The loss of the money was an irritation, Werner, but it can be replaced within six months. I would have thought you would have been more vengeful against the American agent who set the trap and gifted you a tin box for a voice. What was his name? Custer? No, Cutler," she replied.

"It was only business with Cutler. He was doing his job. And thanks to Bauer, he is no longer a problem, although a little late, I might add," the robotic voice said.

"Have you been keeping me in the dark, Werner?" Delegate Frau Uebering probed.

"Not really, just taking care of business. I had Kurt Bauer identify Cutler's close family. After two weeks of research, he found out who they were and where they lived. As you know, Cutler was closing in on us, and I needed a diversion quickly. Anyway, Bauer discovered they had just left for a cruise to Alaska." Werner stopped to take a sip of the local red wine.

"Bauer arranged to get a late booking for the cruise and joined the ship at Vancouver. It took him three days on-board to identify what deck and cabin they were in. Bauer said the ship was like a large town, with over two thousand people on it. This was the same day that Cutler set his trap. That delay cost me my voice." Again, Werner had to take a break and have another sip of wine, as the vocal exertion began to hurt his larynx.

"Bauer targeted the sister; she was young and pretty, and according to his research, Cutler adored her. He followed her at a distance for several hours until he got his chance. She eventually went to the rear of the boat on the topmost deck at night, evidently looking for a signal for her phone," Werner revealed.

"So, he killed Cutler's sister. Did he throw her overboard?" interjected Von-Baer.

"Quiet, my poodle. Let Werner tell us the gory details," she scolded.

"He approached her from behind, but then he heard footsteps, so he retreated into the darkness beside a bulkhead and hidden by the radar mast until the footsteps faded; but they didn't. Evidently, some Asian guy in a wig approached her. Bauer said she appeared to know the man, and called out to him." Werner took another sip of wine, while Delegate Frau Uebering and Von-Baer sat there, quietly engrossed.

"Bauer said the girl was a stunner, but had dressed for the weather. She had a thick, white, hand-knitted sweater on, which made her look in the early stages of pregnancy. Bauer noticed this because he said he would have had a small pang of guilt if he had to kill a baby as well."

"Bauer wouldn't feel guilty if he killed a kindergarten full of kids," Von-Baer stated.

"How many times do I have to tell you, liebling..." the delegate reprimanded.

"Word for word, Bauer said the guy flicked out his right hand and connected with the tip of her nose, and the next thing she was out cold on the deck. He then ripped out a chunk of hair from her head. Within a few moments, her white Aran sweater was deep-red and oozing with blood."

"The Asian guy killed her?" the delegate said, in complete surprise.

"Bauer said the man heard a noise from further down the deck, and quick as a flash she was gone over the side, all this in less than a minute."

"Bruce Lee must have been covered in blood," interposed Von-Baer. This time the delegate just gave him the look a mother gives a naughty child.

"The guy crossed within a metre of Bauer, who was ready with his knife should he be discovered. The Asian pulled out a hose from the bulkhead, went back to the spot, and turned it on himself and the blood stain. Moments later no blood, no crime scene. He then replaced the hose and was gone."

"Why would someone else want to kill her? Had Cutler upset another outfit?" the delegate asked.

"Who knows? But Bauer said we should have hired him; he was that quick."

"Couldn't be that good if he didn't know he was being watched," Von-Baer stated.

"The darkness, noise of the sea and the wind. Bauer said he wouldn't have known if someone were standing next to him with his cock out," Werner cut in.

"So, what did Bauer do then?" Von-Baer asked, ignoring the delegate's look of distaste.

"All this took place the day Cutler set his trap in Bayern for us. Bauer heard from Roderick Friedman by text what had transpired to us. He didn't know if I was alive or dead but decided to stick to the plan and go after Cutler's parents."

"Remind me not to get on the wrong side of you!" Von-Baer said, somewhat jokingly.

"It's not Werner you need to be worried about, leibling," the delegate ventured, losing patience with his constant interruptions.

"Bauer left the ship at Juneau on the next tender, by a stroke of fate so did Cutler's parents. Frantic after the news their daughter was missing, presumed overboard. The next day, Mrs Cutler was transferred to the hospital, evidently in deep shock. Two days later Cutler turned up at the hospital.

With a little financial persuasion, Bauer discovered that an air ambulance was going to airlift the sedated Mrs Cutler and her husband back to Seattle. Bauer assumed the parents and Cutler would be traveling together.

The plane was easy to get to. He cut a hole in the fuel line and patched it with artificial skin spray, the type you would use on scratches and grazes. The skin would hold at rest, but it was only a matter of time before the skin would rupture and the fuel would leak onto the hot engine, which of course it did. And goodbye Mr and Mrs Cutler." Werner stopped again to take a sip of wine.

"And we know Cutler was not on the plane," the delegate deliberated.

"No, but he was out of the game. He was the major risk to our organization, but after his family's deaths, he left the service, and now runs a company looking for missing persons rather than counterfeiters. At least, tat's what I thought. I have some men tracking Richter in Scotland, and who should turn up? Cutler." Werner said, while showing the delegate of a grainy picture of Cutler.

Werner's mobile telephone rang. "Speak," he ordered, and listened intently before continuing.

"Take the shot, fuck the money," Werner mechanical voice commanded.

Both Delegate Frau Uebering and Von-Baer turned towards Werner in expectation.

"Looks like we have located Cutler and Richter. We traced them to Newcastle in the UK, where he had picked up a passport. Richter will be trying to leave the country. It appears Cutler or one of his men took out Falco Jager." Werner took a much needed sip of wine to ease his throat.

"What nationality was the passport?" the delegate inquired.

"American."

"What information did you get out of the forger?" she pressed.

"None. He is well connected and guarded. We did have access to his assistant, he gave us the names on the passport. He also has gone missing," Werner said wearily, as all the talking took a toll on his voice.

"It appears Cutler know what he is doing," she suggested.

"I agree. That is why we have covered the regional airports within a 150-mile radius. They are too astute to go through the bigger airports, so we covered Leeds Bradford and Liverpool airports. That was Lothar on the phone; he has located them in Liverpool Airport," Werner informed them.

"Where are they heading?" questioned Von-Baer.

"Seems they are hopping across to Shannon in Ireland, and from there back to the States, I presume. But he will not get on the plane. Lothar has a vantage point on a factory roof adjoining the airport. The airport loads its passengers by stairs, so each person has to walk in front of the aircraft to board, and Lothar has a clear view over the staging area," Werner explained.

"Hence take the shot," the delegate replied.

What Werner had overlooked when he and Bauer put together the Kurdish team of minders together was that while they were experts in guarding a person, they were not professional all-round security specialists. When Werner took his weekly boat ride, the men went with him. They relied on a security system in the house that had been locally fitted. They did not sweep the house for cameras or microphone bugs; they just made sure no one approached their boss.

Philip Cortez, the Antonio Banderas lookalike Cutler had investigating Werner's gang, had known Werner's whereabouts for several weeks. He had researched all Werner's associates, and with the help of some of his well-placed contacts, and the support of Fabienne Asper, he had soon discovered that Bauer, a well-known associate, had travelled through France and Italy, boarded a ferry to Greece and then onto Kos, and had entered Turkey through Bodrum in a Winnebago, which, he assumed, correctly, contained the hidden Werner.

Once Cortez had observed Werner's routine, it was simple to gain access to the villa and the surrounding areas, such as the pool and gardens. Cortez had planted microphone spy cameras no bigger than the head of a pencil around the outside area, and microphones around the building.

Cortez had listened to every word that Werner, Delegate_Frau Uebering, and Von-Baer had spoken.

He heard them discussing Cutler's demise.

Cortez had to warn Cutler, but kept on getting an 'unobtainable' tone. Cutler had turned his mobile to flight mode.

chapter twenty-five

Cutler had ensured that all three of them—Richter, Hoagie, and himself—had booked in separately onto the Shannon flight. He routed Hoagie through Miami via Chicago and booked a separate direct flight for himself to leave an hour later, landing in Miami an hour earlier. He would reconnoitre the Miami airport before Richter and Hoagie arrived.

Cutler planned to keep Richter for a couple of days in the Everglades before resettling him in Salt Lake City, Utah. Even Richter would be hard-pressed to get himself in trouble in the Mormon state.

Cutler was on edge. He had taken every conceivable precaution to get Richter out of Europe, but every well-laid plan has weak links, and the flights out of the UK were his. All airports had pinch points, somewhere everyone had to congregate at check-in.

Hoagie went into John Lennon Airport's departure terminal first. The terminal had departures and arrivals in the same terminus, situated on opposite sides. He scanned the area, and could see several suspicious persons, but then there were suspicious people in every terminal. Some moving drugs, some moving money, and then some just arriving or departing with more cigarettes than the allowance; they always looked the most conspicuous. But there appeared no ex-military types among them.

Lothar Gottschalk was an albino; he stood out from the crowd, never a good attribute of a hired assassin. Sometimes he dyed his hair and eyebrows and wore coloured contact lenses; sometimes he just wore hooded jackets and a scarf to cover his features. Today he wore a black fleece hoodie and black moleskin trousers. In fact, it was the same outfit as yesterday, as he had not moved off the roof in two days.

Werner had covered three airports that he second-guessed Richter may try to leave from. Werner may have lost his voice, but he had lost none of the acumen that had made him one of the most feared criminal ganglords in Germany, if not in Europe.

Lothar Gottschalk had chosen his site well. There were several factories on the peripheral of the airport: one overlooking the departure area of the airport. The factory-made car seats for Ford and other car manufacturers. Times had been hard for the motor industry, and the company had reduced security staff to one guard and reduced the night shift to a handful of employees. There was no closed-circuit television, which was always an open invitation to a thief or a killer.

Lothar waited until the guard had gone to the toilet and just ducked under the security barrier and jogged to the edge of the factory with his large, black rucksack on his back. There was a ladder with a hooped guard around it fixed against the side of the plant that led to the roof. There was no build-up of debris from the soles of rubber boots on the ladder, so Lothar assumed the access ladder was used very infrequently, and probably just for maintenance.

Despite Werner's orders, Lothar had a minion, Ralph, drive over from Germany, bringing his beloved German Blaser 93 rifle. If Ralph had been caught coming through customs at the Eurotunnel he would simply do the time, as to speak out against one of Werner's men was a death sentence, no matter what prison you were in. As it happened, countries without borders seemed to assist in the transportation of weapons, and his car was not checked.

Lothar had removed the Blaser 93 and had had it modified so he could break it down and place it, along with his ammunition, in the black rucksack. Lothar also had a thermos of coffee, US Army food packs that self-heated, water, adult diapers, and a thin raincoat, as it would undoubtedly rain here.

Ralph had been given a picture of Richter and had settled in at the small coffee shop near to the departure check-in. The first day he had stayed from 0500, which denoted the first check-in of the day, and stayed till 2130. He would then sleep in his car in the parking lot, before starting again at 0500 the next day. It was 2000 hours when he spotted Richter booking in. He was flying Aer Lingus to Shannon, due to leave at 2200. Once Ralph had confirmed the timings, he contacted Lothar over the shortwave radio.

Lothar moved in readiness a further twenty metres down the roof, which would give him a clear view of the stairs leading to flight number EI016 to Shannon. He set the tripod on the roof line and attached the German Blaser 93 onto the tripod, which was barely discernible at ground level.

The passengers began to decant from the departure lounge and were ushered on a yellow-lined, dedicated path they had to follow to the aircraft steps.

It was dark, with bright lights illuminating the path to the plane, and the brightness in the area took a toll on Lothar's night vision, even through the scope. He did not have time to scan the multitude of passengers and concentrated on the one entrance at the front of the aircraft.

Lothar hit the dial on the mobile phone, connected immediately to Werner, and received the kill order.

First Hoagie walked up the aircraft steps and deftly had a backward look to see if anything was out of the ordinary. He could see Richter about twelve passengers back, and Cutler another ten or so behind Richter.

Cutler walked slowly, letting other passengers by as he scanned the area in more depth. Nothing out of the ordinary, he thought, but something nagged him about the area he had just risk rated. Something in his evaluation worried him, so he took a step out of line and scanned the area again. It was a light that did not fit in with the standard airport lights. It appeared right on the edge of the airport, maybe outside the airport, he thought.

Then the mist disappeared. He knew what it was troubling him. It was a laser guide used to fix on targets. He looked up ahead and saw the red spot of the laser jumping from one passenger to another, scanning the passengers.

Cutler was bemused; how could the sniper ever hope to identify his targeted victim from the back of his head? He looked up and saw Richter starting to ascend the aircraft stairs. Now he knew how he was going to identify Richter.

The sniper or help had been in the airport all the time. Somehow, they had managed to rub an illuminated marker on the rear of Richter's coat. Cutler could barely see it, but under a scope it would be as a large bull's-eye illuminating the target.

Cutler pulled off his own jacket while shouting at Richter to hit the floor of the stairs. Richter could just about hear the warning and his name above the idling engines. He did the last thing Cutler had wanted; he turned to face the direction of the shouted warning, rather than follow Cutler's orders.

The force of the bullet caused the same effect as a melon exploding. Men, women, and children on the stairwell were left splattered in Richter's brain matter. The energy of the bullet lifted Richter over the stairwell and onto the rim of the engine that hung below the wing.

Up to that stage, only Richter had been a victim, but pandemonium broke out. Passengers pushed and shoved, trying to get off the stairwell. Other passengers sat in window seats, seeing the carnage, believing it a possible terror attack, and started to run from their positions while shouting instructions to the families and friends sitting beside them. This added to the turmoil and chaos on the stairs.

Passengers fell from the stairs; the smaller ones and children were walked over or crushed in the stampede on the stairs.

Cutler tried his best to pull out the injured and dying from beneath the melee and gave first aid to those that required it most. Within three minutes of the shot, a further eleven passengers were either dead or dying of their injuries. Another twenty-two had severe injuries, of which ten were life-changing injuries.

Lothar broke down his weapon, cling-filled the several diapers, and removed any evidence of himself from the roof. He then turned on hoses located on the roof to wash away any DNA and climbed down the outer building stairwell.

Lother pressed a button on his mobile phone and the small detonator he had placed earlier ignited some fuel that had spilt out from a tank from a bonded area some several hundred metres away; the flames leapt high into the sky within seconds. Lothar watched the security guard run toward the fire, and then he exited the factory complex unseen.

Ralph picked up Lothar on the airport perimeter road and headed away from the airport as convoy after convoy of vehicles with flashing sirens headed toward it.

Cutler recovered quickly from the initial shock and knew immediately that Richter had not survived. He quickly scanned the area looking for Hoagie, but there was so much confusion, and dead and injured bodies lying around, he was unable to locate him. Police swarmed the area and removed the rest of the passengers and Cutler.

Cutler waited in the airport at first, then found out which hospital the injured had been transferred to. He went by taxi to each hospital but still had no news on Hoagie. The next morning Cutler received news that shocked and stunned him. Fabienne hacked into the UK police computer, she had accessed the file on the identification of the dead and injured from the tragic flight. All in all, twenty-one souls were lost. Hoagie had been identified by his DNA. Trapped beneath his body was a small child called Omar.

Fabienne unearthed several statements saying that they had seen the young boy fall at the bottom of the stairwell, and a large man had thrown himself over the boy to stop the sprawling, dying mass of humanity from crushing the child underfoot. Hoagie had used his body as a cage to protect Omar.

It had taken over forty passengers to trample over Hoagie before his neck had broken. In all he had seventy-two fractures; Omar had a broken arm from the initial fall.

Cutler felt proud of his agent and upset at the loss of his colleague and employee. A fallen soldier, brave to the end.

chapter twenty-six

Nathan Colton was as good as his word; he arrived nine hours after his initial phone call with Tuck. He boarded the first flight out of Nassau and touched down less than an hour later in Miami. Colton rented a Mercedes convertible; he refused to drive anything other than a Mercedes or BMW. He admired the German technology and the extra room in the interior to fit his bulk into.

Robert Stahmer had been correct in his assessment of the two men in the car parked fifty yards down the road from the Hilton residence. They surely did not look like they were there to spread the word of God; but more than likely to be undertaking the devil's work. Stahmer was relieved by Tuck, who parked a bit further up the street and out of the pair's line of sight.

Several hours after Stahmer had departed, Nathan Colton knocked lightly on the passenger window and entered the vehicle beside him and passed on greetings and pleasantries. Tuck went on to give him a full briefing on the case and the evidence they had acquired.

"They've been there all night in that black Buick, haven't moved, just watching the house," Tuck said.

"If they've been there all night, they're up to no good," Colton said in his rustic Bahamian accent.

"During school hours there are several patrol cars circulating, with vehicle identity cameras operating. Last thing you want," Tuck stated.

"Makes you think they know the patrol hours. Professional surveillance, possible hit team."

Just as Colton finished his sentence, Mick Hilton exited the house.

"You'd better go now, Tuck. I think they're going to take him out with the car." Colton urged.

Tuck pressed the gas pedal and moved the car towards Mick Hilton. Several seconds later, the target car pulled out and followed Mick Hilton at a short distance.

"The kid has to cross the road at the intersection to get the school bus; look, see the other kids down there? They're going to nail him when he crosses," Colton predicted.

Tuck increased the pressure on the gas at the same time the other car accelerated as Mick Hilton began to cross the street. Mick Hilton looked around to see the two cars veering towards him. He had been alerted by the second car continually using its horn to warn him. Mick Hilton froze there for a second.

Tuck's car was now alongside the Buick, which sped towards the deer trapped in its headlights. The passenger window exploded suddenly as the bullet passed through the glass and embedded itself into Tuck's headrest.

"These fuckers mean business!" shouted Colton, as tiny shards of glass cut his face.

Tuck side-shunted the vehicle, causing it to change its course slightly. The slight movement in the Buick caused its wheels to scrape along the kerb, and Tuck's vehicle bounced off and he redirected back at the Buick with more force.

The Buick hit the kerb again, the force flipping it onto the empty sidewalk. Tuck yanked the wheel over to the right and hit the brakes. They stopped two yards ahead of the Hilton boy, and no more than a couple of feet to his side, Mick Hilton stood frozen to the spot in abject fear.

Tuck exited the vehicle and immediately ran over to the Buick as one of the assailants was dragging himself out of the upturned car, gun in hand. Quickly and efficiently, he stamped down on the gunman's hand and snapped his wrist. He kicked the gun onto the sewer drain edge where it wobbled, then fell in. Tuck punched him once rendering the assailant unconscious.

Colton grabbed the Hilton boy and threw him into the back of his car, Tuck swerved the car back in the direction they had just come from. At the top of the hill Colton exited and closed the door, Tuck pressed down the lock button in case the boy suddenly bolted. He need not have bothered, as Mick Hilton just sat there dumbstruck.

Tuck gave Colton the address of the safe house MIDAS had leased in the area. He followed Tuck back to the address in his Mercedes.

The safe house was a bungalow on the outskirts of Palm Springs.

"Sit," Tuck barked.

"Are you kidnapping me?"

"Look, kid, just shut up and listen to me. You haven't been kidnapped; we just saved your life. The two guys in the Buick just tried to kill you," Tuck informed him.

"But why?" came the stuttered response.

"Don't be stupid, kid. You know why," Colton interjected.

"Anytime you want to leave, you're free to do so, but you'll be dead within the day, you understand that, kid?" Tuck explained.

Mick Hilton just nodded, hoping this was nothing to do with the incident on-board the *Large Pink Boat*, but deep down he knew it was.

"We know you were involved in Don Ross's death. What is more, we have proof from a ring we repossessed with your friend Bernard Rothhelm's DNA on it," Tuck qualified.

"Are you the police?" Mick Hilton inquired.

"We are not the police; we work for an organization called MIDAS that investigates suspicious deaths at sea. And Don Ross's death on the *Large Pink Boat* was suspicious. Do you know we have statements from an Egyptian couple that saw you beating Don up?" detailed Tuck.

"And your friend knows we know. Guess what Daddy is doing to protect him?" Colton declared.

"Mr Rothhelm, Bernard's dad, tried to have me killed?" stuttered Mick Hilton.

"He surely did and would have, had not my friend and I stepped in to save you. And as soon as you leave here, he is going to try again; maybe this time when you are with your mom. As I told you, we know you were involved in the killing of Don Ross, but we don't know if you were dragged into this. We don't believe you were the principal instigator," Tuck continued while the blood drained away from Mick Hilton's face.

"First one to come clean will get the chance to turn state's evidence and get a much-reduced sentence," Colton interjected.

"Reduced sentence; that means prison. I can't go inside!" Hilton began to cry.

"You killed a man; you don't get to walk away from that, kid. But you will not get the death penalty, and you will be young enough when you get out to still have a family. You may even get a light sentence for cooperating, depends on the state's attorney."

"My Mom will go ape,"

"If Rothhelm gets there first, your life is over. Make no mistake that right now his family knows what went on this morning and are already in conference with their attorneys." Tuck spelled out his options as he turned on a recording device on the table.

"It started as a joke. Bernie saw this man having a cigarette at the back of the boat. We were the only ones around, 'because there was some special show going on and nearly everyone was there. Bernie was bored, and we went looking for some fun," Mick Hilton explained, as both Colton and Tuck listened intently.

"Bernie asked the guy for a smoke and he said to come back in about five years. Bernie picked up a stone ashtray from the table like he was offering it to the guy and then: whack, he hit the guy over the head with it! The guy went down like a sack of potatoes, and Bernie started to kick him. He shouted for me to join in and I kicked him once," Mick Hilton said quietly, the shame rising up in his voice.

"Bernie told me to get the cigarettes, and as I bent down to get them, the guy's eyes were wide open. I knew he was dead, and I told Bernie," Hilton indicated.

"Had you boys been drinking or doing drugs?" Colton asked.

"Couple of beers. Bernie was always on the coke, so I'm pretty sure he had a line or two that night," Mick Hilton acknowledged.

"How did Bernie lose the ring?"

"He didn't miss it until the next day. He thought it must have come off when he hit the dead guy with the ashtray. Said it was a bit loose on his finger. We did not go looking for it in case anyone was watching the area.

"My boss has given me the name of a state attorney he knows in the Palm Springs area. We are going to see her, and you are going to tell her exactly what you just said. It's your only chance," Tuck told him. "We'll get in touch with your mother and have her meet us there."

Once Tuck had contacted Carly Bryce, they were in her plush offices in an hour. She had known Cutler for many years and had hidden away her feelings for him for as long as she could remember. They had had a drunken one-night stand several years earlier; Cutler had unknowingly taken her virginity. It was one night of passion and a lasting memory. She would always secretly wish for a second encounter.

Cutler had told her several months earlier about the Don Ross situation, she had laid out the minimum standards required to put forward a case. When he hit that standard, she would be more than happy to assist them.

Well, the Hilton boy's evidence more than met the minimum requirements. Cutler was right; Don Ross had been murdered, and as both boys lived in the Palm Springs area, it was up to her to follow the case up.

Carly had to settle some egos in the police department who wanted to arrest Tuck and Colton for fleeing a crime scene but were persuaded that they had no choice but to go. Several of the officers knew Colton and admired and respected the African American for his work several years earlier on a DEA case in the area.

Two hours after Mick Hilton gave his statement to Carly Bryce; Rothhelm Senior, Bernard Rothhelm, and two attorneys from the most prestigious firm in the city turned up at the district attorney's office wanting to give a statement.

Predictably, they blamed the Hilton boy and went on to describe how Bernard had been terrified of him, and that was why he had not come forward. The attorneys wanted a plea bargain, with no prison time for Bernard, just community service. And Rothhelm foolishly said he would donate a large sum to the local police foundation.

Rothhelm Senior would not get his wish. The interview was stopped inside thirty minutes as two police officers arrived at Carly's office and arrested Rothhelm Senior on conspiracy to murder. Evidently the driver of the Buick came around in the hospital under armed guard. He had decided that twenty-five years in a high-security prison was not for him, and quickly did a deal to turn state's evidence and receive only twelve years for his participation.

Rothhelm Senior liked to act as the big gangster but did not have the organization or respect that the likes of the Werner's of this world attract. Money was not enough to sort this out; MIDAS had seen to that.

It would probably be years of court cases and appeals before Rothhelm Senior was finally sentenced; however, Bernard Rothhelm was not in the same situation.

Carly Bryce restarted the interview with Bernard Rothhelm and only one attorney as the other scuttled off, following the shackled Rothhelm Senior.

"Young man, we don't believe a word you're saying. We have a full statement from Mick Hilton as to your involvement. We also have the DNA of Don Ross on a ring owned by you and found on the ship, not to mention statements from the Yacoubs, who saw you. We are now contacting them to bring them back to the States to formally identify you. In short, we have you; all the evidence points to you. Hilton will be going to prison, but not nearly as long as you are. I'm afraid you'll not be going anywhere for a very long time," avowed Carly.

Bernard Rothhelm was completely dumbstruck for the first time in his life.

"Do something!" he commanded his attorney.

"We need some time, Miss Bryce, if you would," requested his attorney.

Carly Bryce returned to the interview room after a ten-minute break.

"Given his tender age, Miss Bryce, what is your best offer?" requested the attorney.

"Full confession, manslaughter, fifteen to twenty years, first five in a youth offender's correctional facility," Carly stated.

"I can't do fifteen years in prison!" Bernard Rothhelm spoke several octaves higher than normal.

"You'll be doing forty years to life if we go to court. You'll be retired before you see daylight if you don't agree to this in the next five minutes," asserted Carly.

The attorney nodded his agreement.

"What are you doing?" young Rothhelm screeched.

"We were taken on to give you the best advice. My best advice is to make the deal. Your father may not like it, but he has his own problems now, and they have a rock-solid case that even I can't get you out of," the attorney declared.

Carly eventually got through to Tuck Walters, who had returned to the office in Everglade City.

"Hi, Tuck, Carly Bryce from the DA's office. I've been trying to get in touch with Cutler but can't seem to reach him with the news."

"He's over in the UK doing some business at the moment, Miss Bryce."

"Well, I was hoping to give him the good news, but I'm sure you can relay it to him. We got them both; Hilton, and more importantly Rothhelm, who has now admitted to his part. Congratulations on giving us a rock solid case, Tuck," Carly confirmed happily.

As soon as he finished the conversation, he hung up the phone and went in search of Cheryl. Tuck discovered her on the back porch, sitting in the rocking chair with her laptop on her knee. She had been booking the hotels and travel for Robert Stahmer and Ghislaine.

"We got them, Cheryl," Tuck said, with a big, boyish grin.

Cheryl looked up, startled. "Got who?"

"We got Don's killers. Both boys have admitted their guilt, and they are staring at long stretches inside. You were right, Cheryl, it was Hilton and Rothhelm," he stated.

The laptop was sent heavenwards as she jumped up out of the rocking chair.

"We really got them?" she pleaded.

"We really got them, honey," Tuck replied lovingly.

She fell into his arms, and the years of anguish poured forth as she cried and cried and did not stop sobbing in Tuck's arms for over an hour.

chapter twenty-seven

Sebastian had wanted to leave Seattle. He had been sent home after the Port Stanley authorities in the Falklands could not come up with enough evidence to hold him any longer. He had been excluded from leaving the Falklands for over a month. The desire to leave was greater than his constant desire to kill, and he abstained during that period.

He had long ago run out of body hair, and if he were to fulfill the overwhelming desire that was with him day and night, it would be too dangerous to pursue his needs in his home city. He needed to be back traveling the world.

At first Sebastian was shocked to find he had been allocated to re-join *Classical Canta Libra* in Genoa. He had never done a double stint on the same ship; generally they rotated him around the fleet. Sebastian was sure the crew members would know he was under investigation. He hoped that may of the crew had been rotated or on leave.

Sebastian was unaware how much pressure the board of directors had been under to resolve what had occurred in the lifeboat. The bad press and television coverage from the families of the deceased were affecting bookings, and this would lead to a loss of profit and stability of the company—and board members. Most crew members, and the team of artists and musicians, had either been rotated back to the ship, or remained and had leave deferred until after the investigation.

The board had their own security team and investigators, but had taken advice to bring in a set of specialists to avoid accusations of a cover-up. They knew and accepted the risks this would bring, as the investigation would be out of their control. But regardless of the outcome, it had to be better than the negative press they now found themselves exposed to.

After several weeks of identifying potential investigators, Robert Stahmer's name had been put forward by Sean Wright, the director of marketing, who in a previous life had worked for Scotland Yard as head of public relations. He knew that Stahmer now worked for a company called MIDAS, a company the board had never heard of before. But investigations into the managing director, Max Cutler, all came back with glowing reports and reliable recommendations.

Initial contact had been made by Sean Wright through the MIDAS Geneva office, and details had been passed on by Fabienne Asper to Cutler.

The board agreed to Cutler's request that all employees and contractors who had been on the ship at that time would be available in the same location for an interview. They set about revising holidays, rest periods and ship allocations to bring the entire crew back again to the *Classical Canta Libra*. Only two were missing; one had died of cirrhosis the week before, and the other had been injured in a car crash and was unable to fly.

Sebastian re-joined the ship, and realised after several hours that something was amiss. The entire detail of the previous crew had been reassembled, an event that none of them had ever seen before. You could work with the same cruise line operator for life and not see a crew mate for years due to rotation.

Before too long, it became apparent that they had been gathered together intentionally, as the captain gave them the news that there was an investigation team on board who would be joining them on the week-long cruise from Genoa to Istanbul.

Prior to the Liverpool Airport incident and Hoagie's death, Cutler had assigned Stahmer as lead investigator, and Ghislaine Lyman as his translator, due to the multitude of nationalities among the crew. Cutler realized that most would have English as a second language, but some of the ship's maintenance crew and seamen, and some of the housekeeping staff, would have limited or no English.

During the flight to Genoa, Ghislaine refreshed her knowledge of Filipino, as Fabienne's research indicated that forty percent of the crew were from the Philippines. This was mainly due to their hard-working nature, but also, they were some of the cheapest labour on the planet.

Stahmer and Ghislaine landed at 9 am, and the *Classical Canta Libra* was not due to leave its berth in Genoa until 6 pm the following day. The chauffeured Mercedes met them at the main entrance to the airport, and was soon navigating the narrow streets to their hotel. No sooner had they settled into their lush single rooms than Sean Wright called from reception.

Without delay, they were once again circumnavigating the streets of Genoa in the same Mercedes, and under a bright blue and cloudless sky they entered the dock area. They proceeded into the depths of the dockyard until they arrived at a shed; to Stahmer, it looked like an old storage shed that had not been used for many years due to the lack of repair.

They entered the dimly lit building, and Stahmer could see it was basically a ship repair facility used for stripping down parts of marine machinery for reuse on vessels in the fleet of cruise ships owned by the cruise line. Propped up by a wooden jib in the middle of the building was the burnt-out wreckage of what was left of the lifeboat.

Although the roof had had transparent sheeting built into it at intervals, this had long ago become unfit for purpose, after years of damage from acidic rainfall, eliminating the light they once offered.

Stahmer asked Sean Wright to organize some task lighting so he could carefully inspect the wretched craft before him. Within a few minutes, several high-powered halogen lamps were put in place, and the area around the craft was instantly illuminated.

Stahmer had brought along his investigation kit, which included flashlights, evidence containers, a measuring laser, nylon bags, evidence tags, labels, disposable gloves, camera, tape recorder, video recorder, dust mask and respirator, and two white paper overalls for Ghislaine and himself.

Over years of investigating incidents, Stahmer had developed a fixed routine. First, he made a preliminary scene assessment to determine the extent of the damage, proceeding from areas of least damage to areas of greater damage.

Over the next few hours, Stahmer sketched, photographed, and videotaped what was left of the lifeboat. He spoke into a tape recorder of his findings, and Ghislaine took down specialized instructions that would be used by Fabienne in analysing the data. Stahmer's skills only went so far, and like any investigation, it would take a team of experts to get anywhere near the truth.

For six hours, Stahmer clambered in and out of the boat. From the case he had brought along with him, he extracted a laser distance measuring device, amongst other vital investigation equipment, the most important of which were the large and small sterilized nylon bags and containers. He placed samples into the bags and containers of fibreglass, engine parts, and the most crucial piece of evidence that was recovered: the remains of a flare from *inside* the engine compartment.

"I thought there had been a previous investigation into this fire?" Stahmer asked, directing the question to Sean Wright.

"There was a cursory investigation. I'm the first to admit, not an entirely thorough investigation," he said.

"Well, that may well be an exaggeration. Most of the evidence for surface fire has been lost in the sinking and subsequent retrieval of the lifeboat. But there's still evidence of the craft that is intact. On the documents you have provided, the only objective evidence is the post-mortems, which show all the deaths are down to smoke inhalation and burns. Written descriptions of the craft are incomplete; there are no sketches noting burn patterns or ignition point. There is neither photographic evidence nor any meaningful scientific analysis."

"We are quite aware of the shortcomings of the previous investigation and apologize for the lack of the evidence you have discussed. But that is why you are here, Mr Stahmer, to get to the bottom of this," Sean Wright explained.

"Sherlock Holmes once said that many types of investigations are susceptible to prejudgment, but few as often as fire scene investigations. They are destructive by nature, and basically destroy the very evidence needed to identify the cause. However, compound this with the lack of care by the initial investigators, which may have caused cross-contamination. Items may have been removed and not logged down, and the clothes, or what was left of them, have been destroyed!" Stahmer retorted.

Sean Wright reddened slightly. "Can you deduct anything from what you have seen, Mr Stahmer?"

"Well, it's far too early to tell, and I have to have these items shipped back to Geneva for forensic analysis before I can conclusively give you an answer. However, I can tell you I have located where the fire started, and the most likely ignition source. I found tiny pieces, that resemble parts of what appears to be a parachute flare, embedded in metal. Also very telling is that the extinguishers are still in place, meaning no one had time to fight the fire; it was catastrophic and quick. I'm pretty certain this is an act of sabotage, rather than an electrical or cigarette fire, as your internal investigation reported, so we're probably looking at multiple cases of homicide."

"How do you know the flare wasn't set off accidently and this caused the fire?"

"Because the metal the flare was embedded in was the interior of the fuel tank."

"In the fuel tank?" Sean Wright asked, incredulously.

"Exactly. Diesel does not ignite readily, if at all. It is the vapor which ignites; but when it burns, it burns fiercely. You state you only have a minimum amount of diesel in the tanks, to minimize fires, but it is exactly what you should not do, as you have maximum room for the vapours to ignite. The only reason we have anything left of the boat is that when the plastic in the hull melted, the craft sank quickly, dowsing the flames."

"The flares we use have to be manually set up and connected for them to operate."

"The flares you use have a switch on the bottom, which releases a cap and completes a circuit. If the circuit is set a millimetre apart it will not fire, but if you rig it so they come into contact, you have an ignition source. Even the movements of the waves beneath the boat could set off the flare. But like I said, it is a hypothesis at the moment, and we can test this once we get some physical evidence back to our laboratories in London."

Sean Wright sighed, as this was obviously not going to be good news, and he was due to report to the board that very evening, followed by updates each night as the investigation continued.

Following the discussion with Wright, Stahmer patiently laid out all the evidence on the shed floor, and after instructing Ghislaine in the art of photography, she catalogued the parts to ensure a chain of evidence was completed. Stahmer crept back into the craft again to study the smoke patterns on the areas of the hull which remained intact.

Later that evening, Stahmer had just begun to devour his stuffed mushroom appetizer. Ghislaine, who had opted for the calamari, handed him the mobile phone that had vibrated to life in her small black bag. Stahmer listened intently to what Cutler was telling him, and once the conversation ended, so did his appetite, as he moved his plate aside.

It was clear to Ghislaine that the news was not good, but she had not expected it to be so bad.

During the first months of MIDAS, all the team had gathered and had shared a large riverfront house in Everglade City. They had all trained together, devised the protocols together, and eaten each meal together. Undeniable friendships had been forged within this month, and in one or two cases, even more.

The shock of Hoagie's demise brought Ghislaine to tears, as she sat at the table, and Stahmer related what little he knew. She shook her head, as the waiter offered to pour her more of the finest of clarets. Stahmer stood and put his arm around her in a fatherly manner and escorted her out quickly from the prying eyes of the other diners.

Drawn from the lack of sleep and fountain of tears for a man she had only just come to know, she tried to figure out why Hoagie's death had hit her so hard. She felt MIDAS was a family, it was like losing a brother.

By morning, she had shed her last tear, as she joined Stahmer in the Mercedes. They headed with their suitcases to the *Classical Canta Libra*. They sat in silence on the short journey to the ship, Ghislaine reminiscing about her brother, and Stahmer thinking deeply about his departed, beloved wife.

Once aboard the vessel, they were met by the captain, who had been informed he was to give them every assistance. He introduced Stahmer and Ghislaine to the officers first, and then several mass briefings and introductions to the rest of the crew, hospitality staff, and entertainers.

Sebastian had attended the final briefing of the day and looked up at the stage in the theatre at the investigators. His first thought was not about the net being trawled too close to home, as he was certain he had covered his steps. His mind drifted, he thought how lovely the female investigator's hair shone so temptingly with the backlight, and how he would dearly love to rip it out, a strand at a time. But it was pure fantasy, he knew; he would have to curtail his desires, at least until he was off this ship. He was also aware that inviting outside investigators onto the ship was a first; it was the general agreement among the crew that someone must have sabotaged the lifeboat.

Sebastian would have to find another cruise line to work, no matter the outcome of the investigation. He was too close to this, and investigations were not good for business.

Jan Bjork, the ship's Norwegian captain, was as good as his word. He allocated the pair of investigators the unused conference room as their hub for interviews. They sketched out timelines and spider graphs to lay down a basis to start the investigation. All their notes, drawings, speadsheets went back via secure laptops and satellite phones to Fabienne back in Geneva.

Standard procedure for the closed-circuit television revealed that they only recorded in certain areas, and on a twenty-four-hour re-record system. Other cameras were for monitoring in real time, and the captain admitted this was very seldom, as the mainly ex-army security staff had other duties to undertake. The captain did, however, have the foresight to ensure the digital images caught on the CCTV after the lifeboat incident from all recordable cameras was saved to an encrypted file on his computer, which he now gave to Stahmer.

Stahmer copied the images to his laptop and uploaded the unedited file to Fabienne's master computer in Geneva, for it would be she who analysed the pictures. The time-consuming interviews of crew and officers took days. Each night, Stahmer uploaded the oral recorded statements of the day from the crew. Fabienne had created a programme that would transcribe the interviews in seconds and crossmatch the statements to compare any inconsistencies across everyone's statements. Stahmer had established that the lifeboat could only have been sabotaged the night before it exploded. It had been used as a tender the previous afternoon, and had been under constant watch the following morning, as the ship's painters had been plying their trade on balustrades beside the lifeboat station.

Fabienne gave her software programme the name *Speedy Gonzales*, after a cartoon character she had watched as a child. The software had been adjusted by Fabienne to identify where a person had been the previous evening from the individual's statements, cross-reference the person's alibi to others that had been in the same area, and then cross-match to the CCTV, as well as to each and every person's photograph, as supplied by Basmati at the beginning of the investigation. It took more time at Stahmer's end to upload the files than it took Speedy Gonzales to work its magic. Speedy was always the fastest person around, hence the name for the software.

Stahmer knew he would not discover who the perpetrator was in that week. His scope for the week was to interview all 1,025 employees and artists. The captain wanted to restrict interviews to ten minutes per person, Stahmer rejected the time restraints. Both he and Ghislaine worked nineteen hours a day, interviewing and compiling the statements, and after dinner was brought to them in the conference room, Ghislaine would use her translator app on her iPad to confirm the meaning of some of the Latvian and Filipino words that she had not clearly understood during the interviews. Stahmer would upload the files. The last job was to download statements of the interviews Ghislaine had completed.

By the time they had berthed back at the home port of Genoa, they had only two more interviews to undertake, one of which was with Sebastian.

Stahmer found him intriguing and arrogant, as he switched between eight different languages to see if he could catch out the translator. Stahmer told him on four occasions to keep it in English to save time, but to no avail.

Most of the men they had interviewed had kept their gazes normally between Ghislaine's cleavage, but Sebastian was different; he seemed to look at her hair, Stahmer established, as the air conditioning blew strands back and forth across her face, and his eyes appeared to be following the flow.

But in the end, it was an interview like all the rest; fact finding. Kipling's five little soldiers: where, what, how, why and when.

Ghislaine did remark at the end of the interview that she found Sebastian strange, and his gaze uncomfortable, and commented that she thought he was wearing some kind of wig.

Sebastian's interview lasted one and a half hours. Like many others, he had been a little strange, but none of his answers pointed a finger directly at him. While he was listed as a person of interest , he joined a list of theirteen of his crew mates.

Stahmer and Ghislaine collected their interview notes and moved on to their next interviewee Ricky Villa, a dancer from Brazil, who neither looked at Ghislaine's hair or bust, just his own fingernails, his hands, and when possible, other parts of his body, to confirm his own beauty.

With their work on board complete, Stahmer and Ghislaine held a two-hour debriefing with Sean Wright and the captain, explaining that most of the work would now be undertaken in the Geneva office where they had compiled the data. With the help of Speedy Gonzales, they would now go through an elimination process. While making no promises to identify the perpetrator, they could certainly eliminate a good majority of the employees.

Stahmer informed Sean Wright that they had ruled out any involvement by the cruise passengers, as Fabienne had told them the previous night that the closed-circuit television images on one camera had been wiped. Secondly, the closed-circuit television room was deep in the bowels of the ship, and in staff-only areas, with a key or fob access only. It was someone who worked the *Classical Canta Libra* on board.

chapter twenty-eight

Several days after Hoagie was killed, Cutler had turned up, having sought solace in a bottle of bourbon and Cathy's bed in Seattle. Cutler had lost agents before, and no doubt would lose them again, but Hoagie's demise hit him hard, as he had taken him off the reservation. Cathy had put him on a plane to Miami and spoken with Cheryl to ensure he was picked dup at the airport. She worried he was about to regress to the months he spent grieving for his sister and parents. Her strategy was that his colleagues would be feeling upset, so he would have to pull himself together to support them.

Cutler felt as though he was six years old, as he sat uneasily in the soft leather chair. Cheryl Ross sat across the office from him, leaning forward, trying to understand the implications of what she had just heard. The atmosphere was dark and electric, which mirrored the weather that day in Everglade City.

The conversation had been long and drawn out. Cheryl had a hundred and one questions as to why Cutler had omitted to tell her he had carried on investigating the Werner affair after he had left the Secret Service. They were supposed to be partners, and partners do not act like that, she had reprimanded.

The matter of the set-up money for MIDAS was not mentioned, as Cutler did not want to involve her in any future litigation if it ever got out. Plus, he was taking enough flak for one day; deservedly, he thought. Cheryl's anger did not improve when he told her he had used the Geneva office to assist in surveillance.

Then his phone vibrated. He looked down at it and saw Cortez's identification appear on the phone. He looked at his phone and then glanced at Cheryl and shrugged his shoulders.

Cortez spoke only two words, "Code Blue." They had set up a code system beforehand. In essence, Code White was, 'I need you here quickly.' Code Green was, 'Everything is okay.' Code Blue was, 'Get here as fast as you can, and don't come alone.'

Cutler clicked off the phone just as the thunder and lightning filled the room, and the constant splatter of rain began to pour from the heavens.

"I know I haven't been totally honest, and I do regret that. I like to think I was protecting you from it. But after Hoagie, maybe I have been misleading myself, as well as everyone else."

"If you have an open case it is our case, not just yours. Do you think I would have tried to stop you?" Cheryl probed, during their first argument together.

"I accept that, but at the moment I have Cortez, and he needs help. That was what the phone call was about. And I am going to need assistance," Cutler replied hastily.

"Tuck?" she asked worriedly.

"I'm not stupid, Cheryl. I know you have a thing together, so maybe we both have been a little short on honesty. And no, not Tuck this time. I am going to take Manfred Shultz. No doubt I'm going to need you and Fabienne to help as well."

"Where and when do you need the flights from?" she asked in a calmer state.

"Need it today to Bodrum in Turkey via Munich, so I can brief Shultz on the flight," he responded while simultaneously texting Manfred Shultz to be ready for his first mission, today.

There was no mistaking Manfred Shultz as he walked towards Cutler in the departure lounge of the München Franz Josef Strauss Airport, named in memory of the former Bavarian Prime Minister. Shultz was straight-backed, and looked like a military officer in his white shirt, toffee-coloured trousers, black tie, and blazer. He looked much improved from the man Cutler had interviewed for the position previously.

For several hours, as they waited for the flight to Bodrum, they sipped espresso coffees and discussed updates on the Werner case. Cutler explained to Shultz that he was not aware of the reason for the Code Blue, as he and Cortez had agreed not to discuss anything over the phone, but stressed it must be a matter of urgency and importance.

The flight was short and uneventful, as was the short hop down to Bodrum, except for the turbulence generated by the mountains and sea that surround the airport. The pair exited the military-style airport building to be met by Cortez, who looked dishevelled and concerned.

Cortez had hired a nondescript white Seat, which was as anonymous as you could attain in Turkey, as they were everywhere. They drove the mountain pass route from Bodrum to Turkey, driving on steep, unkempt, potholed, narrow lanes, through olive groves and open quarries that supplied the materials for local road building and repairs in the area—just not the road they were on.

As they emerged atop the last mountain before their destination, both Shultz and Cutler were engrossed in the visage of beauty that lay several hundred metres below them. It was breathtaking; the curve of the bay, with the little town of Akbuk spread over sporadic enclaves around the bay, lapped by the warm turquoise sea, dotted with gulets and fishing boats.

Cortez stopped the car on a dirt track beside the lane, and the three emerged. Cortez pointed out the main town, with its minaret from the mosque the highest point in the town. Cortez looked to the south part of the bay.

"See the two villas high up on the hill, set behind the trees, and just down from the airport approach tower?" Cortez said.

Shultz and Cutler removed their sunglasses and strained their eyes in the brilliant sun, allowing a few seconds to cope with the flood of ultraviolet light.

"That's where our boy is. He has six Turkish minders and his German thug, Baer," Cortez reported.

"Six is a reasonable number," Shultz said.

"Bad news is, the other villa is occupied and the occupant has another four minders with her at all times, and a young attorney she is banging whenever she can, and she has diplomatic immunity."

Cutler turned around quickly. "You've identified the delegate, haven't you, Cortez?"

"Delegate Frau Uebering. She is as tight with Werner as a flea on a dog."

Cutler knew Cortez would have done his homework and was professional; he did not need to challenge his words as assumptions. Cortez would never say anything unless he was sure of his facts.

Cutler knew there was more information that Cortez wanted to get over to him but did not press him on the drive down to Akbuk.

Cortez had leased a house just off the main road, a minute or so from the lapping shores of the Aegean. It became apparent why he had picked this house and this spot. The detached house was nestled amongst other similar houses in a small cluster of trees and shrubs. From the two villas high up on the hills to their left, it was indistinguishable from the other properties in the area.

The roof of the villa was a patio, which was open to the elements save for the bamboo shading above them. The previous occupants had installed a sink and BBQ in this area. During the summer months, it was far too hot to cook indoors.

Sitting in prime position at the south end of the patio was a Celestron Reflector Telescope with a thirty-seven-millimetre lens that enabled Cortez to have eyes on the villa. Cutler looked through it and could see through a gap in the foliage the unmistakable figure of Werner, sitting in swimming trunks, bare-chested. Cutler could even pick out the scarring on Werner's chest. Sitting next to him was a stern-looking frump of a woman, who he assumed correctly was the delegate.

"Good work, Shultz. Interpol operates in Turkey. We inform them where Werner is and they will arrest him; there is an international warrant out for his detention. The delegate is a matter for another day. At least we can identify her now, and I have friends in the Secret Service who will be very interested in her," Cutler replied.

"There's more," Cortez said quietly. "And I don't think that will be what you decide on when I tell you."

Cortez looked at Shultz, and the look gave him the invitation to leave.

"Stay, Shultz. You're part of this team and deserve to hear everything." Cutler said.

Cortez shrugged. "You aren't going to like what I tell you," Cortez said in a resigned tone.

"Well, spit it out."

"You know I have been bugging the villa, and it's not exactly legal, so the evidence won't stand up in court."

"Obviously, but when you're dealing with the likes of Werner, in a foreign country, you need to have subterfuge and technology as part of your toolkit, otherwise we'd never get to the truth," Cutler stated.

Cortez seemed to ponder this for several seconds and used the wall surrounding the roof patio as support. Shultz could sense that Cortez was about to reveal something damaging and personal to Cutler. He pulled up a white patio chair and positioned himself in hearing distance of the two and poured himself a stiff brandy from the imitation crystal decanter on the table.

"You may want a snifter of brandy too," Cortez directed at Cutler.

Cutler shifted with impatience. "I'm a big boy, so to repeat myself, spit it out!"

"Well, let me begin by talking about Hoagie. I was listening in when Werner gave the order to shoot Richter on the aircraft steps. I tried to phone you, but evidently you had put your mobile on flight mode."

Cutler remembered the exact time he had put the mobile into flight mode; he had a routine that as soon as he left the departure lounge, he would set it on flight mode. It had been no more than a minute before the shot had hit Richter and all hell broke loose.

Cortez interrupted his thoughts. "The sniper is known throughout the underworld as 'the albino'. His actual name is Lothar Gottschalk. He is a crack shot, and my contacts say he has at least twenty kills to his name."

"So, we have identified who is responsible for Hoagie and the other deaths that night, that's good. We have a name, so we can track him and deal with him. It's the least we can do for Hoagie," Cutler replied.

"You mean kill him," interjected Shultz.

"I said deal with him. I am going to have to give it some thought, but don't you worry. I will deal with it, and I won't involve you if I can't do it legally."

Shultz shrugged his shoulders. "Don't worry about my sensitivity and my involvement, because if I find the bastard who killed my wife, he will be a walking dead man from that moment on."

"That leads me to Newcastle. You killed one of Werner's thugs there, I believe. Again, he and the delegate were discussing the details," declared Cortez.

"Him or us, I'm afraid, not something I'm proud of," confirmed Cutler, referring to the elimination of Falco Jager.

"Not judging you, man, just affirming what is on those tapes. So legal or not legal, we need to wipe them clean, with your permission," suggested Cortez.

"Make transcripts, omit the Newcastle details, and send it over a secure line to Fabienne."

Cortez moved away from the support the wall gave him and filled a balloon glass with a good snifter of brandy. He would need it to move on with his report. After downing the smooth liquid, he felt the soothing heat in his throat and stomach and continued. "Werner was involved in your sister's disappearance, although that is not strictly true; it was Bauer."

Personal was one thing; this information went beyond that and hit Cutler like a sledgehammer. He stumbled back a yard or so until he steadied himself.

"Are you saying Werner had my sister killed, or not?"

"Actually not," Cortez said, and the bemusement was spread wide across Cutler's face.

"I'm confused. Werner sent Bauer to kill Elisa. So, if he didn't kill her, what happened? Did he kidnap her instead?"

"No, I'm afraid she wasn't kidnapped, and I'm sorry I have to tell you this. She is dead; no doubt about it, I'm afraid." Cortez waited a minute for Cutler to absorb the fear that had been his bed partner every night.

"He tracked your family to Canada, and discovered they had left the day before to go on a cruise to Alaska. Bauer purchased a late deal on the Internet, and joined the ship in Vancouver."

Cutler stiffened. "Bauer went to Canada and followed my family?"

"Evidently, from what I heard, he was on-board the ship and had problems locating your family on the ship. The cruise was full so you can imagine trying to locate three individuals amongst all those people. He could hardly go and ask for fear of arousing suspicion."

Cutler stood there, shaking his head from side to side slightly, not wanting to believe what he was hearing, his anger rising.

"Finally, he located your sister and followed her until he became aware of her habits, to lay a trap. Your sister liked calling her friends after dinner, but she had a hard time finding a signal. The only place she could find one was on the top deck.

"Bauer set a trap and hid himself behind a partition on the top deck and waited for her. I think he was planning to kill her and throw her overboard. She came up at her usual time at 10 pm and Bauer was in hiding but within striking distance. According to Werner, when he was telling the German delegate, your sister was joined by some Asian, or half-Asian guy. Your sister appeared to know him as she addressed him as metro or masto, it's unclear on the tape."

Cutler could imagine the scene in his mind's eye; Bauer hidden, Elisa smiling and bidding this guy 'Good evening'. She was always pleasant and courteous. And he could even see the cell phone in her small hands.

"This guy was no ordinary Joe off the street. Bauer said he was trained in some martial art. He was quick on his feet, and he attacked her and killed her in a split second. At least it was not a painful death. The next part is not so sedate, and I can spare you if you wish," offered Cortez.

Shultz interrupted, "You lost your sister on-board a ship just like I lost my wife? I didn't know any of this. Is this why you set up MIDAS?" he asked Cutler.

"Sorry to butt in, Shultz, but that is a conversation for another time. He's only just found out his sister is dead. No disrespect: you know your wife is dead and have had some time to deal with it. He hasn't."

"Tell me how she died," Cutler said angrily, his eyes reflecting the pain.

"The Asian downed her in one blow. She was dead before she hit the deck. Strange thing is, he swooped down on top of her."

"Did he rape her?!" Cutler spat out.

"No, he ripped out a large tuft of her hair and scalp. Bauer went on to say the guy was interrupted by a noise down on the next deck. He picked your sister up, moved away to the side of the ship which, when you look over the side had no balconies or overhanging lower decks, and he coldly threw her overboard. I am sorry, Cutler."

Cutler walked to the edge of the roof patio, holding on tightly to the rails in the sweltering heat, but he felt cold, ice-cold. He stayed there for several minutes until he gained control of his anger and emotions before turning to Cortez.

Cortez finished, "He then washed, turning on a hose to wash the blood off him from your sister's scalp, then walked away casually."

Cutler closed his eyes, re-enacting the scene, torturing himself. After several minutes he had calmed his mind; his brain felt like it was overheating. His thought process returned, and he began to think like an investigator rather than a grieving sibling.

"The split pipe on my parents' plane wasn't an accident, was it?" he directed at Cortez in a barely audible voice.

"No, that was Bauer; they were desperate, and wanted you well away from the case. Triple whammy; your sister, father and mother. Bauer thought you would be on the plane, and even if you weren't, you wouldn't be interested in Werner for a long time."

The plastic patio chair sailed over the edge of the roof as Cutler finally lost his composure and swung his foot, the lip of the seat catching the decanter on the initial upward movement. Cutler swore for several minutes and stamped around among the shards of glass.

His brain was overheating once again; he was shaking with anger as he realized that maybe not his sister, but indeed his parents, had been killed because of his job. He knew his sister would have died too, if not by the Asian martial artist, then by the hands of Bauer. Finally, after what seemed an interminable amount of time to Cortez and Shultz, Cutler regained some small part of his composure.

"Bauer and Werner. Was the delegate involved?"

"Not precisely, but she had put pressure on Werner to try to make you go away," Cortez replied.

"And all three of them are up in those villas right now?" spat out Cutler.

"Yes."

"Can you get me any hardware?" he asked Cortez directly.

"Handguns aren't a problem. Every businessman in Turkey carries one, but anything else may be a bit tricky."

"Get me what you can. Neither of you need to get involved."

"We already are. In for a penny and all that," Cortez replied

"Count me in, Cutler. If we ever get to my wife's killer, I will expect the same courtesy."

"That's a given," Cutler said.

chapter twenty-nine

Esme Ross turned six years old. Her foster parents had tried their best to give her a happy, memorable day. John and Kathi Sturgeon were the kind of people the civilized world could not do without. They received a pittance for fostering Esme, and they had spent a month's fostering fees on taking her to Disney World the previous night.

Kathi Sturgeon had dressed Esme in a yellow dress with black polka dots, and she had two ponytails, with her hair tied back with Minnie Mouse hair clips. She looked ready for her trip to Disney World.

They had crossed the large lagoon on the Mississippi Paddle Boat, and Pinocchio had waterskied past them. They entered Cinderella's Castle onto Main Street, and the Sturgeons had ensured they had purchased the fast-track tickets, so the birthday girl was in front of the queue for any ride she went on.

Esme had insisted on riding on It's A Small World seven times. The Sturgeons thought it was her favourite ride, and happily obliged. What they were unaware of was that Esme had been there three years before, and the park was one of her first memories.

She had been there with her mommy and daddy. One of Esme's first memories was being squashed in the middle of the boat between her two laughing parents. She adored the closeness of the magical ride.

Back home on her nightstand, her foster parents had placed a photograph of her mommy and daddy, with baby Esme held aloft by Daddy while Mickey Mouse had his arms around Mommy. She remembered and missed them both so much.

The Sturgeons knew the little girl was sad, but she had shown steel in attempting to display a sense of enjoyment, not wanting to disappoint them both.

The day before they had left for the park, Cheryl Ross had visited her estranged daughter, as she was allowed to do once a week. It was a source of happiness and pain for Esme. Her mommy was all full of smiles and joy when she arrived, but Esme, through her bedroom window, could see her mommy weeping profusely when she reached her car at the end of the driveway.

For over two years now Cheryl Ross had spent a small fortune on trying to get custody of her little girl. Cheryl was the first to admit she had taken Don's death badly, and for a short while her mental health had suffered. The final straw for the authorities was when she had left Esme with her eighty-year-old grandmother for a week, as she went to Egypt to follow up on the revelation that the Yacoubs had seen her husband being killed.

Grandmother Ross keeled over two days into the trip, a massive stroke, and Esme was there for four hours while she died, moaning and groaning. It was only when Cheryl returned that she discovered the death of her husband's mother, and that her baby had been taken in by the authorities.

The court case the following week had endorsed the social worker's assessment, and Cheryl had been fighting ever since to get her back, to no avail. Cheryl was petrified; if she could not prove she was sane and a good mother, before too long the authorities would put Esme up for adoption, and she would be lost to her forever.

The Sturgeons arrived back to the Miami South Beach property a little after 8 pm, and were surprised to see Chloe, their foster liaison worker on their doorstep. She was accompanied by a man with olive skin, black hair, and a square jaw.

***

Cheryl Ross took the phone call from Fabienne at around 9 pm. She had received the transcripts from Cortez a little over two hours before. At first, Fabienne thought it was the normal transmission from Stahmer and Ghislaine, but then she noticed the name on top: Cortez.

For several weeks, she had been supplying information and analysis to Cortez at Cutler's request. Fabienne realized that this investigation was not what she had initially been briefed on, and she had not met Cortez, yet.

Only that morning she had received a secure call from Cheryl Ross telling her that any information that came in from this investigation that she deemed to be important was to be either e-mailed across to her, or she was to telephone if there was any critical news.

Analysing the transcripts and realizing that this information was not just critical but hit at the heart of the company, as it was highly personal to Cutler, Fabienne followed orders and telephoned Cheryl Ross.

"E-mail me the transcript immediately," were Cheryl's last words before her world changed forever.

The door flew open, and Esme Ross screamed and ran towards Cheryl, who dropped to her knees and burst into tears immediately.

It was several minutes of Cheryl crushing her baby close to her chest, sliding her hand down the back of her hair, and kissing all the available skin on her forehead and face before she said, "I don't understand."

Standing there was Tuck Walters. The tough Maori wiped a tear away from the corner of his left eye as he witnessed the highly charged scene.

"Maybe this card will explain," Tuck said, as he handed her a large card hidden within a large pink envelope. Cheryl would not let go of Esme, and between them both they managed to open the envelope. It said, 'Congratulations, Mommy'. Cheryl missed a breath and caught a sob, as her little girl could not read or write when she left. How much she had missed!

Again, Cheryl let Esme read the card, albeit a little slowly, and some words were accentuated as Esme broke the words down into sizeable chunks, 'A-pol-o-gise'.

Cheryl could read the message far quicker than it was being related to her, but she would not interrupt her baby, not for the world.

'Hope this makes up for not being as open and honest with you, I apologize. Enjoy and have a wonderful day and a beautiful life together,' it read. It was signed by Max Cutler.

Cheryl kissed Esme once again. She moved away from her slightly and adjusted the Minnie Mouse hair ties and looked her little girl up and down. How lovely she looked in her polka dot outfit. And then she hugged her again as the tears began to flow. Cheryl looked up at Tuck. "How?"

"Wyatt Rockman, Cutler's old recruiter from the Secret Service. Evidently, he was a qualified lawyer, and on leaving the Secret Service was fast-tracked as a circuit judge. He is now quite a senior judge for Dade County. Cutler approached him after we had caught the two boys who killed Don and relayed your story. Since then, the judge has moved heaven and earth to get you both reunited, and here she is, yours forever."

The final words became too much, and she clutched Esme tightly again and wept. And because she wept, Esme wept and hung onto her mommy ever so tightly. Tuck smiled and wiped away another tear, a tear of satisfaction.

I am going soft, he thought.

Cheryl somehow came back to reality and let one hand unglue itself from Esme and pointed at the printer.

"Transcript on the printer. Crucial, Tuck."

Tuck pried his eyes away from the cosy scene, and went to the printer to retrieve the e-mail from the top of the stack. He read the contents, becoming increasingly aware of the importance of the e-mail and the likely stratagem that Cutler would put into motion. He went back to Cheryl, kissed her on the head, and stroked Esme's hair.

"Going to leave you two alone to get reacquainted. See you later," Tuck said, on his way out the door.

The night was hot and humid. Even though Tuck had shorts and a T-shirt on, he started to sweat as he left the air-conditioned house. He walked the short stretch to the seafood restaurant that sat atop the inlet from the river system, and asked the waiter for a private table where he could not be overheard.

He sat down and ordered a Coors beer and a bucket of boat trash, his favourite: crab legs and lobster tails with prawns and scampi, and the odd crustacean he had never learned the name of, nor wanted to. From the laptop bag he had grabbed on the way out of Cheryl's office, Tuck removed an iPad and iPhone.

Cutler had issued each member of MIDAS with such a bag. Also inside was a satellite phone for when they were in areas with no mobile towers, and a laptop and external hard drive that were both encrypted with the latest security software.

He video-called Matt Rice first, and after several seconds his face filled a good portion of the screen. After the preliminary banter, Tuck explained what he wanted, and then he phoned Ghislaine, followed by Nathan Colton, his backup in the Hilton case.

Colton was back in Nassau, spending the money he had earned from the Hilton job, and was eager to help, as the cash was draining away fast. Colton was forty-two years of age, and his various appetites, which only excluded drugs, matched the size of his broad shoulders.

Several hours later, Tuck returned to Cheryl's. She was awake and lying prone on the daybed, a sleeping Esme wrapped up in her arms. With some minor protests from Cheryl, Tuck lifted Esme up from her arms and took her into the spare bedroom and put her to bed, fully clothed, and still with the ponytails in her hair.

On returning he found Cheryl quietly weeping and sipping homemade lemonade.

"Thought wine or champagne would have been flowing?" Tuck asked.

She ignored the question. "I know what you're planning, Tuck."

"You know what Cutler is like, Cheryl; he isn't going to walk away while his parents' killers are in the same town, you know it as well as I do."

Cheryl would never leave Cutler exposed, nor would she ever try to influence Tuck's decisions, although part of her screamed inside her head to tell him not to go.

Tuck put his arms around her shoulders and pulled her in tightly. "You just got your daughter back; spend some time with her and let me sort this out."

"You have to be careful; you're going to be a father," she said.

"I would be honoured to be Esme's father, and glad you think I can fill the role. We've come a long way in a short time, Cheryl, and believe me, I'm not one to say this lightly; I love you."

"And I love you, too. You will make a great father to her, and that is why I want you to be careful. This has been one of the best days of my life. I have my daughter back, and I got some news this morning; looks like you are going to be a father twice in one day. So, it is lemonade, I am afraid. Champagne will have to wait for nine months."

chapter thirty

Robert Stahmer was a methodical, instinctive, and dogged investigator. He realized early in the *Classical Canta Libra* investigation that, among all the people he and Ghislaine would interview, there was a high probability they would interview the killer. He was also astute enough to know that the person who could plan the lifeboat explosion would not give himself up willingly in an interview. They were dealing with an extremely intelligent person, with a talent for planning.

Stahmer requested and received the employee digital profiles from the *Classical Canta Libra* human resource director via Sean Wright. He had forwarded them to Fabienne. He asked Fabienne to add some lines to her software to include the fields on intelligence ratings.

He knew the average IQ was 100, and that an IQ of 132 put a person in the top two percent for intelligence. Stahmer reckoned, based on the planning and cunning used in the lifeboat fire, his target had an IQ at the top half of the scale, between an IQ of 110 to 125.

Stahmer was also aware that probably none of the employees aboard the ship would ever have been tested, but there were parameters Fabienne could build into the software to identify previous awards and exam grades, and from this they would certainly be able to exclude some of the employees from the suspect list.

At first, Fabienne had resisted; it was a natural state for her to resist. The work involved was far more in-depth than a few lines of code to the software. She would have to hack and extract information on the subjects from numerous educational facilities across the globe. She constructed an add on software application in a day that would do this while she slept.

Within two days of Stahmer's request, the code had been written. Fabienne did as she did each evening; she went to one of her three favourite restaurants. Tonight it was Domiciles, in the business district of Geneva. She had a routine, and the head waiter always obliged when possible. She would be seated in a quiet area of the establishment, and would eat while working on her iPad. Tonight, she feasted on a cheese fondue slab that melted down onto a drip tray, which she mopped up with Parma ham. It was during this meal that her software search program, Speedy, extracted and highlighted a significant clue.

Stahmer had not ceased his pedantic search for the truth, and this had taken him and Ghislaine to three countries in four days. Stahmer wanted to interview the bereaved families of the victims of the lifeboat disaster. First, they went to France, then to Iceland, and then to England, to interview Christie Rooney and Pam Carter's families, the two entertainers from the *Classical Canta Libra*.

The interviews in France and Iceland had not shed any light on the investigation; they were simply bereaved parents who were looking for answers as to why their loved one had died. None of the families believed the official version, and indeed it had been they who had forced *Classical* to bring in MIDAS.

Stahmer and Ghislaine first travelled to Snow Hill in Birmingham to visit Pam Carter's mother; the father had died of a heart attack shortly after Pam's death, and the mother quite openly blamed the loss of Pam for his demise. The interview was like the previous two, devoid of information they had not already collated.

They travelled by hire car from Birmingham the hundred or so miles to Borehamwood, a suburb on the outskirts of London made famous by Elstree Studios. The hour was late, so they took rooms in the Travelodge to freshen up before interviewing Christie's parents the next day.

They took two rooms, which cost less than a third of what one room would cost ten miles further towards the main city of London. After freshening up, they met in the restaurant situated at the end of the parking lot. No sooner had they begun to share a bottle of Chablis and hot buffet of several meats, Yorkshire pudding, and a variety of vegetables than Ghislaine's phone started to pulse. Tuck was on the end of the line.

Ghislaine explained to Stahmer that she was needed urgently and was to get herself on the next flight to Geneva. They finished the Chablis, and Stahmer ordered her a black cab taxi to Heathrow to catch the red eye to Switzerland.

The following morning, Stahmer went the short distance to the house of Christie's parents. The dwelling was a typical suburban, semi detached house. It had neat lawns to the front, and a man older than his years was stooping down to weed the flower beds.

Stahmer introduced himself and was shepherded into the front room, which seemed smaller than he had first thought, but put this down to the forty-two inch HD television that took pride of place above the mantle.

Mrs Rooney had the appearance of a homemaker in her apron, which had speckles of flour over it; she had obviously been baking in the kitchen. Stahmer accepted the offer of English tea, and was delighted to try the scones she had just baked.

Stahmer did not want to interrupt, as Mr and Mrs Rooney first talked about their daughter, and then got out the photographs from when she was a baby, to the last images of her on stage on the *Classical Canta Libra*.

Stahmer probed whether she had made any enemies, maybe a jealous performer, but the Rooney's assured him that she was loved by everyone. *Not everyone*, Stahmer thought.

Just as Stahmer feared it had been another wasted foray, a tall, handsome young boy of no more than fifteen appeared. He was introduced as Christie's brother, and offered Stahmer his laptop.

"Christie e-mailed me every week. Maybe there is something in the e-mails," he offered.

For the next hour, Stahmer read through the last three months of e-mails. Stahmer was a little uneasy; it was like reading a private diary, he thought. She obviously loved her brother very much, as she had laid out her highs, her lows, and some of her secrets, too.

The words struck him straight away; just one line, but one that stood out from the rest. It was the first significant clue he had had since interviewing all the families.

"The Grim Reaper is back. Every trip I have been on with him someone has gone missing or died, he is a jinx," the sentence read.

No name, no hint of his identification, but a clue, nonetheless. Christie had been on the same ship with him more than once; more than likely a few times for her to make this remark. The Grim Reaper had joined the ship between September and October, otherwise why else would she note on it in her latest e-mail but not in prior e-mails? This was the first clue he had come across, not just after interviewing the parents of the deceased, but also the crew members. Maybe it was something, maybe it was nothing, but Stahmer's intuition and radar were on high alert.

Don't get overexcited, he thought. *It is only a clue, not definitive.* But he knew deep down inside that he had the one clue that could lead him to the killer of all those people aboard the lifeboat.

On leaving the Rooneys, he telephoned Fabienne, and was surprised to hear Ghislaine answering the phone.

"Translator, investigator, and now receptionist, Ghislaine? What gives?" he inquired.

"I know; Fabienne is involved with some crisis involving Cutler, and between us we'll be coordinating. I'm to help out with translation and as you can hear, help with the routine matters in the office," she replied.

"I know you're both busy, but tell Fabienne I need her to check who came onto the ship between September and October prior to the explosion, and to cross-match everyone in that date range against ships and cruises that Christie Rooney has undertaken, and I need it fast."

"You got something from the Rooney family?" Ghislaine asked.

"The Grim Reaper," Stahmer replied.

For the next two hours, Stahmer sat in the café of a local superstore, drinking coffee, and doing the *Times* crossword as he waited with some impatience for the phone call that he knew would be coming. Finally, as he had one clue left to complete, his phone rang.

"Hello, Robert, it's Fabienne."

"Do you have some good news for me, Fabienne?" he asked directly, without his usual banter and greetings.

"Last night Speedy discounted all those at the lower end of the IQ range. At the same time, it was running an analysis of some information that Cutler asked me to run."

"Cutler's on a different case, Fabienne. I don't quite understand."

"I realize that, Robert, and would not bring it up, but the information you asked me to run this morning has generated a link," Fabienne replied.

"Speedy analysed a greeting from Cutler's sister's murder. It was mistro, or matro. So, my beautiful program looked at profiles, names of the crew, witnesses, etc., and came up blank. Speedy has been set up to cross-reference all open cases against keywords, or offer some suggestions related to cruises, and it is eighty percent sure the word is Maestro."

"Maestro," confirmed Stahmer.

"Yes, and Speedy has checked all nicknames or names that are similar and again came up blank. But it did come up with a suggestion; that of a conductor, pianist, or choreographer. And guess what? When you asked this morning to check on staff members who had joined the ship in September and October, and again to cross-reference against past relationships between crew members and related cruises, it came up with one name," she stated.

Stahmer's heart began to beat harder. "What name?"

"There was also reference in the Werner tape to Elisa's assailant pulling out a chunk of her hair and scalp, and I have asked Speedy to cross-reference this unusual action."

"What name please, Fabienne?"

"Ghislaine said you would remember him; the pianist, Sebastian McKenzie."

"Yes, I do remember him; half-white, half-Asian, with a wig or toupee on."

"There is more," Fabienne revealed.

"Don't keep me in suspense, Fabienne."

"He has a clear link with Cutler's sister's murder, and guess what; he was on the ship on which Manfred Shultz's wife went missing."

Stahmer took a deep intake of breath. "Are you saying there is a possibility that he is also responsible for Elisa's death and Manfred's wife?"

"No, I'm saying there is a strong, causal link, firm enough to arouse Speedy to spit his name out several times and to link him to those events."

"You're saying that this guy has done it before. The lifeboat incident sounds entirely different from Cutler's sister's death."

"Maybe he was covering up? Maybe someone found out about him," Fabienne conjectured.

"Maybe, maybe not."

"There's more. When his name popped up, we referenced all known missing persons and events around him. We also referenced missing persons from all the geographical positions he has lived in, and the date he lived there."

"Very astute of you, Fabienne."

"We have links to another twenty missing or dead victims on the ships he has been on. In some cases, body parts have been washed up. Some had the same injuries as Elisa, hair tugged out."

"We've got ourselves a serial killer," Stahmer stated.

"I would say we have a serial killer with trichotillomania tendencies."

"Trichotillomania?" Stahmer inquired.

"Overwhelming desire and need to pull out hair."

"He was wearing a wig. Ghislaine said there was something strange about his hair," Stahmer responded.

"Speedy also spat out another potential victim, but I'm not sure, as our pianist would have only been a little boy when it happened."

"Tell me more."

"A little girl was found twenty years ago stuffed inside a farm slurry tank. The reports state the farm had not used that tank for years, and she went missing when Sebastian McKenzie lived in the area as a child. Although the body was badly decomposed, the post-mortem revealed a head injury that is consistent with hair being ripped out. They also found a rucksack, and a capped bottle of water underneath the body."

"And they didn't do DNA checks in those days," Stahmer added.

"That is correct, but they do keep evidence in vacuum packs on all unsolved cases. I even know the evidence number and location," Fabienne said with a slight air of satisfaction.

"Have you been able to trace a DNA sample from McKenzie?"

"No, he has never been arrested in the US, so we have no DNA, even if we access the evidence. You must understand that a lot of the evidence we have collected is not legal and would not stand up in court. We may have identified him, but we have no reliable evidence to have him arrested," Fabienne ventured.

"We need a sample of his DNA, and we need that evidence. I can get a sample from McKenzie if you or Cutler can use your influence to get the DNA extracted from that evidence," Stahmer said.

"Even if you get his DNA, the years may have degraded the DNA on the water bottle, although I'm sure with the advancement in technology that if there is DNA on the bottle, it will be able to be isolated and identified."

"Cutler needs to know now," Stahmer interjected.

"Sorry, Robert, I've been overruled by Cheryl. She says that Cutler has enough on his plate at the moment and she doesn't want him side-tracked. She says he will still be there next week, when the timing will be better."

"Well, it must be significant, as this was the news Cutler has been waiting for. I am not going to take the chance. McKenzie is still on the *Classical Canta Libra*, and looking at this schedule, they are due to lay off outside Capri the day after tomorrow. I'm going to be there."

"Why don't you wait for Cutler? You have no legal authority over there, and what can you do?" she asked.

"Get a sample of his DNA. Secondly, interview him with the facts, then wait for Cutler to see how he wants to progress the case."

"Take care, Robert. It sounds to me as if you've made your mind up."

chapter thirty-one

ortez visited several non-tourist bars in the Kusadasi area, seventy miles from Akbuk. He had mixed with several unsavoury characters and had expressed an interest in hunting, and maybe hunting boar in the hills around the resort. It had taken long, several bottles of Efes beer to be exact before Mehmet had taken an interest in him.

Mehmet was of Kurdish descent and had moved to the area when the Turkish government had flooded the area he had once lived.

First, he tried to sell Cortez a villa in the local area, then he attempted to sell him an apartment, which was several thousand euros cheaper, all to no avail. Cortez made his situation clear; he was only interested in hunting.

For over twenty years, Mehmet had relied on his charm and sales skills to survive. He had his fingers in lots of little pies, and he had maintained a comfortable life on the back of these skills. For a hundred and fifty euros, he would take Cortez on a guided tour further north, and they could do a little hunting there. Again, when he heard Cortez's reply, he had to change tactics to ensure a sale.

"You want a gun to go shooting wild boar. You do not want any guides, and you want the guns quickly. I must admit this is not a normal transaction we get asked for often; Turkish baths, gulet trips, yes; but weapons, not so much," he stated.

"Not one gun but four guns, as I have three friends who want to go hunting with me as well," Cortez replied.

"How do I know you are not going to use the guns for a robbery? How do I know you are not hitmen?" he asked in excellent English.

"If we were going to do a bank raid, it wouldn't be in Turkey for several reasons. The main reason is we would be nuts, as your prisons are shitholes. We would pick Switzerland or Austria; nicer prisons and the police don't shoot on sight and ask questions later. As for being hitmen, if we were professional hitmen, we would not be very good at our job if we needed to trawl bars to get some guns," Cortez said.

"You do make some good points. Let me make a call and see what I can do," Mehmet said, as he left the bar with the phone already to his ear.

Twenty minutes later, as Cortez finished off his Efes in the corner of the bar, Mehmet returned and ushered him outside, as the bar had become busier with locals and he did not want to be overheard.

"My cousin works in the armoury in Soke barracks. For two thousand euros, you can have four SR-25 semi-automatic special application sniper rifles. They will kill many boars, and if you don't want to be heard, we can give you four suppressors for another thousand euros," Mehmet said.

Cortez knew the rifle, as it was the counterpart to the American M-16. "Seems a fair price," Cortez said, knowing they were worth much more on the open market.

"No, not buy. They are for rent for one week only. Today is Saturday, and they must be back in the armoury before the weekly stock inspection," Mehmet replied.

"Fair enough, I'll take them."

"We need a deposit to ensure you give them back," Mehmet said, expressionless. "You sign the papers for apartment. It is twenty thousand euros. You bring the weapons back you get the deposit back, less my commission on the sale."

"And how much is the commission?" Cortez asked, resigned to being ripped off.

"Twenty percent or four thousand euros, plus an extra hundred dollars for every bullet you use. We have accessed twenty magazines and you can use the lot. My cousin can put the bullets down to training."

"That's a lot of money just to go hunting," Cortez stated.

"It is if you are hunting boar," Mehmet replied.

"Give me an hour and I will sort your cash. It is cash you want, I gather," Cortez said, already knowing the answer.

Cortez gave Mehmet the money only after they met his cousin in the market parking lot, which was large enough for them to be isolated while they did the deal.

"We meet back here Friday at noon," Mehmet ordered, and Cortes nodded.

If I am alive, he thought.

Cortez took it easy in the rental car back to Akbuk, as the last thing he needed was to explain away four SR-25s belonging to the Turkish army. On the way back from Stoke, Cortez made a stop at the new outlet village and picked up four large sports bags to put the guns in.

Less than an hour later he was back in the villa in Akbuk. He found Cutler at the telescope, and Shultz monitoring the listening station.

Cutler joined Cortez in the kitchen area while Shultz was filling three cups with chai, the aromatic Turkish tea. They sat around the small, round table, and Cutler noticed the four sports bags, aware of their contents.

"Why four bags, Cortez? I have already told you this is my problem to sort. This is way beyond the scope of your and Shultz's contract of employment."

Cortez shrugged his shoulders and looked at Shultz.

"Don't remember getting a contract; how about you, Manfred?"

Manfred put both his hands up in the air. "No, I didn't get one."

"Look, I appreciate your loyalty, but we're talking about killing a German delegate, plus anyone who gets in our way, not to mention Werner. They're not coming out of this alive," Cutler stated coldly.

"Well, we didn't think you were going to give them a ticking off and 'Don't do it again' speech," interjected Manfred.

"We are in this together, no arguments. We need to start discussing how we are going to get in there unseen and out again," Cortez suggested.

"Okay, I appreciate this, and I won't forget it. But why four bags when there are only three of us?"

Cutler's question was answered almost immediately as Tuck and Colton walked in through the open door.

"No party without dumb and dumber," Tuck said as he entered.

"I must be dumb," Colton said, "because you are definitely fucking dumber," he said to Tuck, lifting the atmosphere immediately as they all laughed.

Tuck introduced Colton and Shultz and in return, Cutler did the introduction for Cortez.

"Sorry, Colton, thought it was just Tuck on his way over. I have only purchased four guns," Cortez explained.

"Not a problem. I take the gun off the first fucker we come across in that house," Colton said emphatically.

"Next time you get the guns, Tuck. Cortez didn't buy guns, he bought a Turkish villa, and the guns were fittings!" Cutler stated, adding to the laughter.

***

Fabienne sounded strange when Cutler made the routine nightly telephone call to the Geneva office; to Cutler she seemed as if she was hiding something from him. Fabienne had accessed the drawings for the two villas earlier in the day and had sent them over a secure Internet line to Cutler. She had also obtained the security company's drawings of the services, including telephone wires.

While Cortez was tied up in Kusadasi, Shultz monitored the conversations in German between Werner and the delegate, and each night Ghislaine would translate the recordings and produce a written transcript over the Internet to Cutler.

Although Fabienne would never admit it, she was pleased that Ghislaine had been reassigned to assist her in the Geneva office. She had enjoyed the Palestinian's sense of humour and sharp brain.

Fabienne also enjoyed her company each night when they would finish at 10 pm and enjoy a pleasant meal at her favourite restaurant. She was a little jealous when Ghislaine would kiss her farewell and the head waiter would fuss over Ghislaine. The handsome, thirty-something head waiter had never shown an ounce of interest in Fabienne in the two years she had frequented the restaurant, but he had been like a cat on a hot tin roof as soon as Ghislaine arrived on the scene.

So, both Fabienne and Ghislaine, for different reasons, were not overjoyed when Cutler told them he wanted the office manned twenty-four hours a day over the next week. Fabienne volunteered to do the night shift.

Meanwhile, Cutler redirected Matt Rice back to the Everglades. No matter how small the risk, he wanted Cheryl to have some protection, even if it was Basmati, who was more proficient with a camera than a gun.

It was Monday, and the plan was to launch the attack on Wednesday. Cutler put Shultz on the exit plan; Cortez maintained visual and auditory surveillance on the villa. Tuck reconnoitred the area above the villa for an attack plan. A frontal assault was out of the question, as they would be spotted halfway up the hill by Werner's henchmen. Werner maintained a constant lookout at the front of the villas, a duty carried out by his Turkish minders and Delegate Frau Uebering's minders.

The pictures Cortez had taken of the delegate's minders had been sent to Fabienne for identification. Cutler had no appetite to kill agents of the German government, if indeed they were. Cutler and Cortez agreed it was highly unlikely she would have brought her official minders, in case one of them recognized Werner.

Fabienne confirmed their suspicions; the bodyguards were hired minders from Dresden. Ex-East German agents, Stasi thugs in their forties, who had been in the delegate's employ from before the Berlin Wall was demolished. Fabienne had done her research thoroughly. She produced a report for Cutler with their names, and a synopsis of what they had been up to before and after the wall came down. All four were killers; two had been torture specialists for the Stasi during the 1980s.

"The world would be a better place without them," Cutler had confided to Colton.

Cutler had utilized Colton as a sounding board, and as he got to know him better and began to build up a healthy respect for the man and for his knowledge of tactics, he sought his guidance on the attack.

On Tuesday night, Cutler left Cortez to monitor the surveillance. The rest of the group travelled twenty miles through the mountains on the way to Mugla. Fabienne accessed satellite images of the area, and this was the nearest spot she could identify that had no dwellings or activity. The area was a self-sufficient area of olive groves straight out of a scene from the Bible, with rocks interspersed. The area would be flooded with olive pickers when they ripened, but Fabienne informed them that that was months away.

Over the next two hours, they used four of the twenty magazines of bullets. They realigned the sights for their individual use. They set the weapons from semi-automatic to single shot; the targets were not boars, but Coke bottles. Cutler had spaced the bottles at intervals of two hundred yards, seventy yards, and at close quarters.

The only one who would be firing without adjusting the gun would be Cortez. While this was not perfect, Cortez had received excellent training on multiple weapons by the German police, and Cutler was sure he could adjust his firing position rapidly to hit his targets.

Once Cutler was satisfied, they drove back, stopping at a bay along the way for Turkish mezze and pizza. Cutler ordered an extra portion for Cortez, who ate gratefully on their return.

The group sat at the kitchen table until 2 am on Wednesday morning. Tuck outlined his plan for the entry points, and Shultz explained their exit strategy, including clean-up operations. Colton and Cutler apportioned responsibilities and divisions of attack.

Cortez, Shultz, and Tuck agreed with the strategy that Colton and Cutler had come up with to attack both villas simultaneously. Were they just to attack one, they would put themselves at risk of being flanked and cornered by the secondary villa?

Cutler assigned their duties for the following day. There was still equipment to be purchased, as well as other supplies identified to complete their plan.

Finally, when the others had all retired for the night, Cutler telephoned Fabienne.

"Hi, Fabienne, thanks for the latest reports, they're a big help."

"Just doing my job, Herr Cutler," she replied, addressing him as she always did, despite protests from Cutler to just call him by his surname.

"Good, now do your job again and tell me what you didn't say last night."

chapter thirty-two

Glancing over his shoulder to bid the flight attendant goodbye, Stahmer took a deep breath as he descended the aircraft steps. The sharp, acrid aroma of jet fuel was lost on him; the only thing he could smell was blood in the air.

The scent of the hunt was always the same to Stahmer; he thought he had a sixth sense when it came to investigations. No one was more aware than he that facts make a case, not intuition. However, during the final stages of the Houses of Parliament investigation, the quest to catch his wife's killer and latterly the pursuit of Sebastian McKenzie, Stahmer had that elevated consciousness that he was close to an answer.

Classical Canta Libra was moored off the coast of Capri, as the majority of the guests were no doubt enjoying a trip to the beautiful Blue Grotto, a sea cave illuminated by sunlight from an underwater cavity; or having tea in cafes and restaurants once used by the stars of Hollywood.

Stahmer had flown into Naples Airport Capodichino and took a taxi for the short trip to the port of Molo and Calata Porta di Massa. Sean Wright had informed the captain of the *Classical Canta Libra* that Stahmer was on his way, and he organized for a tender to transfer Stahmer to the ship.

During the two hours it took in the calm azure blue of the Tyrrhenian Sea, Stahmer recollected quite clearly his last trip to Naples. For their wedding anniversary, he had arranged a long weekend in the city, followed by a day in Pompeii and the last couple of days in Sorrento. They had spent all day in Pompeii together, traversing the ruins and looking at the magnificent artifacts.

Too soon, the tender had been expertly guided alongside the massive hull of the *Classical Canta Libra*. Even though the sea was calm, the small tender still rose up and down on the swell a few feet, Stahmer needed the strong arm of a general seaman to assist his boarding the ship.

Stahmer was escorted to the palatial quarters that housed the captain's day and night cabins. The captain greeted him in a cordial and professional manner and engaged him in some trivia before getting down to business.

"I believe you wish to re-interview a crew member. Sean Wright reported he had no idea who the crew member was," the captain said, a little perturbed at being kept out of the loop.

"Sean doesn't know. We have only just found a particular piece of evidence; could be something, could be nothing. We wish to re-interview Sebastian McKenzie."

The captain paused for several seconds, trying to put a face to a name, as he had nearly a thousand names and faces to recollect.

"The piano player with the bad hair," he finally said.

"Yes, the piano player. First, I would like to see his cabin, obviously with Mr McKenzie not there," requested Stahmer.

The captain leaned back in his leather chair, swivelled it around, and opened the oak cabinet that was directly behind his desk. Stahmer could see the rows of files with little tabs on them, denoting a crew member's name. He extracted a file from the middle row, Stahmer thinking that must be the row for anyone with M at the beginning of their surname.

"Cabin 17a, sole occupation due to his status as one of the entertainers," the captain stated, as he picked up the phone and dialled the number for the entertainment manager. Several seconds later he asked for Sebastian's schedule and present whereabouts.

"You're in luck, Mr Stahmer; McKenzie is playing classical background music for the next hour in the main restaurant for those guests that find the food much more appetizing than the delights of Capri."

"That is good news, Captain. If you could allocate a guide to show me his cabin, I would be most grateful."

"The subject of a guide, as you call it, has already been taken care of, Mr Stahmer. Much to my annoyance, my rather pleasant lunch was interrupted by a direct telephone call from your Mr Cutler."

Stahmer raised his eyebrows as the captain continued.

"I got the impression that by coming here alone you are breaking with your company protocol. Mr Cutler has requested, and I have granted you, a personal bodyguard while on this ship. Once your interview is completed, you are to return to your hotel and wait for Mr Cutler, who will be with you in the next several days."

"I see," was all Stahmer said.

The captain made another short telephone call, a small, thin Nepalese security guard entered the captain's day room. Stahmer immediately recognized him as a Gurkha, probably ex-British soldier, he thought.

"This is Lachiman. He will be your guard and will not leave your side until we sadly say au revoir to you later today, Mr Stahmer."

Stahmer nodded towards the Gurkha guard.

"Lachiman and his three counterparts are ex-soldiers from the Brigade of Gurkhas. As you probably are aware, all ships have had some problems with Somali pirates. The Gurkhas are some of the toughest men in the world, so you can feel quite safe with him, just as Mr Cutler requested."

"I appreciate the assistance," Stahmer replied.

"Lachiman, like his comrades, would not travel anywhere without his knife, Mr Stahmer. Show him your knife, Lachiman."

The Gurkha just stood there without movement, expressionless.

"Very good, Captain. I get the joke. I know if a Gurkha takes out his khukuri he can't put it back into his scabbard unless he draws blood."

"You are most astute, Mr Stahmer. His khukuri is a work of art. I have never seen the blade, thankfully, but I can tell you the scabbard appears as if it has been crafted by Leonardo da Vinci himself. Would you be so kind, Lachiman, as to show Mr Stahmer the scabbard?"

Lachiman placed it on the captain's table just in front of Robert Stahmer.

Stahmer could see why the captain took every opportunity to display the weapon, for it was a vision of beauty. The forward-curving twelve-inch Nepalese knife was housed in a handmade leather scabbard. It was the ornate handle which stood out; it was carved out from buffalo horn, which had an engraving of a shark, and was separated by a band of gold leaf from a pair of crossed khukuri knives and topped at the top of the handle by a cow's foot. This indicated that it belonged to the Brigade of Gurkha, and as such, its owner had been professionally trained in its use.

"It's very impressive. Thank you for the honour of letting me see it, Lachiman," Stahmer said honestly.

"Well, I'm sure if you wanted to look at beautiful things all day you would have gone the Louvre, so I suppose we had better get on." The captain turned to Lachiman. "Show Mr Stahmer to cabin 17a, and use your master key to let him in. When Mr Stahmer has finished in the cabin, escort him to the conference room on deck six, where I will ensure Mr McKenzie will be waiting for him," he ordered.

Stahmer rose from the chair, which was several inches lower than that of the captain.

"Thank you, Captain, for your hospitality."

The captain looked up and stared at Stahmer for a second.

"You can return the hospitality with the respect to briefing me on what is going on when you finish your interview, Mr Stahmer."

Stahmer realized that the captain was none too happy at having a crew member interviewed by an outsider without prior knowledge of the details.

"Certainly," Stahmer said, as he exited the cabin with his guard.

Stahmer put on latex gloves and spent ten minutes in Sebastian's cabin. He looked through the set of drawers and wardrobe. All the clothes were clean and ironed, and all looked like they had been dry cleaned, which would destroy any usable DNA. The bed was freshly made, and the sheets appeared to be fresh.

In the bathroom, there was a brush, but Stahmer discounted that, as the hair on the brush would be synthetic fibres from Sebastian's wig. There was no toothbrush, as unbeknown to him, Sebastian only used toothbrushes once, and then he would discard them and use a fresh one the following day.

Stahmer began to fret that he would not be able to get a usable DNA sample. He went back to the wardrobe and searched the hidden depths at the rear of the closet floor. "Eureka!" he said to himself, as he extracted a battered old pair of slippers that Sebastian took everywhere with him. Stahmer was sure these were not cleaned every day, and he placed them in a nylon bag.

The conference room on deck six was on the starboard side and had heavy doors that would lead out onto the deck. The lifeboats that hung down from their gravity davits psitoned above the deck, and there were white cylinders containing inflatable lifeboats roped together in cordoned-off areas of the deck.

Inside the room was a podium at the far end. Overhead there was a projector, and a screen was draped down behind the podium. The tables were laid out in a horseshoe shape; there were notepads with the company logo and pencils at the top of the paper. The leather-backed chairs were placed on the outer perimeter of the horseshoe.

Sebastian was sitting at the head of the horseshoe adjacent to the deck door. Stahmer entered and pulled a chair up opposite Sebastian and placed a folder down between them. Lachiman stood at the far end of the room at Stahmer's request.

"Good afternoon, Sebastian."

"Here to see me again so soon, Mr Stahmer? To what do I owe the pleasure?"

"I need to clarify a couple of points and ask you some new questions."

"Just me or the rest of the crew as well?" Sebastian inquired, as he relaxed back into his chair, leaving it balanced on the back legs.

"Just you. I need to ask you again; did you have anything to do with the lifeboat incident?"

Sebastian shook his head.

"Did you know Christie had nicknamed you the Grim Reaper because people tended to die or go missing on ships you both worked on?"

Sebastian leaned forward and the front feet of the seat rested upon the lush red carpet.

"No, I'm not aware of that."

"So, you agree that there was a high proportion of ships you both worked on where people either died or went missing?"

"No, I'm not aware of that, either."

"Some of the body parts from the dead have been identified, and in a couple of cases there was evidence of hair being pulled out."

"I don't see what all this has to do with me."

"Elisa Cutler was attacked by a half-white, half-Asian man, and she had her hair pulled out. Elisa called the man Maestro. Do you know anything about that?"

Stahmer could see the tension suddenly spurt through Sebastian's upper body. *Did I overlook a closed-circuit television?*

How does this investigator know what she called me? Sebastian thought.

"I don't know this girl or anything about what happened."

At that moment, Stahmer's phone vibrated to life. Stahmer glanced down and swiped the phone to open and read the message from Ghislaine. Sebastian could see from Stahmer's wide eyes that the message was important.

"You have to understand that I think you killed all those innocent crew members on the boat because of the Grim Reaper label. I believe that we have links to many other deaths on ships that you have been on," Stahmer stated.

"You should have been a screenwriter. You're putting together innuendo and tragedies and contorting them to fit a theory you have dreamed up from God knows where," Sebastian said in a quiet and controlled voice.

Stahmer ignored the statement. "Do you wear a wig, Mr McKenzie?"

"That's none of your business," Sebastian said in a much sharper tone.

"Do you remember a young girl called Geraldine from when you lived in the UK, Mr McKenzie?"

Sebastian sat upright, shocked at Geraldine's name. *How on earth has he put Geraldine together with me?*

"It's a long time since I lived in the UK, and I was a child. I can't remember my neighbour's name, never mind anyone else's," Sebastian replied, realizing that the man in front of him knew far more about him than he should.

"Do you suffer from trichotillomania?"

"I don't even know what that is," Sebastian replied, rubbing his hands together.

"Strange, you either have dementia or you just lied to me. We have the notes from the psychiatrist your father put you under in Seattle because you kept on pulling out your bodily hairs. You look too young for dementia, so explain to me why you just lied."

Sebastian just shrugged and remained silent, playing with a pencil in his left hand. Lachiman could sense the atmosphere had become highly charged and moved forward a few paces. Sebastian was aware of the movement.

"They discovered Geraldine's body many years ago, before DNA testing. But they found some physical evidence in the slurry pit and we are getting it tested now." Stahmer lied on the last point before continuing, "And while you are the cleanest man I have ever seen, you left slippers in your cabin which I'm certain we can get DNA from. What do you have to say to that, Mr McKenzie?"

"All conjecture."

"We spoke to the Inspector in the Falklands; we know all about your escapades there. He swears blind you killed two people there."

"I was never charged."

"And that was why they could not take your DNA, but that changes now, and we will have your profile sent to him directly. Seems some evidence has cropped up and they are going to see if your DNA matches what they have." Stahmer lied about the DNA.

"Like I said, it's a lot of conjecture and ifs and buts."

"At the moment. I know you have killed many people including your crew mates. Lachiman here will place you under close arrest. You are not leaving this ship until we have pieced together the evidence."

"You can't do that," Sebastian spat out.

"We are tracing every ship you have served on; we are looking at all missing persons, on board and in the area." Stahmer's phone rang.

"Hi Fabienne."

"Speedy has dug up a double murder in Penang. At first the authorities thought it was accidental, but under family pressure they undertook post-mortems, both were murdered. The date they died Sebastian left his ship in Singapore but did not fly home for two days. To cut a long story short, I did some digging and have discovered some CCTV which shows Sebastian getting off a train in George Town. Same day they were killed."

"Thanks, Fabienne," Stahmer leaned closer to Sebastian.

"You have been very careful and precise Sebastian. But today it is impossible to have zero footprint. We have CCTV of you in George Town, the day of a double murder. We are just starting the investigation, and I am a hundred percent sure it is you. When we close this case, it will be a country like Malaysia we send you to. European prisons are too good for you."

"You are good, Mr Stahmer. I have no doubt you and your colleagues will pick away at this until you can prove it's me," Sebastian said quietly.

"So, are you admitting it?"

"You've just made the biggest mistake of your life. I will not spend one day in any prison, Mr Stahmer."

"You will. See, you killed my boss's sister, and one of my colleague's wife. Our company was set up to track you down, and now we have you. Do you think we are going to let you go anywhere?"

Lachiman moved forward a few more steps but was taken completely by surprise by the swiftness of the pianist's reactions. No sooner had Stahmer finished the last words of the sentence than Sebastian had flicked the pencil into the air. The pencil did a one-hundred-eighty-degree spin. Sebastian caught the pencil in his right hand at the apex of the half-circle, and before Stahmer could react, he plunged the sharpened tip with force into Stahmer's left eye.

Stahmer screamed out in pain, and at the same time he fell back from his chair to the floor, where he remained, writhing in agony.

Immediately after Sebastian attacked Stahmer, Lachiman rushed forward and swiftly and adeptly unsheathed the khukuri. He raised his right hand, ready to sweep down across the assailant's chest, and knew in an instant as Sebastian checked the attack that he was facing someone with a high degree of martial arts training.

Lachiman felt no pain but could feel the arterial blood pumping out of the artery. Sebastian had scooped up a second pencil in the microseconds before the Gurkha descended upon him and had blocked the thrust from the khukuri. With his right forearm, while lunging underneath the blocked arm, he expertly plunged the pencil into Lachiman's brachial artery, ensuring he lost the grip on his khukuri.

Lachiman realised if he removed the pencil, he was dead, for presently it stemmed the flow of blood. In typical Gurkha tradition, he maintained the attack, this time surprising Sebastian.

Grabbing Sebastian's attack hand, he headbutted him at the top of the nose. Sebastian tried to move away from the second onslaught, but Lachiman had a tight grip on his arm, and headbutted him again, stunning Sebastian and sending his wig skywards.

Sebastian knew he was in trouble; aware he had met a formidable opponent. He was groggy, if he didn't act fast this former soldier, even though severely wounded, might get the better of him.

Lachiman came back with a third attack, pulling Sebastian to him. This time he could force the nasal bone at the top of the nose backward into Sebastian's brain. A micro-second before his forehead connected for the final attack, Sebastian dropped his head deftly and moved slightly forward. The forward movement and angle of attack reversed the force in relation to the forehead to forehead. Lachiman let go and staggered backward for a second before his shaken brain again became focused.

It only took a second for his vision to clear, but this was all Sebastian needed to exit the door onto the deck. Running after him, the Gurkha bent slightly forward and with his left hand he scooped up the khukuri and followed Sebastian out of the deck exit.

In the second or so that had elapsed from the staggering blow to picking up the khukuri and exiting the door, Sebastian had jumped up on the white cylinders of the inflatable lifeboats. Sebastian leapt outwards, away from the ship's side, hanging in the air for the blink of an eye before he plunged towards the waves some thirty metres below.

It was like a flash of lightning, so quick it was impossible to catch on camera, so fleeting was that moment in the air before plunging into the depths. Lachiman had spent years training for such a moment.

In his time in the army, he had been deployed to Iraq. It was not fulfilling, as it was hard to kill men who were running away from you.

Today he had met an opponent, a worthy enemy, who had hurt the Gurkha and whom he had hurt in return. His mission was to protect the investigator, and he had failed. The least he could do was kill the perpetrator.

The transitory period that Sebastian hung in the nothingness was all that the Gurkha needed to launch his ornate khukuri. He aimed it below Sebastian, his training taking over, and his brain calculating the position of the falling assailant.

The khukuri buried itself deep into Sebastian's left shoulder, down to the hilt, such was the force it entered his body. He fell the thirty metres into the moderate swell, his reflexes moving his body into position to reduce the impact, not sure if he was going to live or die.

chapter thirty-three

The stars pulsated in the clear sky with the thin, reflected line of the moon stretched across the bay's calm waters. The air was still and warm, and the lights of the small fishing vessels plying their trade blinked on and off. It was a perfect evening to visit an excellent restaurant, eat mezze, and drink ice-cold beer. Cortez, Shultz, Tuck, Colton, and Cutler checked each other's equipment on the villa's rooftop, and food was the last thing on their mind.

Once the equipment check was completed, they gathered around Cutler for the final briefing. Cutler went over the plan again. It was the tenth time, but they were all professionals, and accepted the need for repetition. When the briefing was completed, Cutler asked Shultz to stay with him while Cortez, Colton, and Tuck departed in separate cars hired from the local village.

"Fabienne telephoned me a couple of hours ago and I was considering not telling you until after tonight's operation. However, if I do not pass on the information it may destroy your trust in me, Manfred," Cutler said.

"What information? Is it about my wife?" Shultz guessed.

"Your wife and my sister. Between Fabienne, her computer, Stahmer, and Ghislaine, they have come up with a strong link to many missing or suspicious deaths. In short, they have a name, and Stahmer is over there now interviewing him."

Shultz was quiet and moved around the rooftop, shaking his head while thinking.

"He killed my wife and your sister? Stahmer should have waited until you and I could get over there. I will get the truth out of the bastard. What's his name?"

"And he's linked to many more. It would have been better if Stahmer had waited, but we must deal with the situation as it is now. I want to get my hands on him as much as you. His name is Sebastian McKenzie, and he is a ship pianist."

Shultz stood still, thinking back to the ship, to the piano bar, and the pianist she insisted on listening to each night. "There was an Asian guy, a great musician and singer; my wife could not get enough of him. Weird hair, though."

"That's him," Cutler said coldly.

"So, what happens now?" Shultz asked.

"You can go now. There is a flight out at midnight. Or you can wait until tomorrow and fly with me if we are both still alive. I have already spoken to Cortez and Colton, and they are okay with tidying up after the job and returning the weapons. Your choice and no flak if you decide to go."

Shultz had taken several minutes before he answered. "We go tomorrow, on the proviso you let me kill the bastard."

"As long as you do it slowly, I have no problem with that."

"Believe me, it won't be quick," Shultz spat out.

Cutler and Shultz packed the equipment into the car and sped off, driving away from civilization around the bay. They passed the steep lane heading up towards the two villas perched up on the mountain and took the next lane up. The lane was steep, and it had last seen paving many years before. The stones bounced off the chassis continuously.

When they reached the top of the lane, they parked by a building that had once been a shelter for the olive pickers, now it had not been used for over a decade.

Shultz climbed up on Cutler's shoulders until he got a handhold on the huge boulder and climbed to the top with some difficulty. Once he had mounted the rock, he threw down the nylon rope he had tied around his waist. Cutler tied the handle to the sports bag, and it was hauled up.

Cutler manoeuvred the vehicle back down the lane and returned to the village, taking the road that led up over the back of the mountain. He turned off a small, deserted lane that was used for maintenance vehicles to service the tall airport location beacon that flashed its red light throughout the night. He removed a black hooded sweatshirt and put it on, which blended in with his dark trousers. He then went through the same process as the other four earlier and blackened his face with the boot polish they had bought from the local shoe shop.

Cutler used the ladder that the others had left there to climb over the metal fencing surrounding the beacon and met up with Cortez, Colton, and Tuck. They had used the metal railings to secure two abseil lines down to the villas some sixty metres below, and had a similar ladder to get over the railing. This was the tricky bit, as there was not a ladder on the other side, just a sheer sixty-foot drop. They had to shimmy down the railings and reach down to grab the abseil line while holding on with the other hand.

Most abseilers secure the line to a harness, but this was impossible. What made the task harder was they carried about forty pounds each in backpacks.

Clad all in black, they were almost invisible against the rock backdrop. Colton and Cortez went down first, as they were the attacking team for the delegate's villa. Tuck and Cutler went last, as they had chosen Werner's villa.

The frontal view of the villas gave the appearance that they had been built into the rock face, but this was just an illusion. The rear walls ended a yard short of the rock face, and in this gap the ugly air conditioning units were sited and hidden from view.

Both Colton and Cortez had traversed sideward ten yards along the rock face and had landed on the roof of the delegate's villa. All had rubber-soled boots on to minimize any noise on the clay tiles.

Tuck and Cutler ascended the ropes directly onto Werner's roof. Once there, they removed rubber condoms and two bottles from their backpacks. They then removed industrial respirator face masks and put them on. They checked each other's respirator straps to ensure they were sealed to the face correctly.

Tuck held the condom neck open for Cutler and inserted a small funnel into the condom. Cutler poured bleach into the condom until it expanded and was about a third full. Resealing the bleach, they opened and poured in ammonia.

Colton and Cortez removed their weapons and shimmied forward to the apex of the roof.

The waited quietly for ten minutes, and at two minutes to nine exactly, they cut and removed two screws and removed the top of the air conditioning units and placed in the condoms.

Two minutes later, the delegate left Werner's villa to return to her own, with Von Baer and the four German minders. Cortez's observation over the telescope had paid off; this was a nightly ritual.

Stage one of the plan was now underway. Shultz, perched on a boulder some hundred yards to the left, and with a clear view of the front patio area, fired the first shot. The SR-25 sniper rifle was on single shot, and the noise suppressor ensured no one heard the bullet as it spat out, nor saw the spark as the impingent gas ignited, propelling the projectile.

The four German minders were on all sides of the delegate and appeared disciplined and well trained. Von-Baer was lagging. The bullet hit the minder to the front of the delegate and nearest to the villa. His brain would not have time to register what was happening. The bullet entered through his nose, and the gaping exit wound at the back of his head was also the departure point for his brain matter, most of which ended up all over Von-Baer's face.

Von-Baer was stunned and just stood there, wiping his hand over his face, and looking at the contents as he studied his hand. The minders were professionals and quickly recovered. Two of the Germans ushered the delegate inside the villa. The last minder took a Cortez bullet to the spine, snapping his back and killing him instantly.

Cutler, on the roof of Werner's villa, put a large pin into the condom in the air conditioning unit, releasing the chlorine gas which would flood the villa.

Cortez and Colton advanced to the front of the delegate's roof, ready to jump down to the bedroom patio three yards below the edge of the roof. They were surprised to see Von-Baer still standing there beside the infinity pool, obviously in shock. Colton had his weapon on semi-automatic and put a short burst into Von-Baer's chest. The force of the volley lifted him off his feet and propelled him back a couple of metres, and he landed with a mighty splash into the pool, which turned crimson red immediately.

Cutler and Tuck took the same action as their counterparts on the Werner's roof, advancing forward to the front of the roof and jumping down immediately.

The Turkish minders were less professional, and four of the six charged out, spluttering and coughing, weapons held high, ready to fire at the first target. It was unclear who killed whom as Colton and Cortez on the opposite bedroom balcony had a clear view, and Cutler and Tuck on the patio above them had a better view. All four put a short burst into the four minders and they died in each other's blood pools, almost immediately.

Inside, the delegate was trying to use her mobile phone to dial out to the local police. Unbeknown to her, and causing concern and anger to the local population, Tuck had sabotaged the mobile phone reception tower, which was located within the same fenced-off area as the airport beacon. The landlines had been cut at the telegraph poles earlier in the day.

The delegate's two minders ushered her to a downstairs bathroom that had no windows, and which they had classed as the safe room and last resort.

Nathan Colton earlier that day had purchased some saltpeter, a bag of toilet rolls, and a rug. He removed the paper from the rolls, while on the stove he had a skillet in which he had placed three parts saltpeter and one-part sugar. While the mixture heated, he cut out small pieces of rug and taped them to the bottom of the toilet rolls. When he was satisfied the mixture was done, he placed a cup full in each of the prepared toilet rolls. He impregnated strong tissue with the mixture and then twisted the tissue and put it at the other end of the toilet roll, thus creating a fuse. Homemade smoke bombs.

Colton handed three to Cortez and kept three for himself. They moved through the delegate's bedroom, ensuring it was clear. Colton took point, and Cortez came up on the rear. Colton lit a smoke bomb and hurled it over the balustrade, and the smoke bomb burst on contact with the marble floor on the ground floor below. Cortez followed suit, and in total they threw four of the smoke bombs.

Meanwhile, Cutler and Tuck entered Werner's bedroom in the same formation, with Cutler taking point. They kept on sweeping their heads from side to side, as the respirators limited their peripheral vision.

Before they could see the inhabitants of the villa, they could hear them, coughing and spluttering as the chlorine gas took effect on their respiratory systems. The noise emanating from them was men coughing, retching, and babbled shouts in Turkish.

Two of the Turkish minders could stand it no longer and burst out the front door with Uzi submachine guns spraying in all directions. The large Turk to the right continued to fire as he entered the swimming pool backward, as Shultz lined up the shot and the bullet entered the Turk's heart a millisecond later.

The smaller Turk hit the deck immediately to minimize his profile to the sniper. All this achieved was that the next bullet entered his forehead rather than the larger target, his chest.

Cutler ran back to the external patio outside the bedroom in case Shultz had missed his shot, worrying needlessly in case they were flanking Cortez and Colton. Pointing two fingers up and then crossing his throat, he indicated to Tuck: two men down, four to go.

Tuck entered the top of the stairwell, which was a semi-circle of steps down to the ground floor, but he could see clearly to the bottom and saw Werner on the floor, gasping for breath. However, he could not see Bauer, who they all agreed was the most potent threat.

Cutler tied a rope to the balustrade and waited for the moment Bauer was bound to show himself; after all, Tuck had set himself up as a target.

Bullets sprayed upwards in the delegate's villa towards Cortez and Colton, who took shelter in the first bedroom off the stairs. The moment the volley of bullets stopped as the two remaining German minders took a second to reload their magazines, Cortez and Colton ran out of the bedroom and returned the favour. A scream told them one had been hit. Once their guns had run dry of ammunition, Cortez dove back into the bedroom and Colton dove to the right, taking shelter behind a concrete pillar holding the balustrade in place.

Cortez popped his gun out and took one shot towards the German left standing to draw fire. The volley was returned immediately, too quick to get out of the way. Cortez took a round in his right shoulder and slumped backward.

Colton observed Cortez rock back on his feet before sinking to the ground. No sooner had the volley ceased than he leap-frogged the balustrade and began firing on his way down the six-yard drop to the ground floor. He took the German out mid-flight, at around four yards from the floor; his burst ripped the German minder's head apart like a watermelon exploding. The crunch he felt as he landed was his right ankle snapping.

He immediately jumped up on his good leg and hopped around to ensure the minder they had hit from the volley upstairs was dead. He was not and was trying to reload his gun but was hampered, as he had been shot in his leading right arm. Colton also had an empty magazine. The minder was kneeling up, trying to use the floor to leverage the gun while loading a magazine with his unnatural hand. Colton dropped his weapon and rapidly felt at the back of his neck, quickly withdrawing a short, six-inch knife from its sheath beneath his shirt.

The German minder had succeeded and spun towards Colton with his finger reaching for the trigger and wondering why his finger would not move. The knife had entered his left eye, thrown with such force it had pierced the brain, but the second that it took to die was filled with thinking, *Why won't my finger move?*

Cutler, in Werner's villa, had mimicked Colton's move and jumped from the balustrade as Bauer unsuccessfully tried to kill Tuck at the top of the stairs. Tuck was quick and rolled immediately into the bedroom.

Bauer was shocked when Cutler landed on him from above. He lost his weapon immediately and was winded. Werner was unarmed and gasping for breath; the noise was unmistakable as he gasped through his artificial voice box.

Bauer looked up from the floor at the towering man all in black and his face covered by a respirator.

"Who the fuck are you?"

"Take a guess; you killed my parents."

By this time, Tuck had traversed the staircase two steps at a time and had his gun trained on Werner.

Werner sputtered, "Cutler."

"Got it in one."

Cutler surprised Tuck by placing his gun down on a glass table.

"This is where I say I'm going to give you a chance. But if you kill me, Bauer, Tuck over there is going to put a bullet into you anyway."

"I'm going to take you with me." Bauer swept his leg expertly, taking Cutler's legs out from under him, and he slammed to the floor. In the same motion, Bauer took a knife from a sheath on his thigh and jumped onto Cutler. Cutler grabbed Bauer's knife hand with both of his, clasped as in prayer. Tuck swung his gun around to the back of Bauer's head.

"Don't you do it, Tuck. This fucker is mine for what he did to my family!"

Bauer pressed down with all his might and was looking directly into Cutler's eyes.

"Shame I didn't get to your sister first. Nice little titties: could have had some fun there," Bauer spat out.

Cutler flicked Bauer's knee away and brought his own up with force between Bauer's legs, crushing his testicles. He then pushed Bauer off and Cutler stood up, giving his opponent a few seconds to recover, and taking a breath himself.

"After I'm finished with this piece of shit, you're next, Werner," Cutler said coldly as he looked at Werner.

Cutler backed off to the table as Bauer regained his breath and stood, knife in hand, ready to launch another attack. Cutler felt behind him and took a hold of a slate placemat he had spotted when he had placed his gun on the table.

Bauer jumped up several feet and propelled himself at Cutler and tried to stab him on the way down, but Cutler jumped back.

"You've been watching *Hercules in Troy*, you prick! That sort of thing only works in the movies," Cutler goaded him.

Bauer ran at him with his hand half back, ready to stab at Cutler, who was only showing a side profile. As Bauer got within stabbing distance, Cutler spun on his axis, so the thrust went past his left shoulder. Cutler turned to his right instantly and moved his hand that clenched the slate plate, cutting it across Bauer's right thigh. Reflexes and self-preservation took over and Bauer dropped his knife as his hands went to his leg. He tried desperately to stem the flow, firstly to stop the bright red, oxygenated blood that was spurting out from his femoral artery.

"I wouldn't bother, Bauer. You can't stop it, and you have about five minutes left on this planet. Mark Twain once said, 'Heaven is for the climate, and hell is for the company.' I think you're going to have lots of company, not to mention your boss," Cutler said, as he walked over to Werner.

"Herr Werner, last time I saw you, you had your throat ripped out by a bullet. Now you are on the floor gasping like a dog in heat. I never seem to meet you when you're at your best."

"You want me to put a bullet between his eyes, boss?" Tuck said eagerly.

"No, Tuck, go back upstairs and mix one of our condom balloons. We lock this fucker in a bathroom for five minutes; he can hardly breathe now. A bullet is too good for our Herr Werner," Cutler said, as Tuck turned and went back up the stairs.

"Cutler, be reasonable. I have money, millions of euros; it could all be yours," Werner spluttered out in his metallic voice.

"I already have millions, Werner. Who do you think got Richter out?"

Reality hit Werner as Cutler dragged him to a bathroom and threw him to the floor. The bathroom was without windows and was illuminated as bright as daylight with an array of inbuilt LED lights.

Tuck returned. Cutler put a pin prick through the condom and sent it soaring into the bathroom. Cutler slammed the door shut and retrieved a second balloon from Tuck. Toxic chloramine gas from the bleach and ammonia in the condom spread across the bathroom floor and began to rise. Werner choked and began to beat on the door.

"Stay here and check on him in ten minutes. That should do it."

Cutler took his gun and exited the villa. Cortez lined up Cutler in his sights and saw his hair illuminate in his sights. All four of them had washed their hair previously in tonic water; it gave off an unusual glow through the sniper's rifle and enabled Cortez to define foe from friend.

Cortez smiled to himself. "Villa One secure," he said to himself.

Cutler took a quick look through the front entrance door and back out again to analyse what he saw. A second glance told him all he needed to know, and he entered the villa.

Colton was sitting next to Cortez and was administering first aid. He had ripped open the shirt, and Cutler could see that Cortez was grimacing as Colton worked his knife into his shoulder to remove the bullet.

"You a doctor as well?" Cutler said, half in jest.

"You should be asking how we are," Colton replied.

"I can see how you are; in need of more training, looking at Cortez. And you're missing a boot and your ankle looks like an elephant's."

"It's not training we need, its bulletproof vests, you cheapskate," returned the banter.

"Where's the delegate?" Cutler inquired on a more serious note.

"In the bathroom."

Cutler walked over to the bathroom, put a pin in the balloon and threw it in as the delegate screamed abuse.

After several minutes, Tuck walked in. "Didn't take him long to die."

"Get these two into one of the German's Range Rovers. I'll be out in a minute," Cutler replied.

"What about the bodies?" Tuck asked.

They had previously identified an old water well in the mountains with a domed concrete roof that had not been used this century. The well went down over a hundred fifty metres deep, they guessed, by dropping a coin and counting. It was going to be the counterfeiters' final resting place.

"We've got these two out of action; too much damage, too much time. Change of plan. The delegate is locked in the safe room and we have bodies to move and not enough muscle to get the job done."

As Tuck helped Colton and Cortez to the car, Cutler removed his short-wave radio and spoke to Shultz. "Can you see the three liquid petroleum gas bottles at the rear of the building between the house and the side of the cliff?" He waited for the reply. "Good, light those up as soon as we leave, should make for a good cremation. Even in the safe room the fire will take out the generators which are pumping oxygen into the room."

chapter thirty-four

Cutler accompanied Cortez, Shultz and Colton for post-action medicals in a private hospital in Geneva, where Stahmer and Lachiman were recuperating from Sebastian's attack. Tuck wanted to get back to Cheryl, as she was pregnant, he had informed a surprised Cutler.

Shultz and Cutler travelled to the private Ospedale Evangelico Villa Betania hospital in Naples. They visited Stahmer, who had been brought round from an induced coma the night before. They were mightily relieved that his prognosis was good, and he would be back on his feet within two weeks. The bad news was he would either wear a patch on his eye for the rest of his life or would need a glass eye. Stahmer had shrugged it off, saying he was still better looking than Colton and Cortez, even with a patch.

Next, they visited Lachiman.

"We've heard all about you from Mr Stahmer and would like to thank you for saving his life. We would like to offer you a position in our company."

"And I have heard about you, Mr Cutler, and would be honoured to work for you and your organization."

"You may not be aware of it, Lachiman, but the guy who attacked Stahmer killed my sister and Shultz's wife."

"I wasn't conscious of that. You both have my sympathy," Lachiman said in a quiet voice.

"Between the fall and your knife, we thank you for helping kill that bastard."

"He's not dead, Mr Cutler, I'm sorry to say."

"What do you mean he didn't die? You got him with the knife. He fell God knows how far into the sea, and they found no one when they launched the search from the ship," interjected Shultz.

"And you haven't left this hospital since that day, so how do you know he's not dead?" Cutler said.

"When I woke this morning, this was placed underneath my pillow," Lachiman replied, as he retrieved the khukuri carved out from buffalo horn. "There is a fresh carving on it. It is a ship. Last time I saw this it was in McKenzie's back."

In unison, Cutler and Shultz said, "Motherfucker!"

<h1 style="text-align:right">chapter thirty-five</h1>

Mount Etna, or Mongibello—'the beautiful mountain'—as the locals call it, was once again rising from a short sleep. And before the gas slugs and lava flow ceased, she would add another soul to the many she had taken dating back to 1500 BC.

There was an ever-present, pungent smell of sulphur; the aroma was overwhelming. Sitting on an active fault line, the heavier African plate was breaking up the much lighter Ionian microplate. This phenomenon created a vacuum, sucking magma from the Earth's mantle, forcing lava through the crust of Mount Etna.

The eruption happened at a fissure on the flank of the mountain, near to Crateri Silvestri, six thousand feet or two thousand metres above sea level. This was a popular area for tourists to witness recent eruptions and see the local shop buried within an older lava flow.

Mount Etna is reached by driving up the Etna Sud Road, with continuously changing and contrasting landscapes. Vineyards morph into the blackened landscape of previous lava flows. A few yards further on and you can witness the locals picking the green olives from groves which are edged by endemic flora and fauna.

Sebastian had fled to the town of Catania, Sicily. Here he hoped to be reborn with a new identity, one that would allow him free access in and out of mainland Europe. He knew without a doubt there would have been a European arrest warrant issued for him. Indeed, it would not take long for this to circulate to all European ports, airports and what borders remained in a united Europe.

He was aware that pharmacists or doctors would be a port of call for any competent police investigator looking for him. He had to make do with what he had stolen from the hospital when he delivered the khukuri and message back to two investigators from MIDAS.

In hindsight, he realized this was vain and a little stupid, he would have been presumed dead, and people do not look for the dead. Sebastian's psyche was far from normal. No one had beaten him at anything. He had roamed the world killing, unhindered and unknown until the past few days. He would not allow the investigators to believe they had bettered him.

Not killing the Gurkha security guard in his hospital bed was not an act of mercy, it was because he was incapable of killing him with the injury he had sustained.

Once he had delivered the khukuri, Sebastian had rummaged through several unmanned clinical areas. He managed to get more bandages to pack the wound, as the strips of linen he had packed into the wound had started to seep crimson fluid. Sebastian found a storage cupboard with lighting.

With the needle and suture he had discovered, he stitched the damaged ends of the wound together. He applied the little iodine he had taken, and finally after bandaging he found a jacket in one of the side rooms, no doubt left there by a patient or doctor.

Events took a turn for the better as he departed the hospital. In the parking lot, Sebastian noticed a 1975 battered Fiat van idling, the driver standing some way off having a cigarette in a designated smoking area. Either believing no one would steal such a heap of trash or not caring he had left the engine on. Sebastian relieved the negligent driver of the Fiat and headed south. Sebastian stopped at the nearest cashpoint and took the maximum amount of cash the ATM would allow: five hundred Euros.

Sebastian had guessed rightly that too little time had elapsed for the Italian Police to notify Interpol, which would ensure all his known accounts were monitored and funds frozen.

Sebastian had no clothes, little money, and access to his funds would be stopped within days. What the security services would not know was the Swiss account he had set up with the proceeds from the sale of his dead mother's house. The only thing he needed to access the funds was a pin code he had memorized, and he could have money transferred to the nearest bank, no identification required.

Sebastian needed to put some distance between himself and the investigators, so the transfer of cash would have to wait. To the north was mainland Europe, with thousands of eyes across several countries looking for him. To the south lay fewer prying eyes, as he would only have Italian officers on the lookout. Sicily was the obvious place he could rest up and heal while planning for his future.

Sebastian drove east at first, only turning south after accessing cashpoints for several days, to disguise his direction of travel and ultimate destination. On the third day, the ATM retained his card, and Sebastian knew the wheels of justice had begun to turn.

Sebastian purchased a black beret, and clothes more fitting for southern Italy, at the port, where he boarded the ferry for the short trip to Sicily, unhindered or challenged.

Isolated beneath the tallest volcano in Europe, Sebastian leased a converted farmhouse, so he could recover from his wounds and plan for the future. He used the last of his ATM money to pay the deposit. He now had no choice but to set up a transfer from his Swiss account.

***

For several years, Fabienne had been subcontracted out to Government Communicating Headquarters; usually referred to as GCHQ. The covert department owned and run by the British was the epicenter for data and intelligence gathering. Not just throughout Europe, but for the rest of the world.

Within this role, Fabienne had created software for facial mapping used by both American and British intelligence agencies to identify individuals who posed a threat to these nations. This was not a new weapon in their fight against Global Terrorism; it was enhanced technology to positively identify targets. She knew the software would be used to identify targets, locations and would end up with a drone dropping its deadly cargo on top of the individual.

Fabienne had been working for the German Federal Intelligence Service for over twenty years when she was contracted out to GCHQ. She was reared in an orphanage in Geneva, her birth mother giving her up immediately after her introduction to the world.

Once Cutler had begun investigating the German counterfeit gang while working for the American Secret Service, it became apparent to the Germans that there was someone within the German government who was involved.

The German hierarchy became worried a scandal of this nature would knock back the progress Germany had strived to achieve in the post-war years. They also fretted about what information the person involved had access to. Number one priority was to identify the person and quietly eliminate the problem, or better still have Cutler do it for them.

Once Cutler had left the Secret Service and set up MIDAS, Fabienne discovered that Cutler was continuing the investigation into the counterfeit gang. Fabienne maintained high level contacts in the German government, and they fed her some of the information that led to Cutler tracking Werner to Turkey.

Cutler thought they had killed the delegate in the explosion, but she survived, albeit with severe burns. It was Fabienne who had identified Luther Gottschalk as the main sniper for the gang. Gottschalk also did some work for German Intelligence.

Gottschalk was dispatched to Turkey. He was five hundred yards away from the villa when Cutler attacked it. He was perched on the rocks, completely concealed. He had Cutler in his sights and felt the irony when he had been told to protect Cutler's back, rather than cut short his life. German Intelligence paid more than Werner, and he could see Werner's days were over. Fabienne was kept in the loop. The German Intelligence agency had no idea that Gottschalk had killed Hoagie. But Fabienne was not going to let this go.

Delegate Frau Uebering had staggered out of the safe room, smouldering. Gottschalk put a bullet between her eyes, and made his way back to the airport, having ditched his weapon.

Although Fabienne had met Hoagie only a few times, she liked the man. He was part of the MIDAS team, and everyone was upset at his death. The main reason Hoagie died was that Gottschalk shot and killed Richter on the steps of the plane in Liverpool airport, causing a stampede which led to his death. She had monitored Gottschalk's movements, hitching a lift on the satellite feeds from several countries.

With her expertise, she took over a NATO drone that had been returning from the Syrian border. The drone was on surveillance and had the latest camera technology on board. The loss of the NATO drone caused consternation and bemusement back in the control centre. They believed it had either crashed or been brought down. As the drone hovered a thousand feet in the sky above the villas, Fabienne switched the camera on when Gottschalk shot the delegate, and got high-resolution pictures of him as he made his escape.

It only took a minute to route the footage to the Turkish intelligence agency; with notification that a German delegate had been shot. She made it appear the information had come from a NATO source. She then put the drone back under NATO Control.

The Turks do not take kindly to foreign dignitaries being murdered on their home soil, especially by international hitmen. Gottschalk was easily identified, as not many albino men pass through the airport each day. The Turkish police swarmed him as he exited the taxi in front of the Departure lounge at Bodrum airport. No need for a costly trial; the lead officer shot him twice in the chest, claiming that he thought he saw a gun. The taxi driver was in shock as he scraped Gottschalk's innards off his clothes.

Once she knew that Sebastian had survived the injury and the fall from the cruise ship, Fabienne began to track Sebastian. It had taken her two days of hacking for her face recognition software to identify Sebastian at the port, entering Sicily.

With Gottschalk dead, and blamed for the deaths and carnage in the Akbuk villas, she turned her attention to tracking Sebastian down.

Fabienne saw no valid reason to keep Cutler up to date with what she was undertaking. The trail had gone cold for over a fortnight, and Cutler would have been on her back hourly for updates. Fabienne had confirmed two facial images of Sebastian at petrol stations. By backtracking the CCTV she hacked, she discovered the car and number plate Sebastian had driven down the spine of Italy. She had traced it as far as Sicily, but then the trail went cold.

A month later, Speedy software identified a woman going into a bank to withdraw a cash sum. Except it was not a woman; the software gave an indicator reading matching several of Sebastian's features, but not a positive reading of Sebastian. She crunched the numbers; it was only a forty-five percent positive match.

Fabienne hacked into the bank in Catania, and traced the deposit back to an account in Geneva. The account had no name, but was accessed with a passcode. If it was Sebastian, and it was a big 'if', he must be out of money. "Do I tell Cutler or not?" she pondered aloud.

If it is him, he probably thinks he's safe. He would have no idea that we might have the capability to track him through satellites and close circuit cameras throughout Sicily, she thought.

Fabienne waited another week. She wrote a programme to access the motorway and street cameras in Sicily. Once she gained access, it took Speedy less than an hour to locate the 1975 battered Fiat van. Now it was time to tell Cutler. She had a rough location of his sister's killer; he could do the rest.

Cutler was euphoric at the revelation. He had not felt this good since before he had the tragic news of his sister's disappearance. He shared the data with the other members of MIDAS.

Robert Stahmer was recovering from the loss of his eye, and now wore a patch over the missing organ. He had insisted on accompanying Cutler to Sicily. Tuck said he would resign if he were not involved. Ghislaine also insisted they would need an interpreter. Cheryl booked the flights and all four arrived in Sicily two days later.

A further two days of inquiries, and the crossing of many a palm by the four MIDAS operatives, proved fruitful. They identified three new leases for properties in the area, but only one new face.

It was 3 pm on a Friday afternoon as they approached the farmhouse. The sky was blue, only scarred by the small, billowing plume of ash and gas rising from the volcano. Even from that distance, Cutler, Stahmer and Tuck could see the lava flow was a trickle compared to some previous eruptions; the blackened landscape on the mountain bearing witness to past eruptions. The tinge of sulphur in the air caught the back of their throats.

They parked the hire car out of sight, and approached the isolated farm from the south. The land was arable and fertile; vegetation had overtaken the land where crops had grown previously. Cutler guessed that the farm had not been a working farm for several years.

Stahmer broke away and veered right, heading some fifty yards away before turning back towards the farm. As he progressed, he used the vegetation to mask his advance. Stahmer was to be the rear-guard at the back of the property, just in case Sebastian decided that flight was better than fight.

Stealthily Tuck and Cutler edged forward. They could see the battered Fiat that Sebastian had fled in, parked at the side of the property on the stony and unkempt lane.

The heat of the day was at its peak, and both men were sweating in their denims and loose shirts. Cutler carried a haversack on his back. He advanced, looking forward at the farm, while Tuck scanned the ground ahead of them. Suddenly Tuck clamped onto Cutler's shoulder and held him rigidly. He pointed a yard in front of him; Cutler looked down but could not see what Tuck was concerned with.

Tuck knelt and picked up a small branch that was to his side. He whispered to Cutler "the ground has been disturbed." Tuck pressed the branch just forward of their position and forced it downwards. The ground gave way and the stones fell several feet into a small pit, big enough to take a man. The trap door was hinged on both sides and gave way in the middle. Cutler could see the welcome surprise at the bottom of the pit would certainly incapacitate a man, if not kill him outright.

One inch in diameter, sharpened bamboo canes had been cemented into place, pointing upwards awaiting its catch.

"Old Viet Cong tricks," Tuck whispered.

As they circumnavigated the trap, Tuck scanned the area for any other traps that had been constructed. There were two more beneath the downstairs windows looking into the property.

Cutler and Tuck could hear an old piano being played. It may have been ancient, but Sebastian had tuned it the previous day. Wagner's Ring Cycle rose to a crescendo, the sound masking their approach, they hoped.

Tuck kicked the door with force, and it gave way first time. Neither man was armed, as they had not wanted the added risk of trying to buy weapons in the country.

The bald Sebastian sat at the old piano in the corner of the unkempt and tired room. The windows, bereft of curtains or blinds, kept the sunlight at bay with the amount of grime that had built up over the years.

The room stank of wood rot, and smoke from a wood stove that was aflame in the kitchen. This was intermingled with the sweet smell of lemongrass and ginger that had been added to the chicken that was boiling on top of the stove.

Sebastian carried on playing. "Gentlemen, you must be the ones who have been tracking me all these months."

Stahmer entered the room from the rear.

"Ah, I see I was right," he said as he stopped playing and turned to Stahmer. "How's the eye, or lack of it, should I say?"

"In much better shape than you will be in the next few hours, I can assure you," Stahmer replied.

"So, you are not here to arrest me. Sounds personal, is this all over the loss of your eye?" Sebastian said sarcastically.

"No, this is you killing my friend's sister."

Sebastian followed Stahmer's gaze and stared at Cutler.

"Ah, there have been so many; please give me a little more information so I can tell you how she died," Sebastian said with a grin.

"Juneau, Alaska," Cutler spat out.

"Yes, I remember. Beautiful girl, marvellous hair, so tasty."

Cutler moved towards him and kicked the chair from underneath him. Sebastian did not go sprawling as he had expected but landed on his feet and automatically moved side on to Cutler, in a fighting stance.

"Out for revenge, what do they say? Dig two graves, or in this case maybe three or four," Sebastian said calmly.

"We know your capabilities. Unfortunately, you do not know ours," Cutler said.

In the blink of an eye, Sebastian did a roundhouse kick, felling Stahmer in one blow and rendering him unconscious. He turned back to face Cutler.

"Odds a little more even now, don't you think?"

Sebastian leaped up towards Cutler and rose to head height in readiness to launch a flick kick at his temple. The final part of the move did not materialize. Sebastian fell to the floor shuddering.

"Not out for revenge, out for justice," Tuck spat out.

Sebastian was still reverberating to the electric shock that was pulsating through his body from the Taser in Tuck's hand.

"I thought I said no weapons?" Cutler asked slowly.

"This isn't no weapon; this is a toy," Tuck replied theatrically.

Tuck eased off the trigger of the Taser. They wanted him unconscious, not dead. Cutler removed the duct tape he had in the haversack on his back. He started with Sebastian's legs, wrapping them tightly together, but not enough to stop circulation. He then placed his arms together and repeated the process.

Tuck bent over Stahmer, slapping his face lightly to bring him back to consciousness.

"That guy does not like you, Stahmer. First he takes your eye and now he connects with your glass jaw."

Stahmer opened his eyes a little, trying to gain some focus.

"You're an asshole, Tuck," was his drowsy and considered response.

Less than forty minutes later, Tuck and Stahmer were in the hire car, with Sebastian trussed up in the trunk. Cutler had finished by taping his mouth, ensuring that he would not asphyxiate before they got to the destination.

Tuck followed them a little way behind in Sebastian's Fiat. The car struggled to ascend Etna Sud Road as quickly as the hire car.

Ghislaine had not been idle either. Sicilians loved wine, food, and women, in that order. The approach road to the tourist road leading to the crater had been closed by a single barrier, manned by an overweight Sicilian guard.

Fabio had thought all his Christmases had come at once. The beautiful woman had turned up at the wooden shack that had been hastily cobbled together to give him some shelter from the blistering heat of the day and the coolness of the night.

Ghislaine had explained that she had wanted to watch the eruption of Etna at first hand. Would he mind if she spent several hours with him? She could sit by what passed for a window and stare up as the gas slugs erupted some several hundred yards above the shack. But first they would eat from the hamper and drink from the bottle of Chianti and Frascati that was within the food basket.

Fabio was only too happy to oblige. It was his modus operandi to eat a little and drink a lot. When his Dutch courage was enabled, he would try to make a move on this beautiful woman.

Ghislaine guessed right, he was a Chianti drinker. Several glasses later, the sedative she had added took effect. Fabio began to snore heavily, and would not wake for several hours.

When she heard the two cars approach, she lifted the barrier. As instructed by Cutler, she stayed at the barrier in case of any unwanted visitors.

Cutler and Tuck, in the separate cars, made their way through the ancient and not so ancient lava field, through which the road had been carved. Every now and then, a rooftop would sit on top of the lava, the substructure buried for eternity in the rock of life.

Finally, they came up alongside a cone some two hundred yards from Crateri Silvestri. Cutler judged the eruptions, albeit that they were merely small fountains of lava, too dangerous to approach.

From Google, Cutler had learned of these cones and along this flank they were plentiful. They were like the craters but on a much smaller scale. The cinder cones are small, steep-sided volcanic cones built of pyroclastic fragments. They consisted of loose pyroclastic debris formed by explosive eruptions or lava fountains from a single, typically cylindrical, vent.

In the centre of the cone, the lava glowed red and black and rose and fell with the tide of pressure beneath the earth. This particular cone was some twenty yards across, wide enough for what Cutler had in mind.

Tuck set about draining much of the petrol and oil from the Fiat. Cutler did not want the car exploding quickly.

Cutler dragged the trussed form of Sebastian from the hire car. Sebastian was mumbling away beneath the duct tape as Cutler pushed him towards the Fiat.

"Not interested in anything you have to say. Nothing you could say would add anything more to what I know. You killed a beautiful, innocent girl. Now I am sending you straight to Hades."

Stahmer helped to push the struggling Sebastian into the car eventually. He would not bend his legs and Stahmer took no pleasure in breaking both legs with a small lava boulder. Sebastian no longer mumbled; he was trying to stifle the screams from the agony in his lower limbs.

Cutler taped his bounds arms to the steering wheel while Tuck placed a heavy piece of lava rock on the accelerator. Together Cutler, Stahmer, and Tuck manoeuvred the vehicle to about twenty yards from the cone, and it steep sides.

"I believe you like Wagner," Cutler said rhetorically. "Today, I am afraid it's Liszt."

Cutler removed a CD from his jacket and placed it into the car's battered old CD player.

"A symphony to Dante's Comedy, but it's not so comical. It is based on Dante Alighieri's journey through Hell and Purgatory. A journey you are about to embark upon," Cutler said, with ice in his voice.

Both doors were open. Tuck on the right-hand side started the engine and he whined and roared as the gas pedal was to the floor. Once he was clear Cutler leaned in and jammed the engine into gear.

Cutler was dragged along with the car towards the cone and jumped clear with only yards to spare. The intense heat searing and the sulphur fumes choking.

The car stayed in mid-air for a millisecond over the edge of the cone, clearing the steep sides. The car descended into the middle of the fiery hole. A sudden gas slug and fountain of lava spat out. The molten rock did not clear the cone but raised high enough to engulf the car and its screaming occupant.

"The Devil had reached his arms out for one of his own. May the bastard burn for eternity," Cutler said, praying for the first time that there was such a creature.

www.ingramcontent.com/pod-product-compliance
Lightning Source LLC
Chambersburg PA
CBHW030958190726
48285CB00004BB/1365